Praise for

"Brec has outdone herself! What an incredible novel with a refreshing new idea—the tension buildup was masterful. I loved it!"

~ **Jonas Saul**,
Bestselling author of the
Sarah Roberts Series

"Original, clever, riveting, and a fun read from start to finish ... Deftly crafted with novelist Cyndi Brec's distinctively effective and narrative driven storytelling style ... unreservedly recommended ..."

~ **Midwest Book Review**

"Cyndi built a literary bridge into a captivating world of mystery and adventure. This book explores the power of family, the weight of the past, and a quest for identity and belonging. Pick up this novel and prepare for a thrilling self-discovery journey."

~ Dominique "Dom" Brightmon,
Bestselling Author & Host of the
Going North Podcast

"This book is a page-turner that will keep you hooked until the very end in search of the truth. Perfect for teens, The Therans: Secrets Beneath Scars explores themes of grief, friendship, and the power of family, all through the eyes of a character who feels incredibly authentic. Callie's resilience will resonate deeply with readers, making this a must-read! If you love a good fantasy/mystery with heartfelt characters, you won't want to miss out on this enchanting story."

~ Sykereadss
Book Influencer

"Cyndi Brec's *Secrets Beneath Scars* will take you away, where you'll be drawn into Callie's world—a world where her visions are more dangerous than living a lie."

~ Alan Warren
NBC News Radio Host/Producer/Author

"With moving characterization, intriguing storytelling techniques, and a compelling, close-to-heart plot twist. If you thirst for an engrossing, and captivating read, The Secrets Beneath Scars should be your first quenching spot."

~ Peter Okonkwo
Author and Literary Critic
at P English Literature

I like Callie. She's a smart girl with enough grit to do what's right but with just the right amount of teenage angst to make her feel authentic. I most enjoyed when Callie began intensive training and the true nature of what she was capable of — if she had the strength and fortitude to get there — was exceptionally well depicted. I hope the break between book one and two of the series isn't too long ..."

Readers' Favorite

**Cyndi Brec has secured
a 5-star rating from Readers' Favorite.**

BOOKS BY CYNDI BREC

Scarred Legends: Romance on the Run

Scarred Secrets: A Journal

Scarred Lies: Resident Alien & Bathroom confession

THE THERANS: SECRETS BENEATH SCARS

CYNDI BREC

LEGEND PUBLISHING

To my loving husband,
who inspired me throughout
the writing journey to dream big,
I thank you for your faith,
for being with me from the beginning,
and for staying for the long ride.
You hold my heart in your hands, Richard.
Also, to my grandparents, mother, loving in-laws,
and beautiful children—who are more precious than
gold.

secrets
stab
deeper
than
a
blade

Bound by secrets,
Therans shouldered the weight of history
to serve and protect pages that transcend time.
History is the keystone that bridges our future.

~ C. Brec

PREFACE

I've always thought memories shaped my future, which is not so much different than how music can affect my mood, especially when I moved my fingers across the guitar's neck, strumming a softer note. The minor chords set a deep tone and sometimes cut through the pain, but lately, the melody echoed as strongly as the danger of my *faulty* visions.

Death didn't *always* announce itself, but I should've felt or seen it coming. Yet, deciphering images of danger were as deceptive as piecing together sections of my broken past. Clarity was a skill polished by someone with experienced judgment, not a freaky seer with vision malfunctions.

If I've learned anything, the discrepancies between the past, present, and future are a never-ending circle. I'm stuck between who I am, who I want to be, and who I should be.

CHAPTER 1

LIFE

The snow fell in a blinding whirlwind, leaving icy streaks across the car's windshield. When we'd left home, there wasn't even a layer of fog. Now, the hazy-snow mixture left a blur of a mess. The snow smothered the farmlands of northeastern Ohio. The evening gusts had stripped the last leaves from the trees, leaving the branches exposed to a bitter, cruel freeze.

"Nana," I yelled as a horn blasted. "Watch out!"

In a heartbeat, metal groaned against metal, thrusting me forward. I tried to block my face before the airbags deployed. The windshield imploded, showering glass throughout the front seat.

Blackness consumed me. Time slipped by until ... strange noises. Something I couldn't identify stirred my consciousness.

A cold palm pressed against my neck. "Callie, it's Sheriff Travis. Hang in there, girl. Help's on the way."

I forced my eyes open to focus on a hazy form. I blinked. The longer I made eye contact with the stranger–not Sheriff Travis–over the smashed door frame, his eyebrows furrowed, and his lips pinched together in a frown.

The stranger stepped back, a vein pulsing in his jaw. He stared with hardened brown eyes.

Sheriff Travis shifted toward the stranger. "Stay with her. I'm gonna check to see if the others are okay."

I turned my head. "It hurts. *Ohhh ... I hurt.*"

A foul smell of burning rubber filled the air. As acid roiled in my stomach, my lungs agonized for a clean breath. I raised my arm to block the prick of cold against my face and felt a howling ache throughout my chest. A chill crept under my coat, scattering goosebumps across my flesh.

"Don't move. You'll injure yourself worse." His British accent unnerved me.

I sucked in a breath of air and lifted the belt from digging into my rib cage. A bruising pain constricted me. "I-I *hur*t." With each inhale, clouds of steam curled in the air.

"The ambulance is on its way. Try not to move."

"Nana? Where's my ..." I turned but found the stranger's icy palm against my face, restricting my view–but not before I glimpsed Nana's limp, crumpled body in the driver's seat. No movement of her arms or her head. Blood soaked her blue shirt.

"No, Nana, *Nooo* ... Please let her be okay. Don't take her, too."

"Look at me, Callie, please." The stranger's fingers pressed into my jaw, steering my focus back to him–to his eyes. "Yeah, that's it. Look at me."

A painful electrical current radiated beneath my skin, singeing my nerve endings. My fingers curled into fists, fingernails digging into my palms. I closed my eyes against the building pressure, hearing the soothing sound of his words evaporate the rushing of the sirens, my nerve endings drifting into paralysis as if a shot of Novocain deadened my senses.

"Death teaches us that we live in an imperfect, broken world." Pastor Miller spoke heart-wrenching but truthful words.

"I'll never see her again." With each whispered word, my breath turned icy.

Premonition malfunction? Faulty brain wiring? No, my visions didn't warn me about all serious matters. Otherwise, I could've warned Nana, and ... maybe she'd still be alive.

Death followed me like a shadow.

Gramps rested a palm on my shoulder. "Your Nana lives in your heart, Callie. Don't ever forget. She will always be with you. Like your parents, they're a memory away."

The wind blew dirt from my outstretched hand, and soil fell over Nana's casket. Gramps stood a step away from me as Erika held my other hand, anchoring me to Earth. Three years ago, Erika had stood in that same place and had been the only one to attend Skyler's funeral when I'd buried our dog's remains in one of Gramps's old cigar boxes. And over a year ago, Erika stayed with me when I burned my journal—all my secrets went up in smoke, along with my unanswered questions. But even with her next to me, my lungs constricted, tightening.

Why Nana? Why not me? Why did those I love have to die?

Somber faces blended with dark winter coats as mourners' tears fell.

I met Pastor Miller's encouraging smile as he finished the sermon. People strolled away, back to their normal routines, their normal lives. New Cumberlin Falls, Ohio, was my sanctuary, and I was its resident alien.

I inhaled a breath of frosty air. A warm tear broke loose, caressing my cheek. I stepped back, feeling the uneven ground under my feet, and winced, slowly exhaling. I didn't even break a bone, but the seatbelt left a deep bruise from my shoulder, across my chest, and down to my hip bone. I hurt. I *hurt* bad, like a herd of elephants had stampeded over my body, leaving me for dead.

What was worse, Gramps and I had lost Nana. Nothing could bring her back.

"Come, dear, let's get home." Gramps guided me past a couple of headstones and crowds of mourners.

Erika didn't leave my side. Her lack of words eased my frayed nerves.

Muffled whispers and sobs from friends drifted through the trees.

"How's Callie holding up?" someone asked.

"Let us know what we can do," another well-wisher murmured, reaching out to touch my arm.

I cringed, stepping back from her. Gramps's arm wrapped around my shoulders, sending a stab of pain through my body. I sucked in a stabilizing breath, nodded to the supporter, and even though it hurt, I wanted Gramps's hug.

"I'm so sorry for your loss." Mrs. Livingston's familiar voice sounded like a squeaky cry.

Gramps squeezed my shoulder. "Thanks."

Mrs. Livingston wiped a tear from her face. "If there is anything we can do, please let me know. Our thoughts are with you."

I stood stone cold like the surrounding tombstones while Erika and Gramps spoke with friends.

"No one expected the kid to pull out in front of your wife," someone said. "Does anyone know how Mr. Santos is?"

"Heard Mr. Santos came out of surgery this morning," Mrs. Livingston said. "He has a long recovery ahead of him. He broke his leg, even his pelvis. One of the teachers said she'd heard he injured his head."

"Sheriff Travis is holding a meeting. Guess he wants to put a traffic light at the intersection."

A third voice chimed in. "It's irresponsible of the county to wait until several deaths occur before they approve a light. There was a two-car accident just last year, at the same spot."

I balled my hands into fists and looked out over the cemetery. Nana had died in a three-car pileup. A drunk hit our car, lost control, and plowed into Mr. Santos's car. He'd killed Nana, injured Mr. Santos, and left me bruised, mentally broken, and dealing with horrible memories. But the inebriated jerk walked away. Unscathed. I couldn't take it. Everything hurt. What hurt worse was Gramps's troubled grin, a mask of his misery.

"Life isn't fair." Mrs. Livingston nodded and looked over her shoulder at a fresh rectangular mound of dirt. "Why, just five days ago, they buried some professor who taught at Ashworth University. He was so young."

"Murder," Mr. Livingston said. "I tell you, that's what it is. Sheriff Travis must investigate. We can't have crime run amuck."

"Did the professor have any family?" another man asked.

I clenched my teeth. Compassion wormed its way through me. No gravestone marked *his* burial plot. No flowers from loved ones. Did anyone miss him?

"No family that I know of." Mr. Livingston's eyebrows furrowed. "Darn shame, too. I hear he even volunteered at the dog shelter."

"You know." A woman in a frumpy coat pursed her lips. "Death always comes in threes."

I swallowed. The idea of another soul suffering made me sick.

"What will happen to the drunk who killed Adele?" Mr. Livingston asked. "Will Sheriff Travis put him away?"

"That's for the courts to determine." Gramps jammed his hand into a glove. "I don't care."

Part of me wanted to curl up into a ball and avoid the world, while the other part wanted to explode with anger. Why did the good always get hurt? Or die? I flexed my fingers at my side.

"Gramps, can we go?"

"Yes, dear."

"See you later, Callie." Erika squeezed my arm. "Text me, if you can't make it to school this week, I'll tell the others." She left with her family. Hanson, Erika's brother, followed them but kept glancing behind until they got in the car.

Gramps stepped around another cemetery stone, and we walked to his car.

We reached his vehicle, and I looked over my shoulder, scanning the tomb markers. Plastic, ornamental ribbons from wreaths whipped around unkempt graves. My parents' burned remains lay across the country in a cemetery like this one.

I grabbed the door handle and jerked upward. The metal groaned as the handle came off, scratching the paint on the door. I inhaled and cringed. The cold door handle lay in my trembling palm. How would I explain my superhuman strength to Gramps?

An inner warning ignited. *Don't.*

Gramps slid into the car seat and motioned for me to get in. I held up the door handle and winced. He pulled the lever on the passenger door and pushed it open. "What happened?"

"I can't explain." It wasn't a lie.

"I'll have it fixed later. It's chilly. Get in the car, dear."

I slid into the passenger seat. Guilt at the half-truth ripped through me. I couldn't explain everything to Gramps because I didn't understand it myself. I hated lies, but sometimes it was a necessary evil—survival.

My parents' deaths had left me with a list of questions. What knowledge I'd gathered about my existence amounted to a single page in a book: I'd been born with a mark only my parents could see, with powers no human should have.

CHAPTER 2

MARKED

I dried the ends of my hair, wrapped the towel around my body, and threw on my pants. Despite my attempts to avoid looking in Erika's gym locker mirror, I couldn't. I swallowed. The sunken eyes staring back at me didn't look familiar.

Days merged, and weeks became a month. Ever since Nana's death, old feelings from my parents' deaths and my sister's demise had resurfaced. I felt detached from everything. Everyone. I didn't even want to be with Erika, but survival meant going through the motions of life. I knew from previous experiences that things would get better. But depression's darkness had a way of sucking the life out of my soul.

I hated feeling anesthetized to life. Gramps said time would heal all wounds, but I wondered if even Gramps believed the words. His hands trembled when he talked as if he were biting back emotions, and at night, he paced the floors like a caged lion. Gramps lost himself in the mill, and I survived by going through everyday motions. School. Work. Socializing ... numb.

I reached for my shirt, losing my towel around my waist.

"Huhhhhhh."

"Oh, my."

I grabbed the towel and spun to face Lizzy and Marilyn's inquisitive stares.

"Your back." Lizzy pointed at me. "That mark."

No, it's impossible. Bile rose in the back of my throat. She couldn't possibly have seen my birthmark.

I yanked my shirt down over my head, trying to hide my slightly bruised body and scar, and slammed the gym locker door shut. I swiped up my water bottle, wishing it were large enough to conceal me. Dang it, I should've never allowed Erika to talk me into working out at lunch. I thought everyone would've been out of the locker room.

Lizzy's eyes constricted in what I could only assume was surprise. Shallow Lizzy and her friend Marilyn were the two most popular girls at school. "That thing on your back ..."

She did see it. I stood in disbelief as her words slowly registered. I'd never known anyone outside my family who could see my mark. A storm of emotions rampaged in my head.

No internal warnings.

No premonition alerted me to this moment.

Something wasn't right.

"What is it with you?" Lizzy's words interrupted my thoughts. "You look like you're staring off in space."

"I can't believe you can see it," I mumbled.

I reached over and touched my birthmark, feeling the raised edge as my finger traced along the faint crimson line at the highest elevation of my mark, knowing the crimson line divided the luminous lines on each side. Both stars were identical to one another except in size. The smaller star sat at the top of the larger, more evident one.

No matter how familiar I was with every line and my inner strengths, not knowing why I had a mark terrified me.

I was cursed–living with a mark, I didn't understand and couldn't explain.

Both girls looked at me as if I were missing something obvious.

"How could you not?" Lizzy's lips curled in disgust. "It's nasty. Your skin still looks gnarled and puckered up. I don't recommend wearin' any low-back dresses to prom. How did you get the scar?"

My scar. Not my birthmark. Lizzy talked about the jagged reminder of the night my parents were murdered. Not my mark I was branded with since birth. My mark was a constant reminder of my differences–it was even different from my parents' marks.

The memory slipped through my mind, burned there with the horrible image of Dad's death, the feel of the wet blood that had soaked his shirt while he'd held me. He'd told me, "Stay alive. Protect yourself." He'd clutched at his chest, his hand frozen over his birthmark, and fought to say, "S-seran."

I swallowed the cry that threatened to crack what little composure remained. I wished fragments of my memory could be wiped clean.

Still riled up, I spun around and packed my workout clothes in my gym bag. I wouldn't have showered if I had known someone would be in here. This was why I took online gym glasses. Avoiding the locker room was essential. I threw my wet towel in the bin and turned to face the girls.

"I don't care to talk about it." My stomach twisted in a knot. Secrets stabbed deeper than a blade.

"You've gotta tell me." Lizzy's words came quick. "What happened?"

"Lizzy, stop it." Erika's shoes echoed in the locker room. "Callie doesn't have to tell you squat." She came to stand next to me.

"Can't she talk for herself?" I felt Lizzy's eyes bore a hole in my back.

"Yes. But it's none of your business." I bit back another retort. Anything else I said would accelerate my social downfall. I twisted sideways.

"Lizzy, leave her alone." Erika crossed her arms over her chest. "It's only been a month since her grandmother died, and you're hounding her with questions. Butt out."

Wild, sandy hair looped around Lizzy's shoulder. She gazed at my feet, then slowly rose until she made eye contact with me.

"Stay away from Logan. We may be broken up, but I'll get him back. You stay out of my way, or you'll regret it." Lizzy turned, leaving the locker room.

Marilyn's loud shoes clicked on the concrete as she followed her. The gymnasium door slammed shut behind them.

I wiped the sweat from my brow. How can Lizzy go from asking me questions about my scar to her obnoxious ex-boyfriend? I scratched my head. Dang, I couldn't even look at Erika. I never told her about the night my parents were murdered. It was a topic we just never talked about.

I threw my bag over my shoulder, then stepped around her.

"What?" Erika raised her hands, blocking me. "I can't even take a crap without you getting in trouble. What would it hurt to try to make friends with them?" Her soft words hit a nerve. "Or level with her. You don't even like Logan."

"She's territorial. And it won't matter what I do. She thinks every girl in the school is after him."

Even if I didn't want Lizzy and Marilyn as friends, it'd make things easier if I'd said something nice, but I didn't want to hang with either one of them. Lizzy lied with a savage tongue. Drama was her poison and distraction, her weapon.

Her disturbing lies only intensified my anxiety. The ability to read the truth in what others said caused me to wrestle with my own emotions, and that was enough of a battle, but then to have to deal with other people's lies sucked.

"Anyhow, I don't need more friends. I've got you, Steve, Jessica, Camden." Ever since I was seven and moved to New Cumberlin Falls, Erika befriended me. Up until Nana's death, we did almost everything together. Erika and her family were the support that made my reality bearable. What secrets Erika knew about me, she kept. I loved her like a sister.

"Yes, you've got us. But you wouldn't have them if I hadn't begged you to start public school last year."

I groaned, pulling my hair up in a sloppy bun.

Erika's eyes softened. "I'm sorry my words are so rough, but I care about you, and I don't blame you for not talking about things. At least now I understand why you have nightmares. Man, first your family's murdered and then there's Nana's accident. You're so lucky to have your grandfather. Look, I know we've never talked about it, but I'm grasping for answers, and I can only guess you got the scar the night your parents died."

I nodded. Tears weighed down the corner of my eyes.

"Callie, I won't pretend to know what you're feeling. I've only ever lost my uncle, and I didn't even really know him, but I think you need to talk to someone."

"I'm dealing with it."

"Are you?" she whispered. "You don't show signs of dealing with it. You've never talked to me about it, and this is the first I've known about your scar. I bet you've never opened up to a doctor, either. Ever since I've known you, you've had nightmares. And this past month, you've walked around here, numb to the world. You lock yourself away in that dusty old mill, reading books or playing your guitar."

"What would you have me do?" My heart constricted. I'd give anything to dump my pain. To push away and forget my misery, but my sixth sense screamed not to open up. "I don't want to rehash Nana's death or my family's deaths. It opens old wounds."

"I'm not saying I have the answers, but I hate seeing you so lonely. You're missing out on the fun. Maybe go out on a date, do something different for once. Several guys are dying to date you."

"Guys and dating are the last thing on my mind." I bit my lip and released it. "By three o'clock today, Marilyn and Lizzy are going to have added a dramatic soap opera spin to my life. I don't want to deal with my secret spread all over the dang school. Erika, you're the sister of my heart, and I never could've done half of what I have in my life if it weren't for you. You mean the world to me, but I'm not talking about this."

"Okay, I get it." Erika's eyes twinkled. "But admit it, you need to be more open to meeting new people. Do something spontaneous, out of the norm. It will help you forget the tough times. Geesh, anyone would give anything to have your black hair and gorgeous blue eyes, but none of it fazes you. You've lived here almost ten years, and you haven't even let me in. If you won't talk to me, give someone else a chance." She exhaled, shaking her head. "You need a distraction. A fun distraction, something to take you away from all this misery. We're juniors. Next year, we graduate high school. Have some fun. Relax."

A knot in my stomach tightened, and I mentally groaned. A warning flickered—like, with Gramps—don't open up.

"I won't press. I know it doesn't work with you, but I'm here if you're ever ready to talk."

I nodded. Where was all this concern coming from? Erika rarely talked about serious stuff. She was usually into her shopping, or school events. Not that she didn't care about others, but her busy self-centered life made our friendship perfect.

In the end, it didn't matter if I talked with someone. No one could answer my questions. And today's confrontation with Lizzy would fuel speculation and keep high school gossip brewing. People believed what they wanted. It didn't matter how false it was.

"Oh, shoot." Erika glanced at her watch. "I've got to get to class early. I'm sorry about Lizzy, but thanks for working out with me." She hugged me and left.

I gathered up my gear and exited the back door, avoiding anyone I might encounter in the halls. Once I approached the back walkway behind the school, the brisk wind hit my face. My bag slipped off my shoulder, I repositioned it and tucked my chin in my coat. I took a few steps, finding refuge under the tree, soaking up the tranquility the snow offered.

A wave of panic gripped my lungs, squeezing the breath out of me. My head became heavy. I grabbed the tree.

A vision overcame me ...

A single small, yellow flame grew, building with intensity into a blaze of orange, red, and green flames swallowed by the darkness of my vision. A hand reached from beyond the shadows, and I grabbed it.

I gulped for air. When would this happen?

Premonitions were a curse, striking, without warning, day or night. They haunted me until they came true, and headaches accompanied every experience. My mysterious warnings never gave me a precise date or time. Instead, they revealed themselves as the situations they reflected did.

CHAPTER 3

ENCOUNTER

The substitute history teacher sat like a statue, her nose in a book. The whiteboard behind her bare as usual—no lesson again. The class was a joke, another study hall. It had been over a month since the accident, and the school hadn't yet found a replacement for Mr. Santos. Erika and I had gone to see him at the hospital, but he refused visitors.

I stared at the clock as the seconds ticked away. At least it was the last class of the day. At the sound of the bell, I darted into the hallway and slipped my books, papers, and my purse's contents scattered across the hall. I landed on my butt amongst them.

"Jings." I cursed under my breath. Dad's silly Scottish word had a way of easing my troubled thoughts.

A blond male invaded my space, squatting beside me. He picked up a yellow slip of paper at his feet. It looked to be a hall pass. "Are you okay? The floor's wet."

"I noticed." I swiped my stuff off the floor.

He gripped the underside of my arm and helped me to my feet.

He picked up my books as everyone stared. The girl beside him, dressed in a blue shirt and jeans, gawked. She had a beautiful, milky complexion, bright blue eyes, and a brown beauty mark high on her left cheekbone. He shared her complexion but stood a head taller than her. Dark circles underscored his light blue eyes.

"You, okay?" she asked.

"Yes. Ah, thanks."

Her eyes flickered to the floor. I assumed she was scanning for other lost items. She looked back at me. "Hi, I'm Anna. This is my brother, Colin Dougrey. We're checking out the school."

His eyes flashed down the hall. "Yeah, right. More like they're checking us out."

A swarm of kids passed us, heading for their lockers, forcing our circle tighter, pinning me behind the history room door. "Oh, I'm Callie Tresham."

Anna winced as the circle got even tighter. "Is it always like this?"

"Yeah, it's a big school. There are three hundred students in the junior class alone." I stuffed the contents into my purse and zipped it.

Anna frowned.

Colin shifted his stance, avoiding eye contact, and glanced over his shoulder several times.

Last year, I'd been a newbie. Erika helped me with the transition from home school to public school. Perhaps Erika was right. New friends would be a good distraction. "You know, I've got a little time, I can show you around."

"Great." Anna elbowed Colin in the ribcage. He let out a groan.

People cleared the halls. Colin and Anna followed me to my locker. I grabbed my backpack and threw it over my shoulder, tugging at the rising hem of my shirt. We passed classrooms, dodging two people in uniformed shirts and blue jeans working on light fixtures.

"The school's under construction. It will take the next two years to complete."

New Cumberlin Falls High School was an ancient, two-story building. The offices were in the center educational wing, opposite the long corridor where the cafeteria, gymnasium, and lobby were. The glassed-in lobby jutted out in front of the school, connecting to the main part of the building, and breaking up the brick exterior. In the center of the brick courtyard sat a fountain donated by the Gathers, a prominent family in town.

When our tour ended, we sat in the library.

Mr. Sykes, the school janitor, swept the floor, headphones over his ears. He stopped next to a brick column long enough to fasten down the edge of a prom poster that listed the prospective themes for which we would soon be voting.

"Hi, Callie." Erika approached, smiling, my friend Steve trailing behind her.

I scooted my chair back and pushed papers advertising school events out of my way.

"What are you guys up to?"

Erika shifted her backpack over her shoulder. "I had to turn in my English paper. Miss Delong gave me until the end of the day to get it done." Her eyes flickered past me to Anna and came to rest on Colin.

I twisted my messy hair-knot tighter.

"You're new around here," Steve said.

"Steve and Erika, meet Anna and Colin Dougrey."

Colin nodded.

"Oh, yeah." Steve adjusted his glasses and looked at Anna. "You start here next week, right?"

Anna opened her mouth, but before she said anything, Colin stood and moved from the table. She grabbed Colin's wrist, but he jerked away from her.

He cocked his head with a level of alertness.

Unease emanated from them.

I leaned toward her. "Anna, what's wrong?"

She glanced at me for a fraction of a second, and then her eyes flickered to Steve.

"How'd you know?"

Colin crossed his arms over his chest.

"Hey," Steve laughed. "I can't help it if I'm in the right place at the right time. I overheard the office secretary mention two students would start here soon."

"Ignore him." I rolled my eyes and picked up my books from the table. "He thinks he knows everything because he works in the school office."

Anna dropped her shoulders. "We had an appointment with the counselor to pick up the class schedules this afternoon, but she had a family emergency."

Colin glanced at Anna before sitting back in his chair. He slouched away from Steve as if he was a source of discomfort.

My eyes darted between Colin and Anna.

Colin looked up and met my gaze, this time with curiosity in his expression.

I gave a weak smile.

Steve stepped closer to the table, pulled out a chair, and straddled the seat. He rested his arms on the back-rest. "You talk with an accent. Where you from?"

Anna grinned. "We lived in Europe for two years, before that, Africa."

"Wow," Erika murmured. "The most traveling I've done is camping in my backyard."

"Hey, sign me up next time you're moving. I'd do anything to get out of here." Steve jerked his head toward Colin. "What grade are you in?"

"I start at Ashworth University this fall." Colin clenched his jaw. "After I finish some homeschooling requirements. My sister and cousin are juniors."

"What's your major?" Steve asked.

"I'm undecided."

Anna glared at Colin before saying, "Our mom wants him to go to med school. She's afraid he'll waste his talents otherwise."

Colin looked around. "I'm interested in engineering."

Steve chuckled. "My mom would sell our house if she could get me to be a doctor. She's a nurse at Wooster Memorial Hospital."

"Really?" Anna asked. "Our mom just started there. She's an ER physician."

Colin held out his arm and tapped his watch. "Hey, Trystan's waiting outside. We've got to go."

"Trystan?" Steve asked.

Anna unzipped her purse. "My cousin. He came here with us, but when he found out the school counselor had an emergency, he ditched us. He's out in the parking lot."

"Hey, we don't have school tomorrow." Steve tilted his head. "A bunch of us are going to Coccia House Pizza in Wooster. You know, on Pittsburg Ave. We meet around seven. Come if you can."

"No!" Colin said.

"Yes." Anna's eyes lit up.

Colin shook his head. "We got stuff to do at home."

"No," Anna said. "We don't. You do."

Tension radiated under their words. I couldn't figure out what transpired between them. I guess it didn't matter. I zoned out from the conversation, watching two women re-shelve library books. They were Nana's age. Death didn't slow the world down. Others seemed to pick up and move on with their regular routines while I limped along. My heart ached thinking of her.

"Callie?"

I snapped back to the present. "Hmm, yeah?"

"Are you going to Coccia House tonight?" Erika asked.

"Sure," I said.

Erika's smile brightened my dank mood.

"Good." Erika turned around. "I'll catch you later. I must get home and start chores. Come on, Steve." Steve picked up some papers from the table, and they walked out together.

I dragged myself from the chair and flexed my right calf. "Well, I've got to get going. Hope to see you tonight." I put on my coat and followed Anna and Colin outside. Snow salted the ground. The wind whipped under my coat. I pulled it tighter and trudged forward.

Less than a handful of cars remained in the parking lot. A dark-haired guy wearing khaki pants leaned against a blue car parked in the bus loading zone. An orange collared shirt showed around the neck of his snug black coat.

He turned and raised his face.

Our eyes locked. A tingling sensation electrified my spine.

The intensity grew behind his eyes. He blinked fast and shook his head.

I stopped. My nerves became oddly over-energized.

Anna and Colin continued to walk the short distance to the stranger.

I glanced at the trio.

Colin talked to him while the stranger nodded.

This had to be their cousin, Trystan. He had to be seventeen, maybe eighteen, years old.

He gave me another confounding look.

Another tingling sensation gripped me, stronger, like an electrical current. I couldn't move. Twenty paces separated us. I braced my fingertips against the square column at my back to anchor me as they approached. Small pieces of mortar and brick crumbled in my hand. What's going on?

"Callie, this is Trystan. Our cousin." Anna stepped beside me.

Trystan did not resemble them in the slightest. He had dark, curly hair and light brown skin. His facial features, including his square jaw, were much stronger than Colin's. Strength stuck to him.

His dark, restless eyes probed me. "Hi."

"Mmm, uh, hello." My breath caught in my throat. I knew those eyes. Where'd I see them? "You're new here." It was more a question than a statement, but my thoughts scattered under his gaze. "Of course, you're new. What an *awkward* thing to say."

"Awkward." Trystan examined me for a long, uncomfortable moment.

"Don't I know you?"

He blinked several times, shook his head, and pulled up his hood, hiding his face. He spun to face Colin. "I'm cold. Let's get out of here."

Double Dang. Talk about rude. He offered zero explanation and no apology for his abrupt reaction. And what'd I do? I get the chance of meeting several new people, and I end up sounding like an idiot. I already knew he was a *new* student. Why'd I have to ask it? How pathetic. Well, Erika will be happy, I befriended two out of three people.

"Wait, cuz," Anna said. "Callie's friends invited us out for pizza tonight."

Closing his eyes, Colin grimaced. "Not tonight, Anna."

"Neither of you has to go," Anna said. "But I am."

Determined to regain control of myself and defuse the friction—and the conversation—I released my lip. "It's a great hangout, with awesome food." I wasn't going to be rude. Anna and Colin didn't deserve it. I adjusted my bag over my shoulder and pulled my coat tighter as an icy feeling filled me. "Hope to see you later, but I've gotta go. My grandfather's waiting."

"Okay, see you soon." Anna gave me a megawatt smile.

"Sure." My neck prickled, and a hum sounded in my ears. Never felt that way before. Was I coming down with a cold? I turned, missed a step, and would've ended up on the ground if not for Trystan's quick movement and hand under my elbow.

"Good save, cuz," Colin teased. "Second time today, girl. You're not batting a good average in falls, are you?"

"Guess not." I exhaled.

Trystan's hand tightened around my arm. "You okay?"

"I'm fine." I refused to look up at him, my gaze trained on his chest.

"Dang it," Trystan muttered.

It was weird. He sounded like a jerk, but under his cold calm, he showed kindness. I waited for my sixth sense to trigger a warning, but nothing happened. My power to read voice inflections gave me a glimpse of the truth behind people's words, but interpreting that glimpse was hard. It wasn't like reading a neon sign. I could recognize an emotion and whether a person spoke the truth. Yet, it didn't tell me what had caused the emotion or their goal.

He released his grip from my arm and flexed his fingers at his side.

I lowered my eyes to his hand, seeing a black ring on his middle finger as he clenched and opened his hand repeatedly.

"Wait." I inhaled, stepping back. "The accident. You were there. You talked to me."

"Yeah." Trystan raked his fingers through his hair and knocked his hood off. "I was behind your car. I called 911 and stayed with you until the squad arrived."

"Minutes ago, you recognized me. *Why* didn't you tell me?" I tried to block the irritation from filling me.

He went rigid. A low growl reached my ears.

"Why?"

He stared at me, meeting my eyes with the oddest expression on his face—hostile almost. "I didn't want to remind you of the accident."

"Oh, my, gosh." Anna glanced at me. "That was you?"

Colin punched Trystan in the shoulder. "Talk about coincidence."

"Shut up. This isn't funny." Trystan's voice held recognizable pain.

"I didn't mean it, cuz."

"I'm sorry for your loss." Trystan's genuine words penetrated my irritated defenses until he pulled his hood back up. "It's cold. Let's get home." He turned on his heel without another look at me and disappeared around the side of the car.

I didn't even get the chance to thank him before he walked away. Did he suffer from nightmares from the accident? I trekked for my Jeep without looking back.

Anna yelled. "See you later."

The guys said nothing else, and I couldn't blame them. I had to agree with Trystan—meeting him had been awkward. It was easier for me to floss with electrical wire than to meet strangers. Why was I a freak? Annoyance flashed through me—the unfairness of life, the helplessness, vulnerability, and unimaginable horror of losing someone.

After I opened the door to my car, I put my backpack and purse on the passenger seat, climbed in, and slammed the door shut. I placed the key in the ignition after having dropped it, twice on the floor mat. Why'd I feel so strange? What was going on?

I kept my eyes riveted on the road's yellow line until I pulled into my driveway, parked the Jeep, and hurried to the house. Inside, I threw my keys and books on the apple crates. Tesla came running around the corner and licked my hand before I'd even got my arm out of my coat sleeve.

"You're a good boy." Tesla's furry back reached my hip. He nuzzled his cold nose against my palm. "Missed you, too."

Our house was a blacksmith shop Gramps had converted. A thirty-two-foot, hand-hewn beam ran the full length of the structure. I had the main floor bedroom and a bathroom I didn't have to share. Gramps slept upstairs.

"That you, dear?" Gramps's voice was a balm to my anxieties. Since Nana had died, my stomach consisted of small knots, a new one tightening each day. Gramps withdrawing from me hadn't helped. He mourned Nana in silence and went through the motions of everyday life with little rest, using this process as a means of escape.

I opened the cabinet, grabbed a mug, and filled it at the tap. "Ah, uh, yeah."

Gramps and Max came into the kitchen. Max helped Gramps out at the mill during the day. He filled bags of grain while I was at school. Gramps looked comfortable in his bib overalls and a red-collared, button-down shirt. He was an old grizzly bear, a Virginian. He grabbed his wallet from the drawer under the microwave and put it in his back pocket.

Gramps looked at me. "I got a call from the grain convention." His white beard made the dark black circles under his eyes stand out. "They need to meet with us tonight. Dave is in town and leaves for vacation tomorrow. I'm sorry, dear."

"Don't worry. I've got plans." My words came out in a rush as I recalled the awkward encounter with Trystan. I'd have to see him again. I took a breath and slowed my words. "I'm meeting up with Erika and a few others at Coccia House." Tesla's head bumped the underside of my palm. I stroked his back.

"Okay, but don't stay out late." Gramps slipped on his coat and staggered out the door with a clumsy gait as if the world's burdens rested on his shoulders. Max followed like a tired pup.

CHAPTER 4
QUESTIONS

The smell of garlic saturated the air outside Coccia House, making my mouth water and my stomach growl in anticipation. The joke around town was the owner didn't know when to stop piling on the pepperoni. His pizza's crust was crisp, flavorful, and chewy. Nana always said the crust was like flavorful bombs of yummy bites.

Wall sconces lit the long back room, and the crowd was shoulder-to-shoulder. It was a typical night for Wooster, a major hangout for anyone who wanted the best pizza in town.

Erika and I followed the hostess to the back corner. The Dougreys, Steve, Camden, Tony, Jessica, and Sandy were already there. They crowded around a circular booth and added chairs for us. I cringed and took the last seat next to Trystan.

Our server, Hanson, Erika's older brother, placed menus for Erika and me on the table.

"What can I get you to drink?"

"We'll have two pitchers of soda." Steve scanned the table and continued to order with confidence. "Four large pepperoni pizzas." None of the group seemed to mind Steve ordering for them, but I wanted something more.

I cocked my chin, looking over Jessica's head. "Hey, Hanson."

"How're you doing, Callie?"

"I'm good. I'll take an antipasto salad and soda. I'll grab pizza later."

Erika took her fork out of a folded napkin. "Make that two."

Anna cleared her throat. "So, what do most people do for fun around here?"

"Not much," Steve said. "We hang out at each other's houses, go to the movies, and when the weather's better, we ride dirt bikes. Camden and I race four-wheelers out at my granddad's farm. Once the weather breaks, I'm having a party. Nothing big—a bonfire."

Hanson returned with pitchers and glasses.

"How do you like your Jeep?" Camden asked from across the table.

Of all my guy friends, Cam was my favorite. His over helpfulness for others stood out as much as when he incorporated Japanese words into his sentences.

"It's great. I can't wait to take the top off."

Erika put the dessert menu back in the metal ring next to the salt shaker. " It was an Awesome birthday gift. I wish I had my own car."

Steve jumped up onto his chair. The table jerked, creating a foot-long gap between my drink and me.

Trystan grabbed the pitcher before it spilled on my lap.

Steve sang a ridiculous birthday song at the top of his voice while waggling forks in the air like drumsticks.

People turned in our direction. Heat rose to my cheeks, and I hid my head in my hands. Dogs would have howled in pain if they'd had to listen to Steve sing, but he continued as if his captive audience loved him.

Camden stood and tugged on Steve's arm. "You're embarrassing her. Get down, you idiot."

Why was Steve doing this? My birthday was weeks ago. Erika had brought me cupcakes, and Gramps had taken me out to dinner, but it wasn't the same without Nana.

Steve persisted, encouraged by the crowd's applause.

"So help me, if you don't get down from there, Steve," I threatened. "I'll kick your feet out from under you."

"How old are you?" The familiar voice came from the table to my side. Logan Gather, the Falls' basketball hero–Lizzy's ex-boyfriend. He gestured toward the empty seat beside him. "Wanna join us?"

I forced an answer through gritted teeth, hoping I wouldn't have to make good on my promise to Steve. "No, thanks."

Logan's smile grew, stretching from ear to ear.

Tom, Logan's friend, elbowed him. "Ask her."

Logan's green eyes brightened. "Do you want to go to prom?"

The world seemed to go still around me.

Erika nudged my leg.

"Prom's months away." I hated being the center of attention. And ticking off Lizzy didn't sound good.

His eyes narrowed. "So, what's your answer?"

"I'm going with friends."

Logan plastered on a fake smile. "Last chance."

I shook my head and turned around. Steve dropped his drumstick forks on the floor and glared at Logan. Before he could say anything, Camden tugged on his wrist and pulled him from atop the chair.

"Thanks, Camden." I swallowed my words.

Steve looked like he'd sucked on sour grapes. He should've known I didn't want attention.

Hanson's presence broke the friction. He set our salads on the table, gazed over at Logan, and rolled his shoulders back. My unofficial older brother was over-protective.

"Can I help you with something?"

"Hey, I was just asking the girl out. Lighten up, Hanson."

Everyone at our table slipped sidelong glances at one another.

"What a jerk," I mumbled.

Trystan chuckled, and his lips twitched on one side, emphasizing his dimple.

Man, what's wrong with me? Two times today, I spoke my private thoughts aloud. This was a safety hazard I couldn't risk. More puzzling was Trystan's change in behavior. It's as if our ice-breaker-meeting at school reset his mood. That or Anna and Colin worked on him. The more I thought of it, definitely, his cousins worked on his mood swing. Yep. The three of them were strangely tight. Even Colin's tone appeared better.

"We can all agree on that." Erika sat on the edge of her seat. "Hey, I'm so excited. The student council talked about prom themes today. Because of the construction, they've decided to hold it in the lobby."

Steve poured himself a glass of soda. "Prom will suck if they pick any of the themes I've heard."

"It's not that bad." Sandy's eyelids lowered. "They've got some neat ideas. A couple of years ago, Ashland High School did a Monopoly prom. One of my cousins said it was a blast. Something like that would be great."

"New York, New York would be awesome," Steve added.

"Callie's Gramps could supply the decorations." Erika smiled. "They've got stop signs and old streetlights in the attic. He collects that kinda stuff. Anyway, remember, we vote on the theme soon." Erika was part of the decoration committee, which meant she'd be volunteering me to help for prom.

Camden pulled his arm out of his coat sleeve. "I hope they don't do some beach idea, Enchantment Under the Sea or Renaissance theme, something ridiculous like that."

Sandy pulled a straw from her lips. "Ashland's talking about doing some Atlantis theme this year. That's an original idea."

Trystan's eyebrows furrowed. "It's an inventive idea, I'll give you that. Never thought I'd hear it used at a prom."

"It sounds romantic." Sandy pulled her hair over her shoulder. "My cousin's younger sister graduates from there this year. She said they've talked about dressing up in Greek costumes. It's sure to be a hit."

"What's romantic about a man wearing a tantric?" Steve rolled his eyes.

"You said the word wrong." Trystan looked over the rim of his drink. "Not a tantric, but a tunic—or a chiton."

"What did you say?" I asked.

"Chiton. It's a woolen garment worn by the Greeks in ancient times. A tunic is a garment worn at different lengths."

I leaned toward him. "How do you know?"

"My uncle." Trystan set his glass down. "He does IT work for museums. He'd take us along sometimes, and we'd learn about diverse cultures."

Steve dropped his hand. "Atlantis is fiction, a movie gimmick just so producers can make money."

"You're right, and reality TV keeps that stuff alive." Colin grimaced. "Pseudo-archaeology got a foothold in the world with UFO hunters, and there's a popular series about Bigfoot. Yet, no one's ever produced a nine-foot-tall, hairy Sasquatch. Lost civilizations have intrigued the world for centuries."

"Ashland can have their weird prom." Steve crunched on some cubes of ice from his soda. "I hope our school will stick with something that makes sense. So, Anna, Colin, Trystan, what do you think of The Falls so far?"

Hanson returned with silver platters of pizza.

Anna pulled a slice off the tray. "It's quiet."

"There's good people," Colin added. "I like living near the trails."

Camden took a tomato from Erika's salad and popped it into his mouth. "So, you guys live up at the old Markley place?"

Colin nodded.

"Got some good views up there." Camden gave me a grin. "You guys pass Callie's house when you come to town. Now, she's got an awesome place."

"Where do you live?" Anna asked.

I swallowed. "Off Ebby Road."

Erika pulled the fork out of her mouth. "Her grandparents own the old mill. You see it when you come down Cherry Hill."

"It's amazing," Camden said. "Man, the whole thing works using water from an underground river."

Trystan put his glass onto the table and cut it into a gooey slice of pizza. "That gray building with burgundy trim? It's a mill?"

"Mmmhmm." I glanced over at him as a familiar tingling stirred in my gut.

"Callie gives tours," Erika said around a bite of pizza.

"I'd like to see it." Trystan held a half-eaten piece of pizza above his plate. "What do you say?"

"Sure. Would four o'clock next Saturday work? Do Anna and Colin want to come?"

In unison, Anna and Colin shook their heads.

Trystan's face gave way to a cheerful smile. "That's great."

Okay, maybe not a jerk. I'll keep that reserved for Logan. Deciphering guys wasn't my strength. After all, I'd never even had a boyfriend.

"I hear you're starting there this fall?" Sandy fluttered her eyelashes at Colin so fast it looked like she'd start a windstorm.

"Yeah, I've got my courses picked out, including one class I'll take this summer."

"What's your favorite subject?" Sandy asked.

Colin set his pizza on the plate. "Trigonometry. I also like martial arts."

"Callie," Erika said. "Didn't you take martial arts?"

Was martial arts a college elective? I placed my fork on the table. "Uh, yeah, I used to, but I haven't taken it in years."

Erika didn't forget much. She was the only one I'd ever told about my family, and it was always the fun stuff. I thrived on those memories. Dad had taught my sister Ella and me some moves, and I had kept it up and learned some karate techniques from a family friend, Sergeant Beachum, before he'd moved away.

My world revolved around my family. Dad had taught literature at Berkley College, and he and Mom traveled during the summer. He'd freelance for newspapers over the summer, and Ella and I would spend time with Nana and Gramps. My parents would stay at least a month with us during the summer before they'd travel. Nana'd always tried to teach us to sew. We'd dodge her by hiding at the mill. Gramps would take us to Renaissance fairs and historical reenactments. The closest Gramps ever got to reliving his army days.

Thinking of Ella brought back a rush of memories. We'd played for hours at the ocean, making sand angels and baking cookies with Mom. Dad would come home from work and tickle us until we screamed for mercy. Ella was adventurous and daring. Once, she dared me to slide down the banister. That night, I'd found myself in the hospital with a broken arm.

Trystan tapped me on the shoulder and brought me back to the present. "Ah, hey, is the mill a museum?"

"Yeah." I picked up the last piece of pizza, a long strand of cheese oozing from the slice. I bit it and caught the second strand of tasty cheese with my other hand before it hit the table and licked it off my finger, chuckling. "You really like history?"

"Yeah, there's always something new to discover." Trystan looked at his watch.

I set down my half-eaten slice and lifted my glass of pop, smiling over the rim at my friends and Trystan. He wasn't so bad.

A penetrating chill seeped into my gut.

I gasped and swallowed an ice cube, choking on my drink.

A weighted gaze settled across my back, and a deep, inner warning surfaced. Anxiety prickled across my skin, intensifying an ache in my muscles. My heart accelerated–it'd been ten years since I'd felt this intensity.

I scanned the room, seeking the source of my tension.

A woman in the booth across from our table sat up straighter, smiling at her friend. She glanced at Colin. People in the booth beside us put on their coats, and servers cleared messy tables.

Nothing unusual. Everything seemed normal, but the sounds heightened: food sizzled in the kitchen, a fork clattered to a table, and the second hand ticked away on the clock over the mirror on the far wall. My head throbbed.

The vision closed in on me ...

I saw a man's shadowed face in the mirror.

Panic pounded against my chest as unholy eyes gleamed.

His face split into halves, then crumbled, falling into shattered raindrops before me. Each shard depicted an event.

An old wooden chest bound by leather straps, a scarred man's face, and a body floating face down in a sea of turbulent water.

Other pieces, black as night, descended to the ground, carrying a foreboding weight ...

Each shard exploded, shattering into millions of pieces.

Desperate, I wanted to catch each one before it hit the ground. I knew that each shard told a different story—as naturally as I knew, my vision revealed the truth.

Apprehension coiled in my gut. My heart pounded harder. A glass hit the floor, broke, and spilled water. I spun in my seat.

A busboy cleaned the broken glass from the floor as servers dodged the mess.

A middle-aged man dressed in a long black coat turned from my view. With long strides, he shouldered aside several people, dropped something on the ground, smacked money on the counter, and exited Coccia House.

Trystan gripped my forearm, jerking me from my thoughts. The granite intensity of his eyes stirred the brewing uneasiness in my gut.

"Callie?"

Heat crept into my cheeks as words died on my tongue. How long would it take the Dougreys to figure out I was a freak? Why did I even come tonight? Ugh. *Awkwardness* sucked.

Trystan squeezed my arm before he lowered his hand.

"Something's wrong." Erika sat on her heels before me. "You're rubbing your shoulder."

I winced and stopped.

Steve rested his elbow on the table and leaned toward me. "What's wrong with her shoulder?"

"Nothing, Steve." Erika gave me a concerned look. "I don't think I've ever seen you go from white to red to white in a single breath before." She lowered her voice. "Did something trigger a bad thought?"

I avoided looking at Erika and took a deep breath. In. Out. In. Out.

Hanson returned to our table with a crumpled paper in his hand. His eyes zeroed in on me.

"No." I pulled out my keys and slapped a ten on the table. "I need to get home."

Erika stood. "Where do you think you're going?"

"Jings," I cursed. "I'm going home."

"You're not looking right."

"I'm fine, Erika. Don't smother me."

"You're not driving." Hanson took my keys. "My shift ends in fifteen minutes. We'll take you home. By the way, this must be yours." Hanson handed me a thick, shiny, crumpled paper.

"What's this?"

"Don't ask me," Hanson said. "One of the waitresses found it and figured you dropped it."

Everyone went back to their conversations, leaving me alone. I pressed the creases out on my thigh, and an image formed on the page. It wasn't a paper, but a photo of me standing outside the high school three hours ago with Colin, Anna, and Trystan. A black pen mark scorned our faces, then scribbled across the photograph.

What in the hell! Why'd someone take my picture—our picture?

I fisted my hand around the photo and placed it in my pocket, then accepted Erika and Hanson's help. My rattled nerves couldn't handle driving. Couldn't handle the picture.

Most of my friends already thought I was a freak. Now, I'd given them more proof–the Dougreys proof. And why'd the stranger at the counter have that picture?

Less than half an hour later, Erika and Hanson dropped me off at my house.

First, visions of a fire plagued me. Now, this revelation of a shadowed man's face shattering right before my eyes. And the photo? What on earth is happening? The premonition of my family's murder had come before the break-in. I knew now that I should have paid more attention to that vision. How should I manage this one? I had only snapshots, not a complete picture. How was I to stop someone from floating, face down, in the water when I couldn't stop the murder of my own family? Or stop Nana from dying?

Worry mounted. My mind thumbed through my thoughts, dragging me over bed-of-nail images of their brutal murder. I couldn't face it again ...

CHAPTER 5

LEGENDS, MYTHS, & LIES

I crawled into bed, sunk into the pillows, and buried myself beneath a blanket of doubt. I couldn't shake the panic. Why was the vision of the fire plaguing my thoughts? I'd had predictions over the past ten years, but nothing this intense since my family had died. I hadn't even experienced a vision alerting me to the car accident. So, what was tonight's vision about? Why couldn't my parents have prepared me? Talked to me? Given me some clues? Why couldn't I be normal? I was a freak, cursed with predictions. If it weren't for the headaches that accompanied my visions, I could have assumed that they were nightmares. Then again, normal people had nightmares when they slept, not while they were awake, and normal people didn't have the ability to recall visions, as one might boot a saved file from a computer.

Hours later, I mentally kicked myself. I couldn't hide. Answers didn't grow out of thin air.

Spurred by the weird vision, I grabbed a bathrobe and turned on the computer, punched in the passcode, flopped into my chair, and stared at the monitor. Why did I get these visions? Why was I so weird? Did my parents get these? We all had similar birthmarks, but mine was in a different spot.

I wished that they'd given me some clues, but all Dad had said to me at the end was "Seran" as he'd clutched his chest over his mark and died. That's the only time I'd heard any explanation of our history.

I googled "Seran," clicked on the suggested word below it, "Serana," and got information on ancient, pure-blood vampires. Great. It was some game or movie out on the internet. I surfed through everything but found nothing on "Seran."

Forty-five minutes later, I found an interesting site entitled "Do you know where you come from?" The site explained various fragments of factual and mythical evidence that gave a picture of humankind's primitive days. It discussed ancient mysteries and the discovery of scrolls bearing Egyptian hieroglyphics, statues, and copper weapons.

My curiosity piqued as I perused proof of things supposedly unexplainable. The website offered fascinating explanations of how aliens had built the ancient pyramids. Another tidbit discussed was how the five-pointed star had influenced the development of the Egyptian calendar.

I searched for lost civilizations and scrolled from theory to speculation by scientists and archaeologists. I delved into lists of lost empires: the Khmer Empire, the Mycenaean, and two in what is now the United States—the Anasazi and Cahokia.

I rubbed my eyes and peered over at the clock at 1:22 a.m. My finger wandered on the mouse, and my eyes felt dry as words blended, one into another. Some of this information seemed to fit under what Colin called pseudo-archaeology and pseudo-history. Pseudo, meaning false, pretend, or unreal, is a fancy way of saying fake. That would fit what I'd read earlier, discussing the labyrinth associated with Minos. It made my skin crawl to think of a beast called a Minotaur-eating children.

Atlantis and the city of Troy popped up.

Atlantis was the name of a fictional island, a lost paradise, mentioned in Plato's works. I remembered some History Channel documentary I'd watched months back with Gramps talking about several supposed Atlantis locations.

This article said that people argued Atlantis was a fictional story expressing the dangers of greed, a hypothetical utopia that was destroyed.

I tried to click the mouse, but the cursor froze. It wouldn't budge, remaining stuck on the word "Thera." The island of Thera, also called Santorini—reportedly a highly-developed, peaceful society and a major shipping port.

I moved my finger over the cursor, and it finally moved. I explored the site, pictures were everywhere. It seemed they'd loved art and literature. A volcanic explosion had occurred, over a period of days, decimating the island and leaving trails of disaster that stretched for thousands of miles. The island had sunk into the sea, but some people still believed there was a link between the Minoan of Santorini, also known as Thera, and the legend of Atlantis.

I tapped the mouse, and the cursor raced to the bottom of the screen to an image of an ancient coin.

Its caption read: The city of Troy, not a myth. A coin, identified as the currency of the ancient city of Troy, had a woman depicted on it, wearing a wreath of ivy around her head. British archaeologist Frank Calvert, believed to have discovered the legendary city of Troy in northwestern Turkey in 1870, was also credited with finding the jewels that had once belonged to Helen of Troy.

I continued to explore websites.

The words "advanced civilization" and "alien" popped up again and again from articles on various sites. Controversy plagued every page I'd read, but if they could find proof of Homer's epic tale of Helen of Troy and the bones of giants who lived in Ohio, then someday I could find proof of who I really am. One thing was certain, "alien" was a concept too hard for me to believe. However, the truth remained—I had abilities that I didn't even understand.

Mentally drained, I shut down the computer. I wasn't insane. I wasn't fake. My search may have been inconclusive, but it confirmed I wasn't the only one in existence with a murky past.

CHAPTER 6

TROUBLE

Rays of sun peeked around burgundy curtains, and dust particles danced in the air, settling onto the dark furniture in my room. The morning chill crept into my bones. Faint scents of rosemary, onion, and lemon filled the air. I took a deep breath, throwing back the covers.

Gramps walked into my room. "Ah, sleeping in late. That's rare for you. Yesterday must've been rough. What with all that socializing."

"Nope." I lied, wishing I could tell him about my vision of some evil dude. Horrible things are coming, and I'm a freak of nature.

I could ask Gramps questions. Yet, every instinct screamed at me to stop. Don't talk about your mark. Don't talk about your premonitions. Why couldn't I ask Gramps questions? Or Nana?

"I'm fine." I inhaled the aroma of the sauce coming from the kitchen. "You're making spaghetti?"

"Yep." His gaze dropped to my smile. "Get dressed. We have a full day of work ahead of us. Got two new orders to fill." Gramps left my room, closing the door.

I dragged on my clothes and headed to the kitchen. Big bubbles popped in the huge pot on the stove. I dipped my finger into the pan.

"Don't you dare," Gramps threatened as he carried pasta in one hand and napkins in the other. "You'll wait till dinner tonight." He always allowed his sauce to simmer for nine hours before we could eat it. Pure torture. I loved his spaghetti.

"What are you doing?"

"Checking the pantry before I head to the mill. We need to stock up on some goods. Can you swing by the store later?" He put a box of pasta on the counter. "Oh, and Erika's mother could use some of that material your Nana has piled in the sewing room. When you're done, take it to her."

I nodded, avoiding eye contact with Gramps. Nana's favorite room was the last place I wanted to visit if I wanted to keep my emotions in check. I raided the fridge for an oatmeal bar and sprinted to the mill.

I filled flour orders through lunch, past three o'clock, but nothing went right. First, I couldn't find ties to bind the ends of the bags I'd filled. And someone hadn't bought the thirty-gallon trash bags, so I had nowhere to put it when I'd finished clearing the clutter in Gramps's office. At least I cleaned the leather belts and lubricated the bearings, keeping the pulleys from creating enough heat to start a fire when they were in motion.

Once finished, I'd locked the wooden door and made a break for the house. Gray clouds stretched behind white ones in the western sky.

My stomach growled in response to the aroma that filled the kitchen. I lifted the note from the table and read Gramps's handwriting.

PICK UP CANDY BARS WHILE YOU'RE IN TOWN. I WENT TO LIVINGSTON'S TO BORROW A TOOL.

Apparently, I couldn't avoid shopping.

On my way home from the store, gunmetal gray clouds hung in the sky, and I faced the storm head-on. Thunder cracked, splitting the sky and pulling an even darker curtain over it. Rain pelted the window, and lightning fingers reached toward the earth. My windshield wipers couldn't keep up with the flood of rainfall.

I squinted, gauging my path by the white line at the side of the road. My stomach tightened. Something shiny in the middle of the street reflected off the headlights. I swerved wide and went into the other lane.

Something thumped my car twice.

"OMJings."

Feeling the front-end drop, I jerked the wheel to the right, then took my foot off the accelerator and coasted to the edge of the road. I slapped the steering wheel and turned on my hazard lights.

"Crap. What'd I hit?" I opened the door, and rain pelted me.

The front tire was flat with a fist-sized hole right through it. I wiped the rain from my face, but it didn't help. The persistent downpour had already plastered my hair to my face. I had a back seat filled with food and fifteen miles between home and me. Ugh.

Lightning danced in the distance, drawing my attention to an object on the road. I ran over, grabbed a four-inch piece of iron, and threw it into the ditch where it couldn't hurt anyone else.

I set the jack and tire iron on the ground and loosened the lug nuts with my fingers—this was one time I didn't mind being strong. Once the jack was in place, I pushed on the lever and raised the Jeep.

I shivered as cold water seeped through my coat, turning it into a wet sponge. With the Jeep raised now, I removed the nuts with a twist. However, when I tugged on the tire, it wouldn't budge.

I yanked harder at the tire, forcing it off despite the rust that had welded it to the axle.

With a slick shift of gravel and a high-pitched, metallic screech, the jack kicked out from under the car.

"*Move*," someone shouted.

My heart raced. I scrambled backward into the muddy ditch. Filthy water splashed around my waist. The Jeep crashed to the ground, landing on its axle. I wiped the rain from my face. My eyes riveted on the jack on its side next to my Jeep.

Lightning flashed, silhouetting a tall man standing near the front bumper of my car.

Trystan?

My heart stopped in my chest. My ears rang. What's he doing here?

He approached and extended his hand. "Come on, the weather is getting worse. We'll call a tow truck."

I cringed at his sharp words. "Okay."

I tried to stand, but my foot slipped, sending me back down onto my butt. Water rushed into the ditch, all around me.

He stepped into the ditch. His fingers curved, firm but gentle, around my forearm. My instinct was to pull away, but I let him pull me up. His touch was a shock to my body's natural rhythm, but his gaze put my mind at ease, if only for an isolated moment. My gut spun. I cradled my head, losing my footing again. Trystan's hands gripped my waist. My thighs met his as he anchored me.

I took a deep breath and swiped away the rivulets of water from my eyes. Could it rain any harder?

"I'm letting go." His grip released as if I'd scalded him, but his hand stayed inches from my body. "Please don't fall. Where are your keys?" He yelled over a crack of thunder.

"In the J-Jeep." I bit my lower lip.

He pointed to his car. "Can you make it?"

"Yes, but I'm muddy."

"Don't worry. Go."

I pulled open his car door and climbed in. My muscles hurt, and pain inflamed my thigh when I leaned over to look back at him. He disappeared into the darkness, but a set of headlights passing by illuminated his figure, carrying several sacks.

Trystan put the grocery bags on the back seat and climbed into the car. A cold blast of air swept in with him. He leaned between the bucket seats, pulled a frayed towel from the back, and shoved it in my face.

"Here." His cold word intensified my chill.

Why's he so mad? It's not like I could've prevented the accident.

Bright white dash lights came on. Music played.

Confusion invaded my head, making it hurt. I mentally calculated what had happened. He hadn't shown up until after I'd removed the lug nuts, around the time I'd cranked up the jack. I hadn't used inhuman strength to push the Jeep away from me. I'm safe. I lifted my head and gave a forced smile.

"How are you feeling?" His eyes roamed over me like a hawk discovering its prey, but his words rang with genuine concern.

My temperature rose, the heat coating me like a blanket of warmth, caressing my skin and going straight to my toes.

That's odd. I'd become unnaturally warm despite my still-drenched clothes.

"Not the best."

"What happened back there?"

I turned, knees bumping the center console. Why did he talk with a forced calm in his voice?

"I swerved to avoid something in the road. Instead, I hit it and ended up in the ditch."

"I saw your vehicle give way. I didn't know what to do besides yell." His accent grew more pronounced with each sharp word. He peered into the rearview mirror, then shrugged. His hands gripped the wheel at four and eight. "What else do you remember?" His thumbs rubbed the wheel as seconds passed.

"Everything happened so fast. The jack made a noise, my Jeep shifted, you shouted, and I ended up in the ditch." What wasn't he saying?

"Man, I didn't even know you were there." He exhaled, and his shoulders dropped a fraction. "Rescuing you is becoming a regular activity."

"I'm sorry if I messed your night up, but you're okay?" A shiver went down my spine. One minute, I'm freezing, the next, I'm hot.

A car passed us, its taillights swallowed by the fog.

"My brother was killed in an accident on a night like this."

"Recently?"

He turned his head ever so slowly. "No."

His pain tongue-tied me. Besides, if I pried, he would have the right to ask me questions. I wasn't ready for that.

A lock of damp hair fell over my brow. "Can we go? I live fifteen miles down this road."

He turned and looked at me, his lip twitching as if he were suppressing a laugh. "I know." He put the car in drive and pressed the gas. "So, how long have you lived here?"

"Since I was seven." I bit my bottom lip, shivering. It's not as if I told him a secret.

He motioned, pointing with his index finger to the front window. "Does it often rain like this here?"

"It's Ohio. Everything's unpredictable."

"Where'd you live before Ohio?"

"California." My fingers found the door handle. "Where did you live in Europe?"

"We never stayed in one place long." He sighed. "My aunt's job working with the Night Humanitarian Relief Agency kept us traveling. We lived in several countries. Austria and Germany are my favorites."

"I want to see Italy—the Vatican, Rome, and Venice. My dad proposed to my mom in Venice." I mentally kicked myself for saying too much, but talking eased the discomfort.

"From how you talk, I'm guessing you don't intend to stay here."

"No." Cold settled in my bones. The adrenaline rush ended. "I'm leaving as soon as I can. How about you?"

"My dad plans for me to go to Ashworth."

"Your dad?" Curiosity got the best of me. "I thought your parents were dead."

"My mom passed away, and my aunt and uncle raised me. Dad lives out west. He runs a Fortune 500 company." His fingers stretched out along his thigh as he steered with his other hand. "At some point, he expects me to manage it."

He turned down my lane before I said anything. So weird. Of all the places in New Cumberlin Falls for this guy to live, he ends up being my neighbor. A small building we rented out, nestled behind the mill and a pond, appeared over the crest of the hill. Gramps stood on the loading dock of the mill under the overhang.

"That's my grandfather. Come on in. I'll get you something to dry off with."

"Let's grab the groceries first."

We got the bags out of the car and ran toward the house. The fire in the wood burner crackled in the living room, and spaghetti sauce flavored the air.

The door slammed behind us.

Gramps walked in and stood near the kitchen stove. "What happened? You're as wet as a fish." Concern coated his words.

"Got a flat tire, and Trystan helped me. My Jeep's down by Blue Road." I nodded toward Trystan and wrapped my arm around my middle, trying to ignore the coiling pain in my gut. It didn't help that my chest still hurt from the first accident. "He's starting school here."

Trystan nodded and extended his hand. Gramps gripped it. "Hi, nice to meet you. I'm Trystan Dougrey. We moved up Cherry Hill from you."

"Talk about luck," Gramps said. "Thanks for helping her."

"You're welcome."

"What brings you to the Falls?"

"My aunt got a job at the hospital, and my cousin starts at Ashworth University. My other cousin, Anna, and I will be juniors at the high school. We would've started earlier, but there was a mix-up with transfers."

"Ashworth's a good institution," Gramps said.

Trystan sounded like he was reading from a script. Intuition told me he wasn't lying, but I wasn't buying his ready-made speech. I left the kitchen and returned with two towels.

"Hey," Gramps said as I handed Trystan a towel. "I met Dr. Dougrey earlier today. Real nice girl."

My heart twisted. "Gramps, why were you at the hospital?"

"Don't worry, I'm fine." His baby blue eyes smiled at me for the first time in weeks but then dimmed. "Max got hurt on the sheller over at the mill. I'm down a worker for a few days."

"He'll be okay?" I asked.

"Oh, he's hurting. Cut the underside of his hand and two fingers. He needed stitches." Gramps tugged on the end of his beard. "Mark my words. He'll be hitting the Ibuprofen tonight, but he'll be okay."

I glanced at my muddy feet. Shoeprints covered the floor. I pulled the towel tighter around my shoulders and pushed my dark hair behind my ear. I dragged a chair from the kitchen table and sat.

"Do you want to sit?"

Trystan dried his face with the towel and shook his head. "Camden told me about the mill."

Gramps smiled. "It's my pride and joy. It's a functioning water mill, but don't let me ramble." Blue eyes pierced mine, and his smile faded. "You look pale. It's been a long time since you had a cold. I don't think standing here is doing you any good. Go soak in a warm bath."

My shirt clung to my skin like a wet glove. "I'll be fine. I need to eat something."

"Don't fuss about food. Go on. I'll make you some soup. Spaghetti will only upset your tummy." Gramps ran a thumb along his suspender. "You go, dear. I'll get Kirt's

Towing to pick up your Jeep. And don't worry. I'll save you some sauce. It's better the next day anyway." He turned toward Trystan. "When Callie feels better, you must stop back."

I left the kitchen, feeling Trystan's eyes dissecting me.

I flipped the light switch in my room, undressed, turned on the bathwater, and climbed in. As I lay there soaking, the washcloth covered my face, blocking the bathroom lights and leaving me in peaceful darkness. After the water cooled and my skin wrinkled, I got out of the tub, grabbed a towel, and dried off. An engine roared to life. Pulling back the curtains, I saw red lights going down the drive.

Sometimes, Gramps could talk until someone showed wrinkles.

CHAPTER 7

METAMORPHOSIS

I fluffed my pillows, careful to avoid the damp spot. I closed my eyes. Hours later, sleep still eluded me, and discomfort gnawed at me. I threw my blankets back, hit shuffle on my iPod, and opened the window an inch. Nothing eased my pain.

The inconsistent *spack spack speck spack speck* on the windowpane competed with the *ping ping ping* of rain hitting the metal roof. I tried to drown it out with music, but the bass only hammered away within me, increasing my agitation.

My mind tangled with Erika's words from a month ago, "you're missing out on all the fun." What could it hurt to befriend someone new? I'd met three new people this week, and one of them had managed to save my butt twice. Erika was right. I needed some fun.

My heart accelerated. I dug my palm over my chest bone, feeling the spike in my pulse.

Something as bright as a bolt of lightning exploded in my head. I slammed my eyes shut feeling as if my skin had electrified and tightened, stretching across my bones. Pressure compounded within me. The lightning heat struck my core, spilling into my body. Organs lit up. I gasped for air. Every breath I took caused pain. My blood felt as if it had turned to acid. The pain increased and amplified in frequency. It hummed through me, constricting an invisible band on my skin as a deep, clawing pain ate away at my flesh. Muscles constricted.

My mind ached from the intensity–the pain flooded through me with such force that I stopped breathing and screamed from the depths of my soul. My heart knocked against my ribcage as my lungs gasped for air, and hopelessness clung like a weight.

Time passed.

Without warning, the pressure in my head decreased, and an explosion of peaceful bliss consumed me. A vision of golden light surrounded me, red waves coursing through it.

The heat withdrew in increments, and the pain subsided. I took a breath of air and allowed myself to embrace the mental peace as the searing agony eased. I exhaled, catching my breath, and my muscles twitched, falling into rhythmic contractions throughout my body.

My breathing came easier, and with every inhalation, a sense of control came over me. I opened my eyes, pushed my elbows under me, and willed my legs to move. My foot jerked, adding a few wrinkles to the linen. Sweat rolled down my back.

"Thank heaven." Gramps set a glass on the nightstand. "You're awake." I removed the cool washcloth he had pressed to my forehead. "Take these." He handed me two pills. "I ran into Steve's mom. She heard that they'd sent six students home from school with the flu."

I swallowed the pills.

"You scared me, dear. I don't think I can handle any more stress." The quiet pleading in Gramps's voice squeezed my heart for several beats. He moved about the room, the floorboards creaking. "I haven't come to terms with losing my Adele. Then you come down sick."

The creaking stopped. I opened my eyes and met the depths of concern in his.

"What day is it?" My tongue was dry as sawdust.

"It's Sunday morning. Mrs. Sundries checked in on you a couple of times, but she didn't want Erika to come." He shook his head. "I made you some broth, dear. You'll need something in your stomach. Oh, and Erika called to see how you were doing, too." He dropped the washcloth into the hamper. "I'll be back in a few. And don't plan on going to school tomorrow. You need your rest." He left, leaving my door open a crack.

I dragged myself up against the headboard, threw back the covers, and sipped the cool air. Strange as it was, I remembered the first time this had happened. I was seven when I fell ill. Mom had looked after me, frantic with worry. I shuddered at the thought. Later, after that first major illness, I'd begun to experience premonitions, and I'd noticed my ability to read voice intonations. Worst of all, adapting to the *curse* of strength. I had to learn to keep my emotions in check—revealing my powers wasn't a risk I was willing to take.

I dug my fingers into my palm, trying to erase the memory of discovering that I was different from the average person.

I focused on the neon numbers of my alarm clock as a residual ache throbbed in my neck muscles. Over twenty-four hours of hell with the same sickness that had lasted nine hours when I was seven, and I hadn't experienced the golden light that surrounded me.

Jings. What's going on?

In a way, this *sickness* was some changing, a metamorphosis of sorts. If this were anything like my first experience, an emerging ability wouldn't be far behind.

CHAPTER 8

CONFUSION

"Come on, boy." I needed fresh air. Walking would have to work. Anxiety about my illness drained me. And it didn't help that I slept the day away and missed another day of school.

Tesla leaped to my side. I hooked the chain to his collar and went out. The moon was full, and a gentle breeze blew wisps of hair in my face. I pulled my coat tighter around me and put on my gloves.

I stuck to the road's edge, feeling like a prisoner escaping her cell. I breathed in the cool air, disturbed by the flu-like symptoms I had experienced. Since last night, a weird, pulsating current radiated on my skin like some elastic band, humming at a low frequency. Was this connected to the transformation? What would this metamorphosis bring?

My nerves twisted, tightening, remembering that my first premonition had revealed my parents' murder.

I focused on the vision I'd had at Coccia House as I made my way down the long drive. What was the significance of the man's face shattering into smaller actions? Was the other man with the scar a threat? Who was the person floating in the water, and how did these events relate to me? And why'd someone have a picture of me? Us?

Over the years, I'd learned to trust my visions, but the interpretation was difficult. Life had to play out, and I must be ready for anything despite the consequences.

Lost in my thoughts, I hadn't realized I'd returned home. I walked past the last oak tree. Smoke rose from the chimney. Parked by the garage were a blue Jetta and a silver Cadillac. Steve's uncle must be here.

I opened the door and met Erika and Anna sitting at the kitchen table. Gramps was boiling water on the stove. Mr. Lindy, Steve's uncle, stood off to one side, leaning against the fridge. Sheriff Travis poured a cup of coffee.

"You left without saying anything." Gramps lowered his eyes. "You had me worried."

I placed my coat on the hook over the apple crates. "Sorry." I unhooked Tesla's leash and hung it over the wooden peg by the basket.

"Your granddad's right, girl," Lindy said. "Strange things are happening around here. You need to be careful."

"What're you talking about?" Erika asked.

"Not now, Lindy," Sheriff Travis cleared his throat. "This isn't a topic I want to discuss."

Gramps stiffened. "What aren't you sayin', Travis?"

"Everyone will hear of it tomorrow." Lindy pursed his lips. "It's no secret."

Sheriff Travis glared at Lindy. "No, it's not a secret, but it's dang hard to admit the investigation's at a dead end. We can't find the perp who killed the professor."

"What's this world coming to?" Gramps shook his head.

Sheriff Travis's friendship meant the world to me. He helped Gramps sort through his emotions—even the loss of Nana.

Mr. Lindy opened his mouth, but Gramps interrupted. "Let's change the topic, Lindy. I don't want these girls getting nightmares and all."

Gramps's pale face spoke volumes. He didn't like hearing anyone being hurt.

"You're looking better." Erika winked at me. "Maybe you'll be up to going to school tomorrow?"

Missing a day of school sucked. I hated playing catch-up with homework.

"Come sit down, dear." Gramps set three mugs on the table for us girls. "I've made hot cocoa."

Anna took her cup. "Thanks, Mr. Croskney."

Mr. Lindy and Sheriff Travis hung out with Gramps at Wooster Brew, a local coffee shop. Mr. Lindy ran a marina up at Lake Erie. In the off-season, he stayed here. It was good that Gramps's friends visited. He seemed happier being around people. Just before I'd gotten sick, he showed signs of enjoying life again. I had stopped hearing him pace the floors at night.

Mr. Lindy tugged on his sweater sleeve. "How you feeling, Callie?"

I forced a smile. "Much better." Mr. Lindy was the town gossip and Steve's uncle on his mother's side. I had no wish to say anything that would circulate as soon as he walked out the door.

He pulled out a chair and sat next to me, almost blocking Anna from my view. "The flu is going around.

You must have gotten it good. Your granddad said you've been sick."

Gramps cleared his throat. "It didn't do any good. Her getting a flat tire and being stuck out in the pouring rain." He turned to Anna. "It was good your cousin stopped to help. How's the boy doing?"

"Trystan's fine."

"He's a nice young man." Gramps set his mug on the counter. "Most boys wouldn't think of helping someone, especially in nasty conditions."

Mr. Lindy nodded in agreement. "How do you like school?"

"I love it," Anna replied. "Today was my first day. It helped that I met Callie, Erika, and Steve last week. And what's best is, I don't have to wear a uniform."

"You guys had to dress alike?" Erika cringed. "Could students at least wear jewelry?"

Anna grinned. "No, not many students wore jewelry. We went to a private school overseas briefly before we were homeschooled. They were strict. Girls wore blue skirts and white blouses. The boys wore dress pants with white button-down shirts. Home school was much easier."

Erika rolled her eyes. "Man, that would suck. I couldn't give up my clothes—it's what defines me, and I sure wouldn't give up wearing my bracelets." Erika had to find a new bangle almost everywhere we went. She'd break the Guinness Book of World Records with how many she owned.

"Then I'm doing it all wrong," Gramps said playfully. "Here, I thought bib overalls were foxy."

"For train conductors," Mr. Lindy said.

Gramps's hearty snort lifted my spirits.

"All you need is a whistle." I set my hot chocolate down.

Gramps tugged his suspender buckle and snorted again. "Well, I'm not the only one wearing them. Principal Kennedy and his son are wearing them, too."

"His son's four, Gramps." I wrinkled my nose. "Stop saying foxy."

"Mr. Santos wore them when he farmed with my dad." Erika's mug rattled on the table, echoing through the sudden silence in the room. "Oooops."

I stared at Gramps in the corner of the kitchen. "It's okay." He cringed and dropped his heavy head.

"Does anyone know how Mr. Santos is doing?" I asked, breaking the uncomfortable silence. The last word squeaked out. I wanted to see him, but he continued to refuse visitors.

Lindy's mouth opened, but Sheriff Travis spoke first.

"He has months of rehabilitation ahead of him, but he's doing better. Right now, he's in physical therapy." He gave me a weak smile. "How's Max?"

I went to the refrigerator, pulled out the milk, and got the cocoa packet from the cabinet.

"Anyone care for another cup?" I took the pot from the stove and poured it.

Gramps rubbed the back of his neck. "Max is fine. The poor man is going crazy. He came by yesterday, asking if he could do some work. He's a big help around here, and I can't afford him getting hurt again. Doc told him not to make a fist. If he does, he'll tear out those stitches. We needed to hire someone before Max got hurt." Gramps put his mug next to mine, nodding. I tipped over the pot and added hot water to his cup. "With Max down, I hired that Trystan feller."

The pot slipped from my grip. I darted backward, scalding water spilling onto the kitchen floor.

A gasp escaped my lips.

Gramps grabbed my hands. "Dear, did you get hurt?" His eyes narrowed as they took in every inch of me. Anna threw a towel at my feet and dried things up. Tesla licked the floor by my heels. Jings, I'd also spilled the cocoa packet.

"I'm fine. I didn't have a tight grip on the pot." Anxiety festered in me. The idea of Trystan working at the mill set me off. Max worked while I was at school. He would leave me a note, so I picked up and filled in where he left off, but Trystan would be working at the same time as me, which would give me little privacy.

"You're making my hair go gray, girl." He chuckled, but his eyes held a weight of uneasiness, and his tone implied more. "Between needing help at the mill, Kirt's repair cost on your Jeep, and you being sick, I've had all a man can handle."

And Nana died over five weeks ago—my feelings were still raw. "You got an estimate?" I asked, hoping to redirect his attention.

Gramps tugged at his beard. "Yeah, and you'll be driving my car for a while."

Ouch. From Gramps's expression, I'd be working my butt off over the next three months to pay for the repairs.

Anna pushed stray hairs behind her ear. "Callie can ride to school with Trystan and me."

Gramps's hands dropped from his beard, exposing a smile. He looked at the three of us girls. "I like the sound of that."

"Gramps ..." I pursed my lips, giving him a pleading look.

"Don't you go, Gramps-ing me," he said. "It'll do you some good. Car-pooling never hurt no one. They're going to the same place you are. Plus, I like having my car around when I need it." He smiled wider as I frowned. It was a closed subject.

My weekend had gone from unexpected sickness to dependency on others for transportation to school. What was Gramps trying to prove?

Mr. Lindy pushed himself away from the table. "We'll be leaving." Lindy groaned as he stood. "It's not fun, trying to stand on a bad knee."

"Is the church making meals for you?" Gramps asked.

Mr. Lindy and Sheriff Travis put on their coats. "No, I hired a girl to come clean. Steve and his mother will be around to drop off meals. My sister isn't much of a cook, but she prepares a mean TV dinner." He took two steps back and shifted his weight from his bad leg. "I want to get the surgery over with, so I can get back out on the lake. I've had my boat docked up on Erie for the past two summers. With this darn knee, it's been difficult to walk on the deck. You and Callie will have to join me up there this summer." He turned to Anna and Erika. "Callie might like to have some of her friends come along."

"My uncle's got a boat." Anna scratched at her nose. "We love it."

"Callie doesn't like the water," Gramps said. "And you know it, Lindy."

Water, boats, and I don't mix. The first time Mr. Lindy took us to Lake Erie, I ended up hanging over the side of the railing, throwing up, and watching what had once been my lunch float in the wake.

Mr. Lindy adjusted his leather glove. "She doesn't have to go out on the boat. She can use the log cabin off the point." He jerked his chin. "I'll pick up the boat gear sometime later. Thanks for keeping it. I ran out of room in my building, and storage fees are astronomical."

"Glad to help out a friend. I'll see you next time."

Sheriff Travis and Mr. Lindy left.

"I'll clean up in here." Gramps pointed to the living room. "You girls go on."

"I've got to get home. Trystan needs the car." Anna put the wet towel on the counter. "You ready, Erika?"

Erika scooted to the edge of her chair. "I'm glad you're doing better. See you tomorrow at school. Bye." She hugged me, and they left.

I stared out the window as their car disappeared down the drive.

The clink of glass hitting the table brought my attention back to the kitchen. Gramps sat, his eyebrows drawn together, his lips pursed. "You scared me. If I'm not around, leave a note before you go walking the dog."

"Why are you so upset?"

"Upset? No, I'm not upset." He exhaled. "But it's important I know where you're at. You didn't take your phone, and I couldn't get hold of you. What gave me comfort was knowing Tesla wasn't here. It's not easy raising you. I love you, and don't want anything else bad to happen."

The weight of his words crowded my heart. "I'm sorry, Gramps. I didn't think. I just needed some fresh air. I'll be careful, I promise." I nibbled on my lip. "Do you think hiring Trystan's a good idea?"

"He's a good kid, and we'll need the help, especially when grain production picks up in the next few months. The boy won't be starting for a while, so it gives me time to put some things in order at the mill. You'll need to keep up with things until he starts, but I think this will work."

He had never pried or asked questions like this before, nor had he ever asked me to leave a note indicating where I was going. Nana's death caused him to react differently to everything. Still, at least he wasn't withdrawing or avoiding life altogether.

CHAPTER 9

QUICK EXIT

F og rose over the creek at the high side of the mill, and the snow was ankle-deep. I pulled my hair up in a messy ponytail and threw on some clothes. I grabbed my books and dashed outside at the sound of a honk.

Parked by the loading dock sat Trystan's blue Jetta, its passenger window rolled down.

"Hi, Callie." Anna hitched her thumb over her shoulder. "Hop in."

Trystan peered back at me. "Hi. You feeling better?"

I gazed at him as an electrical current zipped through me. "Ah, uh. Somewhat." I blinked, trying to concentrate. Okay, why'd I feel this electrical weirdness around him?

The first bell had already rung by the time we got to school. I plunged into the chaos of the main hall and bumped someone's elbow as I maneuvered through the crowd. We passed the lobby, heading toward the central office's hallway.

"Ouch." Anna adjusted her books in her arms. "Man, I've been poked and jabbed so often this morning that I feel like a soccer ball at a scrimmage."

"That's one reason why I'm glad my locker's on the second floor, across from my history class. It's in the alcove, where it's not so crowded." The construction had caused students to crowd certain hallways.

Anna looked over her shoulder. "I forgot to tell you. Principal Kennedy has us sharing a locker."

"Cool." I bit my lip.

Trystan followed us but walked past my locker to reach the last one on the opposite side. Ashton Van De-camp threw his books and coat into his locker. Trystan waited and put in his stuff once Ashton walked off with his girlfriend. The guys didn't talk.

Steve met up with us. He hung out, talking while Anna and I stuffed things inside. I gathered my books and listened to the morning gossip.

"Hey, did you know Miss Delong has a pop quiz planned this week?" Steve flung his coat over his shoulder.

"No, No. No. Please tell me you're joking." Erika stood behind me, drawing the others' attention. "If I don't pass this next English quiz, my parents won't let me drive."

"Drop the class," Steve said.

"I can't." Erika grimaced, clutching her coat. "What do your parents do if your grades suck?"

"Nothing." Steve shrugged, shutting my locker door. "I make my own rules. My dad left us, and Mom gave up."

"Why didn't you tell us?" I knew his parents had divorced, but I hadn't known his mom wasn't trying anymore, and his dad was gone. It went against Steve's typical behavior. He usually had to be the first to report the latest news.

"It ain't a big deal. Anyway, it's no secret. They finalized the divorce last month. I like it this way. I get my pick of TV dinners, Mom does her thing, and I do mine."

The second bell rang.

Steve's glasses slipped on his nose. He pushed them back. "Oh, did you hear—"

"Callie?" My name sounded from across the hall. Logan and the other basketball players approached, and people moved to the edge of the hallway. "What happened to your Jeep? You weren't driving it this morning."

"It's in the shop," Steve said. "I told you that already."

Logan's eyes blazed. The skin around them crinkled in contempt. "I'm asking her, Steve." Logan jerked his chin at me.

I scanned the hall for a quick exit. Trystan leaned against his locker. I met his gaze, and a tingle shivered down my spine.

He smiled and nodded.

"Callie." Logan snapped his fingers in my face. "Yoo-hoo. Callie."

"Yeah," I said, turning to face Logan.

Logan's gaze flickered over my shoulder at Trystan. "Next time, bring it to the dealership." Logan adjusted his Ray-Ban sunglasses. "My dad's mechanics could repair it."

"My granddad got it taken care of." Why was Logan talking to me? We haven't said two words to each other all year except at Coccia House the other night.

"You're cute when you're flustered, Tresham." Logan gave a weak grin. "My dad got Dylan and me each a new car. Call me if you ever need a ride. See you around." Logan and his gang left.

Steve stepped closer to me and tugged on my arm.

I twisted my combo lock. "Logan's never shown interest in me before. Now, all of a sudden, he does. What's up?"

The warning bell rang, and students poured into their classrooms, except Erika, Anna, and Steve, who stood, mute as mimes.

Erika cleared her throat. "My guess is Logan likes the challenge of being your first boyfriend."

My dating life was non-existent, but not for lack of Erika's matchmaking efforts. Dating wasn't an option for me. I preferred my anonymity, which dictated distance between others and myself. While I was okay with cautious friendships, I'd never considered serious dating.

And I never thought someone might like the challenge.

A pressure like an elastic band tightened above my skin. An edgy vibration slowly increased in frequency. I glanced at Steve. "Why is Logan aggravated with you?"

Steve shrugged.

Why wasn't he talking? Usually, he wouldn't shut up. This was stupid. I wasn't so distracted I couldn't tell he was hiding something.

Erika lowered her eyelids. "Logan's mad because Steve likes you, too."

Steve blanched. "Erika, you promised not to say anything."

I gave him an awkward smile. This was the last thing I'd expected. I'm glad Erika told me. Steve was cool. I could handle him, but I didn't like Logan's attention.

Morning classes crawled by. Twice, Logan and I crossed paths in the hall between lessons, but I avoided him. The last thing I wanted to do was give him any encouragement. I'd already said no to prom.

Finally, the bell rang for lunch. The cafeteria was alive with conversation. Anna and Trystan sat with Camden,

Tony, Jessica, and Sandy. Steve set down his tray as Erika and I approached the table. Steve wet his lips and stood back, away from me. I smiled, trying to put him at ease. He sat down as far away from me as the table allowed. It wasn't Steve's fault Logan saw me as a conquest. Steve must have been trying to mention to me this morning Logan liked me when he interrupted him. I'd never cared about gossip, but Logan's breakup with Lizzy was still on everyone's lips. I didn't intend to be the next prize.

Chatter echoed around the table.

Despite all my thinking, it was Trystan who held my attention. He pulled food to the one side of his plate with his fork, never taking a bite, while he talked with Camden. His eyes seemed pained in some unmistakable way, as if unpleasant thoughts distracted him. He sat with quiet confidence, his back against the wall. One thing was certain, conversations weren't going to be boring, what with everyone attracted to our table.

CHAPTER 10
EMOTIONS

An earthy scent crowded me. I ran my fingers across the worn leather belt in the grain room, feeling a light layer of dust. I'd have to clean it. I caught up on all the grain Gramps hadn't finished. I'd gotten it cleaned, shelled, and bagged. It was a mindless, repetitive process, filling bag after bag. I packed the full bags in the cooler before shutting down the pulley system and lights.

I sat on Dad's old wooden workbench at the windowsill. It was a shrine, just as my dad had left it before dying.

I seldom came into this room. When we visited, my dad hung out in the woodshop more than in any other room. This is where he made things with us. He had some old books on the shelf next to his bench. Almost every night, Dad would read us poetry at bedtime.

I scrunched my eyes shut, pushing memories away, and rubbed my shoulder. Loneliness ached within me as I traced my fingers along the raised crimson edge of the birthmark under my shirt. I'd never known anyone outside of my family who could see it. No matter how familiar I was with every line, living with a mark I hardly understood wasn't easy. A mark I couldn't explain.

Since the night I had gotten sick, an elastic current remained present, humming in a low tone above my skin. I knew the pulsation had a direct link to my birthmark. Yesterday, when I couldn't figure out what was happening with Steve, and I'd become flustered, the current had hummed in my ear at a higher frequency. How did this feeling fit into my reality?

I hugged my midriff and leaned back against the windowsill, closing my eyes. More was at play here than what I could see. Strong emotions and energy pulsated through me with increased urgency, and visions flashed cryptic snapshots. I wished I knew what I was dealing with ... then again, maybe I didn't want to know.

The sewing room door swung wide. A daybed sat in the far corner, and piles of fabric were stacked against the wall. I put off cleaning. In a sick, twisted way, I felt like my actions would disturb the dead. We'd left Dad's space at the mill alone. Why not Nana's? Gramps wanted it done, but I wasn't ready to do it. I closed the door and headed to my room.

After a shower, I put on my robe and went to the kitchen. The answering machine flashed a red neon number one. Maybe Trystan had called to cancel the tour we'd planned for this afternoon. I toweled my damp hair, dried the ends, and pressed the playback button.

"Dear, I'm running behind," Gramps's voice garbled from the machine. "They didn't have our orders filled, so I'll be home late. Go on with your plans. I'll catch up with you later. Oh, and it looks like I'll have to go to PA sometime in April. I wish I'd never taken the seat as treasurer with the National Grain Association. No one can make decisions. See you shortly, dear. Oh, and don't cook me anything tonight. I'll grab some food with Johnny Simms."

CHAPTER II

DIFFERENCES

I dreaded it all day. Part of me hoped Trystan would call and cancel the appointment, or he'd forgotten about our scheduled tour. But Tesla's bark told me a different story. I watched his Jetta coming down the gravel drive. Knots tightened in my stomach. I grabbed my coat, stepped off the front porch, and approached Trystan. He stood before the mill, looking up at the roofline, hands deep in his coat pockets.

He turned and faced me, his eyes dancing. "This is your Gramps's baby." His grin lifted into a smile, and a warm zing shot through my stomach.

I stepped back.

The odd sensations I experienced when around him confused me. My inner radar registered no serious warnings. But my sixth sense told me something, and

I had to learn to trust my instinct—the sensation never failed me yet.

I cleared my throat. "Umm, well, not only his baby but all of New Cumberlin Falls' actually. The mill was the first industry in Wayne County. The old water wheel is what draws people." I stepped forward and walked toward the mill. "We get people from all over the States." I opened the double door as it creaked.

"How old is this place?"

This was no typical tour. Trystan had to know how things functioned if he planned to work here. Someone always around, hovering and working with me—the thought sickened me. What if I had another vision? And he witnessed me having it? He'd see me for the freak I was.

I swallowed a groan, pushing away the thoughts. "Samuel Nemon built the mill in 1816."

We walked toward a wooden circle with spokes and a bucket hanging above it tied to a rope. "This is the bull wheel. It controls the main-line shaft over there, and all the pulleys run off it." Two long metal shafts ran across the ceiling, and leather belts and metal wheels hung from them. "There are five components to the mill: cider press, sawmill, grist mill, metal shop, and woodshop. The metal and wood shops share the same space, but it's a humongous room. And this area remains like a museum. My grandpa doesn't want to ruin the historical look, plus the Department of Interior protects it. Of the four stories, Gramps permits only one room to use electrical power. Everything else runs solely off the power of the waterwheel."

"In which area are most people interested?"

"The woodshop. Come on, I'll show you." We entered that room and moved closer to the bull wheel. "You might want to plug your ears. It'll get loud in here, and watch your head. Getting hit in the head by a moving pulley can cause one heck of a headache. Been there."

"It'd sure knock some sense into you." We both laughed.

"You got that right. Felt that monster's wrath more than once." I stopped before the line shaft control and gestured for him to take hold. The seven-foot-long stick hung down from the ceiling, allowing someone to turn on the wheel. "Don't let go." We lifted the shaft, and the room came to life.

The floor shook, and a low rumble sounded under our feet. A roaring whine echoed throughout the room. Belts and pulleys pulsated above our heads in all different directions. An earthy scent stirred. The control vibrated beneath our grasps. His eyes moved from object to object.

The control handle jerked. Trystan gazed at me. I gave him a reassuring nod, and his gaze wandered again. He stayed transfixed on another object in the far corner. I pulled the control shaft down, lowering the watergate. Everything went still.

"The jerking sensation is the change in rhythmic response to the water going over the wheel. It doesn't always maintain a constant speed. It's important to watch the wheel. If the mill shakes uncontrollably, it means the water wheel is out of balance. It could destroy the internal gears if the wheel doesn't stay balanced with the right amount of water pressure. With practice, you'll learn how to gauge the mill's quirks."

"This place is awesome." He gave me a megawatt smile. "I can see you love it."

I hesitated, but the words fell too easily. "It's as close as I can get to being home." A nervous chuckle escaped my lips. It helped staunch the ache in my throat and kept the memories at bay. His penetrating gaze didn't bother me this time. "This is the actual heart of the mill. Every line shaft is like an artery going to an organ. The water is the blood, supplying the energy to operate everything."

He put his hands in his jacket. "How come you know so much about the property?"

"History has always fascinated me. My dad fostered my interest. We'd spend our summers here, and Dad always tinkered, building and repairing equipment or collecting old material for tours." I took a breath. "The information sat for years, but about five years ago, we started using it." I sat down on the steps.

He joined me, sitting inches away. "Despite all our traveling, I'd never seen anything like this. The mill's technology is astounding."

"You do a lot with your family."

"Last year, we went rock climbing in Colorado. Colin's trying to talk me into parasailing with him this summer. My aunt and uncle want to go east to the ocean. It beats the unpredictable Ohio weather we've had. Have you ever been rock climbing?"

"The extent of my adventures begins and ends with opening a book." Safe lie? "And a little hiking and running. I even do some photography and play guitar." The way he talked about his family made me miss mine.

His eyebrows drew together, assessing my words as if he'd expected me to say something altogether different. "You're not the adventurous type?"

"One can't get too adventurous living with an old guy like Gramps."

"If you were given a choice of anything ... anything you could do, what would it be?"

"I don't know."

"What's the first thing that comes to your mind?"

"Run a marathon. Learn to swim. I'd like to travel around Europe."

His smile showed his dimple. "You told me about traveling the other night. Are you going to attend Ashworth University?"

"Haven't given it much thought. I'd like to do something in journalism or writing, maybe teaching. I've even thought about antiquing, but that doesn't require a major. How about you—wait, you're going to Ashworth, right?"

"That's the plan."

"You don't sound as if you want to go." Erika had talked about what her brother, Trevor, had to do when he'd gone to college. The idea of sharing a bedroom with strangers, not to mention bathrooms, made me cringe.

"Mmm, it's safest to say I am my dad's"—he held up his hands and made quotation marks with his fingers—"lost cause."

What a loaded statement to dump on a person. What wasn't he saying? Had his real parents given up on him? Were his aunt and uncle his last hope? Could he have—no, stop thinking as if you gotta question everyone's history.

I swallowed and steered the conversation to a neutral topic. I didn't want it to end. "Do you like Mustangs?"

"Horses or cars?"

I rolled my eyes. "Funny."

"What year?" he asked.

"'67."

"That's the best year. I like the body style."

"Gramps has one. I haven't ridden in it much. I wouldn't be surprised if my grandmother never had."

He lowered his head. "Your voice softens when you speak of her."

"She meant the world to me. By the way, I never thanked you for staying with me during the accident."

"It's nothing." He waved a hand once. "Anyone would've done it."

"I miss her ... It's hard, her being gone." Callie glanced down at her hands as she fiddled with a nail. "She understood me. In ways, Gramps doesn't. I think it's a girl thing, but her compassion helped me deal with the loss of my family. She didn't let me get down for long. She believed in keeping the mind and the hands working. When I'd have a black mood, she made me work my frustration off, bagging grain." I turned, accidentally bumping his knee, and bit my lip. I was talking too much. "You don't mind the idea of grinding grain? It can be hard, lugging twenty-five and fifty-pound bags all day." To a normal person, anyway.

"No, I don't mind. Colin started working up at Mr. Sidle's farm last week. He regrets his decision." Trystan smothered a laugh behind his palm. "He comes home smelling like manure."

The Sidles were the nicest family in our neighborhood. "Why doesn't he quit?"

Trystan smiled, resting his elbow on his knee. "He likes the Sidles, and he made a commitment for this year."

"What, because he made a commitment, he has to stay?"

"It's not cemented in stone, but Colin gave his word he'd work for them through the year."

I stood, stretched my arms above my head, and watched over my shoulder as he moved one step down from me. "That's old-fashioned, kinda bizarre."

"Is it bizarre for one's word to have value?" Tension colored his tone.

It struck me. He spoke like he'd walked out of a historical novel. He didn't use words typical of a teenager.

"No. It's not. It's just few people feel that way today, but it means a lot to me. This world would be much better if people cared and stuck to their word." Gramps had lived an honest life, and everything in me believed my parents had, too. "Do you think you'll like the Falls?"

"I like it so far." His eyebrow rose, counterbalancing a mischievous smile. "But we've never settled anywhere for long."

I turned on the landing and faced him. He stood two steps down from me. I could see directly into his eyes and noted the inexplicable longing. There had to be more to his life story. "Is your aunt the reason you travel?"

"My aunt's a great physician. My uncle would never get in her way. He can work from his computer any-where, even at home in his pajamas. His job as an IT specialist allowed him to homeschool us." His voice was thick with implication. Something flashed in his eyes. Hesitation or reluctance, whatever it was, I couldn't get a good reading. I turned and walked the rest of the way up the stairs. I wasn't going to push the topic. I knew what it was like to be an insect on a pin, always scrutinized.

BANG!

"What the—"

We ran up the steps to find Gramps's hard shell safety hat on the office floor.

"How'd that happen?"

I chuckled. "Ghosts?"

"You're kidding, right?"

"Yes, silly. It's happened before. Sometimes, the vi-bration from running the waterwheel shifts something upstairs. Especially if it's on a workbench. Gramps's tools fall, too."

We walked through the office and into a large room crowded with equipment and tools where Gramps had a TV on the wall in case he got bored.

"This is the woodshop, and this section is the metal shop. A lot of the equipment downstairs was made or repaired in this very room." Three workbenches butted up against the far wall, and a huge metal lathe separated the woodworking from the metal equipment.

"Anyone ever die in here?"

"Not that I know of, but it's funny you ask." I chuckled. "Gramps is always accusing a ghost of moving his tools. He swears every time he puts a screwdriver down, it shows up somewhere else."

"Maybe he misplaced it."

"Could be." What could I say? I hated the idea of Gramps mentally forgetting where he'd put something. It showed his age.

Trystan ran a hand down Dad's bench. "Every room is spotless, no cobwebs, debris, or dust"—he turned his palm and looked at the filth—"except this one. You don't open this room to many tourists."

"You're very observant." Most people wouldn't have noticed.

His eyes took in every inch, but Dad's bench transfixed him. Dust-coated books stacked the bench, and tools lay everywhere. He picked up a Znapple bottle from the windowsill. "I assume this is your favorite spot."

"How did you know?"

"The Peach Znapple's a dead giveaway. Especially since you had three empty bottles on the floorboard of the Jeep the night, I found you stranded."

"My dad and I spent a lot of time here."

"Did you make many things with him?"

"I guess—as much as a six-year-old could." My voice became hoarse, but I continued. "This birdhouse was our last project. Ella's, my sister's, is over there. It isn't finished."

"Were you and your sister close?"

"Yes. No. I mean ..."

He surprised me with a smile.

"What I meant to say is, yes. She was two years older than me."

He raised one eyebrow, waiting for a response.

I knew his interest wouldn't stop there. Anyone else would have accepted my response.

"We were typical sisters. We always played together, but if she wanted something, she'd pull on my hair until I gave it to her."

"Colin's my best friend, but even we don't share everything."

I was grateful when we moved on to a different topic.

"How'd you come to live with your granddad?" he asked.

I took a deep breath, making the mistake of meeting his tranquil gaze. "My parents died." A serene feeling, like a soft blanket, warmed me. "I don't think I'll ever get over it. Heck, I still carry their obituary in my purse."

He paused, leaned against the bench, and looked out the window. "My mom died, too. She gave up on life after Sebastian's car accident. My dad," Trystan rubbed his eyebrow, his gaze distant, "in some ways, he's given up on me." His countenance, which had seemed okay a moment ago, changed to a strange, tell—nothing expression. Before he ended the sentence, I could tell he'd never intended to say this. "We all deal with grief differently."

Trystan picked up a wrench and turned it over in his palm. A low chuckle cleared his throat. "Things were much simpler long ago. Men's main purpose was putting food on the table and tilling fields, and women cooked and preserved food. We didn't have all the choices we have now."

I didn't want to interrupt. One minute, we talked about family, and the next, history.

He took a deep breath. "In Europe, we'd visit museums and learn about customs, medieval practices, and various cultures. Realizing how far humankind has come in the past two centuries just amazes me."

"It still surprises me you like history."

"Of course, I love it." He smiled and rolled his eyes. "What, did you think I'd come over to spy on you?"

I bit my lip, stepping back, putting distance between us. My mind sprang to the burglars who had killed my parents. They'd scouted our neighborhood before breaking into several houses, including ours, and killing my family. Ice cubes prickled down my spine. Maybe opening up was too much of a risk. I didn't know anything about him, after all. Why did he move so often? Was I being too trusting?

But I wanted this friendship.

Trystan's hand rested on my shoulder. "Callie."

I jerked away from him.

"Whoa!" He raised his arms. "I didn't mean it to come out the way it sounded." Concern filled his voice. "I'm not used to talking. In some ways, sarcasm seems easier for me."

"Never tease me about scouting ... I mean, spying." I searched his face, hating he could read my body language so well.

He sat on the bench, placed the heel of his foot on the shelf below, and picked up an old pencil. "Damn. This is hard. Before I even start a friendship, I'm losing it." The pencil snapped, and, for several heartbeats, he stared at his hands. He looked at me, his Adam's apple bobbing. "I was just trying to be playful." He took a breath and tapped the broken pencil on the bench. His eyes monitored my expressions. "The first day I met you, there was something different about you."

I sucked in air. I wanted to back up, but something screamed at me to stay.

One word I hated—different. I was unlike my parents and sister.

The pain in his eyes unnerved me. "I wanted to know you." His voice sounded hopeful, giving weight to each word. "It's hard, moving all the time and meeting new people."

"You're talking about *our* friendship?" Impatience faded, and caution slipped to intrigue.

He nodded. "Yeah. I think you're cool and smart, but I can see I've got a lot to learn about girls." His cheeks reddened, and his lips twitched into a smile.

I met his stare.

His shoulders dropped as he heaved a sigh.

I waited to hear the word "freak" but it never passed his lips. "And we both like history."

I chuckled. "Have to admit—conversations aren't boring when you're around."

Tesla's whimper dissolved what was left of the tension as he joined our tour.

"Wow," Trystan said. "Who's this big fellow?"

"That's Tesla." The mutt tracked wet paw prints across the wooden floor. "He must've been playing in the snow."

"Ah, so, is Tesla named after the man who invented the polyphase alternating current system?" He ruffled Tesla's ears. "He's huge."

I nodded. "He's a horse."

Trystan petted Tesla behind his ears again. "What breed?"

Tesla cocked his head and stared at me with his puppy eyes.

"Labradoodle, but he's mixed with something else, too. I used to ride his dad when I was little. He seems to like you. I'm surprised. Usually, he doesn't take to strangers. He doesn't even care for Max, who's an old fixture around here."

"Your grandfather's helper?" Trystan asked.

"Good memory."

Boots dragged on the floor outside the shop door. "Did I hear some reference to an old fixture?" Gramps set some bags on the turret lathe. "Are you talking about me?"

We burst out laughing.

Gramps's eyes gleamed with amusement. "She's showing you around?"

"Yes." Trystan winked at me. "We're finished."

Gramps loaded one bag onto the wooden cart. Trystan picked up the other and placed it next to the first one. "Good. Glad to hear that. Something's come up. Can you start in a couple of weeks?"

"Yes, I'll let my aunt and uncle know." Trystan looked over at me. "I know it's short notice, but Anna invited Erika to dinner tomorrow night. Can you come?"

"Why not? When Callie's done with work, she'll have nothing better to do." Gramps tugged on his beard and looked at me. "You go tomorrow and have fun."

I bit the inside of my cheek. Gramps hadn't given me time to make an excuse.

"Great," Trystan said. "If you have any movies you want to watch, bring them." The theme music from the movie *Jaws* blared from his coat pocket.

Gramps's brows rose.

"Give me a minute." Trystan pulled out his phone and tapped the screen. "Excuse me." He walked past the lathe into the office.

"Well," Gramps said. "These bags aren't going to move themselves. Give me a hand."

Gramps and I went outside, unloaded the car's back end, and placed the rest of the bags in the wooden cart. Tesla growled at our shadows as they moved about the floor.

Gramps pulled out his hanky and wiped the sweat from his brow. "Hiring Trystan is going to save my back." He braced both palms over the base of his spine and arched back. "I'm hiring me one of those masseuses."

"You mean massage therapists?"

"Whatever they call them girls," he said.

"Where's the receipt for the grain?"

He tucked the hanky in his pants pocket and pulled out a long, white paper.

"Here, can you put it in the office? I'm going to the house. Lock up when you're done here." Gramps exited, leaving Tesla behind.

"Come on, boy. Let's see what Trystan's up to."

I swung open the office door. Trystan was still on the phone. He stood with his back toward me, looking out the window at the long metal sluice.

"Rubbish, Dad. One minute, you want me attending Ashworth. The next, you want me with you. I don't know what's going on, but I'm not moving to California. Get it through your head. You can't tell me what to do. You lost that right when you gave me up." He slammed the phone down on a sack of grain.

I took several steps backward and bumped into the door, which swung open.

Trystan turned, eyes blazing with anger. "You heard?"

I nodded.

He rubbed the bridge of his nose. "My dad wants me to move back in with him. He'd do anything to get me." Trystan stopped. Contempt coated his words. "One minute, he wants me at Ashworth. The next, he wants me in California. He thinks he can pull my strings like I'm a puppet. I don't want to leave my family."

I bit my lip to hide a smile. "They mean the world to you." He nodded. We had that in common. "Then tell him you can't break your commitment to Gramps." Anxiety seeped out of my body as Trystan laughed. Tesla nuzzled Trystan's palm.

His eyes sparkled back at me. "You're funny."

Today was awesome. Our friendship was good.

By the time I went to bed, all my concerns about being careful around Trystan had vanished from my mind.

Dysfunctional families had become the norm, and each family had its secrets. What made us different was how we hid those secrets.

CHAPTER 12

INSPECTION

I dug deeper into my dresser drawer. "Jings, where is my shirt?" I bent over and wiggled under my bed. "I know it's around here somewhere." I sighed. "Achoo."

"Surprise me. Tell me you've got dirt under there?"

"Ouch." Startled, I hit my head on the underside frame. What's Erika doing here?

I squirmed from under the bed frame and rested on my bottom in a sea of discarded clothes. A tornado had hit my bedroom. I'd tried nearly every outfit I owned but couldn't find my favorite blue shirt. "Erika. I thought we were meeting at the Dougrey's house. Trystan will be here soon."

"There's a change in plans. Oh, I met your granddad on the way in. He wants you to know he's headed over to Max's."

I pushed aside a couple of shirts and sat on the bed. "Okay, thanks. So, what happened? Trystan said he'd pick me up."

"I had to come. You won't believe it." Erika rubbed her palms together. "My mom gave in. I can buy a prom dress."

"How'd that happen?"

Erika pulled on her necklace, sliding the pendant up and down the chain. "Well, the dresses my cousin had me look at didn't work out, and Camden asked me to prom."

"Wow. That's great." Camden was a catch–the perfect guy for Erika.

"There's one condition," Erika said. "My mom wants to take us both shopping for dresses."

"And here I thought she'd freaked out since you hadn't mentioned it in a while."

"Nope. It pays to be the only girl." She leaned against the doorframe and scanned the room. "What's possessed you?" Erika took in my messy bedroom and peeked around the walk-in closet door. "Wow, you've still got price tags on some of these shirts. Thought you didn't like shopping."

I shut the dresser drawer. "You know I don't. Nana picked them out."

She walked farther into the closet and fanned through my clothes.

"If it's got a tag, you can have it."

"Are you serious?"

"Some shirts are a couple of years old and out of fashion."

"I can make anything fashionable." She gave a megawatt smile. "Thanks. What are you doing? You look like you're cleaning."

"No. I'm trying to find the blue V-neck shirt I bought at Christmas last year."

"You mean something like this." Erika pulled a yellow V-neck shirt off its hanger.

"Yeah, but not that one."

"Here." She peeked around the closet door and held up a blue shirt. "This would look great on you tonight." She held up a blue, open-necked shirt with small, beaded sparkles. "It's not fancy, but it's better than wearing different colored T-shirts all the time. Especially after all the fuss you put into French braiding your hair."

I gripped the end of my braid. "I like it this way."

"I do, too, but usually it's just braided. You've fancied it up." She swung her palm out over the clothes on the bed. "Since when do you care how you look?" She gave me an all-knowing smirk.

Why did I care? Meeting Trystan's aunt and uncle wasn't a big deal. So, what was my problem? I went to the closet and switched shirts.

My phone on the bed rang.

"I bet that's Steve," Erika said. "He's pestered me all day."

"I doubt it. He doesn't usually call me."

I swiped my cell from the bed. "Hello?"

No one answered.

"Is anybody there?"

Heavy breathing came from the other end of the phone as if it were broadcast over the radio.

"Hello?"

"Who is it?" Erika asked.

"I've got no idea." I ended the call. "Probably some telemarketer."

"My mom hates it. They call all the time."

I tossed the phone back on the bed. "So, why are you here?"

"Picking your sorry butt up." She raised a hand play-fully. "No—Trystan wanted to help his aunt with some last-minute stuff. I offered to get you. Anyhow, I wanted to tell you about Camden. And help you get fixed up."

The phone rang again.

"Give me a second. This could be Gramps." I grabbed my cell and swiped the button from green to red. "Hello."

Again, labored breathing.

"Hello?"

The line died.

"That's fricken' weird." I pressed end on the phone and saw the word RESTRICTED.

CHAPTER 13

HIDDEN THREATS

We turned onto a snow-covered drive and crested a hill. A two-story, dark-gray Cape Cod sat nestled in a cove of trees. Three gray outbuildings stretched across the property. We pulled up beside Trystan's Jetta near a makeshift garage. A massive seven-foot stone wall near the outbuilding closest to the house had one of the hugest fire pits and open-pit grill areas. The previous owners must've entertained on a grand scale because this cooking area was explosive in size.

I flipped down the sun visor and looked into the mirror. I sparkled in my new shirt and jeans. Wisps of my black hair hung over my shoulder from the French braid. Colin appeared from behind the building. I zipped up my coat and grabbed my duffel bag when my cell rang again. When I pulled out my phone, the same word was on my screen—RESTRICTED.

"You're popular today." Erika smiled at me.

I shoved my phone back into my pocket.

"What took so long?" Colin teased, tossing a snowball back and forth in his gloved palms. "Thought you'd be here half an hour ago."

"Callie's been rearranging her room." Erika looked at me, her eyes dancing with mischief. "She couldn't figure out what to wear."

I propped the open bag on my knee and gave Erika a smirk. "It's not a crime to make a good impression."

Anna burst out of the house, slid her arm into her coat sleeve, and ran toward us.

"Hi, Anna."

"Good, you're here." Anna saw my bag and tugged the mouth of the sack wider. "Hey, you brought movies. I haven't seen this one." She pulled out the DVD case.

"Gramps and I watched *Pride and Prejudice* last month. I brought the movie *Revenge*, too."

"Trystan's dying to see *Revenge*." Anna put the movie back in the bag and linked arms with Erika and me. "Come on. Trystan's out back."

We'd strolled past the garage and turned the corner when a snowball hit me in the back of the head. Frozen chunks slid between my shirt and coat. A squeal escaped my lips right before another snowball landed on my shoulder. Anna jerked away, and Erika sprinted toward another building.

"Nice shot, Trystan," Colin yelled from behind a bush.

I shook off the snow and dropped my bag on the plowed driveway. I stared at Trystan, open-mouthed, and a tingle went down my back.

He winked, bent to gather more snow, and ran toward Colin.

"Get him, Callie," Anna screamed over her shoulder.

Within seconds, snowballs were flying in every direction—Guys against girls. Anna came up behind me and nailed Trystan in the back.

He spun around, giving us a wicked grin. I pitched a snowball at him. It struck him on the forehead, reddening his skin. His eyes brightened with excitement. He wiggled his shoulders, shaking off more snow and balancing a snowball in his other hand.

A snowball flew over my head. I ducked behind the car and shrieked. I gathered ammunition and used the car as a shield. Erika hid behind some bushes near the house twenty feet away.

Anna crouched behind the woodpile in front of the car, stacking snowballs. She was awesome, already building up an arsenal, and almost every missile she threw met its mark.

I yelled over my shoulder, "Erika, do what Anna's doing."

I packed several more balls, peeked over the car, and ducked as two snowballs landed behind me, hitting Erika's car. I snuck out from between the vehicles and threw a bullet right at Colin, hitting him in the rear. I burst out laughing and got a mouthful of snow.

Trystan hooted so hard tears streaked his face.

I ran, trying to get away, but snow crunched behind me. Then someone caught me by the elbow. I whirled around and faced my attacker.

Trystan released me and backed up several steps.

I turned my focus to the lopsided snowball in Trystan's hand. "You're crazy."

His smirk stretched into a smile.

"Do it, and you'll pay," I teased.

He tossed the ball.

I caught it, and it held its shape. I tossed it back and forth between my hands.

"Trystan," Anna shouted from behind me.

His grin faded, his laughter dying out.

I bent over to pack more snow around my stolen snowball.

Curses assailed the air as missiles of deadly snowballs whooshed past me and nailed Trystan. Another targeted Colin.

"Girls stick together, cuz." Anna wiped her hands on her coat and ran past me, chuckling. Before anything could start up again, I grabbed my bag and followed her into the house.

Anna opened the front door to reveal a foyer and a large staircase curved at its base. Three rooms opened into one large area, with the living room at the center. A wooden mantle hung over a stone fireplace. Warmth radiated throughout the house as glimpses of the setting sun shone through the window over the foyer, reflecting off the crystal chandelier.

Everything was neutral: the walls, furniture, and decorations. Black-and-white photographs of older people with stern facial expressions patterned the wall up the stairs. The women in the paintings wore gowns, and the men were dressed in cravats with old, stylish suits. The house was a snapshot from another era. Everything was spaced with precision, and nothing was out of place.

"Mom, these are my friends, Callie and Erika," Anna said as we walked into the kitchen. "This is my mom and dad, Selma and Mark Dougrey."

I pulled off my coat. "Thanks for having us."

Trystan took my coat and draped it over the back of a chair.

"Oh, it's our pleasure." Mrs. Dougrey scratched her nose. "I've heard so much about you two from the kids these past few weeks. It's nice to put faces with your names." She glanced at me. "I hope your grandfather didn't mind Trystan staying so long yesterday."

"No, he's pretty cool about things."

Mrs. Dougrey had olive-colored skin and short, caramel-blond hair. Anna resembled her mother, with the same high cheekbones and feminine jawlines. Colin was a mixture of both his parents. Mr. Dougrey was darker, with chocolate-brown hair, tall and lean. Trystan looked like his uncle but with broad shoulders and wavy, dark hair. No one shared Trystan's warm brown eyes.

Erika and I followed Anna into the living room, where the fire blazed. I held out my hands to warm them. "The fire feels so good."

Anna bumped me in the arm and handed me a paper towel. "The ends of your hair are wet."

I accepted it with a muffled "Thanks" and dried my hair.

"What are you whispering about?" Colin asked from the kitchen, gazing at us girls. "I see it's three against two. We'd better be on our best behavior now. Anna's got friends, Trystan."

Anna smiled at Colin and reached into my unzipped bag. "Mom, Callie brought *Pride and Prejudice*—the one with Keira Knightly."

Colin let out a groan of disapproval, but Mrs. Dougrey wiggled her way in between us girls.

"You're kidding me. It's an old chick flick." Colin grabbed his throat, giving a strangled sound of suffering. He should become an actor, for he actually sounded tortured.

I loved the era of gallantry. Some beauty in loyalty and honesty always captivated me, perhaps because I'd had enough misery to last a lifetime.

Colin scrunched down in the chair, wincing. "You couldn't pay me to watch that stuff."

I tossed the *Revenge* DVD to him. "Maybe we'll have enough time for two movies."

Colin caught the plastic case and read the title. "You're a keeper."

Mr. Dougrey cleared his throat. "Dinner's ready."

We made our way to the dining room. Carrots, celery, and potatoes filled the platter on the table, alongside a couple of cans of pop. I accepted the salad and passed it along. It'd been over a month since I'd eaten with anyone at a table, except on Mondays when Gramps had Max over, and they talked about mill business.

Mrs. Dougrey and Anna laughed. Colin talked with Erika. At times, Mrs. Dougrey jumped in with questions for Erika. Bubbly, Erika answered them as if she had predicted the question before it was even asked.

"Callie." Mrs. Dougrey glanced at me. "I hear you play guitar."

"Hmm?"

"Weren't you paying attention?" Erika chuckled.

"Sorry." I swallowed. "Yes, I play some guitar." I couldn't believe Erika told the Dougreys.

"Two years ago, if she wasn't reading or playing guitar, she was taking pictures."

I smiled at Erika. "And now, I'm so busy with public school. I rarely do anything."

Erika winked.

My social life existed because Erika included me in everything.

"Hobbies are so important." Mrs. Dougrey glanced at me. "What's your favorite subject, Callie?"

My phone rang. "Ah, history ... and literature." I pulled my phone from my pocket. RESTRICTED flashed across the screen again. It wasn't Gramps. Pushing decline on the screen, I caught Erika's scrunched eyebrows. I shook my head and continued to listen to Mrs. Dougrey. I didn't want to make a bad first impression.

"You and Trystan have that in common." Mrs. Dougrey took a bite of salad. "In Baden-Baden, Trystan would go to museums with Mark. They'd spend hours looking at artifacts. Mark works from home for the Cleveland Museum," she added. "But he has to go on-site weekly to check up on things." She dabbed the corners of her mouth, put the napkin on her lap, and focused on me. "Do you prefer to read fictional or non-fictional literature?"

I took some carrots from the platter. "I like non-fiction, but I read some fiction, too—mostly historical romance."

Trystan sat across from me. He swallowed, pointing his fork in my direction. "What kind of non-fiction do you like?"

"Anything on travel destinations—especially places I hope to travel to."

Erika set down her glass. "A group from the school is touring France and Germany this summer."

"I loved Germany." Anna leaned back in her chair.

Colin tossed a carrot across the table at Anna. "You said that about Africa, too."

"Have you girls done much traveling?" Mark scowled at Colin and replaced his napkin on his lap. "It's good to see the world before one starts college."

Erika took a bite and shook her head.

"Never outside the country," I replied. "I traveled with my grandparents during breaks from homeschooling. I've been out west, but never northwest. I'd like to see Mount Rushmore sometime. We've also traveled the east coast. My grandmother loved Myrtle Beach."

"Do you girls play any sports or games?" Selma asked.

Erika wiped her mouth with her sleeve. "No time in the day for sports. Callie and I play chess some."

"Mark and Trystan love chess," Selma said. "Sometimes they play late into the night."

"I'm grateful my kids aren't addicted to video games," Mark said.

"Anna was telling us you live with your grandfather, Callie. Is that right?" Selma asked.

"Ah, yes." I would've looked at Erika for reassurance, but she sat beside me. This was uncomfortable territory—when people went digging for answers to what they didn't understand about my home life.

Trystan cleared his throat. "Oh, Mr. Croskney's going to start me working at the mill in a couple of weeks."

I exhaled. Great rescue.

My phone rang again.

Erika cocked her head.

How annoying. I clenched my fist, not wanting to answer the phone, and shoved it under my thigh.

"It will be a lot of weekend work," Trystan continued. "Some hours during the week. Oh, and Monday nights. Mr. Croskney has meetings to discuss mill business, but he'll feed me dinner if it gets too late."

"Sounds good, but remember, school comes first." Mark smiled. "And I want the rest of the basement unpacked. This move has been another adjustment for the three of you, but I still expect you to keep up with the chores."

Anna fanned herself with her hand. "Colin's the one who's going to have a problem keeping up with chores, work, and now dating. He found a red-headed girl on campus the other day."

"Wait, how did you know?" Colin looked at Trystan, who shrugged, shaking his head. "Man." Colin dropped his fork onto his plate. "Stop eavesdropping, Anna. You're always in my business. You've become a pest."

"Colin, that's enough," Dr. Dougrey added. "We all know you've got a girlfriend."

"Yeah, it's not top-secret military info." Anna elbowed Colin.

I bit my lip, trying to hide a chuckle. Anna really liked to dig at Colin's last nerve. There were some perks to not having siblings.

"You're not the only one dating," Anna said with a smug smile. Camden asked Erika to prom."

Erika pushed her plate away from her and locked eyes with Anna. "Can you believe it? I'm so excited. My mom's taking Callie and me shopping. We've got room if you wanna come, too?"

Anna put the salt back on the table. "Sounds great."

Erika was on the edge of her seat, her hands gesturing excitedly. "Oh, student council voted to do the New York, New York theme. Everyone will find out Monday morning over the announcements."

"Isn't it a little early to be deciding all this?" I asked.

Erika poured a glass of pop. "There's not enough money in the decorating budget, so we decided to start early and make the props for prom. It will take months to get everything ready. But it will be awesome. The plan is to make a big city skyline along the lobby window and put lights above it." She tapped her finger on her chin. "Now, we just need to find dates for you guys."

"You're not setting me up," I countered.

"Why not?" Erika sipped her drink. "It's one night."

I grabbed a cherry tomato from my salad. "You like to play matchmaker, and I'm not into it. I'll go to prom, but no one's fixing me up. Besides, I can't tell my right foot from my left, let alone dance."

"I'm with Callie on this one." Anna leaned forward, her elbow resting on the table. "I'll go to prom, but I don't need a date."

I hadn't expected Anna's interest in prom. Reluctantly, I nodded. I didn't want to squelch her excitement. Anyhow, I'd planned to go, just not with a date.

"You guys won't mind helping decorate?" Erika asked.

I agreed.

Trystan tossed his napkin onto his plate and glanced across the table at me. "You up for a game of chess?"

"Hmm. Sure."

We helped Selma clear the table while Trystan set up the game by the fireplace. After we finished cleaning, I grabbed my soda and joined him. A picture on the fireplace mantle caught my eye.

"That's my dad." Trystan pointed at the wooden frame. "We took the picture two months before my mom passed away."

Trystan's mom was the most beautiful lady I'd ever seen. Her dark skin emphasized her gorgeous smile. What confidence. I loved the way she held Trystan so tenderly. One could tell so much from a picture.

"Your accent?"

"Ahh, I picked up my accent in Europe. My mom's dad's side of the family is from Nubia, but her mom's side is from England. My mom grew up in England. She worked for the European banking system. That's k-kinda"—he cleared his throat—"how my parents met. Dad was stationed there when he was in the Marines. I was born in England." He winced. "Shortly after she died, I moved in with my aunt and uncle. And my dad continued to work. As he always did."

I sat opposite Trystan and put my drink next to the chessboard.

My phone rang again.

"Didn't you turn off the ringer?" Erika chimed in from the kitchen.

"Nope." I grabbed my phone. Uneasiness wormed its way through me at seeing RESTRICTED on the screen.

"Ignore it," Anna said.

I couldn't! "Hello?" I made eye contact with Trystan.

Again, the raspy breathing came from the other end.

"Is anybody there?" I asked.

Trystan arched his eyebrow.

"Callie?" the stranger on the phone whispered.

My heart skittered to an abrupt stop as the silence stretched between the stranger and me. How did he know my name? I sure as heck couldn't place his voice.

"Yes?"

"*Tsk. Tsk.*" The phone died.

Trepidation gave me the chills. I held the cell away from my ear and stared at the black screen.

Trystan took the phone from my hand. "What's going on?"

"I keep getting these restricted calls. Some guy breathes heavy on the other end. And he tsked tsked me after saying my name."

"Someone's playing a prank," Erika added.

Trystan set my phone next to my Coke. "You okay?"

"Ah, sure. I'm fine." I rubbed my hands together, trying to push away the edginess. "You're probably right, Erika. It's just a hoax." I glanced at Trystan. "You ready to play?"

No words were exchanged between us. No words were needed.

There was too much tension in the air—not from the restricted caller—but from the emotional moment. He cared. That wasn't something I was used to. It wasn't something I could ever allow. Never.

"Hey, do you want to be black or white?" Trystan held the knight in his hand.

"White." I smiled as if his gaze hadn't left my trembling fingers.

I was thankful for the change of topic, although this wasn't the first time I'd gotten pranked. Trevor and Hanson knew some dude who phone-pranked older folks. They eventually got caught, but I'd never had a male friend who cared enough.

"Do you play a lot?"

"Yeah, used to, and I've always chosen white over black. It was an inside joke." I chuckled. "My dad played with me for hours. He believed the chessboard was a symbol of life challenges."

Trystan and I played. He made quick decisions, capturing some of my chess pieces early. His strategy reminded me of when I'd play with my dad—quick and decisive. On the other hand, I always questioned my decisions even after making them.

Trystan's fingers tapped the table, his eyes shifting over the board. I frowned at my options, knowing I had blocked myself into a bad spot. My choices were limited. The warmth of the room, people laughing, Colin bantering with Erika and Anna, it all distracted me. Trystan took another sip from his glass, leaned forward, and moved his castle to take my king.

Trystan's lips twitched into a smile. "You overthink. You could've had my castle three moves back. Go with your gut instinct." He put the pieces back into the box. "Come on, let's watch a movie."

The night breezed by as we watched movies. The guys muted the romantic scenes and took creative liberties, modernizing lines in *Pride and Prejudice*. It was so funny. Next, we watched *Revenge* and fast-forwarded the action scenes, supplying any dialog in a *Looney Toons*-cartoonish voice. By the time Erika took me home, my head ached from laughing so hard.

I lay in bed after playing guitar for the first time in a long time, thinking of Anna and Selma clearing the table and doing dishes. They were close, sharing a bond I'd never experienced. It was a bittersweet thought. I missed my family more than ever.

Tonight, I hadn't felt like an outsider, but I was jealous—jealous of a future I would never have.

CHAPTER 14
UNCHARTED

"Everyone, grab a seat. I'm Mr. Taylor, your new American history teacher." He paced before the desk. "Whichever seat you choose now will remain yours for the semester." He had thick, reddish-brown hair and freckles. He looked to be in his early thirties. Wire-rimmed Euro glasses magnified his beady eyes—a raspy sound carried in his voice.

Four rows of desks filled the room, and a swarm of kids filled the chairs, leaving five empty seats in the back. I walked down the aisle and took one, dropping my bag on the floor. This should be interesting. Until now, every substitute teacher spent more time reading than teaching.

He had lists printed on the whiteboard behind him: The War of 1812, Civil War, and World War II. Some names appeared on the board closest to the window:

Martin Luther King, Jr., Nikola Tesla, Albert Einstein, and Thomas Edison.

Three students entered the room. The door slammed behind them. Two students raced to the back of the class, leaving Trystan alone at the front of the room. One of the boys, Tom Perry, slammed his book onto the desk and planted his butt onto a seat next to mine. He turned and gave me a megawatt smile.

I faced the front of the room, ignoring his stare.

Trystan approached Mr. Taylor's desk. "May I have a syllabus?"

"Sure. You must be the new student." Taylor handed Trystan a paper. "Pick an open seat. It'll be yours for the semester."

Trystan walked past me to the far side of the room.

"Hey, you're cute," Tom Perry teased.

Taylor cleared his throat. "Is there something you would like to share with the class, Mr. ...?"

"Nope. And the name's Tom." He slunk down in his chair like some hipster and shot Taylor a challenging look. "I got nothing to share."

"Well, Tom, I can see this seating arrangement won't work. You're here to learn, not to flirt."

"But you said we could pick a seat."

I covered my mouth to muffle a chuckle. This teacher seemed intent on teaching. This might be perfect.

"Not in your case. Change seats with Trystan."

"Come on, Teach."

Taylor crossed his arms over his chest. "It's Mr. Taylor, and do as you're told."

Tom picked up his book, passed Trystan, and high-fived the other boy who had come in late.

Trystan took the seat next to me. I flushed cranberry red. Carbonated bubbles popped in my stomach. Guaranteed—I wouldn't be watching the clock in this class anymore. I kept my eyes on the desk as Lizzy passed out the papers Mr. Taylor had given her.

"Real quick," Taylor began. "I'll be taking over Mr. Santos's classes for the remainder of the year. I graduated four years ago from Ohio State University and have a master's degree in education and counseling. I have an open-door policy. I take a different approach than most teachers on teaching, as well. I believe students can't get interested in history unless they appreciate their backgrounds, but I'll get to that later this semester." He paced the distance of the room, stopping to look at each of us in turn.

He pushed his glasses up on his nose. "I've asked Lizzy to place a quiz on each desk. You'll have thirty minutes to finish as much as you can. You may begin." Everyone flipped over their papers.

Before I turned over my page, I gazed three rows over. Lizzy gave me a don't-you-mess-with-me look. Jings! What was it with her idiotic obsession with Logan? I sure as heck didn't want him.

The quiz had basic questions. The first few were easy—where is the capital of the U.S.A.? Explain the significance of symbols—i.e., stars, stripes, red, white, and blue.

I finished the quiz, flipped over the page, and noticed that Trystan had also finished. "How'd you end up in here?" I whispered.

He gave a muffled huff. "Mix up in transfers."

"Well, Mr. Taylor's already given us more work than the other substitute teachers combined. With them, it was just a study hall."

"Can't believe how easy the test was." He placed a pencil behind his ear and cupped his mouth with his palm. "Shhh ... shh. Taylor's looking this way." Taylor focused back on some papers on his desk.

We opened our books, pretending to be busy but talking as if no one else existed.

"Wait." My cell vibrated in my pocket. I pulled it out, kept it under the desk, and covered the screen with my palm to hide the glare of the light. "Awesome. Gramps texted." I did a little jig in my seat. "My Jeep's done. Gramps just paid for the repairs. I can pick it up any time."

His eyes were warm. "I'll take you after school."

"Are you sure?" Slammed with sudden pain, I shut my eyes. My muscles constricted. Pressure hammered in my head. Notnownotnownotnow. My body temperature shifted from cold to warm, and that feeling vibrating above my skin increased its frequency. I dropped my head into my palms. Hearing sharpened.

"Callie," Trystan whispered.

I ignored Trystan's question.

Taylor's voice rang loud. "Thirty minutes are up. Now, pass the quizzes forward."

People passed the tests up. Taylor collected them and licked his finger, turning from page to page. Time stretched.

"I'm impressed with the responses on your tests," Taylor said from the front of the classroom. "Other than a few questions I randomly selected, most came from the citizenship test the government gives." I heard Mr. Taylor lick his finger again. "Trystan, for being home-schooled, you're on the ball. Good job. You only missed one question."

Everything slowed down.

"Cheeeeater," someone spat from the front of the room, muffling the word under a cough.

Someone's foot tapped the floor. A chair screeched against the linoleum, echoing in my mind like fingernails across a chalkboard. The rhythmic commotion agitated me.

"Which question did I miss?" Trystan asked.

I embraced the vision ...

Snapshot of ... *Open, double glass doors ... fire on both sides of the opening ... large, long, open areas, and narrow archways ... a red ax behind a glass case ...*

The snapshot focused on a door, and I knew it was locked.

The fire vision—again.

Footsteps echoed, getting louder.

The warmth from Trystan's hand on my back invaded my thoughts.

"Are you okay?" Trystan's words penetrated my fears.

The footsteps stopped.

I opened my eyes and blinked.

Black, beady eyes stared back at me. "Miss Tresham, your head was down. I thought you might have fallen asleep?"

Immediately, a suffocating sensation slapped me in the face, cutting me off from my surroundings, and a strong pulling feeling from the top layer of my skin gripped me, releasing an elastic band. A transparent wall of gold light stretched before me, enfolding me in bubble wrap. I gasped in awe. A crimson light electrified within the golden one in an undulating pulse throughout the transparent barrier. Heat penetrated from the light.

What was this ability? What was going on?

Trystan lowered his hand, and the feeling of security went with it.

I pressed against the back of my chair, away from Taylor.

"No," I forced myself to say calmly. I turned and glanced at Trystan.

His eyes narrowed with alarm. "Let me take you to the nurse. It could be a drop in your blood sugar." Trystan leaned proprietorially close to me.

With what strength I could muster, I pushed my chair away from my desk. Forty-eight eyes, including Mr. Taylor's, watched my every move, but Taylor's alone bore into me as if he searched for answers. Searched my psyche.

"No, I'm n-not sleeping," I said. "I'm fine. And I don't need a nurse." The last part I hoped Trystan heard.

"Well, then." Taylor turned and strode back to the front of the room. "Please join the discussion."

I sat back in my chair and concentrated on Trystan, sensing his honesty. The stimulation of everything overwhelmed me. A compulsory nudging–a niggle of something unknown gained intensity within me. I turned and looked out the window.

This transparent wall complicated my already convoluted life.

I had to learn on the job how to channel my visions. My parents had died before I could ask questions about my visions and birthmark. And no training manual existed.

"Callie, are you sure?" Trystan asked.

My skin buzzed, but I had no more discomfort. "I'm fine."

His eyes were black. He shifted in his chair, leaving my space.

The golden crimson light separated me from everyone. Afraid to react, not knowing how the barrier would respond, I stayed in my seat and tried to listen to Taylor.

Mr. Taylor called Trystan's name, drawing my attention. He adjusted the glasses on his nose.

"You missed the question which asked who said, 'Give me liberty or give me death?'"

"It's Patrick Henry," Trystan said.

Taylor's brow rose. "No, actually, it was Grant."

"Patrick Henry did say it." The words came out strong but ended up strangled on my tongue.

"Whooo, she just contradicted the teacher," Lizzy said.

I stiffened.

The bell rang. I grabbed my books and followed Trystan and Tony toward the exit.

"Callie?" I turned, facing Taylor. "The next time you decide to talk, get permission first."

"Yes." Regardless of the fact he'd been wrong, I should have raised my hand. He unnerved me.

We exited the room. I ignored everyone—and my barrier—around me. I went to my locker, exchanged my books, spun the dial on the lock, and threw my backpack over my shoulder. I plowed through a sea of people, intent on finding Trystan's car. I should've walked with him, but I'd needed to get out of this sardine box of a school.

I hadn't made an excellent first impression on Mr. Taylor, but I didn't care.

Kids flooded out of the school toward the parking lot, and I spotted Trystan standing in front of his car. As I approached, I could see his eyes burning with questions.

I wrapped shaky arms around my middle and sucked in the cool air, realizing the red barrier within the gold light had disappeared. And the gold light still wrapped around me.

I reached Trystan.

He jerked his thumb back at the school. "What happened?"

"What do you mean?"

He slid between the passenger door and me, blocking me from opening the door. "Are you sick?"

I needed a moment of normalcy—time without threatening visions, superior teachers, and questions from friends. I dropped my backpack on the ground, blew a tendril of hair away from my eyes, and scowled at his perfect face. "Sick? What are you talking about?"

"Ouch, Callie," Erika said. "Calm down."

I spun around and met Erika's stare. Anna and Camden stood by the hood of the car. I took a deep breath, ready to face off with everyone.

Trystan opened the passenger door. "Erika, I'm taking Callie to pick up her Jeep. Could you take Anna home?"

"I can," Camden said. "Erika rode with me this morning."

Trystan yanked the door open farther. "Let's go."

I stiffened at his words, at the worry in his eyes. I moved to get into the car.

A door slammed behind me. "What's going on over here?"

I jerked my head toward the sound.

A few spaces away from us, a group of nine or ten guys collected between two new parked cars. They were laughing. Tom Perry, one of Logan's friends, and Dylan, his brother, were watching us from inside the crowded circle.

Lizzy waited amongst the crowd, her foot tapping, watching my every move.

Tom's foot rested on the red Charger's bumper. "Aw, sounds like they're having a fight."

Logan kicked Tom's foot and knocked him off balance. "Don't be a jerk."

He fist-bumped his older brother, Dylan, before focusing his attention back on us.

Why was Dylan here? Wasn't he in college? This day couldn't get any worse. Logan was an idiot, but Dylan was trouble.

"Hey, Callie," Dylan called. "Who's the dude and the girl?"

"My friends, Anna and Trystan," I snapped.

Logan approached us. "So, he's not your boyfriend?"

My lips pursed. I hated audiences. Hated inquisitions. Hated the uncertainty of my life. "I don't report to you. Butt out."

"Burn. Man, she burned you," some idiot said. "Don't think she's going to prom with you now."

Tom's fist clenched at his side.

I moved away from Trystan, but he gripped my arm. His hold secured me. A flicker of red appeared, pulsating through the ever-present transparent barrier before it disappeared. A tornado of emotions swirled within me. I ignored the barrier. Ignored Trystan. I hated arrogance.

"Hell will freeze over before I ever go to prom with you."

"Leave, Logan." Trystan's authoritative words seemed natural.

"You're a loser." Logan's right hand cradled his clenched left fist. "You can't come here and take what's not yours."

I tried shaking off Trystan's hold, but he kept me close. "I'm *not* a possession."

Like fresh air, a serene sensation pressed against me, easing my tension and draining my heightened sense of agitation. What was happening?

"Let me know when you want a man." Logan dropped his arms, and his face melted into a placid expression. He and his friends got into their cars and drove away.

I lowered my eyes. Trystan's grip on my arm had broken through the barrier. This inexplicable barricade didn't stop physical objects. What did it stop? What was its function? And where did it come from?

Camden slid up next to me. "I know you already know it, Callie, but the dish on Logan's not good. After the basketball game last week, he bragged he kissed a girl in an empty stairwell. And from the later talk, he wasn't nice about it, either."

"Thanks." I croaked, avoiding Trystan's eyes. "Can we go?"

I tossed my jacket onto the car floor and pulled the band from my hair, letting it cascade over my shoulders. Trystan slid behind the wheel. Between my bizarre behavior in class and the argument with Logan, Trystan probably thought I was a freak. I took a deep breath, avoiding eye contact. How could I explain this?

He backed out of the parking spot, and we were on the main drag before long. Snow covered the sides of the road. Houses began to look alike.

"What's the address?"

"It's on Moreland Road. Kirt's got a sign out for auto repair."

"Did you buy your Jeep from him?" he asked.

"Yeah, Kirt is Gramps's friend." We chatted about my Jeep, which eased my mind.

We passed the cemetery and some grand old houses on Madison Hill. ATI College buzzed with students crossing the walkway. He took the right lane at the fork in the road and continued driving.

"Callie, I hate to ask." His eyelashes lowered. "Are you sick?"

"What makes you think so?"

"Twice since I've known you, you've spaced out." He was probably referring to the night at the restaurant. "I ask as a friend."

I recalled all the psychologists who had prodded me with questions after my family's murder. All in an attempt to help. Those inquisitions felt like they'd lasted for days. Over the years, Nana had taken me to doctors. After a while, she'd stopped. One of us had to give in.

Trystan pulled into the graveled parking lot at Kirt's Towing. An old Sinclair gas pump separated two tow trucks from five vehicles with For Sale signs in their windows. The garage doors were open. Men and women worked under cars on lifts.

Trystan turned off the engine and looked at me.

"No, I'm not sick."

He leaned against the door and gazed at me through narrowed eyes. "Do you suffer from headaches?"

"Yes." Heat crept into my cheeks, and I struggled for words. "*Jings.*"

"That's *gosh* in Scottish."

"How'd you know?"

He crossed his arms, smiling. "I love languages."

I searched his face but couldn't find the lie.

"I've gotten headaches since I was a child. Medicine doesn't help." Visions brought headaches, which disappeared when the vision had played. My living nightmare. My curse. I wasn't going to tell him that.

He tapped the steering wheel, his eyes brimming with questions.

There was a tap on the window.

Talk about perfect timing. Bob Kirt, the towing company's owner, waited for Trystan to lower the window.

Relief flooded through me. I'd escaped the conversation.

"Couldn't wait, could you?" Kirt's missing tooth gave character to his wide smile. "Knew you'd show up today."

I opened the passenger door and smiled at him. "I've been dying to get my wheels back."

"So, this is the lucky boy chauffeuring you." Kirt stuck out his hand, and they exchanged a shake. "Al

Croskney's told me about you. Heard your aunt works at the hospital."

"Yes," Trystan said.

"Nice lady. She fixed Max up real good." Kirt lowered the baseball cap over his eyes. "Come on. Let me show you what I did to the Jeep." We rounded the corner of the garage, where my Jeep sat next to an old Cutlass.

"Wow. That's a beauty." Trystan ran his finger down the body of the candy-apple red Cutlass. "How much are you asking for her?"

Kirt took off his cap and tucked it under his arm. "I've never thought about selling it."

"My uncle might be interested if the price is right." Trystan continued to examine the parked Cutlass.

"I'll think on it," Kirt said. "Now you, girly, you damaged your Jeep but good. I understand why the dust shield got buggered up from hitting the road when it fell, but I can't figure out how you managed to dent a customized bumper made of two-inch steel tubing." He jerked up his chin. "I had to put heat to it to straighten it." Kirt raised his hand, showing four fingers. "This wide. It was a devil to get out."

Trystan stuffed his fingers into his pants pockets and kicked gravel under his feet, sending pebble-sized stones toward the sign. Dark hair framed the angles of his rigid, intellectual face.

"That night was nasty," Trystan muttered.

"Yes, it was," Kirt said. He dipped his head toward his shoulder and rubbed his jaw. "But it doesn't explain how the vehicle got damaged."

I didn't care. I'd had enough unanswered questions in my life. I wanted to go home and forget today had ever happened.

Kirt gave up and tossed me the keys. "Well, you be careful."

We said goodbye, and I thanked Trystan.

He pulled out onto the main road. I got into my Jeep and gripped the steering wheel. The sun shone through the front windshield, lifting my spirits as freedom coursed through me.

My mind focused, my thoughts sharpened, and my determination sparked. I had to find out about this barrier and what connection it had to the visions. This was serious. My power of premonition had developed, followed by my family's murder. Could the emergence of this new power mean another catastrophe was coming?

CHAPTER 15

DISCOVERY

I didn't go straight home. I drove around for hours, my mind tripping over ideas as speculation about the barrier grew until I pulled up to the loading dock at the mill. No floodlights came on. Cloaked in black, the night possessed an ominous feel. I shivered, grabbed my jacket and books, and bolted for the kitchen door. Tesla barked. I fumbled with the keys and unlocked the door. A gust of wind slammed it behind me. I flicked the light switch. Nothing.

The breaker must be out.

Tesla bounced at my side. "Hi, boy."

Once my eyes adjusted to the darkness, I moved around the island and inhaled a hint of tobacco. Gramps had better not be smoking cigars again. Nana had made him give it up three years ago when he had cancer treatment.

At the top of the stairs that led to the basement, I paused, then took the first step and descended into the basement. Eeriness surrounded me. I made it to the corner and flicked the switch on the control panel. Lights flooded on upstairs, leaking through the cracked door at the main level.

"Come on, boy. I'm starving."

I went back upstairs and dumped food for Tesla, changed into sweats, and cranked up the bass on the iPod. Hidden speakers brought the music to life. I went to the kitchen, made coffee, and found leftover meatloaf in the refrigerator. I threw a couple of baked potatoes into the microwave and began cutting tomatoes for a salad.

Gramps opened the kitchen door, Max on his heels. "How can you think with that racket blaring?" Dark circles emphasized Gramps's eyes. "See, you got the Jeep back. How's it handling?"

Max sat at the kitchen island.

I lowered the music's volume. "It's great." I smiled. "Dinner will be ready in thirty minutes."

Gramps took off his coat, slouched into a chair, and rubbed his eyes. "How'd your day go?"

Unbelievably horrible. "Fine."

Loneliness crushed me. I wanted to run into Gramps's arms and let him chase away my fears. If Nana had been here, she'd have listened, even if I couldn't tell her everything.

I kept my back to them and continued to prepare the vegetables. "Typical Monday," I said, brushing a tear away with my hand.

"Oh, since you didn't pack up your grandmother's sewing room, I started it. I want to get rid of the stuff soon. Someone else could use the material."

I placed the knife on the cutting board and took a deep breath. "After supper, I'll get on it."

"Thanks, dear." Gramps came up behind me and bumped my shoulder as he reached for a coffee mug. "Glad you got your wheels back?"

"Yeah, I'll pay you back."

He waved his palm. "Keep up your grades, and forget about paying me." Gramps set a mug in front of Max, scanned the mail on the table, and then tucked an envelope in his pocket. "I'll be back."

"Callie," Max said. "When was Tesla to the vet last?"

"Just before Christmas. Why?"

Max set his cup on the table. "I came over last night, helped your granddad with some filing at the mill." He rested his arm over the back of the seat. "Tesla was acting all weird. He charged a customer."

"That's strange."

Tesla's ears perked up at the mention of his name.

"He doesn't need a vet," Gramps interjected. "But he's been wandering off. Mr. Livingston said Tesla's been walking back along the creek, even near the fen. I've had to hose him off twice recently."

"He's a dog." I sliced through a cucumber. "Tesla did this when we first got him, too, remember?"

Gramps chuckled. "Yeah, and the vet said neutering him would fix it."

After supper, I placed the leftovers in the fridge. Bottled-up energy was driving me nuts, so I hooked up Tesla and escaped for a run. The cold soaked into my body, and the distance I ran didn't ease my frustration. I didn't trust my judgment between the emerging barrier and increased edginess.

I rushed into the house, locking out the cool air. I unhooked Tesla's leash. He made a dash for his dog bowl as I made for the sewing room. Stacks of boxes filled with fabric and assorted sewing paraphernalia hugged the wall. Books covered Nana's rocking chair. The room looked disorganized.

I sat on the floor and ran my palm over Nana's things. My heart ached. A faint chocolate scent hung in the air. Memories rushed in Nana baking cookies with Ella and me. Her pinching my cheek, giving me a half-grin when she'd caught me with my fingers in the mixing bowl. A quiet tremor rippled through me.

To stop the memories, I grabbed a box and, over the next hour, packed stuff from the floor. It seemed Gramps had no method for organizing other than putting similarly sized objects together. I continued stacking boxes until my space became crowded. I pushed more boxes to the side, moved back into the closet, and pulled out miscellaneous stuff. Nothing rested on the shelf over the coats at the back wall, but I separated some old clothes hanging there, assessing what else needed gotten rid of.

On the floor sat a wooden chest, bound on both sides by a dirty leather strap. I ran my fingers down the splintered edges that time had worn.

Anxiety stirred within me. This was the very chest from my vision, which I'd seen the same night as the shattered, shadowed man's face.

Upon closer inspection, the markings and familiar scratches became obvious.

It had been my mom's.

I thought the fire had destroyed everything when they'd died. Why is it here?

Mom had lit candles all over the house but never on *this* trunk. Ella and I had played on it with our dollies. Mom said it had come from her side of the family.

I lifted the bulky chest from the closet and carried it to my bedroom. It was awkward to hold but light, considering my unnatural strength. I set it on the bed and opened the lid. It creaked on rusty hinges, and I inhaled a musty scent. Dust stirred. A tattered, faded purple blanket lay inside. I pulled it out, the frayed edges reaching for the floor.

I sat on the bed and laid the blanket on my lap. A woven symbol dangled from one threadbare corner. Embroidered in the material was a coat of arms, something one would see in a history book. An eagle's wings spread wide. Its talons clutched a single star. I touched my stomach as a frisson of apprehension twisted my gut.

After setting the blanket on the bed, I touched the patina on the chest which sent an icy feeling throughout my body. Pressure in my head gripped me and a vision sprang forth.

A gold ring with blue stones.

Curiosity prodded me to kneel on the bed and dig another blanket from the chest. I peered into the trunk. My heart skipped a beat as I choked, trying to suck in air.

Four small eyes stared back at me—two blue, two green. I lifted the redhead, Ella's baby doll, first. Our parents had made them to resemble each of us. We had played with them for endless hours.

I picked up Tori. Her coal-black hair hung, braided, down her back. Her red lips, rosy cheeks, and blue eyes stared back at me. Both dolls were dirty and discolored, their dresses torn at the seams from use.

I set the dolls on the bed and continued rooting through the chest. The back of my hand brushed something cold. I pulled out my mom's old, silver-handled mirror and hairbrush. The sight of her brush reminded me of the times when she'd combed her fingers through my hair while humming a tune. The scent of vanilla surrounded me as I imagined her fingers' caress, easing my loneliness. I set the mirror and brush on the pillow and searched.

My hand settled on a solid object toward the chest's bottom. I lifted out a jeweled box about the size of Gramps's empty cigar box. I'd never seen this before. I crawled over the items from the chest, which I'd placed on my bed and set against the headboard, coming to rest with the box on my lap. I traced my hand over a small crest with small precious stones on its lid. Another coat of arms was stamped here, an antique scale imprinted on a shield. Four books filled one surface on the scale, perfectly balanced with—I blinked—two stars suspended in the air above the other platform. A trickle of unease wormed through me. Same position. Same sizes. Just like my mark.

The eagle in the other coat of arms on the blanket held a single star. Did that reflect my parents' mark?

I raised the top. A leather-bound book rested on red velvet. I eased it out. The book was two times the size of my palm's width. I opened it, and a folded paper fell onto the bed. I tucked it back into the thick pages, distracted by the beautifully scripted words in the book, and read between watermarked sentences.

My Dearest daughters,

If you are reading this, then the prediction has come to fruition. This is not how your father and I envisioned our futures. Make no mistake. You girls are the joys of our lives, and we grieve knowing we won't see you grow.

I closed my eyes. Anger surged within me. Even knowing of my parents' imminent demise, my visions hadn't been able to predict the exact time to save them. My heart squeezed.

Mom and Dad believed that Ella lived, too.

IT WEIGHS HEAVILY ON MY HEART TO REVEAL WHAT I MUST MAKE KNOWN TO YOU. OUR INTENTION HAD ALWAYS BEEN TO SHARE THIS WITH YOU WHEN YOU WERE OLDER AND BETTER PREPARED TO ACCEPT IT. NOW, THIS LETTER IS THE ONLY WAY TO ARMOR YOU WITH THE WISDOM YOU NEED.

THERE IS NO PERFECT PLACE TO BEGIN.

WE'RE CALLED THERAN.

With reverence and wonder, I spoke the name aloud, "Theran." I had been on the right path when I'd googled lost civilizations. Dad had died trying to say "Theran," not "Seran."

IT IS CUSTOMARY FOR THERANS TO ALLOW ONE'S ELDERS TO ARRANGE A MARRIAGE, BUT YOUR FATHER, CYRUS, AND I KNEW FROM THE MOMENT WE'D MET THAT WE WERE DESTINED TO BE TOGETHER. WE

WENT AGAINST THE ELDERS' ORDERS. DESPITE THE SCANDAL, MY PARENTS WERE WILLING TO HELP CYRUS AND ME. ALTHOUGH THEY HAD HAD AN ARRANGED MARRIAGE, MY PARENTS LOVED ONE ANOTHER AND SYMPATHIZED WITH US. MY FATHER, RICHARD ANSTLEY, DISAPPROVED OF THE MATCH THE ELDERS HAD MADE FOR ME. CYRUS AND I ESCAPED IN SECRECY, TAKING REFUGE AMONG HUMANS, FINDING COMFORT WITHIN THEIR MASSES. WITH SOME EFFORT, WE WERE ABLE TO CHANGE OUR LAST NAME FROM YOUR FATHER'S GIVEN NAME TRESMEIRE TO TRESHAM.

IT GRIEVES ME TO TELL YOU THAT YOU ARE NOT BIOLOGICAL SISTERS.

My heart skipped another beat as my fingers tightened on the book. The room grew colder. I pulled the blanket over my legs.

CYRUS AND I BEFRIENDED A HUMAN WOMAN, A FOSTER PARENT IN GUARDIA LOMBARDI AVELLINO, ITALY, BY THE NAME OF MRS. CHILSON. SHE'D TAKEN IN A ONE-YEAR-OLD BABY WITH NO LIVING RELATIVES TO CLAIM HER. WE FELL IN LOVE WITH YOU, ELLA. TO OUR SURPRISE, WE DISCOVERED YOU ALSO

HAD A BIRTHMARK. WE ONLY KNEW THAT WE COULD UNDERSTAND YOU MORE THAN ANY HUMAN WOULD, AND SO WE DECIDED TO ADOPT YOU. IT SEEMED LIKE FOREVER, BUT FINALLY, THE ADOPTION WAS OFFICIAL, AND YOU WERE OURS. THE AGENCY HAD NO MORE DETAILS ABOUT YOUR PARENTS, BUT THEY WERE ABLE TO TELL US YOUR NAME WAS MARGARET. THE AGENCY ALSO GAVE US A PURPLE BLANKET, THE ONE THEY FOUND YOU BUNDLED IN ON THE NIGHT YOU CAME TO THEM.

ELLA, DEAR, YOU ARE THE CHILD OF OUR HEARTS. NEVER FORGET THAT. WE KEPT YOUR ORIGINAL NAME, MARGARET, AND GAVE YOU THE MIDDLE NAME OF ELIZABETH AFTER YOUR FATHER'S MOTHER, ELIZA-BETH TRESMEIRE.

I slumped against the pillows and pulled the blanket tighter, reality soaking in. Ella wasn't my biological sister. They must have adopted her shortly after they'd gotten married in Italy. I glanced at the purple blanket next to the chest, flipped the thick page and continued reading past smeared marks.

IT'S ODD HOW ONE CHOICE CAN INDIRECT-LY AFFECT ANOTHER. WE DIDN'T KNOW THAT BY LEAVING OUR FAMILIES, WE WERE

PROTECTING YOUR FUTURE, CALLIE. YOUR MARK IS LIKE NONE WE'D EVER SEEN.

I took a deep breath. Mom and Dad must not have recognized the symbol on the jewelry box.

I KNEW YOU HAD A SPECIAL PURPOSE IN LIFE. YOU MAY BE ANGRY THAT YOUR FATHER AND I NEVER EXPLAINED WHY YOUR MARK IS DIFFERENT FROM OURS. THE TRUTH, MY DAUGHTER, IS WE DID NOT UNDERSTAND IT OURSELVES. AFTER LEAVING THE REMNANT ELDERS, OUR SOURCES WERE LIMITED, AND THE ONE CHILDHOOD FRIEND WE TRUSTED WASN'T AROUND TO ASK

WE KNOW IT'S HARD, BUT, IN MANY WAYS, IT'S ALSO A BLESSING WE DIDN'T UNDER-STAND THE MEANING OF YOUR MARK. HAD WE UNDERSTOOD, WE WOULD, PERHAPS, HAVE MISGUIDED YOU OR INTERFERED WITH YOUR TRUE CALLING.

WHILE YOU ARE NO DOUBT UPSET THAT YOU COULDN'T SAVE US, YOUR VISION DID AID US IN PREPARING FOR YOUR FUTURES. WE PLACED YOU GIRLS IN THE LOVING ARMS OF OUR DEAREST FRIENDS, MR. CROSKNEY

AND HIS WIFE. THEY'RE NOT YOUR BIOLOGI-
CAL GRANDPARENTS, BUT THAT MAKES NO
DIFFERENCE. I ASK YOU TO REMEMBER THAT
IT IS NOT ONLY BLOOD THAT BINDS BUT ALSO
THE MEMORIES OF THE HEART.

I slammed the book shut and vaulted off the bed to pace
the floor. This was a nightmare coming to life. How was
I to comprehend anything? Yeah, I could understand my
parents not wanting to tell me when I was younger, but
why couldn't Gramps have told Nana or me before she'd
died? Bitterness seeped into my thoughts. Wait. There
must be more Therans. There must be others out there
who could answer my questions.

I flopped back onto the bed and flipped to the next
page.

WHAT I'M ABOUT TO TELL YOU MAY BE
CONFUSING, BUT IT IS SIGNIFICANT. OUR
HERITAGE GOES BACK TO THERA, THE IS-
LAND OF SANTORINI. LONG AGO, A VOLCANO
ERUPTED. ACCORDING TO LEGEND, OUR PEO-
PLE ESCAPED THE EXPLOSION BY FLEEING TO
EGYPT, HEEDING THE WARNING OF A SEER.
WHAT I TELL YOU NOW IS CRUCIAL.

THOUSANDS OF YEARS AGO, A MAN NAMED
PTOLEMY PREDICTED A WAR OF CATA-
CLYSMIC PROPORTIONS. A FEW MONTHS
LATER, A WAR CALLED THE WAR OF KNOWL-

EDGE BROKE OUT IN ALEXANDRIA, EGYPT, CAUSING A DIVIDE BETWEEN HUMANS AND THERANS.

DURING THE WAR OF KNOWLEDGE, A SMALL FACTION, WHICH INCLUDED BOTH YOUR FATHER'S AND MY ANCESTORS, SEPARATED FROM THOSE THERANS WHO DIDN'T BELIEVE IN PTOLEMY'S VISION. OURS WAS A SMALL GROUP COMPARED TO THOSE THERANS STILL IN ALEXANDRIA. WE CALLED OURSELVES THE REMNANTS.

IN AN EFFORT TO COVER THE REMNANTS' TRACKS, OUR ANCESTORS ENCOURAGED OTHERS TO BELIEVE MANY OF US HAD DIED IN THE FIGHTING IN THE WAR OF KNOWLEDGE. OUR ANCESTORS ALSO SET A FIRE TO COVER OUR ESCAPE. WE HAD TO PRESERVE THE POWER WITHIN OUR BLOODLINE FROM THE DANGERS IN EGYPT.

I took a deep breath and flipped to the next page.

OUR FAMILIES SET ROOTS IN SCOTLAND, ASSUMING NEW IDENTITIES. HOWEVER, THE WAR OF KNOWLEDGE HADN'T STOPPED PTOLEMY FROM SEEING THE SAME RECUR-

RING VISION. ANOTHER PREDICTION HAS YET TO HAPPEN.

CALLIE, SWEETHEART, IT IS OUR FEAR THAT YOUR MARK HAS ASSIGNED YOU A MISSION, A PART OF THE FULFILLMENT OF PTOLEMY'S PREMONITION. I CAN'T STRESS ENOUGH THE IMPORTANCE OF DISCERNMENT IN ALL MATTERS. LEARN BY WITNESSING OTHERS. BE SLOW TO SPEAK AND LEAN NOT ON YOUR UNDERSTANDING BUT TRUST IN YOUR GOD-GIVEN INSTINCTS. INTUITION HAS ALWAYS BEEN YOUR FATHER'S STRENGTH. IT'S MY HOPE YOU'VE INHERITED THIS INSIGHT. HEED IT.

WE LOVE YOU GIRLS WITH ALL OUR HEARTS,

AFFECTIONATELY, YOUR MOTHER,

VICTORIA CALERINE TRESMEIRE

I took a deep breath, closed my eyes, and worked to control my thoughts. So, there had originally been one group of Therans before a smaller section, to which my parents belonged, had broken off, calling themselves the Remnants. What'd they call the other group?

I opened my eyes and noticed a sparkle from the box. I picked up a single gold band with an intricately placed sapphire. One side of the ring had an irregular flat space.

Why did someone leave a ring in here? I searched again but came up with nothing. However, remembering the paper I'd stuffed back in the book, I pulled it out and saw Elizabeth Tresham's adoption certificate.

I picked up the book again and flipped through the pages. Below my mother's signature, the line read ...

CALLIE, KEEP THIS RING WITH YOU. I DO NOT UNDERSTAND ITS IMPORTANCE, BUT MY AUNT GAVE IT TO ME ON THE NIGHT WE LEFT OUR FAMILIES, ASKING ME TO GIVE IT TO YOU. SHE, TOO, WAS A SEER. SHE BELIEVED THERANS EVOLVE WITH THE TIMES. YOUR MARK PROVES MY AUNT'S BELIEF AND WHY SHE IS ESSENTIAL TO THE REMNANT ELDERS. HEED MY WARNING, TRUST YOUR INSTINCTS IN ALL MATTERS.

I slid the ring onto my left finger—a perfect fit. A brilliant blue stone gleamed back at me. What was significant about this ring? And what had Mom's aunt seen that made it important?

"I see you found the chest."

I spun around and almost dumped everything on the floor.

Jaw tight, head cocked, Gramps stood, ash-gray against the doorframe, eyes half-closed. His white hands gripped his suspenders.

"I knew ..." His voice broke into a gravelly sound. "I knew it was time to tell you." He came in and sat on the corner of my bed.

"Gramps?"

Palm outward, he stopped me mid-sentence. "Please, give me a chance to say what I must." His Adam's apple jerked. "A week or so before your parents' and sister's murder, your mother sent us the chest for you girls. We were not to open it." He pulled the purple blanket toward him and traced the eagle with his finger. "I've known since the day you were born you were different. Unlike us ... humans." His fingers trembled. "Your mom was the prettiest little thing, but she packed a punch. She was powerful. I ain't never seen anything like it before. I only witnessed it once. And we never discussed it in detail."

He lowered his chin to his chest. "It's because of your mom I'm still alive. Before you were born, your mom visited your dad for lunch one day at the university. We were in the basement cafeteria with the other teachers when the ground trembled, shifting the floor under our feet. Tables slid clear across the cafeteria. Next, the floor opened up and swallowed us, burying us under rubble. Your mother knocked one girl out of the way and managed to prevent an eight-foot slab of concrete from crushing me at the same time. She got us all out of there."

I watched him speak with reverence in his voice.

Gramps continued. "Since then, I have sworn to keep your mother's secret. And I've come to believe God had a purpose for me that day in letting me learn about your mom." His baby-blue eyes pierced mine. "In the end, it was to be here to protect you. I have learned to trust God more than ever and to keep my mouth shut. Having a security clearance in the Army has helped. Your mom never explained matters, and I don't know I'd understand if she had because what I witnessed that day would make Superman real." His chin dipped. "We may not be related, but you'll always be my granddaughter."

His words robbed my lungs of air. I wrapped my arms around his waist. I should have been angry because no one had told me he wasn't my true grandfather, but I'd lost Nana, my parents, and Ella. The thought of losing Gramps over this gripped my heart.

He accepted me and loved me, all the while knowing that I wasn't his biological grandchild. I swallowed the ache of knowing I was something other than human. I couldn't share everything with him, but he made my life richer. He'd always be my Gramps.

He dropped one arm from my waist and wiped away a tear.

"I've got things to do, dear." He patted my hand and left my room.

I crawled into bed, sat back against the headboard, and re-read the letter in the book. My mom's message was crowded with information. My mind twisted around the word Theran. The two-syllable word felt so foreign. What did it mean? I'd had years to accept I had powers, but I'd never known what I was, only that I was different from my friends. But I hadn't thought I was *this* different. I kept coming back to Mom's concern, linking Ptolemy's catastrophic vision and my mark. Were they connected? And how did the barrier I'd seen in Taylor's class fit together with everything?

Before this day, what I'd known of my existence amounted to a page in a book—today filled a chapter.

CHAPTER 16

ARMOR

The weeks slipped by, and I had little time to myself between school, homework, and work. April was around the corner, and the weather was unseasonably warm. I arrived early at school and walked through the courtyard toward the picnic table, where Erika sat with Camden. She bubbled enthusiastically, discussing how the committee decided to decorate for prom. She spoke about nothing but the dance on the way to my locker. Her eagerness verged on annoying. I even volunteered to watch a psycho-thriller just to get her to talk about something else.

Anna and Trystan hung out at his locker, talking more like whispering.

I nodded as he waved. A shot of electricity zinged through my stomach. The electrical current was so familiar. I didn't question it. Also, if I did, he'd think I was weird. Anyhow, there were no consequences—positive, negative, or neutral—besides how awkward it made me feel.

"Callie." Steve dashed up the stairs. "Oh my gosh. You won't believe it."

"What's up?" I shut my locker.

Steve scooted close, invading my personal space. His sunken-in, chaotic eyes darted around the alcove and watched other kids passing us.

"Come on, Steve. I don't have time—"

"Shh." He huffed. "You gotta hear this. It's gonna be all over school by three today."

"What?" I rolled my eyes, taking a step away from him.

"Sheriff left maybe an hour before the school doors opened. Someone vandalized the school library."

"OMJings. Did they catch the culprit?"

"No, not that I've heard. But this is the weird thing." He licked his lips. "From what I overheard in the office. They ransacked the school yearbooks. Nothing else. But the photos of kids in our school."

"Who'd be so stupid to destroy pictures?"

"They even damaged the elementary school yearbooks. Rumor has it that Lizzy broke in last night and destroyed the pictures of all Logan's ex-girlfriends." He whispered the last word. "You need to stay the heck away from Logan. I can't imagine what she'd do to any girl who showed interest in him now."

The bell rang, robbing me of my words, but it gave me an excuse to leave Steve. I hustled down the stairs as he took off to spread the news.

The morning classes dragged by. It was hard to stay in my seat with all this bottled-up energy inside me. I was determined to find a secluded place and try to recreate the barrier after school. I had to make sense of my world. Last night, after I'd finished my homework, I'd reread

Mom's letter. I'd then spent an hour or more on the internet, hoping to find something that would give me more information. Instead, it gave me more questions.

The lunch bell rang. It didn't come soon enough. I headed through the maze of corridors toward the cafeteria with Erika and Anna. People crowded the halls in a mad rush to fill their stomachs. I darted behind one person only to smack into Mr. Sykes. His broom handle dropped, and a Windex bottle skidded across the floor.

Two hands grabbed my shoulders.

"Oops. My bad."

"If I let go"—Mr. Sykes grimaced—"can you stay upright?"

I shrugged and kicked up my heel. "Two-left feet."

His arms dropped from my shoulders. He bent over, swiped the Windex bottle, and left without a word.

"Callie, come on." Anna tapped her foot. "If you keep this up, we'll have to eat lunch awfully fast." She grabbed my wrist, towing me along.

"Oh," Erika said. "My mom left me a text. Beautiful Felony has gowns on sale. They've got awesome deals. Last year, Lizzy's older sister got her dress there."

"Beautiful Felony?" Anna said. "That's an oxymoron if I ever heard one."

"Better than Nicely Cluttered Antiques." I snorted.

"Where's Beautiful Felony?" Anna asked as we reached the lunch line, and she grabbed a tray.

Erika seized a fork and a napkin. "At the Outlet Mall."

"I'm in." Anna snatched a hot sandwich. "Your mom's going, right?"

"Yeah," Erika said. "But she has errands to do first on the other end of town. Can we meet you there around 5:30ish?"

"Prom's not until the end of May. We've got over a month and a half before we need dresses. What's the hurry?" I asked.

"It's best to start early. Everyone's searching for a dress, not just us." Erika pulled cash from her pocket. "Besides, it'll be fun."

I pulled out my cell and texted Gramps. "If I can go, I'd have to swing by the house and grab some money."

"Cool." Anna paid the cashier. "I'll drive if you navigate, Callie. But I've got to pick up Colin at Ashworth at nine tonight."

I nodded, filled my tray, and scouted for a table. Our usual spot was empty, but Logan's crew sat only a table away. He generally sat by the soda machines. With no other vacant seats but in our typical area, I trudged forward.

"Hey." Steve elbowed me in the ribs. "What are you girls doing this weekend?"

Anna and Erika dashed past us and claimed seats. "I'm working. Don't know what they're doing."

"I'm having a bonfire Friday night." Steve's eyes darted to Logan. "I've invited Erika and the others."

I glanced at Logan. He sat with Ashton van Decamp and Tom by the windows. His arms whirled around his head like he was swinging at a bee. "Will Logan be there?"

Steve halted mid-stride. "He's popular. I couldn't just tell him no."

"He's a troublemaker. And just as bad as Lizzy." I lowered my tray. "Why have you been hanging around him and his brother the last few months?"

"Logan's not that bad. Rough around the edges, but he's cool."

"Steve, you know Lizzy will show up at the party if she catches wind about Logan being there."

"Come to the party, but just stay away from Logan."

Steve frustrated me. One minute, he warned me against hanging out with Logan because of Lizzy's jealousy, and the next, he acted like things were okay. Go figure.

We walked to the table. Trystan swung into a seat next to Anna. His warm smile melted my dark thoughts.

Erika grabbed her fork. "Was Steve trying to talk you into going Friday?"

"Yes," I rolled my eyes, pulling out my phone. "But I've got plans."

"Whoa." Logan came up behind us and swatted Steve on the back. "Told you, man, if she turned me down, she ain't going to prom with you."

Logan's words slid down my back, igniting my anger. Why was it some people felt the need to comment on a conversation when they hadn't even heard it? Could Steve not see Logan was a jerk? I had to get out of here.

Logan's presence threatened to push me over the edge. His words seemed more than a challenge, almost a warning. Yet, his arm wrapped around Steve's shoulder like they were best buds. Logan even squeezed Steve harder.

Steve stepped back from Logan. "No one's talking about prom. I'm seeing who's coming to the party."

Logan's brows drew together. "You going, Callie?"

I plastered a smile on my face. "Nope." I turned and faced Anna and Erika. "I'll be ready at five." I excused myself, crossed the cafeteria, snatched my drink off the tray, and dumped my burning frustration in the trash. I had no intention of hanging around Logan and his idiot group.

CHAPTER 17

PRACTICE – NOT PERFECT

I ditched my books on the kitchen table and dashed to the secluded field behind the mill. I had two hours before Anna would be here. A gigantic oak tree shaded some of the meadow from the sun. A huge limb that was big enough to climb hung over some rocks. The sun danced from behind the trees near the boulders. I walked into the open expanse of the field and raised my face, feeling the sun's warmth caress my skin.

You can do this.

I raised my arm and willed the barrier to appear.

Nothing happened.

I tried again. I commanded the barrier to show itself. The only things that stood up were the hairs on my arm from the breeze. After a while, curse words filled my head.

The first actual tingle of fear slithered within my mind. I had fallen into learning about my other capabilities under pressure or by accident. My first premonition had been a horrible vision of my parents' murder, and on that terrible night, I'd discovered I was stronger than a normal girl. The thought chilled me through to the marrow of my bones.

What purpose did the barrier have? It had kept me separated from everyone else in the classroom–like a barricade. Could it be a shield?

"Shield," I said aloud. The word felt right.

But if it were a protective wall, why didn't it stop Trystan from touching me? His hand was on my back when the barrier had electrified around me. I paced the ground. That could mean the shield didn't protect me from physical harm.

Something mental?

My mind reeled with the implications. All those movie and game characters, I sifted through on the internet for information about Theran—some characters had telekinesis and ESP. Could someone read my mind?

I had the ability to read lies, not to know what had caused them. Yet, I was at risk if someone else could read my mind.

The good thing was Trystan hadn't shown signs of having seen the barrier. So I didn't have to freak out if it popped up again. If it went off, I'd pretend nothing had happened.

Waiting was the best course of action. Eventually, someone would screw up and reveal more.

Mom was right. I had to be vigilant, trust my instincts, and practice using my powers.

I stared at my hand as the sapphire stone danced in the light, my mind wandering. The more time passed, the more concerned I became about the holes in my memories surrounding my parents' deaths. Pieces of that night came to me in glimpses.

The police had reported it as a random burglary, all evidence destroyed in the fire.

I stood, stretched, and massaged my lower back. I had to figure out the shield's function. Would I be able to control it? Or could I navigate it as I did my visions once they initially showed the premonition snapshots?

CHAPTER 18

BARRIER

People packed the outlet mall. Anna and I followed the signs to Beautiful Felony, stopping once for a small-scale train on rails that carried passengers through the parking lot. My mind buzzed with ways to control the shield while Anna talked non-stop.

"Where do you think they can be?" Anna looked at the clock on the dashboard. We were five minutes late.

I scanned the row of shops and the outside entrance to Beautiful Felony, then spotted Erika with her mom in front of Old Navy Outlet.

"Come on, they're over there." We exited the car and trudged around shoppers carrying bags into the parking lot. The warmer weather brought out all the shoppers.

"Hi," I said, approaching Mrs. Sundries and Erika.

Mrs. Sundries adjusted her sunglasses and rested them on her head. "Glad you girls could make it." She rubbed her hands together. "Come on, I'm excited to see what they've got on sale."

I opened the door. Three long walls and two center displays carried many dress selections. A shopper stood before a three-way mirror, trying on a light blue gown, pulling a strap over her shoulder.

"May I help you?" A gray-haired woman with glasses in her shirt pocket approached us.

"Yes," Mrs. Sundries said. "I've got three girls here who need to be fitted for prom gowns."

"I'd be glad to help you. Please follow me." We passed several mannequins dressed in bright colors on our way to the store's back corner.

"Tell me, is there a preference, a certain style of gown?" the clerk asked.

Erika pulled out a picture. "Do you happen to have this dress?"

"Yes, yes, we do," she said, leading us to a rack near the back of the store. The sales clerk pulled a dress off a rack of bright gowns and held it in front of her.

Erika had found her dress, the one from the magazine article. Mrs. Sundries' face brightened, and a smile tugged at her cheek when she pulled on the sales tag.

A little bit later, Erika was wearing *her* dress—a red satin sweetheart gown with a beaded bodice.

I'd bet Mrs. Sundries would be altering the slit up the side. Erika disappeared, changed back into her clothes, leaving the gown with her mother, and hunted for accessories. Anna tried on every green dress available. Her determination to find one laced up around the bodice and neckline impressed me.

I fanned through the dresses and waited for Anna to come out of the fitting room. None of the dresses caught my interest. They all exposed more skin than I was comfortable showing.

"Callie." A beautiful sapphire satin dress layered with a sheer blue and hunter-green chiffon was draped over Erika's arms.

The sales clerk cleared her throat and set down a couple of shoeboxes on the floor. "Your friend believes this one's made for you. The chiffon is lightweight. Once it's on, wrap the extra sheer over your shoulders. It can act as a wrap."

I hugged Erika. "Thank you."

Anna stood in front of the three-way mirror, wearing a stunning green gown. "Hurry, go try it on."

"Wait," the sales clerk said. "You'll need these, too." I accepted the shoeboxes and followed Erika into the dressing room.

"I'll wait until you need help."

I pulled the gown over my hips as bi-colored sheers flowed onto the floor. I pulled it up over my breasts and saw the sweetheart neckline sizzled with a small teardrop crystal. I took a deep breath.

"All right, you can come in."

Erika pulled the curtain back. I faced her. She held up her finger and rotated it.

I dropped my shoulders and turned around. She zipped the back and laced up the chiffon. The dress hid my scar, the layers of chiffon, my birthmark. "You look beautiful."

Putting on the one-inch blue heels lifted my spirits. I'd be certain to have a memorable night at prom. Before we left the store, I consulted with the clerk and asked the tailor to add extra material to the sweetheart neckline. Anna loved my gown and had managed to find herself a green dress that looked stunning on her. Mrs. Sundries wiped a misty tear from her cheek, giving us all a warm smile.

I pressed my palms against my temple as my head ached. A vision rose in my consciousness of ... *a smoke-filled hall and a red exit sign suspended from a ceiling, nothing more.*

Erika put her hand on my arm. "Are you all right?"

"Mmm-hmm. Just a headache."

We exited with bags full of accessories and three gowns. I was starving. "Can we grab some grub?"

Mrs. Sundries looked at her watch.

"We've got to help with chores yet." Erika hugged me, and they left us at the mall's cafeteria.

Anna raised the bags in her hands. "These are getting heavy. Let's put this stuff in my car, then grab a bite to eat."

Once we'd returned to the food court empty-handed, I asked, "What are you hungry for?"

"What about pizza or subs?"

"I'm game for a hot sub."

We ordered and sat outside. The warmth airbrushed my skin. I unwrapped the paper from my sub and took a bite. Lights illuminated the parking lot and sidewalk café. Kids tossed coins in a fountain near the train conductor's hut while their parents ate. The train dropped off several kids, took on new passengers, and circled the mall's buildings.

"Slow down, Callie," Anna said. "You're going to choke. I know you didn't eat lunch at school, but didn't you grab a bite afterward?"

"No. I didn't have time."

"It's good Trystan's started working at the mill. I can see from the dark crescents under your eyes you've been working too hard. You're not studying for finals already, are you?"

Trystan's training was with Gramps most of the time, but when I'd show him some of the operational adjustments that had to be made, surprisingly, Trystan's questions weren't annoying, and his silence was comforting.

Was my lack of sleep noticeable? "No, Max's injury has healed, so he's back to work."

I took another bite, watching birds eat crumbs from the ground. Finals were the last thing on my mind.

"Didn't expect to see you here," Mr. Lindy said.

I covered my mouth, swallowed my last bite, and nodded to Steve, who stood beside his uncle. "Wow. You're up and walking. Looks like surgery helped your knee."

He picked up his cane. "I've got a few more weeks before I can get rid of this stick and get back out on my boat." He smiled. "It's the best thing I could've done."

"How you doing?" Steve asked, looking at Anna.

"Great." Anna rolled her sub wrapper into a ball. Moving to throw it toward the garbage can, she stopped, saying, "Hi, Mr. Taylor."

Taylor and a blonde female skirted around Steve and Mr. Lindy as shoppers passed behind us.

"Hi," Taylor scanned the courtyard. "Since it's gotten nicer, it seems like everyone's shopping."

I stood. "Hello."

Taylor nodded.

"This is Mr. Lindy, Steve's uncle," I said.

Taylor dipped in to shake the extended hand Mr. Lindy offered. "This is Samantha, my girlfriend." He took off his Euro glasses. "Good night to hang out." He bit on the frame, looking at me. "Didn't take you for the shopping type."

Samantha rested her red fingertips on Taylor's forearm. "Now, Teddy, every girl likes to shop." The woman's eyes shifted restlessly.

Taylor's girlfriend wasn't from around here. She was a walking mannequin in stiletto heels, long blonde hair, and cosmetically altered lips.

"Callie's not a shopper." Steve smiled. "You'd have better luck finding her stacking grain or bagging flour."

Taylor's eyes crinkled. "I see."

Anna took a swig of her pop. "We bought our prom gowns."

Samantha's hands danced before us in excitement. "Oh, Anna, I'd love to see them."

Anna became animated, explaining our dresses.

I froze. Alarm hit me, sending a stampede of spiders down my spine. My barrier burst forth, I stepped back, bumping the back of my leg on the chair behind me. How'd Samantha know Anna's name? I hadn't introduced her.

Taylor's eyes locked in on Anna, darkening. He stepped back, and his heavy-lidded eyes dropped, glancing at me.

My surroundings scattered from my thoughts. My peripheral blurred and refocused in tunnel vision. Something outside of my understanding was happening here.

My sixth sense flared. An intruding force. Taylor had some mental ability.

Everything happened so quickly. So unexpectedly.

Crimson light exploded into view, a solid wall within my shield changed it to a shade of orange—at its darkest, right in front of me. I narrowed my eyes, and the color amplified, glowing like a fireball about the size of a quarter, in the same localized spot at which Mr. Taylor and I had made eye contact.

I dipped my head but kept my eyes narrowed. The orange light stayed within the shield's wall, always in eyesight and responding to the direction of my stare.

A thunderous *pop* broke my concentration.

I jerked my head. Power filled me. Where'd that sound come from?

The harder I focused—the vision tightened again—the more the world blurred around me, centering to a quarter-sized beam that shot from the glow of my shield, striking a large light in the parking lot behind a truck that backfired.

The light shattered, and glass dropped to the ground. Shoppers below scattered, panicked at the explosion.

"What the ...?" The words strangled on my tongue. Did I do that? How? And why did the beam look like wrinkles in the air?

"Wow. What the heck happened?" Mr. Lindy jerked back and looked over his shoulder. "I hope no one got hurt."

Taylor turned away from the parking lot. "Let's hope not. Regardless, someone's got a major clean-up job." He pushed his glasses back on his face and pulled out his keys. "We've got to go." He dipped his chin, dismissing us.

"Do have fun." Samantha flicked up her palm, waving.

Anna jerked her purse up over her shoulder. "Oh, jeez, I almost forgot about picking up Colin. Come on, Callie."

I pitched my trash in the garbage can. "See you, Mr. Lindy, Steve."

The barrier dropped like a curtain as it dawned on me. Mr. Taylor and Samantha were Theran. My shield's color had changed in reaction to something Mr. Taylor had done. And yet, no one noticed I destroyed the parking lot light. ... Oh, no! I cringed, biting hard on my lower lip. Had the truck not backfired, distracting me, I could've hurt someone with my powers.

I swallowed heavily, feeling cornered by my thoughts, paralyzed, unable to move. My inner insecurities plagued me ...

CHAPTER 19

INTIMIDATION

Wait here for me. I'll get Colin. It should only take a few minutes." Anna slammed the car into park, across from a row of buildings on Ashworth Campus and jumped out. Lampposts lit the brick sidewalk and street. Students crossed in front of the cars that traveled past.

It was weird. The shield had appeared without warning—both times when I was vulnerable and around Taylor. Was he the shadowed man from my vision? I closed my eyes and replayed the vision, reaching out with intuition. Something about Taylor didn't fit. He couldn't be the shadowed man. But what did he want?

The shield seemed to be a radar detector for those using their powers against me. It had to deflect mental power—that was the only way to explain how it reacted when Taylor looked at me. And the red and golden colors combined to make a dangerous weapon.

Laughter pulled me from my thoughts. People crossed the street and entered the Boundary Fitness Center where Anna had gone. Restless, I got out and followed them inside.

Gym equipment and weights covered the floor. Muted televisions displayed newscasters reporting from a local news station. No one greeted me. An organized chant echoed from the back hall. I trailed the row of chairs along the wall and peeked into a massive private room. Mirrors covered three walls, like in a dance studio, while forty or more people moved in unison. Some sort of karate dance. Dad had called it a Kata back during my lessons.

My eyes homed in on one of the six black-belt instructors. Colin faced the mass of students wearing differently colored belts. "Wow, he's a black belt."

"Callie?" Anna came from the side hallway. Her lips pinched. "I thought you were in the car."

I raised my eyebrow. "What's wrong?"

She looked over her shoulder.

Colin stood, poker straight. His students still moved in synchronized formation.

"Come on." She tugged on my shirt and pulled me back toward the entrance. "Colin's class is running late."

"I had no idea he taught."

Her lips parted, but she didn't speak.

"Callie," Colin interrupted, coming up behind Anna.

I spun around, swallowing my anxiety. Maybe I should bone up on my moves. "How does one take lessons here?"

Colin tilted his head. "You want instruction in martial arts?"

"Yes."

"This place is for ..." Anna looked over at Colin.

"College students," Colin stated matter-of-factly. "But, between Trystan and me, we could teach you some techniques over the summer."

"Sure."

"Hey. Get back here." Two guys with brown hair and reddish highlights barreled out of the back room where Colin had been teaching, followed by an older black-belt instructor. "You've got to work on your techniques." The black-belt instructor's words stopped when he saw us.

"We've got better things to do than practice," the taller of the two students said, dismissing the instructor. They stopped at Anna's side. One gave her a dazzling smile. "Did your brother let you out to play?"

Anna hurried toward me.

"Get away from her, Jon." Colin's crisp words alarmed me. "If you're not going to take practice seriously, then leave."

"You aren't my boss. Nor is your uncle." Jon then looked at me. "You look familiar."

"We've never met." What was up with this idiot?

Jon stepped up to me, leaned into my neck, and inhaled. "I'd like to get to know you better." The hot air from his breath caressed my cheek.

"Back up." I gritted my teeth.

The other guy grabbed Jon, wrenching him away from me.

Jon walked out around us and flipped the sign on the window to CLOSED. "This place stinks."

The other boy exited behind him. The door slammed shut, punctuating the awkward moment.

"Now, that's creepy." I kept my voice low so as not to sound urgent. "Anna, I've got to get home." This time, *I* tugged on *her* shirt.

"Harrumph." Colin gripped the ends of his black belt, never taking his eyes off the two guys. "I'll catch up in a minute. Let me tell my sensei I'm leaving."

Five minutes later, the three of us packed into the car. I had even more questions cramming my brain, like what was up with Colin's bizarre attitude? And where'd I see that guy before? I sure didn't recognize him.

CHAPTER 20
WILLINGLY

The sun shone through the lobby's glass windows. Chaos seemed a mild word to describe thirty students in the large reception area hammering, moving 2x4s, and coloring prom posters. The room buzzed with excitement. We cut out cardboard building patterns to transform the lobby into a romantic New York City skyline. School officials and the decorating committee decided to have us work weekends to avoid interfering with the construction crew. This meant limited days and extended weekend hours.

I scouted the room. "Look over there."

Erika glanced toward the metal scissor gate that separated the lobby from the wide hallway going to the gym.

"Mr. Sykes doesn't seem happy."

"Would *you* be happy if you had to clean up after construction workers and us?" Every inch of the lobby screamed prom. "I'd hate to pick all this up."

"Well, right now, that's not a concern." Erika snatched newspapers and climbed the ladder. "Hey, hand me the tape over there."

"Here."

"Thanks." Erika grabbed it. "Did Trystan ditch you?"

My head jerked up. "What?"

Her eyes crinkled. "Thought you were training him tonight at the mill."

"Oh, no, he's been working with Gramps. Aren't you going to Steve's party later?"

"That doesn't start till seven. I thought I'd put some time in here and decorate first before I meet up with Anna. We've got room for you if you change your mind."

"No, thanks." I tried to sound enthusiastic but didn't think I fooled her. My night would be boring, but I preferred that to hanging out with Logan.

She smiled crookedly.

I glanced at the construction workers. They had stacked their tools in the corner. "But I'll help out with decorating again next weekend."

She smiled. "Catch you later."

"Have fun." I left the lobby and headed to my car as guilt consumed me. Birds flew over the courtyard, and cars passed on the main road. Part of me wanted to stay and help Erika, but I'd spent several nights wrestling with the shield and still couldn't conjure it up on command. It worked, but to what extent? It was great that I had a weapon, but it was useless if I couldn't control it.

I needed to kick back and chill at home. Gramps had worked like a zombie on adrenaline this past week, even training Trystan, which was going better than I'd expected. Trystan showed every indication of grasping the bagging process.

I pulled up under the loading dock and shifted the Jeep into park. A truck I didn't recognize was parked by the outbuilding and mill. Before I shut the door, a scream came from the mill. I rushed up the steps into the mill office and came to a dead stop. Flour covered every inch of the grain room.

My eyes zipped toward Trystan. He stood next to Gramps in the wide doorway. A white dusting covered their hair and shoulders. Tesla pushed his way between Gramps and Trystan and licked Trystan's fingers. Mud darkened Tesla's already brown coat, and doggy, flour-mud tracks covered the floor.

Max came running in from the woodshop. A bright smile stretched across his face.

I burst out laughing and used my phone to snap a picture.

Gramps flicked grain from his sleeve. "Dang dog comes scurrying in here, and I drop flour everywhere."

A flash went off behind Max. Our neighbor, Harry Livingston, held up his phone and snapped another picture. "This'll be good for blackmailing."

Gramps cleared his throat. "You act like those darn-fool paparazzi with those cameras. Excuse me. Trystan, come on, let's get cleaned up."

I looked at Mr. Livingston with a smile. Sweat beaded below his hairline.

"Please don't tell me Tesla was out at your place again."

He frowned.

My grin withered.

"What's up?" Max pocketed his cell phone.

Mr. Livingston looked over at Tesla.

Concern niggled at my consciousness. What had Tesla done?

Gramps rounded the corner with Trystan three steps behind him, wiping his hands on a towel. He smiled at me, his eyes wrinkled at the corners. He cocked his head, giving me a questioning look.

"What can I do for you, Harry?" Gramps asked.

Mr. Livingston tapped his foot on the floor. "No sweet way to put it, Al. I came home to find some kids spray painting the side of my barn with graffiti. Your dog," he raised his jaw toward Tesla, "chased them off. I guess Holmes County has experienced some barn burnings over the last two months."

"What?" The word escaped my mouth. I hadn't expected this.

"Don't worry," Mr. Livingston said. "Sheriff Travis is sure the sheriff in Holmes County will catch them soon. I just hope being their neighboring county won't make their problems ours."

"This district made a smart move, electing Sheriff Travis," Max commented.

"That we did." Livingston huffed. "You might want to make sure your floodlights are working. I'd suggest keeping some lights on inside the mill, too." He looked down at Tesla and laughed. "Leave him inside here. With that bark, he'll scare off just about anyone."

Gramps threw his towel over his shoulder. "Thanks. Max and I are meeting Sheriff Travis later after we check on Mr. Santos. Let's hope he's found a lead."

"Mr. Santos still isn't accepting visitors," Livingston said.

Gramps grinned at me. "Well, I guess that makes tonight easier."

He looked over at Max. "We'd better get ready if we're going to get a decent seat at the restaurant. You did a good job, Trystan. Keep them notes and study hard. I'll see you bright and early tomorrow. Thanks for coming tonight and letting us know what's going on, Harry. If I hear something, I'll call you." Gramps pulled the towel from his shoulder.

"He's a keeper." Livingston petted Tesla behind the ear before leaving.

Max jerked his thumb over his shoulder. "I'm gonna finish picking up below. Meet you at the car in five."

Tesla trotted over to me and sat down. "You're such a good boy." I ruffled my fingers through his hair.

"What are you two doing tonight?" Gramps looked from me to Trystan.

My stomach growled, and a blush crawled into my cheeks.

Trystan's eyes sparkled, and he shrugged.

A gurgle erupted. I slapped my stomach like one would muffle a burp behind one's palm. My eyes widened, and I sucked on my lips.

"We can talk about it." Trystan's mouth stretched into a wide grin, showing his laugh lines. "Let me clean up the rest of the flour."

"Mmm. Okay." What could I say after Gramps suggested Trystan and I hang out? "I'm going to grab a book from the woodshop."

"Well," Gramps used the towel and swatted gently at Tesla's nose. "It sounds like you need some grub. I'll leave money on the table for some food." He winked and exited the mill.

Trystan wandered off into the office.

I hurried away, red-faced and dying of humiliation. Had Gramps done it on purpose? Jings.

Dad had a book I intended to take over to the house. When I moved to pick it up, Ella's birdhouse caught my eye. I ran my fingers over the unfinished edge. We would've completed it had ...

I pushed myself back on the bench by the window and grabbed the birdhouse. My best times were watching Gramps and Dad woodwork together, making live-edge furniture. My dad's talent in crafting even went to timber-frame sheds. His skills—his passion—were unstoppable.

Snap.

I cringed, seeing a fracture in the birdhouse.

Light from the sunset filtered in through the window. Bright orange, pink, and light purple rested on the treetops on the horizon. I leaned my head against the frame and stared out into space. Why did people have to hurt one another? Vandalize? Kill?

A memory resurfaced—I was sitting outside, below an open window, listening to my parents' conversation and watching the birds eat from the feeder.

"She told you this?"

"Callie wouldn't lie to me, Cyrus."

"Victoria, I've never known one to show an ability before the age of eighteen. It's rare to have a power. None of this makes sense. She is but seven."

"Her mark is different."

"Truth has never changed. We evolve with the demands of our times."

"How do we protect her? Cyrus, she saw our death. She doesn't know it now. She is too little to understand what she described to me, but it was our death, yours, and mine."

"Who can we trust?"

The painful memory of my parents' demise filled my mind. My heart twisted, squeezing in my chest. However, the words were as clear as if they'd been written on my heart. My parents died, knowing I had to live.

Footfalls echoed on the floor.

"I got you a mug of hot cocoa. Gotta love that machine."

"What?" I didn't take my eyes from Ella's birdhouse.

"Didn't you hear a word I said?"

"No. I'm sorry." I didn't look up.

Trystan stopped short of the lathe. His black tennis shoes were now covered with flecks of flour. "I was commenting on the cocoa machine your Gramps has in his office. Here."

I set the birdhouse on my lap and accepted the mug. I stared up at him, searching. His gaze was deep, reaching, moving me. This man had called 911 after the accident, stayed with me until the ambulance arrived, stopped to help me, a virtual stranger in the middle of a lightning storm, and showed concern the first time I'd seen my shield. He hadn't treated me like a freak, only comforted me.

He'd proven to be a good friend.

"You're thinking again." Under black, curly hair, his eyebrows danced. "I can tell that look from a mile away." His chuckle eased some of my concerns. He recognized when I struggled and tried to weave humor into the conversation.

The enormity of what I was about to reveal hit me. For half a second, I considered my decision. I listened, half expecting my sixth sense to warn me against this, but it didn't.

I exhaled to steady my pulse, running my finger again over the birdhouse. "My sist ... sister." The words edged out. "This is the last thing she tried to make with o-our dad. She and I used to play with our doll babies, watching the birds out the window." I touched the cool glass that separated us from the outside. "She'd made this and couldn't finish it before we left that summer to go back to

California. They had intended to complete it but never got the chance."

Trystan didn't respond. He leaned against the bench, and it jerked.

The words came easier. "Most people here think they died in a fire. Information gets distorted on the news. That's how my grandparents left it. We never explained or confirmed the details." I forced myself to meet his eyes as I touched my scar. "Have you heard any of the rumors?"

His chin dropped to his chest, breaking eye contact.

Ah, he had. I silently weighed the moment. Something about the stillness reassured me.

"How they died wasn't a secret." I swallowed the swell of pain. "But, still, giving details to people was like confirming the brutal reality of it. For a while, the newspapers spread it all over California. The airwaves spouted my family's name, but it eventually died. They became another statistic. Some here may know the truth, but I ..." I took a deep breath and continued. "That night, Dad tucked us into bed. We said our prayers, and he recited Little Boy Blue. It was our nightly ritual." I closed my eyes and gave in to the memory. I let the words rush forth. "I awoke to their screams." I crossed my arms over my chest. "It was the last time I saw my sister, Ella. She ran downstairs, trying to find Mom and Dad, but I couldn't. I hid under my bed. It was only after I heard her scream that I came out."—I was dragged out.

My heart accelerated, remembering the intruder's tight, fierce grip as he dragged me out from under the bed. I'd dug my nails into the floor until splinters rooted under my nails.

I choked on air. "I heard shots ... three of them." I paused, uncertain of my next words, and traced a deep gash in the wood of Dad's bench with my fingertip. "I fought the man in my room." I had to be careful not to say too much. "We struggled, but I got away."

Trystan's gentle eyes were encouraging.

"Downstairs, candles lit the entire house." And an iron scent of blood scorched my lungs. "It didn't seem real until I saw my mother."

Trystan moved closer, his hip bumping my knee.

"Mom was draped over the couch like a rag doll. Dad's body lay over Mom's." I wiped a traitorous tear away. "I know he tried to protect Mom. When I found him, he wasn't d-dead." Tears streamed from me as the words lodged in my throat.

I drew my knees up under my chin and hugged my arms around my shoulders, trying to find comfort, tracing my mark. I stared straight into the depths of Trystan's soul.

"He held me," I remembered his words, *Stay alive. Protect yourself.* "Later that night, I woke up to discover the house was on fire, and I was outside, near the shed. I still haven't put all of the pieces together. I don't even know how I made it out."

We sat there for a long time. I held his stare, seeing the compassion in his eyes. He might not understand everything, but he wasn't a stranger to grief.

Finally, he broke his silence. "There was more than one person?"

I massaged my temples. "There were three intruders. The police reported it as a burglary. A string of them had occurred in the area. Ours was the first to result in murder."

"Did the police catch them?" I didn't miss the thread of tension in his tone.

"Gramps told me it'd taken them a few days to catch the murderers. They're all in jail now." I paused and collected my thoughts. "That night, the police took me to the hospital. The social workers gave up after what seemed an age of intense questioning because I wouldn't talk to anyone. A lifetime seemed to pass before Gramps and Nana came to get me from the orphanage. There were major problems locating my grandparents. And the doctors said I hadn't spoken a word until I'd seen them." I clamped my fingers together to stop them from trembling.

I made eye contact with Trystan. He rubbed a hand over his face. When he pulled his hand away, his eyes had taken on a strange, dark hue. I couldn't take the intensity of his stare, so I gazed over his shoulder at the stationary gear.

"Your sister?" His tone soothed my exposed nerves.

"I never saw her again." I tried to shake off the vision of how it would have looked to see my sister dead like my mother and father.

My memory slipped into overdrive, allowing me to hear, again, the snap of the switchblade open behind me and to remember the searing pain of the blade piercing my flesh. "W-while Dad held me, one of them stabbed me in the back." I cleared my throat. "The police reported a candle had started the fire. I guess it was knocked over during the struggle. I can't understand why they were taken from m ... me." I took a deep breath. "But I can't keep hiding my feelings. Erika tells me I need to open up."

Concern crowded his eyes. I found warmth in his unease. "You've never told this to anyone before, have you?"

I shook my head. Up until now, I'd never felt comfortable enough. "Sometimes, I feel so empty. The hardest thing for me to accept is I'll never know why. It's hard to let go when some memories are so fresh." I choked on my words. "Sometimes, I remember how Dad chased us around the house. Ella and I would run from him, laughing. We'd jump off the steps to avoid him. My parents used to do so much with us. It seems like the good memories get all mixed up with the painful ones." I sighed. "A couple of days ago, I found a chest full of things."

"So, not everything got destroyed in the house fire?"

I played with the etched marks on the table for a moment. "Mom had sent some things to my grandparents' house before she died."

"I'm glad you have your grandfather." He glanced down at his shoes. "It's obvious he cares. In some ways, I'm envious."

"What would make you say that?" I picked up my mug and took a sip of lukewarm cocoa.

"It's the way you two talk with each other. The warmth you show him." His jaw tightened, lips pursing as he looked out the window. He took a deep breath and faced me. "Life is what we make it—with the deck of cards that life deals. My parents weren't the least bit affectionate. They raised us with a firm hand—no praise, compassion, or warmth. Sebastian was ten years older than me. They destroyed his life. He tried so hard to be perfect, to earn their love. They pushed us both to meet impossible expectations."

Trystan blinked and balled his palm into a fist. "They believed that extreme measures had to be taken for us to be strong and self-sufficient. As if showing us love would spoil us." A hint of sarcasm marred his tone. "My parents groomed Sebastian to take over the family business." He dipped his chin. "My brother destroyed himself trying to meet their expectations. Sometimes, I think my parents only gave birth to us because that's what was expected of them, especially my father. We were pawns for his ambitions. He drummed this into us. We had to be warriors—to protect our heritage, history, and family. By age eight, I could recite our family lineage by name, like a student might recite the US presidents in junior high." A dark chuckle escaped from his lips. "My father's a proud, overbearing man, and I'm his biggest disappointment." He paused, squaring his shoulders. "I only found support after I rebelled. My aunt and uncle saved me from my brother's fate. It still amazes me that two people could be raised in the same family and household and be polar opposites."

I had no idea if he was speaking about his brother and himself or his dad and uncle.

He gazed at the ceiling, his fingers weaving through his hair. I recognized the movement as a sign of his nervousness. He took my empty mug from my hand. The clink of the mug on the workbench tightened my nerves, but the warmth of his hand as he interwove our fingers kept me entranced. Butterflies brightened in my stomach. His touch made me feel safe as he brushed the top of my knuckles with his thumb.

As troubling as the conversation was, it was an important moment in our friendship. I couldn't reveal everything, but I wanted him to know me. I loved that he didn't try to soften my reality with words of support—he just listened and shared.

He squeezed my hand, and my stomach gurgled to life.

This time, I didn't attempt to muffle the sounds.

"Come on." He tugged my hand and stepped away from the bench. "I don't want your Gramps accusing me of starving you. Let's grab a bite to eat."

I flashed him a grin. "Sounds great. I'll beat you." I raced Trystan out the door and to the car.

We drove down Liberty, pulled off the street, and parked in front of Coccia House.

"We need to hurry," he said. "Your stomach's demanding food."

I gripped the car door handle as my face turned beet red. I opened the door, but he was standing on my side of the car when my feet hit the ground. He extended his hand, and I took it.

We entered the restaurant. The owner waved to us from the back. Without letting go of my hand, Trystan headed to the table at the rear.

"What can I get you, Callie?" Hanson's eyes darted between Trystan and me.

I unwrapped the napkin from the silverware, not wanting to answer Hanson's unspoken question. "Can you bring us a pitcher of soda?"

"Coming right up." Hanson dashed around the partition, leaving us alone in the dark corner.

"What do you like on your pizza? We can split a large."

I smiled. "I'm hungry enough to eat three pieces."

"Cool."

My mouth inched up at the corners. "I love onions."

He laughed. "I like mine loaded with everything but anchovies."

Hanson came back with our drinks and filled the glasses.

"Okay, we'd like a large pizza, half with everything, the other half with pepperoni and onions."

"Ah." Hanson grinned. "You've got Callie's number. She loves a good pepperoni-and-onion pizza."

Time evaporated, and the world around us became a backdrop. Trystan's animated expressions kept my focus. We talked and laughed, waiting for our food.

"One large pizza," Hanson interrupted us, placing a round aluminum pizza tray on the table. "Enjoy."

I scooped up a slice and took a bite. Cheese dripped from the sides. There was no end to it. I rushed, taking quick, small bites, but the cheese still oozed over my fingers. I reached for my napkin and missed spilling my drink by inches.

Trystan wiped his mouth with his tablecloth. "This is fantastic. The cheese practically falls off the pizza. How can they make a profit with all the cheese they put on here?"

I picked up my drink and took a sip. "I don't know, but I'm not complaining."

"I wasn't criticizing, but wow." His eyes twinkled. "Last time we were here, I thought it had been a fluke that the food was so great. The exterior confused me cause it's a house. Looks can be so misleading."

"It's a local secret. People actually have this pizza shipped overseas."

"Man, that'd cost an arm."

"Oh, but it's soooo worth it." I smiled and pressed my back against the seat. "I'm glad you're adjusting to the Falls."

"I really like it here." He smiled. "It's intriguing."

"Never thought I'd hear the Falls called intriguing. It's about the most boring place on Earth." Until Mr. Taylor–and Trystan–had shown up.

He put down his crust and licked his fingers, his eyes examining my face. "Sometimes, you start to say something and then fail to fill in the rest of the words." Trystan cocked his head, a smile playing on his lips.

I shrugged. "So, what's so interesting about the Falls?" I threw the last bite into my mouth.

"You."

"Me?" Did he say ...

He cleared his throat. "Will you go to prom with me?"

Caution evaporated. "Yes, but I must confess I'm a walking time bomb in heels."

Trystan's eyes sparkled. "Awesome." His shoulders dropped, and he took a deep breath. He unzipped his sweatshirt. "Don't you think it's a little warm in here?"

I smiled and devoured three more slices while listening to his stories about Colin, Anna, and him in France, at a museum where the security guards had caught them playing hide-and-seek. It seemed we'd both learned to accept the cards we'd been dealt and make a *new* family from the affection of others. By the time we'd finished dinner, a sense of understanding overcame me.

Trystan cracked my dark moods. Maybe I couldn't live a dream, but for one night at a dance, I could try.

CHAPTER 21

COUNTDOWN

The folds of the cotton curtain slipped through my fingers, cutting off the view of late April's flowers. I turned on the faucet and filled my mug.

Over the past few weeks, Trystan and I had established an easy rhythm while working at the mill. I found myself thinking more of prom. Happiness bubbled within me at the thought of going to the dance. His friendship filled an empty spot I hadn't known needed filled. Work and school consumed almost every free moment, but I stole moments to practice calling up the shield, with no results.

And I had no results with figuring out my visions either. What I had were scattered snapshots of two separate visions. One a burning building. The other, a shadowed man's face, splitting in half. My sixth sense somehow tied the second vision to Mr. Taylor, but how did everything correlate? Or were they two separate incidents? My gut clenched, tightening at the thought of another fire.

One of the vision fragments had come true—the chest in the sewing room had revealed my mom's letter, which had only survived the house fire because it had been with Nana and Gramps. I could only assume the second would, too.

Tesla's nails clicked across the floor. The chair's legs screeched. "I'm grateful we don't pay for water."

I turned off the faucet. "Sorry."

Gramps frowned. "Before I can set eyes on you, you're barreling out the door, running off to school, or working at the mill. At the rate you're going, your feet will fall off. And don't think I haven't seen you hiking up to that field." He held out his palm. "Don't try to explain it. I knew in raising you there would be much I wouldn't understand." His right shoulder dropped. "Now, sit. I want to talk."

I set my mug on the kitchen counter, half-smiling.

He cleared his throat. "I've given this a lot of thought. You're not an ordinary girl."

"Gramps."

"Listen, dear." Gramps arched a brow. "I see how you work around here. You don't argue with me like most teens would. It's important to me I give back to you all the joy you've given me. Had you not been here after your Nana's ..." His chin trembled as he stared down at his hand. "Well, the thing is, I'm thinking we need a vacation."

I dropped into a chair and set my phone down. "When?"

"This summer." He beamed. "Max can handle things for a while. If you want to bring someone, we can do that.

Your Nana always wanted to take you to Italy. I want to do it for her. And for you, my dear."

"But the cost."

A bark of laughter erupted from him. "Money's not a concern. Your parents left you financially secure."

My mouth fell open. "I thought we didn't have much."

"What good would it have done to tell you there's money? Nothing. I still wouldn't have raised you any different. You gotta work for what you want, and you gotta carve out–"

"You gotta carve out your own life. Ain't nobody going to make you happy but you. I haven't forgotten, Gramps."

"Good. So, what do you think?"

"Yes." I jumped out of my chair and wrapped my arms around his neck. "Can we see Venice?" The thought warmed my heart.

"We'll work out the details later." He patted my back. "We've got to get passports first. Now, if you're decorating for prom later, you'd better hurry. Trystan will be here soon, and the paint needs loading. Max's already put the 2x4s in your Jeep."

"Thanks, Gramps." I pecked him on the cheek and bolted for the door, grabbing the toolbox and paint. Tesla barked, wagging his tail. He dashed outside, and I followed.

Trystan's car pulled up next to my Jeep. He got out and shut the door behind him.

"Callie, we'll never make it in time," Trystan said when he saw the paint and toolbox in my arms. "We're already late." He took the box from my hand.

"I'm sorry." I adjusted the gallon of paint. "Gramps wanted to talk, and I forgot we had to load all the stuff Erika wanted. I don't see why we need to bring this paint. She's already got some in the storage room."

He lifted the hatch and loaded the trunk. "It's not your fault. I'm running behind, too." He exhaled. "My dad's still putting pressure on me to move in with him." He gave me a look stripped of warmth.

"Can he make you?"

He shook his head and shut the hatch. "Right now, he's giving me a list of options, or as he puts it, incentives for joining him."

I got into the Jeep. "Are you moving?"

"No." He shut the Jeep door and winked. "I like living here."

We exited the drive as gravel hit the underside of the Jeep. I pressed the button until the window retracted. "If I get pulled over with all this stuff blocking my rearview mirror, I'm sending Erika the ticket." I gazed at a billboard along the road. "I'm excited about prom, but the decorating committee is getting crazy. Erika said they'd argued over the color of lights for the skyline. They're trying to get everything just right. It's so stupid. As soon as it's over, everything'll be thrown away."

"Don't even say it, or Erika will ask you to pull the trailer to haul the junk."

This was a drawback of owning a reliable vehicle with a hitch. "Oh, Erika had me bring an old stoplight. It works. I think it'll be cool. She wants to put it in the corner, near the—"

An engine roared beside us.

"Callie!"

I snapped a look out the driver's window as my tires vibrated against the rough gravel on the side road.

A silver Camaro straddled the double yellow lines, keeping pace with us. Music blared from the car, and tinted windows prevented me from seeing inside.

We approached an incline. I backed off the gas and maneuvered the Jeep to the right.

A horn blared. A semi-truck crested the hill, barreling down on the Camaro in his lane.

I jerked my wheel farther over the white line. The Camaro sped up and slipped between the semi and us.

I slammed on the brakes and screeched to a stop at the side of the road. Paint and wood shifted, banging around in the Jeep.

The semi thundered past, close enough that its draft brushed my face. Up ahead, the silver Camaro ran a red light and disappeared.

I caught my breath. The thought flashed through my mind ... Nana had died at that very intersection. Sheriff Travis had installed a light to ensure people's safety, and this idiot sped right through it.

A brick drive-thru sat catty-corner to an open field, where Sheriff Travis said Mr. Santos's car had flipped three times. I clutched the wheel and looked straight at Trystan.

"Jackasses. Jerks. Idiots." My heart pumped hard in my chest. "They could have killed us."

Trystan sat soldier straight, one palm bracing the dashboard, the other gripping the emergency brake.

I took a moment to steady my nerves and pressed my head back against the headrest.

"Callie, let me drive."

I glanced at him.

Trystan fisted his hand, and his knuckles cracked. "You're in no shape to drive." He grabbed the keys from the ignition and turned off the Jeep. "Look at your hands."

My fingers trembled.

His eyes didn't stray from mine. "You're shaken up. I'm not risking either one of our lives. You've been strung tighter than wire for a while now." Muscles clenched near his jawline.

I didn't argue with him.

I glanced at the clock and saw we were almost half an hour late. We switched seats, and he drove. Silence hung between us, anxiety sizzling along my nerves. He was right. I had been wound up lately.

Since my shield had shown up, I'd spent hours looking through the chest, trying to piece things together. I'd even skipped two outings with Erika and Anna. The only things I'd been consistent with were work and school.

Eagerness to talk consumed me, but how could I tell him I'd been hiding out, trying to control a bizarre shield that detaches from my body because our new history teacher has powers? Oh, and by the way, you didn't know this, but I was born with a mark ... but you can't see it. Oh, and I forgot, I can see the future. An evil man has something horrible planned. So awful that I saw a figure floating, face down, in the water.

How quickly did I want to find myself in a straitjacket? His aunt would have connections in the psych ward.

We pulled into the parking lot. Erika was directing cars up to the courtyard lawn to unload supplies. She flailed her arms, directing another vehicle toward the lobby. Trystan slowed the Jeep and pulled up beside her.

"About time." Erika pointed at the school. "You're late. Everything's falling apart. We had to change ideas on props because they wouldn't stay on the wall. Mr. Sykes didn't show up. The blasted gate is down, so we can't access the prop room unless we go through the main entrance. Thank goodness Principal Kennedy had the keys to the lobby doors, or we'd be completely stuck."

Neither of us gave an excuse or explained about the jackass in the Camaro. I didn't want to relive the event by explaining it.

We parked. It'd be easier to make several trips back and forth from the Jeep than to fight the crowd to unload supplies. We began to unpack the Jeep. I lifted several cans of paint, turned, and saw Erika run to the lobby entrance, passing Mr. Taylor on his way out.

I fought the bile that rose in my throat at the sight of Taylor. Something about him dug at my exposed nerves. I bit my lip and ignored him.

Rock music blared in the background while we worked away the hours. The sounds of hammering and laughter filled the lobby. I went through the motions, painting a cardboard building, noting that the windows still needed to be cut out and the shadows needed more definition. Everyone was lost in a project. Teachers helped us nail the 2x4s together, and Mr. Taylor buzzed from one end of the lobby to the other, usually carrying supplies.

As if from nowhere, an inner warning ignited. My head throbbed. I dropped the paintbrush and rubbed my eyes.

Fire alarms echoed throughout the lobby.

A scream erupted. "Fire."

My memory traveled back with a vivid flash, my back pressed to the stable doors, watching the flaming fingers of death grip, inch by inch, with determination, as fire destroyed the home in which I'd lived as a child.

My body hummed with its last remnant of tension, and several things happened simultaneously.

My headache increased. I pushed my childhood thoughts away, and a premonition took hold. *Orange ... red flames ...*

A voice buzzed in my ear. Trystan.

Pressure tightened around my wrist.

I tried to pull myself from Trystan's hold, but it became tighter. Stronger.

"No ... stop."

Trystan swung me over his shoulder.

I kicked and swung my arms, pounding. My fists met a solid wall. I fought against him, but his arms anchored my legs, restraining my movement.

My vision went blank. "I can't see ..."

I opened my eyes. Everything was upside down.

People were pushing and shoving, trying to get out. Some shouted in panic, finding the only exit blocked by the people ahead of them.

We made it outside. Cool air played with my shirt. My head pounded as chaos surrounded me.

Once my feet met solid ground, I scanned everywhere, soaking up details. There must've been forty of us scattered across the parking lot.

Teachers yelled for everyone to stay back while some made lists of all students present.

Smoke billowed from the southwestern corner of the gymnasium roof.

Seconds passed.

Trystan's eyes narrowed in on me as people huddled in small groups, hugging and reassuring one another.

Mr. Kennedy cupped his hands around his mouth and shouted, "The fire department is on its way. Is everyone out of the school?"

"Where's Anna?" I froze at Erika's scream and watched Trystan's pained expression crumble into despair.

"No." I shrieked, dropping my shoulders and twisting out of his hold. "She's still inside."

He grabbed my hand, but I yanked it away and ran for the double doors.

Trystan's footsteps thundered behind me, breaking up the rhythm of my shoes hitting the sidewalk.

Fear gnawed at me. Could I keep Trystan alive? Could I find Anna in time?

We dodged spectators in the parking lot and rushed through the courtyard toward the double doors.

When I entered the school, I followed where my vision led me, Trystan on my heels. We ran down the main corridor, past the school offices near the lobby's locked mesh gate, and turned the corner into another long hall.

At the opposite end, three figures burst out of the gym's wide-open doors, turned left, exited through the narrow hall behind the cafeteria, and then disappeared.

We stopped.

Bright orange, red, and blue flames climbed the wall, engulfing the school banner and eating away the words *Welcome to New Cumberlin Falls*. A blaze danced on the wooden bleachers, and smoke seeped into the hallway. It cast an eerie light over the vast darkness of the passage stretching before us, illuminated by the emergency lights of the exit signs.

"Look for an ax."

"Dang it." Trystan grabbed my hand. "Callie?"

"DON'T. Just trust me." I spoke with assurance—false assurance. "We've got minutes before the hallway is consumed with smoke. Find an ax, *now*."

The lobby had tools.

The wide, mesh gate wall stood before us, separating us from the tools scattered on the floor, but I couldn't see an ax.

Improvise.

My mind mapped out an alternative plan as smoke filtered down the hall.

Trystan followed me toward the gym, where every step led us into a giant sauna.

"Someone help me. Please." Anna screamed from behind a door.

Following Anna's voice, Trystan pulled me into a narrow hallway with several doors. This was the primary storage wing for the props.

"HELP."

Relief flooded through me, knowing Anna was alive.

More smoke filled the hall as a haze hovered around our heads.

Trystan grabbed the storage room knob.

"Wait." I scanned the hall. "Get the fire extinguisher."

Trystan's eyes locked on the extinguisher on the opposite wall. He lunged at it, breaking the glass with his fist.

I couldn't wait.

When he turned around, I used my body to conceal my movements and, in one twist, ripped the knob off the door and pushed it open.

A wall of smoke filled the hallway.

When Trystan saw Anna, he shoved the extinguisher at me and took her in his arms. Tears fell from her face.

I set the extinguisher and knob down and snatched Trystan's arm, placing his hand on the back of my shirt.

"Come on. Let's get out of here. Stay low." I slunk down and crawled along the floor, feeling with my fingers.

My sixth sense screamed with urgency, but I pushed it aside. My muscles ached.

Once we hit the main hall, a thick haze hovered in the air. A red EXIT sign glowed near the ceiling.

The red sign caught my attention, and my intuition flared—this direction wasn't safe. It took all my mental strength to ignore this way out and follow my intuition.

Smoke filled my lungs, choking me. The only option was to return the way we had come, through the narrow hall with the storage rooms.

"Turn around," I yelled, the words burning my throat. I didn't wait to see their reactions, but Trystan's grip tightened on my shirt. We swung around. Sweat rolled off my back. My face burned from the heat. The emergency lights in the main hall weren't lighting up our space. I picked up the extinguisher I'd left lying on the ground and dragged it with us. I listened, hearing nothing but Anna's broken sobs. We reached the last door in the hallway.

I gave the handle a quick twist. Locked. Thick air filtered into our narrow hall. With nothing to distract them, I couldn't use my strength. I got to my feet and, with one quick swing of the extinguisher took the knob off the door. Once it was open, we crawled inside, and Trystan slammed it shut.

Soaked with sweat and drenched with fear, I sagged against the door. My lungs burned, and my eyes stung from the smoke as the room took shape. The full moon shone through the windows, revealing storage boxes, poster boards, and athletic supplies.

Trystan shifted, blocking the view of the moon. Amidst the silence, the sound of glass erupted. He turned around, and blood dripped from his hand. "Come on. Let's get out of here."

Trystan helped Anna slide out the window. He turned, squeezed my hand, and then helped me climb out.

Reality smothered me–I had survived again–and so had Trystan and Anna.

CHAPTER 22

IMPOSSIBLE

I took my first breath of fresh air and stood on sheer adrenaline outside the storage room window. After reassuring ourselves we were okay, we walked around the corner of the school to find swarms of people in the parking lot. Blue and red lights reflected off car windows. Yellow and red firetrucks parked on sidewalks near the southeast entrance of the school. Police contained the public behind barriers while firefighters fought the fire. Frightened cries echoed through the night.

"Look ... *look*." A brown-haired man's words drowned out sobs. He pointed past us. "Look, over there."

I glanced over my shoulder to see what he was pointing at. Angry flames danced on the gymnasium roof. Then, medical personnel pounced on us.

"They're alive," someone yelled.

The medical staff split up the three of us.

I sat on the end of an EMS vehicle as I was examined.

"No soot around the mouth or nose." They put a pressure cuff on my arm. Numb anxiety gripped me. I watched them lower Anna onto a gurney and place a mask over her mouth.

Firefighters hooked up an extension hose running toward the school with it propped upon their shoulders. People hung on the outskirts, watching the crew's work.

A firefighter approached me, blocking the chaos in the parking lot. "I'm Chief Rick. We need to ask you some questions." My heart warmed seeing Sheriff Travis beside the firefighter.

I nodded.

"I don't know whether to scold you or hug you, Callie," Travis said. "That was a dangerous move you and that boy made."

I cleared my throat. "I had no choice." The words felt like they'd clawed their way over course sandpaper as they exited my mouth.

"You should have waited," Sheriff Travis countered.

I knew I should have, but I wasn't about to watch another person die when I could prevent it.

Chief Rick took off his hat. "What can you tell us about the fire?"

I recounted everything I could from the time we arrived at the school until now, but I avoided giving any details that would raise questions about my behavior or abilities.

The fire chief faced Travis. "This corroborates Trystan's story. Three people running from the fire, out a side door."

I scanned faces, medical crews' and firefighters' faces, as they raced around me.

"Callie." Sheriff Travis captured my attention. "I hate to ask more questions, but our best hope of finding the culprits is to collect solid information when events are freshest in the minds of those involved. Can you think of anything else?" He patted my forearm.

I was aware of every heartbeat and every breath of fresh air I inhaled. Anger gripped me. Too much was happening, too quickly. Splinters of memory shot through my mind: Nana's death, a photo of my face scored, my visions, a dysfunctional shield, Mr. Taylor's powers.

I stood, accidentally jerking the pressure-cuff cord from the machine. With the culmination of everything that'd happened, my anger spiked. I hated being the focus of all this attention.

"Some idiots in a silver Camaro ran us off the road, with a semi barreling down on us. A friend of mine almost died. I don't need this."

I shut my mouth and dropped back onto the bumper of the EMS vehicle. I couldn't take out my frustration on them. They were only doing their jobs. I watched as Chief Rick whispered in Sheriff Travis's ear.

"What can you tell us about this car?" Sheriff Travis asked.

I shook my head and sighed. "Not much. Everything happened so quick." I rubbed the flat of my palm over the bridge of my nose. "It was a Camaro. A silver one. I don't know the year, but it was a newer model." I tucked a stray strand of hair behind my ear. "The car had tinted windows and a crooked license plate stuck near the back taillights. It wasn't even secured to the body of the car." I exhaled, seeing the crowd build up around us. "I'd like to go home."

"EMS wants to take you to the hospital." Sheriff Travis shifted his stance. "We may want to talk with you tomorrow. By the way, your grandfather's been contacted." He looked off to the right, past a firetruck. "Uh, he's actually here."

I took a deep breath. As much respect as I had for nurses and doctors, I hated being a frequent flier to the hospital.

Gramps squeezed through the circle of people and looked down at me with weary-riddled eyes. "Callie, my dear."

I burrowed myself into Gramps's embrace. I didn't want to deal with anyone. A depressive shock consumed my mind.

They put me in a private room close to the nurses' station. The nurses hooked me up to another blood pressure cuff and inserted an intravenous drip. Gramps hadn't left my side except when they'd taken me down for chest X-rays. They'd poked me so many times to draw blood that I wanted to scream. A nurse came into the room, adjusted the cuff on my arm, and fussed with the monitor.

A man wearing white entered my room, carrying a laptop. "I'm Doctor De Henery. I'm sorry we've kept you so long." He put a pen and a small piece of paper into his white jacket pocket. "From what we can tell from the X-rays, your lungs are clear, and your oxygen levels are normal. However, smoke inhalation can be tricky. Upon arrival, a patient could appear asymptomatic but may develop significant problems up to thirty-six hours after exposure. Our main concern is pulmonary edema, but it doesn't appear likely you are in danger of that."

Gramps's fingers brushed the creases of his forehead. "So, she's all right?"

The doctor patted Gramps on the shoulder. "I've been practicing for over twenty-five years. I can't make any promises, but I believe your granddaughter will be fine. Before you leave, a nurse will review the discharge papers with you."

"How are Anna and Trystan?" I asked.

Dr. De Henery's expression of friendliness relieved me. "There was no permanent injury to Trystan's hand, and, like you, he's shown no signs of smoke inhalation. He's been discharged. He's visiting with his cousin. He's still a little edgy from the fire."

Gramps cocked his head. "Thanks, Dr. De Henery. And for you, dear, I want to get you home." Gramps's tone of disapproval concerned me. He looked like he'd aged several years since yesterday.

I threw my legs over the side of the bed and hopped down. "Can I see them?"

"Not Anna. A nurse is admitting her for overnight observation," Dr. De Henery said. "She's still shaken up, and we're trying to keep her calm, but you may see Trystan. You've risked a lot today. Let us take care of them. You go home and rest. You're free to leave once Nurse Friday has reviewed the discharge papers with you."

"Thanks, Dr. De Henery." Gramps shook the doctor's hand.

"You're welcome." The doctor looked back over at me. "And you, take care of yourself."

Shortly after that, the nurse excused herself from the room, having handed me a packet of papers, including one on which Doc had written an excuse to dismiss me from school on Monday. I wasn't sure that it would be necessary with the damage to the gymnasium. Maybe they'd have to cancel school.

CHAPTER 23

SCARRED

Gray-blue walls intensified the depressing atmosphere of the hospital's waiting room. People filtered in and out as my eyes narrowed on Trystan standing in the wide hallway. His hands were jammed into his pockets, and one heel rested against the wall. He pushed himself away from the wall and walked toward us.

"Are you okay?" he asked.

"I'm fine. Doc told me you were with Anna. How's she doing?"

He took a deep breath. "She'll be okay."

"Trystan." Gramps slid his arm through the sleeve of his jacket. "You take a few days off and rest your hand. Don't worry about work. Call me when you're ready to come back."

Trystan pulled his hands out of his pockets. White, sterile gauze covered the palm and wrist of his hand. "Thanks."

Gramps looked back and forth between Trystan and me. "I'll go get the car, dear."

Gramps exited through the automatic doors.

Trystan stepped forward, stopped, then rocked back onto his heels. His restless eyes searched my face, narrowing. "Thanks for saving Anna's life."

The temporary silence took a bite out of my courage.

I hugged my middle. "How'd Anna ever get stuck in the storage room?"

He stood ramrod straight. "She said she had been pulling stuff off a shelf, then when she went to leave, she couldn't twist the knob. One of the sheriffs said something had been jammed into the mechanism of the doorknob."

"Anna's alive, that's what matters."

His jaw tightened. "I'll see you soon." Then he stepped away and left.

"Bye," I said to his back. I couldn't think of anything else to say, and evidently, he couldn't either. What do you say to someone when you've lived through a nightmare together?

As I turned to leave, a nurse pushed an older man in a wheelchair past the line of flowers along the nurses' station. A younger woman walked past him and smiled.

"Callie?"

I glanced toward the familiar voice. "Mr. Santos?" I gulped a breath of air.

"Don't be scared." A scar ran down the left side of his face from above his eye down across his cheek. "It's not pretty." His fingers covered part of the deep scar. His brown hair was longer than when he'd taught class. He wore a black T-shirt and sweatpants.

I searched the canvas of his face and waited for my shield to pop up. Something should have happened, but it didn't. Yet, his scar was the one I'd seen in my vision. His face in the vision hadn't been clear, only the disfigurement.

"I hadn't expected this reaction." Mr. Santos's eyes glazed over with worry. "Several nurses have told me the scar makes me better looking." He laughed. "I had a nurse threaten that once I start to walk better, she's going to take me out on the town."

I swallowed and crouched in front of the wheelchair, still waiting for my shield to flash. Is this why he hadn't wanted visitors? Because of the scar?

"How are you?"

"Okay. But I think I should be asking you that."

"I'm fine."

"After my surgery, I asked about you. None of the nurses could tell me anything because of the privacy laws. But they did tell me you and Erika had come to visit."

"I suffered bruises, but I'm fine." I placed my hand over my shoulder, where most of my discomfort from the accident remained.

"I'm hoping they'll release me soon." He twisted a cap on the soda bottle in his drink holder. "Physical therapy is going well. I'm walking okay. That's a blessing. They had to do some reconstructive surgery, but I'm hanging in there. I hear life hasn't been easy for you, either. I overheard one of the nurses talking about the school fire. The hospital's buzzing with news of your heroic efforts."

I released my lower lip from a nervous bite. "Anna, my friend, got trapped in a props room."

"I'm glad you could save her." His shoulders sagged. "I'm so sorry about your grandmother."

"Thanks. Gramps and I wanted to visit, but everyone said you'd refused visitors."

He looked around the waiting room. "When you're in rehab, you don't get much of a break. And to be honest," he touched the wheelchair, "it's been hard to accept my physical limitations." He leaned forward, grabbed my hand off my knee, and tapped my finger with his thumb. "Callie, I don't know how to tell you this. I have wanted to speak with you ever since last September." His voice grew quiet. "Your parents and I were friends."

My mouth went dry. "You knew them?"

"Yes. Both Cyrus and Victoria were my childhood friends."

"You're ..."

"Theran," he finished my question before the words slipped my lips.

I couldn't believe it. He wasn't human. "My parents left their family so they could marry. Did you stay in contact with them?"

"Remnants cast them out." Mr. Santos's eyebrows knitted together. "I didn't. I kept in touch with your parents until I left California when you were four. When I returned from an assignment overseas, I learned your parents had passed on." His voice resonated with truth.

"Why are you telling me this now?" I tried to jerk my hand from his grip. "You were my teacher for half a year. Why now?"

"I thought I had time. I wanted to build your trust, then tell you. I never thought I'd wind up in a hospital." He frowned, his eyes searching mine. "I've wanted to tell you many times, but none of this is anything you discuss around humans. I'm taking a risk now, just talking. And, more importantly, I didn't know how much you knew about your circumstances." His thumb tapped my finger.

I pulled my hand from his. "None of this is happening." I stood, feeling disbelief, crowding my thoughts. So often, I'd wanted answers that no one could give me. Now, all of a sudden, others with powers magically appeared. "This is too much." Overwhelmed, I stepped back.

Mr. Santos pulled a piece of paper from the corner of a crossword puzzle booklet he'd had tucked in the side of the wheelchair and scribbled something on it. "My cell number." He placed it in my palm and folded my fingers down over it. "When you're ready, I will explain whatever you want to know."

The automatic doors opened. "Callie, I'm ready when you are."

"Gramps." My thumb stroked the sapphire ring. "This is Mr. Santos."

"Ah, hello." Gramps blanched. "This isn't how I'd hoped to meet you. My friends and I have tried to visit you."

Mr. Santos straightened in his chair and winced. "I wish we were meeting under different circumstances."

"Callie's had a rough day." Gramps shifted on his feet. "When she's better, we can get together, but she needs rest right now."

Santos smirked. "I hope to be discharged next month at the latest."

Gramps rubbed his eye and nodded. "That sounds good." He pressed his other hand into the small of my back and steered me out the exit door.

My mind raced. No shield. No bad vibes. Could I trust Mr. Santos?

CHAPTER 24
UNEXPECTED

I looked like something that had crawled out of a grave. My smile faded into a frown as I peered at my reflection in the locker mirror. I fumbled in my purse, pulled out concealer, and applied it to the dark shadows under my eyes. I had to admit it, Erika gave good advice. The cover-up made me look more normal. I replaced the concealer in my purse and slammed the locker shut.

"Why do you look mad?" Anna asked.

"How am I supposed to feel when Trystan up and disappears?" Leaving me to deal with everything. I wanted to find a small corner and hide.

It'd been five days since the fire, and speculation had gone viral. The Sunday *Gazette* had printed an article, and everyone had their spin on it, especially regarding the three individuals we'd seen leaving the school. Clean-up crews had worked hard to put the school back in order before we returned. They'd blocked the main hallway and gym off with a metal gate. The decorating committee would have to replace the damaged prom items.

I wished they had closed the school for the entire week. Instead, we had to show up on Friday.

I found myself the center of attention. People patted me on the back. Some, whom I didn't even know, called me a hero. Classrooms became silent when I entered them, but it didn't take long before everyone crowded me with questions.

Anna swung her purse over her shoulder. "He didn't just disappear. He's under a lot of pressure from his dad, and the fire didn't help. With the way he's been acting, you'd think he'd been the one stuck in that storage room. My parents think the fire has hit him hard."

"I don't mean to sound angry." I just wish he were here.

I'd tried twice to visit Mr. Santos and left frustrated—between his scheduled therapies and other visits. He'd had no time for me. Questions piled up, and Trystan's disappearance had filled me with worry. I didn't like how we'd parted at the hospital last weekend. From Anna, I knew Trystan had been on a plane to California within twelve hours of his discharge from the hospital.

"Callie." Anna's shoulder sagged. "Thank you for what you did. You saved my life, and if I could explain Trystan's behavior, I would. Since we moved here, he's changed. He's distanced himself, even from Colin." She cocked her head. "I don't want to see you get hurt."

"What?" I bit my lip to stop the flow of words.

"I know Trystan asked you to prom."

Where was this going?

"It's not that I don't think you should go with him. I'm just suggesting you don't get too attached. Trystan's dad has his life mapped out for him."

Yeah, with unrealistic expectations—anyone who'd have their kids memorize their lineage was nuts. After all, it wasn't the 1800s.

"Do you like your uncle?"

She lifted her hand to scratch between her brows. "I don't know my uncle well."

"Trystan didn't have time to recover from the fire, and his dad hauled him off. If his dad cared, he should've been on an airplane to come here and see him. And what about you? You're his niece."

She winced.

My heart constricted. "I'm sorry, Anna. I know my attitude sucks. Just so much is happening. It's good Trystan has you guys."

"You know, he comes back tomorrow," Anna said.

"Oh, I'm glad to hear that. Unfortunately, Gramps leaves tonight for PA."

"Why's he going there?"

I tucked wisps of hair behind my ear. "Some grain convention. He'll be gone just shy of a week."

"You could stay with us."

I smiled. "I might take you up on that later, but right now, I'm fine. I wouldn't be surprised if Sheriff Travis himself checks in on me."

Anna chuckled. "I'm surprised he's leaving."

I didn't like the idea of him being gone, but he didn't have a choice. "He sits on the grain committee. I guess they've got some hot issues to vote on this year." The halls were empty, except for us. "I'm studying for finals tonight, and knowing Gramps, he hasn't packed half of his things yet. We'd better go." I threw my backpack over my shoulder, and we left.

The air outside was warm. Clouds hung low on the horizon, and birds flew around the school.

"Oh, shoot." I skidded to a stop. "I forgot my history book. Go ahead. I'll see you later." I turned and ran back through the courtyard, slid through the lobby doors, and bounded up the stairs. I puffed air, blew the hair from my eyes, clicked open the locker, and grabbed my book.

"Why, Miss Tresham, you're here late."

My shield popped as a sickening sensation swelled in my stomach. I spun around to see Mr. Taylor and Principal Kennedy. "I forgot my book."

"You're a very serious student." Taylor took a pencil from behind his ear. "I like that."

He nodded toward Mr. Kennedy.

"Do you have a minute?" Principal Kennedy asked. "We'd like to talk."

I lowered my chin, keeping my eyes fixed on Taylor. If Taylor had asked, I'd have told him I had plans to study and help Gramps, but I couldn't do that with Principal Kennedy. I trailed them into Taylor's classroom.

Taylor stood by his chair and bit the end of his pencil. "We'd like you to consider tutoring students this summer. I've been telling Principal Kennedy how much I appreciate your insight and knowledge." He chuckled. "Remember the first day we met? Somehow, I messed up, and you corrected me." His jaw clenched.

He appreciates my insight and knowledge—What? We haven't spoken except a few times since our initial meeting. And he scolded me for correcting him in class. Why'd he lie?

Taylor repositioned the pencil behind his ear and opened his desk drawer. "Let me see." He grabbed a page with some handwriting on it and flipped it over. "Well, the schedule shows history class will be offered each Tuesday morning. We have several students needing assistance, although you'd only have three or four students to tutor over the summer. What do you think?"

"I'm sorry, but I can't."

Mr. Kennedy tugged at the cuff of his shirtsleeve. "This would look great on a college application."

My bag hit the surface of Taylor's desk, and I stuffed my history book inside it. "Thanks for the offer."

"Callie," Kennedy said. "Your granddad has talked with the school counselor. He wants you to look at colleges. Mr. Taylor happened to overhear and spoke with your granddad, suggesting you'd be a good candidate to tutor individuals. And, like I said, this would look great on your college applications." His eyebrows knitted together. "Consider it and get back to one of us."

Blood boiled in my gut. I hated Mr. Taylor knowing anything about me.

Taylor put the schedule back in the drawer, but not before my eyes fixed on a thick, rolled-up piece of paper with what looked like an imprint of black wax. My fingers flexed at my side, desiring to snatch it. The dense, white paper looked similar to what my mother used to write to me.

I nodded and exited the room before my mouth or fingers got me into trouble.

CHAPTER 25

DREAD

I pulled up under the loading dock and shifted into park, my mind racing with confused thoughts. I knew my powers were all that could protect me from what lay ahead. So far, my premonitions had come true, although in surprising ways. The fact my shield had not flickered once in his presence, nor had I caught him in a lie, indicated Mr. Santos was a friend. Perhaps he was the one Mom had mentioned in her note. But who was Mr. Taylor?

I glanced up and saw Gramps, his foot tapping on the loading dock. I opened the Jeep door.

"How long have you been here?"

"Long enough to see you're upset."

My mind raced. Should I tell him everything? He already knew I was different. Nausea roiled in my gut at the thought. I knew I couldn't do that. Gramps's safety meant keeping him in the dark about Taylor. Gramps seemed stressed enough as it was. "Mr. Kennedy said you spoke with a school counselor."

He raised his eyebrow and leaned forward against the railing. "Yes, I did. And it's time you be thinking about college. The counselor put me in touch with Mr. Taylor. He asked me if you'd be up to tutoring this summer."

Why'd Taylor want me to tutor? I clenched my eyes shut and rubbed my temple. "Did you commit me to tutoring?"

"No. I told him I'd speak with you."

I opened my eyes and lowered my hands.

He came down the steps and approached me. His snowy white beard hid his frown lines. "You don't like the teacher?"

"No."

"I didn't like my teachers, either." He frowned. "It takes time to get used to their ways. But I don't like leaving for the grain convention with that troubled look on your face."

"I'm fine, Gramps." I forced a grin.

"Okay." His frown stretched into a smile. "Well, now. I just remembered, you can't tutor this summer. We're going to Italy."

"Great." Relief surged through me. At least I didn't have to dig up an excuse if Taylor or Principal Kennedy asked me again.

He flipped open his phone. "Which reminds me, I'm all packed for tonight's trip. While I've got time, why don't we go ahead and get our pictures taken, so we can send our applications in next week."

I took a deep breath, suddenly feeling thirty pounds lighter.

After we had our pictures taken and eaten dinner, Gramps left, and I sat alone with Tesla, staring at the four walls of the living room.

What was in the rolled-up paper on Taylor's desk? And how could I get my hands on it?

Sleep eluded me yet again. The next morning, I dragged myself to the mill. By noon, chores were done, and Max began working on Monday's grain orders.

I craved fresh air—away from people. I called for Tesla, swiped a water bottle from the refrigerator, and headed toward the meadow. The closer I got, the more tension evaporated. Grass blew in the breeze, spreading the scent of pine. I sat and soaked in the air for a while, and Tesla played near the trees.

An impending sense of doom pushed me to practice calling up the shield.

I faced the boulders and closed my eyes, hoping that recreating the feeling of the shield would bring it forth. I tried, but nothing happened.

Tesla lay curled up at the base of the boulders. Shadows shifted on the ground as the sun lowered, and I wasn't any closer to conjuring the barrier. Ideas bubbled through my mind. Visualize. Focus.

My vulnerability activated the shield. When I focused on the parking lot light at the outlet mall, it responded to my eye movements, combining the color elements and firing a beam.

I drew deep breaths, concentrating on my feet, and visualized the golden-white light. A sensation zipped through me, and a flicker appeared at my heel. As quickly as it had appeared, it disappeared.

Current flowed through my muscles.

OMJings.

I tried again, and a powerful glow encircled my feet this time. I wrapped my mind around it and pulled it up like a tangible object. I visually held it at waist height.

"Wow."

A flash erupted, wrapping me completely within the translucent shield. Thirty seconds later, the gold was electrified with crimson.

I braced my feet apart and closed my mind to the crimson light. It disappeared. Clearly, the colors acted as two separate energies—one offensive, the other defensive. The golden shield protected me from Mr. Taylor's invasive mental power. The crimson energy, on the other hand, was a weapon.

"This is awesome." I continued to practice working with my shield, occasionally having to tell Tesla to keep back from me. I didn't know exactly how it worked and didn't want to take the chance of hurting him.

Questions rippled through my mind, draining my focus, and the shield disappeared. I grabbed the water bottle, gulped, and dumped the rest over my head. Sweat and water dripped down my back, so I pulled out the rubberband in my hair, combed it with my fingers, and squeezed the ends.

This was pivotal. Control of the shield put me at an advantage. How else would I be able to defend against Taylor's mental attacks? He'd probably had years of practice. I had to get this right.

CHAPTER 26

CRIMSON-BLOOD

"Come on, boy, let's go." Tesla jerked to a stand and followed.

I walked down the path toward the pond, taking the long way home. I fanned my hands through the lush grass, prickly plant life scraping the tips of my fingers. Different shades of green danced in the sun. Pond water shimmered, distorting the reflection of overhanging branches. Tesla played by the boulders as someone drove a car down our lane. He bolted down the hill. I followed but stopped when I spotted Trystan walking out of the mill with Max.

Trystan wore a tight, purple button-down shirt and dark shorts. He waved goodbye to Max and hiked the hill, Tesla barking at his side.

"What are you doing here?" I bit my inner cheek.

Trystan, smiling, carried two Znapple bottles. "Came to visit. Max and I saw you from the loading dock." His eyes canvassed the pond. "Boy, this is a private refuge."

I followed Trystan deeper into the meadow, away from the mill.

"Your flight landed early. Anna said you wouldn't be in until later."

"Yeah, I got in over an hour ago. It helps Dad has his own jet. I hope you don't mind. I took two bottles from the office fridge." He set down the bottles and squatted in front of Tesla, petting him behind his ears, his eyes holding mine the entire time. "I missed you."

"I missed you, too." I swallowed. "I thought you'd be with your cousins."

"No one was home, so I came over to see you. Oh, and I spoke with Max. I'd like to pick my hours back up. I hated ditching your grandfather." His voice dropped to a lower register. "And you."

"Then why'd you leave?" Frustration built within me—the fire, Mr. Santos's unavailability, Mr. Taylor and his bizarre behavior, Trystan leaving without a word. The pressure of it all was drowning me. "Doctors hadn't even discharged Anna. And you were on an airplane headed west."

His jaw clenched. "Something serious happened. Dad summoned me."

"Summoned?"

"I had to go back. You wouldn't understand."

"You're right. If Gramps were in the hospital, a tow truck couldn't pull me from him." My heart pounded in my chest. His dad didn't seem to care about his own family.

Trystan pressed his finger under my chin, coaxing my face upward. "He's all business, Callie. And I don't want to discuss him." I pushed his hand away, but he grabbed my wrist. His eyes locked on our hands. "Can you pull from my clasp?"

"What?"

He raised his fingers, allowing his thumb and middle finger to circle my wrist. "Break loose."

"I ... can't."

"That's not true." He caressed the underside of my wrist with his thumb. "Your pulse is racing." He inched closer and released his grasp long enough to interweave our fingers. "I assumed that by watching you, I'd learn your secrets, but I've found I can't wait any longer."

Fear spread through my body like poison.

He met my stare. "The night of the fire, you beat the hell out of my back when I carried you from the school. Then, you had me grab the fire extinguisher because you couldn't risk breaking the door handle with me watching—but you did anyhow when my back was turned. Did you think I wouldn't notice the knob on the ground?"

My knees weakened.

Trystan swung an arm around my waist, the other still holding my hand. My forehead rested on his chest. Did my radar have a malfunction? If not, why didn't it go off? It was one thing to discuss my family, but talking about my capabilities with a human was something else. How do I explain something I'm just beginning to understand?

"I'm no threat to you." His words tickled my ear. The air was thick with unspoken words, and our heartbeats slowed. "Come. Sit." He eased away from me, giving me time to adjust to my unsteady feet. He picked up the Znapples.

I sat and leaned against a boulder. He joined me, our legs touching. He set a bottle on the ground at my hip. Sunlight flickered through the shifting branches, and shadows danced on the ground.

"How'd you figure it out?"

He twisted the lid off his bottle. "It was pure speculation until the fire, but the constant electrical charge I feel whenever you're around confused me. Especially the intensity of the charge I felt at the car accident." He took a sip of his drink. "That's how I knew it was you the night of the storm. I'm sorry I was such a jerk that night, but I was sure I'd exposed myself to you by pushing the Jeep away."

Reality took root as my mind relived the past few months' events. The crash. And the night of the fire, I hit him. Hard. Could it be he was so mad because he was afraid of exposure? To me?

Wait. How had the signs slipped by me? A mental image of Taylor flashed before my eyes. I'd been so distracted by Taylor that I missed the clues in front of my face. Trystan had slipped under my radar.

"Electrical charge? Wait, what?"

I faced him and unfastened the first button of his shirt. He didn't attempt to stop me as he watched in puzzlement. If he had a mark, it'd explain our undeniable connection. My hands trembled on his chest as I unbuttoned the second button and then stopped.

Traitorous tears slid down my cheek. I dropped my hands from his chest, released my fears, and gave in to the one truth I could trust—my intuition. Excitement and nervousness coursed through my veins and twisted with anticipation, heightened by the chill of the afternoon shade. Our eyes never parted. I had to know. I raised my hands again, unfastening each button. I opened his shirt and touched his mark's slight, raised edge. My parents had marks just like that.

He flinched away from me. "You can see it?"

I nodded. "You're Theran?"

A smile threatened to curl his lips. "You're educated?"

"No. I've taken a crash course without an instructor."

His forehead creased. "But, your grandfather?"

"We're not blood relatives." My mouth went dry as his eyes blackened. "It's a long story, Trystan. One I'm not ready to share." I moved away and took a sip of sweetened tea.

Trystan stared past me at the treetops for an immeasurable amount of time. He pinched the bridge of his nose. "I won't pry. We have time to talk, but just because I'm not pushing you to talk tonight doesn't mean I'm not interested in your life story, Callie. The night of the fire, I heard you scream, 'I can't see.'" He leaned closer. "You had a vision, didn't you?"

"Mmmhmm, yes."

"That's how you found Anna? You have the power of premonition?" He jumped up and spouted off questions. "How accurate are your visions? Have they ever been wrong? Can you call up a vision by holding an inanimate object? Can you locate missing people?"

"What? I'm not a visionary bloodhound."

He blew out a puff of air. "Over the past week, I've used the Theran population books and the computer to track every bloodline recorded over the past two hundred years. I couldn't find a trace of your family name, so you can't be a crimson blood, but no human could see my mark. That leaves one possibility, but half-bloods are forbidden. Have been for centuries, but none of this explains the strength of your power. You're a walking conundrum."

But Tresham's not my real last name. "Powers?"

"Theran powers are believed to have developed through genetic variance." He scanned my face, pausing for the longest time. "You really don't know what I'm talking about, do you?"

"No, my parents never had a chance to explain."

"Mmm. Okay, the rough version is that accounts and legends speak of a meteorite that came down some five thousand years ago and exposed our ancestors to micro-organisms. It also exposed other groups native to present-day Northern Sudan and southern Egypt. This virus infected the host, a human living on Thera's island, with a DNA fragment. Over time, this fragment mutated our molecular structure, changing our bloodlines and giving us capabilities, somehow increasing cognitive function. Essentially, we're hybrids. We call ourselves Therans to differentiate ourselves from humans. With MRI technology, physicians have recently discovered anomalies in Therans' frontal cortices. They believed these to be tumors. In reality, Therans have an extra temporal lobe."

"Okkaayy." So, I wasn't an alien but a member of some ancient lost civilization that had got infected by foreign micro-organisms. Our powers come from the mutation in our blood. Curiosity prodded me. "What's crimson-blood?"

"It means both parents are Theran."

Then, I'm crimson-blood. The word seemed so cold—a level of supremacy over half-blood. Half-blood was a union between a Theran and a human.

Trystan planted himself in front of me. "Callie, my dad summoned me because someone was murdered. We don't know who's behind it. Your ability of sight, directed by the right mentor, could be vital to finding out who committed this murder. Man, I wish my brother Sebastian were here. He'd be able to train you." Fingers raked through his hair. "It puzzles me that a half-blood could be the key to all this. I've never heard of a half-breed possessing sight, but, of course, half-breeds are forbidden. Although, long ago, studies showed some half-breeds possessed abilities related to the healing arts or superhuman strength, but never premonition."

There was something so vulnerable and raw about revealing myself to him. For some reason, I couldn't stomach correcting him. "A mentor?"

He leaned back on his heels. Exasperation creased his forehead. "Ashworth University is a camp—essentially, a training ground. I'm sure they'd accommodate you with your ability, but they'd want to track your lineage."

Track my lineage? No way. In their search for my family's heritage, the Remnant Faction could be revealed, along with Mr. Santos. I was the link between the two groups. The Remnants' safety meant keeping my mouth shut.

I recalled my encounter with Colin at the fitness center.

"Does Colin have an ability?" I searched his eyes. Trystan turned away, a pained look on his face. "I'm willing to help, but I want to know more before I agree to anything."

Trystan sighed, long and heavy. "Colin's power is strength, and he's great with weapons."

"What about Anna?"

"Her power is in the healing arts." He sat down.

An uncomfortable silence grew between us.

"You know my ability, Trystan. What are you holding back?"

His eyes bore into mine, searching. "My family doesn't know about our abilities."

"They won't learn it from me." Man, if his group found out about my history, how many people would be at risk? "I'll help, but only under the condition, you won't tell anyone about me. I'll work with you."

"Done. I will do what's necessary to keep your secret—and you—safe, but I want honesty between us."

The depth of feeling behind his words soothed my frayed nerves. I would be as truthful as I could, but I sure wasn't going to divulge all my secrets.

"What's your ability?"

He let out a slow breath of air. "Translator." He fidgeted with the crease on his shorts. "I'm also able to diffuse anxiety, and if I focus long enough, I can diminish physical pain, almost like a painkiller."

"The accident. You deadened my pain, didn't you?"

"Yeah, I couldn't stomach seeing you suffer."

"Thanks. I owe you." Images of Nana filled my mind—things she said, things we did together. I closed my eyes against the memories and changed the topic. "So, your love of languages stems from this power?"

"Yes." He gave me a toothy grin. "Translators are rare. We're the communication bridge between civilizations. Like seers, few of us exist."

"Do all Therans have abilities?"

"No." He lowered his gaze, shaking his head. "I don't think even forty percent of us have abilities."

I picked up a blade of grass. Questions danced in my head. When did you learn you had power? Why are half-bloods forbidden?

"Why the secrecy from your parents about your powers?"

He played with the lid of his Znapple. "My brother, Sebastian, was a seer–the first in over a thousand years."

I caressed the sapphire ring. My great aunt was a seer for the Remnant Faction.

"Sebastian made a horrible prediction before he died." He let his Znapple lid fall to the ground. "He told Colin and me to tell no one of our powers until the time came to reveal them. He said we'd know. The governing council's mission is to prevent the devastation my brother foresaw, but the council is chasing shadows. Now, there's been a murder."

I sucked in air. Could it be that Sebastian's vision dealt with the shadowed man's face from my vision? How did this fit with my mom's thoughts of Ptolemy's prediction? None of this was clear to me. How was it all connected?

Something shifted in his eyes, and they narrowed into slits.

Before I could question him more, my phone vibrated. I tugged it out of my pocket and touched the screen, grateful the jerk who'd pranked me hadn't called.

"What's up, Erika?"

Trystan rose, then settled onto a boulder, lowering his face in his hands.

My legs became restless. I got up and stretched, rotating my shoulders back. "When does the movie start? Who's going?" I stopped a few steps from Trystan. "Ah, everyone. Including Colin and Anna."

Trystan bounded off the rock and shook his head.

"Hmm. Uh-huh. I'll try to convince Trystan." I tilted my head and gave him a questioning look.

He threw his palm to his forehead.

"Yeah, he's here." I shrugged. "See you tonight." I ended the call.

Trystan kicked the grass with his foot. "You shouldn't have told them I'm here."

"Why not?"

He rubbed his hand across his face. "My family is dead set against us dating. Once they heard about prom, they went ballistic."

Mom's words rang in my ears. It is customary to allow one's elders to arrange a marriage. "Your governing elders wouldn't approve of us?"

"No, because of you being a half-blood. You have to understand that my bloodline is among Therans's strongest. But my family thinks you're human. My dad doesn't want us involved with one another."

Human! I reached over my shoulder and traced my mark, searching the canvas of his face.

"What's your feeling about half-bloods?" Instinct screamed to spill my guts and tell him everything, but other lives than mine were at stake.

"Half-blood, crimson-blood. I don't care." He stepped closer, held my hand, and interlocked our fingers. "My initial hope was to ease into this relationship, allowing my family time to adjust, but whether they know you are part Theran or not, they'll have to deal with us dating."

The idea of my mind and gut being in sync swelled my heart. The compulsion to spill everything was strong, but this was enough to digest for one day.

His thumb caressed my palm. "This relationship won't be easy. Dad and I have already fought about it, but I have leverage. My father sits on the Council of Elders. In our government, seats are inherited. I'm last in our direct family line, then it goes to my uncle's side. I told my dad that if he attempted to interfere in our relationship, I wouldn't assume his position, allowing it to pass to my uncle and Colin." His thumb stilled. "He's insinuated that my involvement with you is a rebellious act—a teenager's fling."

Dislike and anger fought for priority in my mind. "What do you mean by your dad's seat?"

"Our system is similar to the old British peerage but is much older. Although we've adapted to the modern world, many archaic rules still exist, including the use of the term 'lords' for council members."

Ah, they have their sense of nobility. Wait. Could they stop him from taking me to prom?

"So, the prom's still on?" The silly words slipped out.

"Yeah."

I shuddered at the bleakness in his voice but welcomed the relief that flooded me, knowing he still wanted to be a part of my life.

His pursed lips grew into a slight smile. "And, since you've committed us to the movies, we'd best hurry. I don't want to give my family any more reason for being concerned about us, but don't think we're done talking about all this."

We walked down to the house, and I changed clothes. We piled into his car and headed to the north end of Wooster.

"Tell me more about this council."

He focused on the road. "Think of it like this. Amish people live in contemporary society but have their own laws and beliefs, including limitations on technology and even particular regulations concerning clothes and men's beards. Their local bishops guide them in this. We, Theran, also have our laws and beliefs. We marry within our race, protect the libraries, and keep our existence a secret."

Therans masquerading as humans? Libraries? And what was wrong with half-bloods?

"I've yet to understand your background, Callie, but there was a time when our rules were broken, and it took centuries to clean up the mess—the consequences were horrible. For our safety and humans, it's best we maintain our laws."

"So. Ah, half-blood means one human parent, one Theran?"

"Yeah." He flicked the heater to low. "And one with two pure-blooded Theran parents is called a crimson-blood."

Thoughts collected in my head, but my mouth stayed shut. My questions would have to wait. Lights flashed around the theater sign, and Trystan pulled into a parking spot.

My gut clenched. Our friends had collected on the sidewalk near the ticket stall.

"Hmm. How do we handle them?"

He pulled open the glove compartment and a soapy scent filled my nose. He took his wallet out. "Just like any couple dating."

I grabbed his arm. "Colin and Anna don't know?"

"I've said nothing to them about thinking you're Theran. And Anna never questioned me on how we found her." He laid his hand on mine.

"Cool." The confirmation eased my mind. My secret was safe, but how would they react to us?

Trystan came around to my door and opened it. He took my hand, and we walked toward the entrance.

Erika made a mad dash toward us. Colin and Anna stayed on the fringe of the circle, behind Camden, Steve, Jessica, and Sandy. I didn't recognize the person standing behind Sandy.

Erika glanced down at our clasped hands. "I get full details later. Oh, before we get up there, you should know Sandy brought a date."

"Okay."

Erika winced. "Camden doesn't like him. They've already exchanged looks."

"Why?" I glanced at the approaching guy. He must be at least twenty. "Don't say anything. They're behind you," I whispered.

Sandy stepped up beside Erika. "Callie, Trystan, this is Draco Manson, my date."

Sandy giggled, showing off her trophy of a man. Draco leered at Jessica, who hung close to Steve's arm, while Steve glared at Trystan's and my interlocked hands. Camden latched onto Erika's arm.

Slimy would have been a better name for the tall, gangly male. Adding Draco to our mixture of friends was like combining rubbing alcohol and bleach, and it looked to be Sandy's health that was in question. Draco looked at her like she was a piece of meat. Nana had always told me, "Older guys have no business with young girls." From the reactions of my other friends, it seemed likely before the evening was out, someone would tell Sandy the guy was too old for her.

Anna crept over from behind the circle. "Callie, how are you?"

Trystan's fingers stiffened around mine.

"Great." I inhaled. "Hi, Colin."

Colin grinned. "Looks like another movie night."

"What are we watching?" Relief surged through me. Colin and Anna were still talking to me.

"They've chosen *Travistine Hall.*" Colin smiled. "Not a regency romance." Colin's eyes pierced Trystan, his stare lowered, stopping for a second on our interlocked fingers.

I cringed, but he still grinned at me. Did Colin believe this was a teenage fling, too?

"Oh." Erika jammed her thumb into her front pocket. "Cam and I are shopping for his tux. Do you two care to go?"

"Sounds good," Trystan said.

Air escaped my pursed lips. "I'm in."

Everyone headed to the outside ticket booth, walking more slowly than usual.

"Hey." Trystan tugged on my hand. "If you bring a swatch of your dress, we can match my tux with it."

"Sure," I said. "What do you make of the new guy?"

"He's too old for Sandy, but I don't think he'll be with her long. He's too much of a player. Look at the way he eyed Jessica."

"Sandy's really into him. I don't want to see her hurt."

"I don't think anyone liked him. Someone will say something."

I was being overly sensitive. Not everything was *normal,* but Anna and Colin seemed okay with Trystan and me.

Within an hour, I regretted coming to the movie. Every time an action scene showed, kissing sounds from behind us amplified.

Anna slouched in her seat with her hands over her mouth, Erika's face smothered in her shoulder. Both looked to be having seizures from laughing. Erika kept elbowing me on one side while Trystan held my hand. I couldn't get a take on Camden's reaction since he and Steve sat closest to the wall.

Wow. Finally. Credits.

The lights came on, and people's faces became visible. I stood, stretched, and stepped into the aisle next to Trystan.

Sandy and Slimy had moved during the movie and were now in the back corner seats. She applied makeup while Slimy licked his lips, trying to get another kiss. She nudged him away and flashed her teeth as if she were about to accept an Emmy.

So, Sandy and Slimy were the kissing bandits.

Trystan slid his fingers into mine and winked.

Excitement fizzed up in me like foam in a shaken bottle of soda. Would Trystan ever kiss me?

CHAPTER 27

RESERVATIONS

The floor jerked, and metal elevator doors opened onto the rehab floor. People dressed in scrubs and white coats paced the long corridor. My hopes of talking to Mr. Santos shrank with each step I took. On my past two attempts, his therapy sessions had prevented me from talking to him. I shuffled past several rooms and stopped at the nurses' station.

A dark-haired nurse looked up from the computer. "What can I do for you?"

I clutched my brown purse. "I'm here to see Mr. Santos."

She clicked a button on the computer and pulled out a piece of paper. "They moved to the other end of the rehab floor. Follow me," Jade said.

Gramps always taught me to pay attention to name tags.

Two tall men in suits walked by us. The white hallway reeked of ammonia, tempered by a strong cologne scent.

Nurse Jade and I turned the corner, almost bumping into Samantha.

Dressed in blue scrubs, her collagen-enhanced lips stretched into a bright smirk. "Why, Miss Callie, twice we meet."

"You two know each other?" Jade asked.

"Yes." Samantha closed the computer lid she carried. "My boyfriend is her history teacher."

"Ah," Jade said. "She's here to see Mr. Santos."

Samantha raised an eyebrow. "Ahh, that's right. He was your teacher last fall."

How long had she worked here? Had she seen Santos's mark? Did she know about the Remnant Therans?

I forced a grin. "He was injured in the same accident that killed my grandmother." I hated using Nana as an excuse.

Jade's hands smacked over her mouth. "You're Callie Tresham."

I nodded.

"Your gramps is such a dear man. He's sent chocolates to Mr. Santos and freshened up the flowers in his room several times."

Not once had Gramps mentioned he'd sent flowers to Santos.

"Oh, I heard rumors about that accident," Samantha said.

She'd heard more than rumors. I squared my shoulders and smiled at Jade. "Could you point me to his room?"

"Why, yes." Jade turned. "Come."

"Mrs. Jameson." Samantha clutched her computer to her chest as she spoke to Jade. "I'd be happy to take Miss Tresham for you."

"It's not a problem," Nurse Jameson said. "I'm already headed that way. You go about your orders."

I turned, not waiting to see Samantha's expression, feeling as if she'd pinned a target made of questions onto my back.

We passed several closed wooden doors. Jameson stopped at the last door in the corridor just before a door opened. A smaller corridor broke off to the right. Nurse Jade grinned at me before knocking.

"Come in." A gruff voice sounded from behind the door.

"Thank you." I grinned back at the nurse.

The nurse's retreating shoes brought a sense of momentary relief. I pushed open the door and closed it behind me. Santos sat, reclining in his chair.

"Hi."

I held up my hand to stop him from saying anything else. He cocked his head, raising his eyebrows. I pointed directly at him, moved my two fingers in front of my eyes, and mouthed with my lips, *You're being watched*.

He straightened.

I held one finger to my pursed lips, scanned the room, and pulled at the blank placemat below his breakfast tray. I pointed to the pen on the crossword puzzle near the vases of flowers. He stretched over, grabbed it, and handed it to me.

"You're looking good." With quick fingers, I wrote.

Nurse Samantha is a Theran, working with a teacher named Mr. Taylor.

I handed the placemat and pen to him. "I've been wondering how your therapy is going," I commented, trying to separate the two lines of thought.

"Good." He read my note and looked at me, his eyebrows squishing together. "Much better since I got rid of the walker."

I moved the breakfast tray and squatted at the side of his recliner, taking the placemat from him as he continued to speak. I scribbled.

I've got no idea what they're after, but it's not good, and if my instincts are correct, they know about you. Do you know them?

I handed it back.
    He read. "No."
    I nodded.
    He took the pen and wrote.

THEY MUST BE MEMBERS OF THE ANCIENT THERANS. I'D KNOW IF REMNANTS WERE HERE.

He handed me the paper and leaned back in his seat.
    It was going to take time to get used to these foreign words. I cocked my head.
    He snatched the paper from me and wrote.

ANCIENT THERANS DON'T BELONG TO THE FACTION FROM WHICH YOUR PARENTS AND I COME. DON'T WORRY. I'VE RETIRED FROM THE THERAN SECRET SERVICE. BUT, IF

CONFRONTED, I CAN WHIP UP A GOOD COVER STORY.

This wasn't the place to divulge details. We'd taken a risk even talking this much. "When do you get out of here?"

"Shortly. Rehab's going great. I had what Dr. Jaski calls a high-impact pelvic fracture, but my hip's healing nicely. I should be out soon." He flexed his left arm over his head, the pen still in his grip. "But I don't intend to return to teaching until maybe next year. I don't like the idea of all that walking. I'll pick up working on the Sundries' farm later. The bad news is the lease is up on my apartment, so I'll have to hunt for a new place."

"Stop by and talk with Gramps." I shifted from my knees to my butt. "We've got a first-floor, two-bedroom place behind the mill."

"Are you sure? He didn't look happy to see me when we met."

"It's not been easy on him, raising me," I whispered. "Anyhow, he cares enough to send flowers."

"Your granddad's a good man. He's respected around town." He pinched his lips together and wrote while I kept talking.

He lowered the placemat to me, and I scanned it.

HAD I KNOWN WHAT HAD HAPPENED TO YOUR PARENTS AND SISTER, I WOULD HAVE RE-TURNED FROM MY MISSION SOONER. YOU HAVE TO BELIEVE ME. MY OCCUPATION DIDN'T GIVE ME ACCESS TO THE OUTSIDE WORLD.

A squeak from behind alerted me to the door opening.

My shield sprang forth like a tidal wave. Samantha—my protective shield was proving useful.

"I miss teaching. Miss all you kids." His intentional change in topic helped ease my mind.

I stuffed our paper conversation inside my purse. "I'm glad you're doing better, Mr. Santos. I'll let the other kids know how you're doing." I stood and turned to see Samantha.

Her eyes flickered ever so slightly, probing me. "I just came to see how our patient is doing." She walked over with a pitcher of water and filled Santos's cup.

She must have a power since my shield popped up. Thank goodness she couldn't sense squat with my shield activated. I must look like any regular human to her.

I pasted a smile on my face. "It's good to know nurses around here are so helpful."

"Well." Samantha flipped a strand of loose blond hair over her shoulder. "We're short-staffed, so everyone has to pitch in."

Papers shuffled, and as I slanted a look at Santos, he closed his crossword puzzle book.

"Get going. Tell your Gramps I'll see him soon."

I hated leaving him with her. What was her power? And who did she and Mr. Taylor work for? What I knew for sure was that neither one was the shadowed figure in my vision.

CHAPTER 28

MURDER

I stuffed my phone back inside my pants pocket. Trystan hadn't called yet, nor Erika. I'd been ready to go shopping since after lunch. I pulled a pencil from behind my ear and flopped back onto my stomach, looking at the book before me. Finals were just over a month away, right after prom.

For the first time since my family's deaths, the world appeared brighter and different in an inexplicable way. Anxiety still had a hold of my life—what with all the unanswered questions, especially not knowing what my mark meant—and, more than anything, I wanted to hear about Sebastian's vision. Still, despite all the mounting pressure of keeping the mill running, dealing with Mr. Taylor, and understanding my differences, Trystan's friendship had lifted a weight from my life. One I hadn't known could be elevated.

My pocket vibrated. I withdrew my phone and, seeing it was Erika, activated the speakerphone. "Hello, Erika."

"What are you doing?"

"I'm trying to study for exams—something you should consider."

"Not happening." She chuckled. "So, give me all the juicy details."

I dropped my pencil on the bed and rolled over onto my back. "It's weird. You know when you feel like something fits ... a piece of a puzzle in your life you never knew you needed until you found it?"

"Callie, are you sure you're studying and not reading some romance novel?"

"Yep—I'm reading textbooks, not romance." I snickered.

"Well, I'm happy for you. Now, we both have awesome guys. Oh, Camden called. He talked with Trystan already. He's gonna pick you up first, and then he'll come for Camden and me around two."

"Cool. I'll be ready." The phone beeped. "Erika, I've got to go. Someone else is calling."

I transferred the call. "Hello."

"Good to hear your voice."

I sat on the bed and pulled my legs up under my chin. "Gramps. How's PA?"

"Just fine, dear. The line sounds garbled. Can you hear me, okay?"

"I've got you on speakerphone. I was talking to Erika before you called."

The phone beeped. I ignored it, not wanting to interrupt Gramps.

"Ah-ha." A yawn sounded from his end. "I'm tired. The mattress is lumpy. I can't wait to get home. Is everything going well there? Don't forget to use money from the secretary drawer if you need to get more groceries."

"I know. I know. Everything's fine here," I said as Tesla whined. "Other than Tesla missing you. He can hear your voice over the phone."

Gramps chuckled. "Hug the mutt for me. He ain't used to me being gone. The trouble is, it's looking like I might have to return to PA next month."

"Not at the end of May?"

"Not if I can help it. I want to see you in your ruffles and frills. I'm glad Trystan's taking you to prom. He's a good boy. I like him. Your Nana has some really nice necklaces you can borrow if you'd like."

"Thanks, Gramps."

"I'll see you Wednesday, dear."

"I can't wait."

I ended the phone call and gazed at my T-shirt and jeans. I bolted up, ran to the closet, and pulled on a blue, short-sleeved shirt. At least it was different from what I always wore. The swatch of material from my prom gown lay on the dresser. I grabbed it on my way out and stuffed it in my purse.

"Be a good boy." Tesla perked up his ears.

Trystan pulled into the drive and got out of the Jetta. I locked the house door and turned around, feeling the now-familiar stream of electricity. Lately, the sensation I experienced when we made eye contact felt natural—somehow, it tethered us together.

I settled into the passenger seat and buckled my seatbelt. He climbed back into the driver's side.

Trystan snickered, looking across the bushes at the house's front window. Tesla had his nose pushed up against the glass. "Seems Tesla's upset you're leaving."

"Nah, he doesn't care if I'm gone. He hates being stuck inside."

"You know"—he put the car in reverse—"he's been up to our house a few times."

"You're kidding. I had no idea he wandered so far."

Trystan pulled onto the main road. "Don't worry. My aunt loves animals. She thinks it's great he scared off the vandals at Mr. Livingston's."

"I hate that Mr. Livingston's barn got vandalized."

"It looks bad." Trystan turned onto another road. "Sometimes, our mailman delivers our mail to them, and Mrs. Livingston comes by to drop it off to us."

He ran his fingers through his hair.

"Trystan, you're playing with your hair. You do that when you're nervous. What's up?"

He took a corner a little too fast, turned onto Erika's drive, and then swerved, missing one of the ducks by the lane. His silence drove me crazy. We came to a stop, and he threw the car into park.

"We need to talk, but we don't have time now."

I cocked an eyebrow.

"It's about the guy who was murdered." Trystan's mouth drew into a straight line. "He was one of Dad's friends. A council member."

"Oh, no. Does this have anything to do with the professor who got killed at Ashworth?"

"Theran investigators don't know exactly how they're linked."

The front door of Erika's house swung open, and Camden stepped out onto the porch. He held up his index finger, motioning for us to wait a minute.

The conversation drifted into silence. I smashed my eyes shut. I so bad wanted to talk to him. Since last night, he'd seemed different, more relaxed. At least I knew he was willing to speak, if not right now. Guilt settled into my thoughts. I wondered what he would do if I told him the truth about my family. Did I have a right to keep information from him? What would he do if I told him about the difference in our marks? Was I protecting

Santos and my history? Trystan wasn't asking questions, but I wondered, was I making the right choice.

Even though my instinct screamed at me to confess, I wasn't going to open up.

"Earth to Callie."

I opened my eyes. Light bounced off the barn's metal rooftop.

Trystan's brows furrowed. "You're deep in thought."

I grinned. "As you said, we'll talk later."

It seemed he looked straight through the confusion in my head and was willing to give me the space I needed to sort it out. "Do you have the swatch?"

"Ah. Yeah." I opened my purse, dug around, and felt for the material. "It's in here somewhere."

"Your purse isn't that big that you won't be able to find it."

I pulled out a wad of papers, set them on my lap, and continued to empty my purse. Keys and coins jingled at the bottom. Did it fall out? This would be a good reason to start zipping it.

"Ah, here it is." I pulled it out of my bag.

"It's blue satin." He chuckled. "It'll bring out your eyes."

Camden approached, placed two palms on the hood of Trystan's car, and pushed up and down, jostling the vehicle. Erika tugged Camden and pulled him around to the back door. They climbed in.

Trystan turned left out of the drive and, in no time, caught the main highway.

"I can't believe I got away." Erika smacked her lips together. "Dad's been like a drill sergeant ever since Trevor left. I can't wait until Mr. Santos gets better. Dad could use him full time."

"It'll be months before he can do any work. He's still in therapy."

"Were you able to see him?"

I shifted to see into the back seat. "Yeah, he's doing better, but he's doing a lot of physical therapy."

"I'd have gone with you if you'd called," Erika said.

Trystan cleared his throat. "Who's Mr. Santos?"

"Callie's favorite teacher." Erika bumped the back of my seat. "Taylor's taken over teaching his class."

I clutched my purse. I didn't have the stomach to tell Trystan Santos had been in the car accident with Nana. The thought of the accident pained me. What I didn't tell him, he'd collect from others. "So, are we headed to Canton?"

"No," Camden said. "There's a new place in Mansfield that's got some cool tuxes."

Trystan looked at Camden in the rearview mirror. "No one's getting me into an orange vest."

Camden smacked his knee with his hand. "You still haven't figured it out? I was teasing this morning. Neon orange was the craze *last* year."

Trystan turned up the music and harmonized with the radio's singer in a soothing tenor. He tapped his thumb on the wheel. Erika hit the back of my seat, keeping to the beat, and Camden muffled loud bass beats under his breath like a rapper. I lip-synced, enjoying the sound of Trystan's voice.

We laughed almost the entire drive. We pulled into a parking spot. A red and blue OPEN sign hung in the store window. This wasn't anywhere near the mall but in a large, L-shaped complex near a bridal gallery.

"Come on." Camden exited the car, and the rest of us followed.

"Oh, look." Erika pointed. "We've got to go over and check out Body Fragrances. I love that store."

Once we were in front of the display window, Erika screwed her face into a weird look, gesturing with her hand over her shoulder, mimicking the figure behind her. "Look, three mannequins." She deepened her voice to impersonate a male. "*We* look like penguins."

Trystan held open the door, and we all filed inside the store.

A blond man greeted us. "Hello, I'm Brian. How can I help you?"

Camden stepped forward. "Two of us would like to be fitted for tuxes."

"Definitely not the four of us," Erika murmured with a chuckle. "Can you imagine—some girls actually wear these things?" She pulled on a nearby mannequin's coat-tail. "I wouldn't look good in one."

"Some girls can pull the look off really good." Camden's eyebrows danced.

Brian clapped his hands together. "Stan, we have customers."

A thin, older man stuck his head out from behind the ceiling-to-floor curtains toward the back of the store.

We spent the next hour trying on tuxes but ended up picking out a blue-black, shimmery suit. His tie matched my swatch.

Neither of us spoke about the murders again. Trystan was a solid rock in the middle of my uncertain ocean. He'd become the friend I needed, my anchor to the shore.

CHAPTER 29

STEWARDS OF HISTORY

English class bored me to death. I tapped the pen on my table. What were the chances of the scroll still being in Taylor's desk drawer? I'd been back to school for four days and still couldn't search his classroom. Gramps's return home last night from PA had kept me so busy doing his laundry and catching him up on what had happened with the mill that I'd fallen asleep from mental exhaustion.

The bell rang. I gathered my books, made a dash for the door, slipped behind some guy in blue, and stopped. Trystan stood across the hall. Jings. As much as I wanted to be with him, I needed time to find the scroll.

"Callie." Steve's voice rang with excitement from behind me. "Wait up."

I turned against the flood of teenagers spilling out into the hall from their classes.

"What's up? I'm in a hurry."

"I'm gonna flunk English if you don't help me."

"I thought you didn't care."

Lizzy, wide-eyed, spun around to look at me as I swallowed my bitter retort. She left, and I regretted my harsh words.

Steve stepped back. "Miss Delong said I'll need a seventy-six percent to pass." Desperation colored his tone. "Please."

The knot in my stomach tightened. "Fine, I'll help tonight."

"Cool. What about five at my house? My mom's working."

"Fine."

"Great. See you later." Steve winked and left.

I spun around.

"Hi." Trystan hadn't moved an inch. He held a sub bag. "My aunt dropped off lunch for Anna, but she wasn't interested. How'd you like a roast beef sub for lunch?"

"Sounds good." Instead of heading to the cafeteria like everyone else, Trystan opened the glass door and stepped onto the sidewalk leading to the track field a good distance away, opposite the parking lot.

Garbage dumpsters located outside the gymnasium killed any romantic notion, but at least it was private. We walked a few steps and found a patch of grass nestled under a willow tree. When I sat, the cool grass felt welcoming to my already-stretched nerves.

Trystan pulled back the wrapper and offered me half the sub.

"Thanks."

"You were a little short with Steve."

"I'm stressed." I plucked a tomato from the sub and popped it into my mouth.

The flame in his eyes dimmed. "It wouldn't have anything to do with us, would it?"

"No." The wind blew, sending shivers coursing over my skin. Although the weather had warmed considerably this past week, I felt cold.

"Do you want to talk about it?"

I chewed and swallowed. "There's so much going on with school and so many unanswered questions with ... you know." Us. Therans.

"Ask me anything you want."

I gave him a sidelong glance. "The other day, you mentioned something about libraries. What did you mean?"

He set down his sub, scanning the landscape. "We, our kind, protect the libraries. Essentially, we're stewards of history. We guard history because humans are quick to destroy—even to attempt to control—in the name of a cause. I like to joke that we're 'history keepers.'"

"History keepers. That's got a nice ring to it."

"History is significant. It plays so much a part of our future."

I cocked my head.

"For a girl who professes to love history so much, you don't seem–"

"I know history is important." Etched memories of Nana reading the Bible surfaced. "My grandmother always said one of the reasons the Old Testament was important is because it told the truth of future events."

"That's true. But it's also a way to learn from past wrongs in order not to repeat them."

"Maybe we should become archeologists and travel the world." I chuckled.

"Sign me up." Trystan smiled. "Amazingly, there's still so much we have yet to collect. Each Theran library is a time capsule filled with hidden treasures, rare books, and artifacts. I've heard rumors there's even information about forgotten civilizations in the Egyptian library—something to do with a golden chamber. My dad describes it as one of the 'underground wonders of the world.'" He smiled, picking up his sub.

I sighed, and the breeze stirred the air. "So, how many Therans live here?"

"There could be thousands. Ashworth University is the biggest education center in America for Therans, second in the world to a university in Alexandria, Egypt, but humans attend the university, too."

I swallowed. Thousands? "So, they come here to attend Ashworth?"

"Some of the greatest." His voice lowered. "Theran minds come here to learn, but nothing compares to the Alexandrian Library. Millenniums ago, it was the collecting center for the entire world's knowledge. Ptolemy, a great astronomer from Egypt, went to great lengths to discover and possess rare and original masterpieces. Some say he gave outrageous sums of money to other countries, like Greece and China, to borrow their masterworks. Then, he made two copies of whatever he'd borrowed. He would send one back to the country from which he had borrowed the original. The second print he would supposedly keep on a shelf in the library, which was, at its peak, estimated to have stored 400,000 to 700,000 parchment scrolls."

"What happened to the original books?"

"Speculation is a fire destroyed everything." His eyes roamed the tops of the trees. "But legend has it Ptolemy had a secret library. We may be stewards, but we don't even know everything. Our world's riddled with myths. The Italian library has dedicated a room to the unsolvable, rightly called the Room of Legends. That's why translators are so valuable. We help reveal the history of our past, although we even have limits on what we can transcribe."

Could Taylor's interest in New Cumberlin Falls be its proximity to Ashworth University? Does he use his ability on unsuspecting humans?

"So, the greatest minds, even the council members, come here?"

He nodded. "Since the late 1800s, Wooster's been where all the Theran action happens. Civil unrest forced us to make America our home base. Americans are known for their humanitarian efforts and acceptance of others. And Wooster being an agricultural area just seemed right."

"So, there are three libraries?"

He grinned. "Yes, and all three libraries are underground. Humans are not permitted inside them, although the library in Alexandria has an above-ground, public area, making some finds available to humans." He leaned back and glanced up at me. "I guess after two thousand years, we've decided to work with humans again."

"Work with them again?"

He sat up and rolled his wrapper into a ball. "It's rather in-depth and depressing. I told you two thousand years ago that Alexandria was a cultural learning center for the greatest Theran minds in the world. What I didn't say is that Therans used it as a place to help advance humans' understanding, not just our own. In the end, the War of Knowledge happened, and the library caught on fire—the Fire of Unknown Cause. He scratched his head. "They built a new library there over ten years ago. If I remember rightly, it's called Bibliotheca. It's near the site of the old library." He lowered his head and grimaced. "I'll explain the rest later. We don't have much time before the bell rings."

That triggered a memory of my mother's letter.

IN AN EFFORT TO COVER THE REMNANTS' TRACKS, OUR ANCESTORS ENCOURAGED OTHERS TO BELIEVE MANY OF US HAD DIED IN THE FIGHTING IN THE WAR OF KNOWLEDGE. OUR ANCESTORS ALSO SET A FIRE TO COVER OUR ESCAPE. WE HAD TO PRESERVE THE POWER WITHIN OUR BLOODLINE FROM THE DANGERS IN EGYPT.

This must be how they'd escaped from Alexandria. They'd started a fire and formed the Remnant Faction.

"Hey, how long will you study with Steve tonight?" Trystan asked.

"Hopefully, only a few hours."

"I'll give you a call. Colin wants to practice some karate techniques with me."

There were moments when I wished I could read his thoughts. It was like he'd purposely ended the conversation. I pushed myself up onto my knees. "Wait. I've got one more question."

"What?"

"Are there other ways to tell a person is ...?" I pointed at his chest.

His brows drew together. "No. The mark is what distinguishes us from humans. If not for having witnessed you on the night of the fire, I'd never have known unless ..." His gaze dropped to my chest.

A blush crawled into my cheeks. *Oh my!* Not what I expected.

CHAPTER 30

STALKER

I'd no sooner pulled the keys from the ignition and opened the car door than Steve hustled out of his house and strolled down the sidewalk.

"Right on time," Steve said.

"Well, I'd hate to let you flunk out."

He chuckled and took my books from my hands. "Oh, Erika called and said she couldn't reach you. She left a message on voicemail. Camden's having a bonfire tomorrow night, and she wants you to come. She also said something about working at the school tomorrow for the decorating committee."

I could use a relaxing evening with friends. "If Trystan goes, I'll go. Are you going?"

"Yeah, I guess. Camden's only invited a few of us."

"Cool." We entered the house, and the door slammed behind me.

Steve scattered his books across the dining room table. We spent an hour or more focusing on Miss Delong's study guide questions, writing in the margins.

"You know, Callie, your study method of using different colors of pens and writing in the margins makes it easier to focus on the right things for tests."

"It's worked for me, but it doesn't help when I transpose numbers."

Steve put down the colored pen. "You reverse numbers?"

"Sometimes words. Mostly when I'm stressed, dyslexia sucks."

"Hey." Steve stood and pushed his chair back. "Can I get you a pop?"

"That'd be great."

Steve made a dash downstairs, and I took the opportunity to stretch and massage my lower back. An engine mower kicked up outside. I pulled the lace curtains back. A chuckle escaped my lips. Taylor and Steve were neighbors. Awesome.

Steve came up the steps and handed me a cold can of soda. "Mr. Taylor's the envy of every guy around here. Since he moved into the neighborhood, two other guys purchased convertible mowers. Those things are amazing. You can walk behind *or* ride on them." He plopped back into his chair and popped the can open.

My excitement grew over the next hour as we finished the study guide. A thought took root—I couldn't search the house as Taylor would find me, but I could keep watch.

After I left Steve's place, the warm sky colors fell away, leaving the dark night in its place. Finally, I had a chance to check Taylor out. I parked in an alley off a remote sideroad. I got out of the Jeep and tossed my phone on the seat.

Darkness cloaked me. I skirted around the backs of the ranch houses until I reached Taylor's home. Several windows were a couple of inches ajar. There wasn't enough space for me to climb inside, and, with my luck, any attempts to raise the windows high enough to create the space for me to do so would cause creaking noises, alerting him to my presence. I inhaled. A rank odor gagged me. Large piles of dung covered the ground.

I stayed low, hiding behind the bushes, using the cool, metal siding as a guide, and slipped around the corner. Dim lights from inside cast a soft glow onto the green shrubs. I concealed myself in the shadows and peered into the house.

Taylor sat on a couch with his back toward me. Samantha laid stretched out on the floor in a pink nightie with an assortment of colored nail polish spread across the wooden floor.

"How'd things go at the hospital?"

"Still nothing." She blew on her fingernails. "But he's popular with the kids. He's got a string of them checking up on him."

"Has Callie been back?" he asked.

"Nope, just that once."

Ah, so they don't know about my other attempts to see Santos.

"Good. I don't like the girl." He leaned forward on the couch and petted the head of a large black dog. Taylor blocked my view of the animal. I couldn't make out the breed.

Samantha sat up, crossing her legs in front of her and looking at her hand. "She's human. You can't expect much."

The dog's growl reached my ears.

Startled, I pressed back against the cool wall. I couldn't risk getting caught by the dog. I ducked down and backtracked to the Jeep, where I burrowed in and watched the house—I'd turned into a stalker.

A bitter chill seeped into my bones, and an ache dug into my side. Time passed. A lot of time passed.

I yawned, stretching my arm above my head, and opened my eyes. Bright colors sculpted the horizon, and the seatbelt clasp poked into my side. I sat up.

"OMJings." I'd fallen asleep on the seat. I scrambled for my keys and found my phone—Gramps had called nine times. I had left it on vibrate. I should've turned the ringer on when Steve told me Erika tried to call. Ugh. I slept through the entire freakin' night. Once I found my keys, I hit the road and called Gramps.

He picked up on the first ring. "*Callie*, you okay?"

"I'm fine."

"You didn't answer your phone. Where are you?"

"I'll be home in fifteen minutes. I'll explain." I ended the call. There was no way out of it. Gramps was going to drill me with questions. I'd have to tell him. And it was already after seven, not leaving me much time before school started.

Once I pulled in, Gramps stepped out on the front porch with his hands on his hips. I slammed the car door shut.

"Girl, you've got some explaining to do." His face flushed red. He jerked open the screen door, and I slipped inside. "You'd better have a good explanation. Your friends are worried sick. Steve said you studied with him, then left. Mrs. Sundries has called me several times. Trystan stopped by to see you last night, and Mr. Santos called." Gramps flipped his hands around in the air. "And he mentioned something about wanting to rent the apartment."

I set my books on the counter and spun around. "When's he getting discharged?"

"Don't you dare ask another question." He paced the floor, and Tesla slunk to the ground. "Where were you last night?"

"With Steve." I clutched my stomach with my palm and went against my instinct. "Then, I spied on Mr. Taylor and his girlfriend, who are Theran."

Gramps stopped in his tracks. His head jerked up.

"There are thousands of Therans here, and if my intuition is correct, something dangerous is going to happen. Taylor and his girlfriend are at the center of it."

"Dear God in Heaven, please, give me strength." Gramps sunk into the kitchen chair, all color drained from his face.

I knelt beside him and pressed my palm to his knee. His cold hand slid over mine.

"You've got to trust me. I don't understand everything that's going on, but right now, I need you to be patient with me."

His eyes glassed over, and a tear escaped his eye, trailing his worry lines. "Are you like your mom?"

He was asking if I had powers. "Yes."

"You're strong, like her." It wasn't a question. "I suspected you were different on the day of your grandmother's funeral when you pulled off the doorknob. My guess is, you did something during the fire to rescue Anna, too. Up until that point, you'd hid your strength well, even when you worked at the mill."

"Why didn't you say anything?"

"Your parents never explained, and I wasn't about to go rooting into something that made Marvel comics come to life, especially since I'd had a hard time grasping your mom's power."

"Well, you need to know, Gramps. It's the only way I can make sure you stay safe." I adjusted myself and sat on the floor, recounting everything that had happened over the past few months since the night I'd gotten sick–but not my new powers. I explained Trystan and his family were Therans, and Mr. Santos. I didn't go into details about the Council of Elders or the Remnant group, and I stressed to him he must not mention Mr. Santos's name to anyone. I didn't want Trystan or his family to learn of the Remnants by mistake. When I'd explained Mom and Dad were friends with Mr. Santos, Gramps's facial features seemed to ease. I had to trust telling Gramps had been the right move, even going against my gut instinct. At least now he'd know the bad guys from the good.

"I don't like any of this." He placed both hands on the table. "But one thing I learned from sergeant—who busted out a quote for any situation–is Edmund Burke's, 'All that is necessary for evil to triumph is that good men do nothing.'" He looked down at his palms. "Do you think Taylor knows about you?"

"No. Best I can tell, I'm just a thorn in his side." Switching topics seemed like a good idea. "What's up with Mr. Santos?"

"He's being discharged sooner than he thought, and he wants to rent the apartment out back." He glanced at me with a faint smile. "I take it you two have talked."

"It'd be good to have him here."

His finger traced along the seam in the table slat. "I'm scared, dear. I won't lie to you."

Doubt landed in my mind. For a second, I wished I'd never said anything. I had robbed him of what little peace he'd found since Nana's death. But how could I not tell him? It was time. He had to know. I couldn't move forward with the knowledge that whenever I made a decision, I'd be causing friction between us. I didn't want excuses or lies. Being straightforward with him was best. Mom and Dad had trusted him to raise me, so I had to arm him with information that could protect him.

An hour later, I pulled up in front of the school. We'd agreed that acting normal was best. Gramps had come up with the excuse that I'd fallen asleep in the rental property while I'd been getting it prepared for Mr. Santos. Taylor already knew we were friends. Nana's death was just another reason to allow Santos to move onto our property. Gramps made calls to our friends and explained my absence to them while I tackled the explanations at school.

I pushed the button next to the glass doors.

"How may I help you?"

I adjusted the books in my arms. "It's me, Mrs. Glass, Callie." I looked into the school camera.

"Come to the office," Mrs. Glass said.

The door buzzed, and I opened it.

The school office was quiet. Mrs. Glass typed away at the desk while Counselor Davis mumbled something to Coach, causing his eyes to go wide and his jaw to drop.

Mrs. Glass tapped the surface in front of me, breaking my concentration. "Your granddad called and explained your tardiness." She handed me a gray slip of paper. "There are a few minutes before the third-period bell rings. Get your first-and second-period teachers to sign this and return it to me later today."

Third period breezed by. The bell rang, and I made a beeline to my locker.

Steve leaned against the row of lockers, talking with Erika, Anna, and Trystan.

"What happened last night?" Steve asked before Trystan could say a word.

I bumped Steve on the shoulder, spun the dial, and opened the locker. "I fell asleep in the apartment." Keeping my English book with me, I set my other books on the shelf and glanced at Anna, who lowered her eyes. What the heck? Why isn't she looking at me?

"How could your gramps not find you?" Erika asked.

I chewed on my lower lip, wishing I could push the guilt away. "It slipped my mind to tell him what I was doing." I spun around and faced Erika.

She smacked her lips together, chewing gum. "Your gramps was frantic."

"With dead bodies surfacing, who could blame him?" Steve said.

"What. Did. You. Say?" I asked, knowing my whisper was harsh.

Steve's eyes sparked. "It's all over the news. They found some person's body—bound, gagged, and wrapped in a tarp—floating in the swamp this morning. I guess the cops have questioned some old woman who'd been out walking her dog after sunset. She called the police, pissed, complaining people were littering in the marsh."

Nausea swelled in my stomach, and a tear trickled down my cheek. I whirled around, pressed my forehead to the cool locker, and clutched my book to my midsection. Bound and gagged? What had happened? Taylor—he and Samantha were home last night at sunset. Was this the person from my vision who'd drowned? Something wasn't right. Steve said there was a tarp around the body. I didn't see that. In my vision, the body's arms were floating freely on either side of their head, which was submerged, face down in the water.

Were both murders connected?

Trystan's arms swallowed me up. I inhaled a spicy scent of musk. "Shh ... shh." The bell rang, but I stayed plastered to him. Man, I wanted to climb into his skin and soak up his strength. Students scattered, and silence eventually consumed the hall. Trystan's hold around my waist eased.

I pushed against his chest and stared deep into his eyes. "We need to talk, but not here."

His warm thumb brushed a tear away from my face. "Dadgummit, Callie. You scared the hell out of me."

"I know. I'm sorry, but I've been through this with Gramps."

His grip lingered above my hip. "You weren't home last night. I searched. Where'd you go after you left Steve's house?"

I sighed. "Not here. I'll explain tonight."

Trystan stared at me, an edge of frustration creeping into his voice. "I'd like to skip the bonfire, but Camden's expecting Anna and me. He's invited Colin, too. Callie, I don't want the edited version." He leaned into me, whispering, "Your disappearing act made me insane with worry. I should've told you, but I didn't want to ruin our night. Remember the day we went to pick out my suit for prom, and I tried to tell you about the council member who'd been murdered?"

I cocked my head.

"The man was Lord Avalon. Someone had murdered him in Egypt a few days before I flew out to be with my dad. He'd summoned me because of Avalon's murder. The man the police found bound and gagged in the swamp is Samuel Avalon, the youngest son of Lord Avalon. My dad's coming in late tonight, and he is planning to start a Theran investigation."

The door behind us opened with a squeal. "That's enough, PDA. Get to your classes."

My body went poker straight in Trystan's grip. I wanted to turn around and scream at Taylor from the depths of my soul. Instead, I closed my eyes, the reality of it dawning on me, burning a hole in my mind—I was

Taylor's alibi—I could confirm they were home when the murder was committed.

CHAPTER 31

CAUGHT

I left English class and headed for the main office. After pulling the signed gray slip from my pocket, I slapped it onto the secretary's desk. My stomach growled, but determination propelled me forward. I exited the school office and headed to my locker.

Trystan was the answer. I needed to level with him. I couldn't do this alone. Anyway, it was time to find out what had transpired in Sebastian's vision. My premonitions had guided me to save Anna's life. Whatever devastation Sebastian's vision revealed, it convinced the Ancient Council to investigate, as well as Trystan, Colin, and Anna, to keep their powers a secret from even their parents.

But what drove Taylor? He'd shown little interest in me unless I was with another Theran. He'd made no move against the Dougrey family—at least, not as far as I could tell. How did this murder fit with everything else?

Anna's fingers snapped in front of my face, pulling me from my thoughts. "What's up with you? You're acting all weird."

"I'm sorry." I dropped my books inside our locker, which gave me a perfect view of Taylor's classroom. No students were in it.

Anna pushed the door open farther, smacking her lips together. "Are you nervous about finals?"

"No."

"Well, we're late for lunch. Are you coming?"

Two teachers and Principal Kennedy walked past us near the trophy wall, toward the steps. Taylor buzzed out of his room with a few file folders in his hand.

"Mr. Kennedy," Taylor said. "I got the results back. Do you have a minute?"

Anna waved her hand in front of me. "Yoo-hoo. Are you coming or not?"

"Mmm. No." I stared down the empty hall. "I'm going to ... uh, I've got something I want to do before the next class. I'll be down shortly."

She shrugged and left.

I dashed straight for Mr. Taylor's desk. There were several stacks of paper, three historic tomes, and his computer–which he'd left on–scattered across his desk. I tugged open the drawer. Nothing. The scroll was gone. I opened the other drawers and sifted through everything. My heart raced. Not a blasted thing. I slammed the drawers shut, then made my way to his closet and turned the knob. Unlocked.

I opened it and fished through his jacket pockets, finding his keys and wallet. After opening his wallet, I found a Visa card, his medical information, and a driver's license, all named Theodore Taylor. Noises came from the hall, and fear crept into my brain.

I had to get out of there.

I stashed everything back inside his pockets, closed the door, and slipped past the desk. Before I rounded the door jam, I plowed into the checkered plaid of Mr. Taylor's slender chest.

Mr. Taylor's hands gripped my shoulders, stopping me in place. "What are you doing in my classroom?"

"I ... I forgot my pencil." Stupid. Stupid. Stupid.

"Pencil?" Excitement rose in his voice as my tummy burned with acid. I couldn't get caught. I couldn't let them think I was onto them. I just couldn't.

I bit my lip as doubt snaked its way through the holes in my story. "Ah, yeah."

Taylor looked over at his desk and then back at me. "And where is this forgotten pencil?"

I pulled a wooden mechanical pencil from my back pocket. Nervous energy made me tap my foot. I hated lies. Hated them.

"Where'd you get this?" Taylor blinked several times and took the pencil from me. "This shank, it's hand-made, isn't it?"

"Uhm, yeah." It wasn't a lie. "Sergeant made it for my grandad."

"I can see why you wouldn't want to lose this." He stroked his thumb over the wood grain. "I've seen Amish make these pencils and pens. It takes skill to make the shank on a lathe without blowing the wooden cylinder." He handed the pencil back to me.

"Ah, thanks. Well, I've got to go. I don't want to miss lunch." I froze, momentarily at a loss while waiting for his response.

His face melted into a warm, tight smile. "Go. Get out of here."

"Ah, bye." I dashed to the cafeteria.

Frustration pounded in my head, expanding with every unanswered question and hardening my resolve. I needed answers. But one thing was true: Taylor couldn't tell the truth from falsehood.

CHAPTER 32

DISTRACTIONS

I might've escaped Taylor's wrath before lunch when I investigated his room, but no one escaped it during class.

Taylor's eyes narrowed to slits, and fear spread throughout the classroom. "Tommy, how will you succeed when you plagiarize someone else's work?" He tossed a pile of papers onto his desk. "I wash my hands of you ..."

Human. My mind filled in where Taylor's words failed.

The final bell rang. I pushed back my chair, swiped my book from the desk, and forced a smile as I made eye contact with Trystan. "I'm grabbing a soda from the cafeteria." I pushed past others without waiting for his response and managed to avoid Taylor on my way out the door.

This was one time intuition could clearly link fact and uncertainty. While Taylor may not have thrown the body into the swamp, I was certain he knew who was responsible.

In the hall, I noticed Steve and Anna by our locker. I nodded, turned the corner, and quickly took the steps. I flexed my fingers at my side. A current burned deep within—I thirsted for a fight. Since the fire, my emotions had been volatile. Trystan was a grounding wire.

Taylor and Samantha had been at home last night. So, someone else was in control of their movements behind the scenes. A chuckle bubbled up in my throat. Ironically, what I'd once thought a curse was actually my protection. My shield and premonitions meant self-preservation for my friends and myself. And that meant I had to learn to control my powers, but how far would I have to go to protect them?

I crossed the threshold of the cafeteria and fished in my pocket for quarters. Band kids passed in front of me, heading in the direction from which I'd come. I caught a glimpse of the scissor gate latched to the floor, still blocking the gym.

"Mmm, don't you look good?"

The words pricked my instinct like pins being jabbed into my palms. I snatched my soda from the machine and turned. Logan's cheesy smile radiated with a sense of mischief. Tom stood behind Logan and fidgeted with his zipper.

"Logan, what do you want?" Other students flowed past us, using the cafeteria for a through-way as Mr. Sykes swept the floor.

"I heard you hooked up with the loser." His eyes lowered until he'd taken in every inch of me. "But there's nothing wrong with datin' two guys. Go to the movies with me?"

I gritted my teeth. "No."

"Aw, come on, give me a chance. I could name twenty girls who would die to be where you are."

"Ask one of them."

"Ah, but you're the one I want." He stepped closer. "I'll pick you up Saturday at seven."

"Back off. I'm not interested." Can't the guy take a rejection?

His lips curled into a mischievous smile. "Don't play hard to get."

My frayed nerves coiled at the ends. I took a step back, seeking refuge against the wall as anger made me want to punch him.

People collected on the outskirts of the room, closing in on us.

His eyes lowered to the cross around my neck—Nana's necklace. "I like your necklace. Tell me, have you been a good girl?"

Lizzy worked her way to the inner circle of our peers.

"Logan. I'm not interested in you. I don't want you. You can't even respect Lizzy enough to keep your lips off other girls. I'm not stupid."

"Back away, Logan." Trystan's words rang from the other side of the cafeteria.

"Feisty—I like that." The words oozed from his slimy lips.

"*Logan!* Get away from her, *now*." Tension drained from my body at hearing Trystan's voice.

"The girl's got a right to date more than one guy." Logan's words echoed.

"She's not interested." Trystan's coal-black eyes bore into mine. He approached from behind Logan.

"You've got good hearing for a loser." Logan's face twisted into a scowl. "This ain't your business."

Erika and Anna entered the cafeteria, Steve on their tail.

"Come on," Logan said. "Go out with me on Saturday. I guarantee you'll have fun. Coccia House has a pizza contest we can enter."

Tom snickered. "We're all going."

"*No.*" I raked him with freezing contempt. "Not every female wants you."

A screech from behind Logan drew my attention. Trystan pushed up a chair and it bumped into the back of Logan's legs. Logan fell back under his own weight, away from me, landing in the chair. Trystan spun the chair around to face him and leaned over Logan, caging him in the chair with his arms.

"Stay away from her. Don't talk, look, or even breathe in her direction." Trystan straightened and kicked the chair from him. Logan skittered back across the scarred floor into the support column as a squeal echoed through the room.

When the chair stopped, Logan stood and flexed his muscles, rolling back his shoulders. "The hell with you. She isn't your property."

"Make no mistake. She's. My. Girl." Trystan's authoritative tone carried a threat.

My face turned tomato red. Everyone heard his words.

I stepped between them and put my hand on Trystan's chest. His muscles constricted under my palms. Deep pain flickered in the shadows of his dark eyes. He pushed me behind him, protecting me.

The crowd parted behind Logan, and Mr. Kennedy entered through the double glass doors with Sheriff Travis at his side, followed by two uniformed officers.

Not taking his eyes off Trystan, Logan yelled, "You're a total loser. Always sticking your nose where it's not wanted."

I saw Steve tugging on Tom's arm.

Trystan squared his shoulders. "Really? Well, I didn't stick my nose into your business while you painted orange and black on the stop signs out back by the track field."

Logan's eyes narrowed. "Who gives a damn?"

Tom stepped closer to Logan and elbowed him in the arm. "You tell him."

I cringed. Couldn't Logan and Tom sense the sheriff's presence behind them?

"You think you've got everything figured out, don't you?" Spittle dripped from Logan's lips.

A group of onlookers parted as movement over Trystan's shoulder caught my attention. A round of snickers rose around us. I shot a glance at the sheriff and his deputies, who stood a short distance behind Logan and Tom, soaking up the conversation.

"Ahh ..." Trystan said. "Well, what about your reckless driving in that black Mustang?"

Tom chuckled. "You idiot. Logan wasn't even with us. And it wasn't a black Mustang. It's a silver Camaro. Can't you even tell the difference?"

Sheriff Travis lowered his chin, his eyes glittering with amusement.

Steve's nostrils flared. "Shut the hell up, Tom!"

My mind whirled.

Tom's jaw dropped.

Logan jerked his head toward Steve.

Steve's face turned purple with rage.

"Enough," Mr. Kennedy barked. "Break this up. Everyone, clear the cafeteria. You guys"—he pointed at each of us—"my office. Now."

Other teachers appeared, guiding students outside.

Trystan reached toward me and grabbed my hand. I closed my mouth, clutched my book and soda in one hand, Trystan's hand in the other, and followed him to Principal Kennedy's office.

Shoes dragged on the floor behind us, followed by the echo of a staccato beat. We entered Principal Kennedy's office, and the others piled in behind us.

"I'm Sheriff Travis. These here are Deputies Marks and Thomas." One of them had his hand resting on his billy club. Sheriff Travis looked at Tom and said, "I take it you're Tom Perry."

Tom's eyes widened.

Sheriff Travis glared at Logan and Steve. "I know you two."

Logan flinched. "What's going on? I've done nothing. You can't arrest me. When my dad hears about this."

"Your dad's the reason we're here," Sheriff Travis said.

Logan paled.

Deputy Marks released his grip on his billy club. "I'm advising you to say nothing."

"Logan Gather, you are not under arrest, but continue with this behavior, and you'll find your butt in jail, right next to Steve and Tom." Logan inched back, leaving Steve and Tom front and center.

A beat of silence stretched into an age. Sheriff Travis nodded to his deputies. Marks and Thomas took out their handcuffs and cuffed Steve and Tom.

"Both of your parents have been notified and will meet you at the station." The sheriff patted them down. "Steve Sellers, Tom Perry—you're under arrest for unauthorized use of a vehicle. You have the right to remain silent. Anything you say can and will be used against you in a court of law. You have the right to an attorney before answering questions. If you cannot afford one, one will be appointed to you. You have a right to have your parents present during questioning. Do you understand these rights?" Steve nodded, glaring at Tom. "Take them to the station. I'll see you back at the station shortly." Sheriff Travis pierced me with his eyes.

"How did you know?" I asked.

"We didn't know for sure." Sheriff Travis lowered his eyes. "Still. We would've caught them sooner had we not been distracted by the barn burnings. It seemed the cases were linked for a while, but investigative work cleared that up." Sheriff Travis looked at me. "Usually, the most valuable information for these cases comes within the first forty-eight hours of the incident, when events are freshest in the witnesses' minds. When we were looking back through your report recently, we noted you'd mentioned the reckless driver who'd run you off the road had the license plate stuck to the back of the car, near the taillights. That prompted us to search numbers for any vehicles with plates attached in case they'd recently gotten speeding tickets."

Sheriff Travis continued, shaking his head. "When that didn't pan out, one of my deputies suggested we try looking at dealership tags. We were desperate and called up local dealers, including Mr. Gather. Let's just say a surveillance video is worth a thousand words. And Tom incriminating himself in public today didn't hurt." Sheriff Travis glared at Logan. "Whatever excuse you had to avoid joining them, count yourself lucky."

Why hadn't I sensed Steve's involvement? I swallowed my anger. "Are they responsible for the school's fire?"

"I don't know." Sheriff Travis's face split into a wide grin. "We'll find out. One of them will talk, and he'll rat out the others."

"What happens now?" Trystan asked.

Sheriff Travis put both his hands on his waist. "We'll see what happens with the interrogation. The evidence we have on them is enough to convict them on the lesser of the charges. If we find they were involved in the fire, more charges will be filed against them, but that's for the courts to determine. You don't need to concern yourselves with it. I appreciate both of you cooperating with us. Kids like you make our jobs much easier." Sheriff Travis looked at Trystan and me, but not at Logan, and left without another word.

Mr. Kennedy's eyes darted back and forth among the three of us. "I don't know what transpired between the three of you, but I hope with everything that's happened already, we can come to the agreement that, until the end of this year, you will stay away from one another—at least at school—unless you can be civilized. I will not tolerate any more problems this year." Principal Kennedy pointed his finger in disapproval at Logan. "And don't think for a minute, Logan, this discussion is completely over. Next week, we will talk about your part in defacing school property."

Logan nodded and left the room. We followed shortly after that.

Trystan's body didn't ease up until we were in the parking lot with Anna, Camden, and Erika.

Camden shifted his stance. "You guys, I'm canceling the bonfire tonight."

"Okay, Camden." Trystan pulled the keys from his pocket. "I'm taking Callie home. Anna, would you take my car back to the house?" He tossed her the keys.

Anna caught them. "What about your dad?"

"He'll be there when I get home."

My gaze darted to Trystan, who looked at me a split second later. He turned from the others and took my hand. We walked to the Jeep, and I handed him my keys.

Minutes later, he pulled onto the main road. Silence hung heavy between us. Uneasiness stirred in me as we passed familiar landmarks.

Once inside my house, I flung myself onto the couch. Numb to the world, I ignored Tesla's nudges at my palm. Trystan reached under my arm, across my middle, and dragged me into his lap. I curled up in the crook of his arm as calm seeped into my body and my mental exhaustion eased. I closed my eyes and slept.

The door banged open, waking us.

"Ah, good, you're home," Gramps said.

I rubbed my eyes, and Trystan sat up straighter, bumping the back of my head with his elbow.

"Gramps, it's not been a good day."

"So, I heard." Gramps set a gallon of milk on the table. "Sheriff Travis called and explained. By the looks of it, neither of you wants to tell me about it."

I was grateful to Gramps for not prying. He set the milk in the fridge. "I don't mean to rush you, Trystan, but I'm thinking you're wanted at home. You both need to get some rest."

"Give us five minutes, okay, Gramps?"

"I'll put the mutt out," Gramps said.

Tesla bounced to the kitchen door.

I leaned back against Trystan. "I can't believe I didn't notice Steve's involvement."

"You're not a mind reader," he murmured.

"I wish I were. It'd be much more useful than my ability to read voice inflections. Although, if I'd heard him speak of it, maybe I could've sensed his involvement, but we never talked about the fire. That should've alerted me. Before, he was always the first one to share gossip."

Trystan stiffened under me. "What did you say?—about reading voice modulations?"

I swallowed. "There's much I don't know about my life, Trystan. I won't lie to you. We've got to talk, and I know we don't have time for all of it right now, but there's something else I've got to tell you before you leave."

The *Jaws* theme song came from his phone. Trystan cursed under his breath, pulled out his phone, and pushed a button. He listened for a second. I could hear a man's voice on the other end, but I couldn't make out the words.

"You what?" He bolted upright, knocking me aside. "To heck with you. No way. You can't do that. I won't submit myself to those tests." Pause. "Good. You can't make us. Screw the elders." Trystan ended the call and swung around to face me.

"What happened?"

"I've got to go. My dad's putting Anna, Colin, and me under intense observation to see if we have abilities."

"Why are you so reluctant to tell your family?"

He raked his fingers through his hair. "It's not the right time to tell anyone. I don't know how I know or why it's not—I just know. Colin agreed last week that it wasn't. Dad's confused about why Colin doesn't have powers yet, since our bloodlines are so strong, and he's over eighteen. He says the elders are desperate. These dead bodies have made him think there's more importance to my brother's visions than he'd thought. My dad's pissed that Anna and Colin have refused to submit themselves to observations. Sebastian and his prophetic vision have pushed Dad to seek if we might have powers." His tone dropped. "I'm sorry, but I've got to get home before my dad starts to work on Anna. She's the one he'll target first to get information. We'll talk about Logan and this mess soon, but I've got to go deal with my dad."

I grabbed for him, grasping nothing but thin air. He was already exiting the house, slamming the door behind him.

I sat alone. Trystan's absence robbed me of the relief I'd felt. A somber reality filled the silent vacuum of my living room. A mental image of the bound-and-gagged man took shape. What was happening?

CHAPTER 33

LONELINESS

"He's gone." Gramps came around the couch and sat next to me. "You know, I miss the nights we use to bunk out here in the living room and fall asleep watching the flames in the wood burner."

I brought my legs up onto the cushion, wrapped my arms around them, and propped my head on my knees. "I used to dread sleeping alone. Nana made a game of putting me to bed or sleeping in here with me so I could get some rest."

"She always knew what to do, just like your mom." Gramps moved closer to me. "There are two couches. We can bunk out here if you'd like, maybe watch a comedy."

"Sounds good." My words faltered.

Gramps pushed himself up and bounded for the kitchen. "I'll make popcorn. You find a movie to throw in."

I fanned through the selections, picked *Baby's Adventure*, then flipped on the TV and surfed the channels. Reality shows consumed most of the stations. I flicked to the local station and noticed a news-alert ribbon running across the bottom of the screen. I turned up the volume.

"The body of Ashworth University graduate Librarian Samuel Avalon was found early this morning near swamps in Wooster, Ohio." As the ticker tape repeated itself at the bottom of the screen, the newscaster onscreen offered details about the incident. "Mr. Avalon was found bound and gagged in the swamps near Brown's Bog. Recent reports confirm that, weeks ago, Roger Avalon, father of the deceased, was found with a single gunshot wound to the head in Egypt. An investigation is underway to see how these murders are linked. Roger Avalon, until recently, worked as a librarian in Alexandria, Egypt. Both men are credited with having assisted in setting up the newly resurrected Library of Alexandria. Ohio Govenor Edward Sanderson had this to say, 'They both cherished life and will be sorely missed.'"

Gramps clicked the power button on the remote. The TV went blank. "You might not have explained much to me, girl, but I'm not too *countrified* to see it's not common for a librarian to have friends in political places." He dropped the remote on the table. "Are you sure you'll be safe with Santos here while I'm gone?"

It had slipped my mind. Gramps planned to leave for PA again. "Yes. It's others I'm worried about, not myself." And the farther you get from here, the safer you'll be.

Tesla sat on his haunches, watched a fly circle around his head, and snapped at it a few times. If only my life could be so easy.

We skipped the movie, and neither one of us could stomach eating the popcorn, but I grabbed one couch, Gramps the other. Tesla curled up on the floor, and, with heavy-lidded eyes, I gave in to sleep. Exhaustion won.

CHAPTER 34

OPPOSITION

"This is the last of the plants." Erika set the potted foliage by the refreshment table inside the cafeteria. Half a dozen people were making final touches to the NYC skyline and other prom decorations. A tall girl with short-cropped hair painted yellow lines on a mock road leading to a photo booth with a working traffic light. The deejay's area had taken on the appearance of the Empire State Building.

I put the fake tree I'd been holding behind the others. "All that's missing is King Kong."

The days after Steve and Tom's arrest had turned to weeks. May hadn't been an easy month. Work and prom decorating had swallowed up my time. And Trystan's dad had stolen every moment when Trystan and I could've talked. Even when he'd show up to work, someone—or something—got in the way. School was a different story. I might have been able to find the time to talk with him alone there, but Taylor showed up at the weirdest times, putting me in defense mode and limiting the right time to talk.

Moods crashed through me like a hurricane.

Erika glanced at the fake Empire State Building and chuckled. "You're a little touchy."

I sat and lowered my head toward my lap. "It's been horrible."

"I couldn't agree more. Everyone's lost it. The locksmith on Second Street is the only one happy about what's been going on lately. Mom told me the owner couldn't keep deadbolts on the shelf. You'd think weeks later, they'd have some idea who murdered that poor guy." She sat in the chair beside me, bumping my leg. "Nothing's been easy since Steve's arrest, not to mention Tom's. It's sad. Steve won't be back this school year other than for final exams. And then to find out Logan's brother, Dylan, instigated taking the car. Dylan was already a prime candidate for jail. But to stoop so low as to burn the school."

"He's the biggest idiot, Erika. He's got everything in the world. Good parents. Good homelife. And he can't even appreciate it."

"I'm glad I have Camden. He's been so protective of me since all this stuff happened. He's earned points with my parents, too. It stinks that Trystan's dad is taking up so much of his time since he's come in from California."

I raised my head. "His family doesn't want us together."

"Why?" Erika sucked in air.

How do I answer that? "Hmm, his dad thinks I'm a distraction." It stung to say the words.

"You're a distraction? Isn't his dad the one that caused Trystan and Anna to miss two school days?" Erika scooped her hair onto her shoulder. "Talk about luck. They're getting a five-day weekend since we don't have school Monday." She stiffened. "Wait. You don't think his dad will stop him from taking you to prom, do you?"

"His dad might not like us dating, but Trystan won't let him get in the way. He's the type that lives up to his commitments." I rubbed my eyes. "Erika, I've got to find a way to talk to him, face to face."

"Go over tonight."

I dropped my hand from my lap. "I can't. I'm meeting Mr. Santos. He's going to move into the apartment."

"His dad's not the only thing interfering with your relationship. How'd you manage to get that apartment cleaned? It must've been worse than my bedroom. I still can't believe Mr. Santos is moving in there. My dad's glad he plans to return to work at the farm, but I'm sure it will take time for him to acclimate to things. Mr. Santos is a hard worker. It won't be easy next fall when he picks up teaching, too." She shook her head. "I'll bet your gramps is glad someone will be around for you after he leaves on Sunday."

"He wouldn't leave for the grain convention if Mr. Santos weren't staying."

"Callie, you're miserable. Trystan missed school. Find Mrs. Glass and see if you can take him his homework. They'll have to let you see him then."

I turned to Erika and gave her a big hug. "Great idea, thanks."

"What are besties for? Why—oh, shoot. Don't forget our hair appointment."

"I won't."

Ten minutes later, I texted Santos to tell him I'd be late and gave him the location of the spare key. I dashed to the main office and caught Principal Kennedy on his way out. After he heard my request, he assisted me in getting Trystan's and Anna's make-up work and books.

If I banged any harder on the Dougrey's door, I would break it. The entry swung open to reveal an elegantly dressed man in a black suit and blue tie. White streaks peppered his dark, curly hair.

"Mr. Dougrey?"

He lowered his head. "Yes?"

"I'm Callie Tresham." The calculating light in his eyes sent a chill pulsating through my nerves. "I'm here to drop off Anna and Trystan's schoolwork."

"Ah." One haughty eyebrow arched. "Do come in, please." He stepped back, folded his arms across his chest, and eyed me with disapproval.

Get to the point. "Are they here?"

"No, my son and Anna went to Ashworth University to talk with Colin." He looked over at the mantle clock. "Which is where I should be."

Invite me in, and then tell me you're leaving. I can play that game, too. I tilted my chin. I marched right into the living room and bit my inner cheek. Sunlight fell upon the floors.

"It's a lovely day, isn't it?"

A beat of silence stretched before a low chuckle broke the odd moment. "My, oh my, you are amusing. I can see why my son's drawn to you." He closed the door behind him and crossed his arms over his chest again. "You are not at all what I expected."

You have no idea how right you are. "Where would you like me to put these books?"

"Over there on the table will do."

I placed the books on the cherry surface. "Can you tell them I stopped by?"

"That I will."

He grabbed an orange from the basket on the table. "You know this relationship can't go on for long. Trystan has responsibilities in California after he graduates next year."

"Yes, he mentioned working at your company." Implicating that Trystan would be taking over the reins at his father's business someday seemed safer than saying, *I know that you're a Theran and that your son will someday take your place on the council.*

His eyes flickered to mine. "Let's get to the point, my dear. This infatuation will die down, and, over time, it will disappear."

I smiled. "Then you've nothing to fear."

"Clever and direct. For what it's worth, I like you, and I don't want you to get hurt. You may as well accept it now. Eventually, you will grow apart, attend different colleges, and my son will come to work with me after graduating from Ashworth."

I forced a wider smile. "A lot can happen in a year."

He tilted his head a fraction and gave me a perplexed look. "You are the one contention on which my son will not waiver. For the sake of peace in this house, I will not contest your prom plans."

We parted. I took a deep breath, my lungs filling with relief. Mr. Dougrey wasn't horrible. Just a businessman concerned about his investment—his son.

CHAPTER 35

INFORMATION OVERLOAD

I turned onto the drive, glimpsing the tree line in the distance. The foliage reached for the horizon. Tesla greeted me before I'd managed to get the Jeep door shut.

"How'd you get out, boy?"

"Your granddad left him with Max and me." Santos walked over, leaning on his cane. "Max's in the mill, grinding grain. You know, I like your granddad."

I adjusted my purse while Santos caught up with me. "Sorry, I wasn't here on time."

"No problem." He smiled. "Friends helped me move into the apartment."

People crowded my space at school. Was this to be the case at home now, too? "You have friends that live around here?"

He lifted his eyes to meet mine. "It was unavoidable. My associates from the agency knew I would need help with moving. I couldn't turn them down."

I turned. One foot was placed on the porch step. "You mean you let others..."

"Other Therans, your great-aunt's friends, helped me move."

Air seeped from my lungs. I leaned against the railing and slipped down onto my butt.

"She's still alive?"

"Yes, she is. Our group is small compared to the ancients, but she is a wise woman who leads the agency and us. She's the reason we can infiltrate the Ancient Faction." Mr. Santos sat down on the stoop and rested his cane on the railing near a couple of broken sticks in the flowerbed. Tesla at his side, his tail dusting the ground. "I'm glad her existence isn't a surprise to you. She'll curse me for not telling her we've met, but I don't feel it's my place to tell her. Anyhow, I want to discover what you know of our existence."

Anxiety sank its claws into me. All these bits of facts surrounded me. Ancients. Remnants. Crimson-blood. Half-blood. Dead people. And it was all localized here, at my doorstep.

"What do I know?"

"Did your parents ever talk about the libraries?"

I rubbed the strap of my purse between my fingers. "I've heard of them." I didn't lie.

He leaned over and patted Tesla on the head. "For millenniums, Ancient Therans protected libraries. These libraries are sacred as they hold all of history's past treasures that transcend time. Truth be told, we've yet to uncover the significance of every object." His voice was congenial. "Thousands of years ago, each Theran had one of three tasks. Searchers were one group. From what studies show, they were detectives."

"Wait. Wait. Are you saying long ago they had detectives?"

"Not necessarily. However, their job was to investigate and explore. Call it what you want, Callie."

"No, I want to get this right." I toyed with a string that hung from my shirt. "I know how important history is."

"Then it's safer to say that searchers were known to root out information and find ancient historical treasures. Despite their existence, we have not discovered every secret the world knows. The Dead Sea Scrolls are a good example of a missing treasure. They weren't found until the twentieth century."

He rubbed his thumb over the top of the cane handle. "I've learned all this from research. Since the War of Knowledge, there's been a great disconnect between the past and present. Most Therans—nearly eighty percent, according to some reports—fell to the second task. They assisted in documenting and storing the scrolls or tomes that were found by the searchers, keeping records of each treasure's lineage. These Therans were known as collectors.

"Wow! This is really cool information. So, in other words, librarians."

"'That's a way of looking at it." He raised his shoulder a fraction. "Some argue there was another group that had a duty, called protectors. There is no proof they ever existed."

I swallowed. "Then, how can you mention them?"

"Because there's an ancient tome which speaks of them."

"Do you believe?"

"Anything's possible," Mr. Santos said. "But then I chase mysteries for a living."

"Where'd you find this information?" I pulled at my shirt.

"What little is known comes from various ancient tomes, which could easily have been misread and misinterpreted. Only a couple of Therans have deciphered the ancient writings over the past two thousand years."

That would make Trystan very valuable.

His lips formed a straight line. "Researchers have speculated fewer than three percent of Therans were protectors."

I gasped. "Three percent. Wait! That's not many."

He glanced at my hands as I pulled the stitch from my shirt. "Don't hold me to that figure. It could even be less. Of course, this was long ago, before the War of Knowledge, when the Remnants broke from the Ancients' Faction. Theories have been circulating for centuries. Some say the protectors were the most powerful of the three. Supposedly, protectors' abilities were more powerful than what Therans possess today." He shrugged. "It doesn't matter. If they did or didn't exist, they're an extinct breed, now."

"Extinct breed?" My stomach lurched, causing me to tug the string from my shirt, leaving a frayed edge. I held the long thread before me. "Oops! Didn't mean to do that."

"You seem awfully nervous."

"Nervous?" I flicked the strand on the deck. "Ahh, no. This is just interesting. So, you were saying."

His eyes narrowed. "I'm glad you're taking an interest. But if you're not careful, you might destroy your shirt."

"It's old. No big deal." I flicked my wrist. "So, you were saying."

"Never forgetting history is important." He looked past me, facing the mill. "But things have changed for us now. Ancient Therans control through influence. They infiltrate the human world and conceal the libraries' locations. Some Therans work in political positions, but most work in other fields—as journalists or scientists. Confusion is the major tool ancients used in limiting the humans' knowledge of the libraries' locations. However, the ancients have also had to use other measures. Human archaeologists are the biggest threat. They like to unearth discoveries, and some work close to library sites. That's when political influence is used. Given the right incentives, countries will ban digs in certain areas.

"We may rely on these measures, but it's still important to focus on education, even for humans who have access to the Alexandrian Library—if only to that above-ground section. Knowledge strengthens the mind, allowing Therans and humans to live freely. We've seen countries controlled because civilians have limited access to information. This is dangerous. After several generations of suppressing humans' access to knowledge, an established paradigm exists, making it easier to keep humans under control. Because humans outnumber us significantly, keeping universities and colleges open is paramount. When people fear the administration, there is tyranny. In areas of dictatorships, one's decisions are no longer one's own, but when the controlling leadership fears the people, the people have liberty. Ancient and Remnant Therans agree that knowledge is the true power source."

That was a lot to swallow. "What's wrong with them knowing about us?"

"Long ago, some humans did know of us and the contents in the catacombs beneath the Alexandrian Library." He picked up a stick and tore a piece of bark from it. "Therans shared information with select humans. However, our bloodlines were being depleted because some Therans believed it was okay to marry humans. Intermarriage between Therans and humans over time decreased the power in the bloodline of our children, and our Theran seal—or, as others would say, birthmark—faded. Our birthmarks began to disappear, having been depleted by human blood. That's why we only marry within our kind."

"This is so much information." The words died on my tongue.

"Yes, it is. I'm explaining this because you may not understand that the Theran blood builds and strengthens the longer the bloodlines stay pure."

Santos's sorrowful eyes flickered at me. "Sometime later, the power struggle over the Alexandrian Library culminated in the War of Knowledge. Some humans and Therans fought to possess the contents of the library—and over the practice of Human-Theran intermarriage. Ancients won the battle and control of the library but didn't stop the practice of intermarriage with humans until much later with the Remnant Faction—that is, those Therans, our ancestors, who'd escaped during the war." He shifted his leg. "Humans have short-term memories, and keeping history alive is important. It's the only way to avoid repetition of a horrifying past."

I gasped. "Horrifying past?"

The stick in Santos's hand snapped in two. "Some humans who mated with Therans actually developed and maintained their capabilities—strength or healing wisdom—passing these on to their human ancestors, wreaking havoc on the world. They created the witch trials and burned innocent people at the stake."

"No, no." I clutched my chest. "That can't be."

"I'm telling you the truth. For some, Therans possessed powers, whereas humans didn't. Humans became scared of what they couldn't understand. Freedom of education, any kind of information, is paramount to understanding the world. If we forget our history, we're doomed to repeat it." He cleared his throat. "Fear of repeating our past mistakes keeps us from revealing who we are, and it's why it's prohibited for us to be intimately involved with humans. This unwritten law protects them as much as it does us." Mr. Santos glanced down, avoiding eye contact. "While some Therans and humans have been known to befriend one another, even to date, their relationships are always monitored closely by Theran elders."

My palms became sweaty. My heart beat faster, louder, in my ear. How closely did the elders watch Trystan? Did they watch me?

"How do they keep track of one another?"

He arched an eyebrow. "Once a Theran mother has a child, she's eager to report it to the elders. From there, the name is registered in the Ancients Central Information Bank. Remnants keep track of their offspring, separately, but also in a central information bank."

I tapped my fingers on my knee. "Is that how they find out about others' abilities?"

"Around one's eighteenth birthday, if one has power, one goes through a sort of transformation, not unlike the metamorphic stage of a butterfly. Afterward, one goes to a camp. Around here, it's Ashworth University—and ancient professors assess one's value and whether one has a true capability. If so, they work to help develop it."

I waited seconds, allowing this information to sink in. Everything he said confirmed Trystan's words and my mother's letter, but Mr. Santos gave me an in-depth viewpoint, filling in the areas I hadn't understood.

Are those the skill tests Mr. Dougrey wanted for Trystan, Colin, and Anna? My gut clenched with concern. "You've learned a lot about the ancients."

He flicked a piece of bark off his lap. "I infiltrated their ranks years ago and have lived among them since."

"Why?"

"There's a trickle-down effect. What happens to humans indirectly affects us, the same as the ancients. Remnant military is dispatched to keep track of what transpires in the ancient and human world."

"So, for thousands of years, Remnants have lived on the sidelines and observed ancients so that they can ... what?"

The skin around his eyes crinkled. "Remnants have two goals: to keep our bloodlines pure and to hunt for the lost library. We have managed to keep our bloodlines *purer* much longer than the ancients."

"Okay, but both factions believe in keeping the bloodlines pure. So, why not reveal yourselves to the Ancient Faction?"

"We like our secrecy, Callie. And our motives are still different from the Ancient Faction. We seek the lost library. Most ancients don't believe it exists."

He preaches freedom of information and openness but wants to keep the Remnants hidden. Why? What was this lost library? And why did the Remnants hide in the dark and let the ancients take risks? My stomach swirled with anger, draining me of what energy I'd had. More questions surfaced. I didn't have time to make sense of this lost library.

"What do you make of Samantha and Taylor being here?"

"Ancients tend to stick together."

"Yeah, and there's Ashworth University," I said. Santos might believe it, but I didn't. I couldn't shake loose the niggling suspicion that they were here for something more. Taylor, having used his powers, was an ominous sign.

Santos picked up his cane, stood, and rubbed at his thigh. "You don't believe it?"

"It doesn't take a mathematician to figure out two dead Therans from the same family equals trouble. And the dead professor. Humans have even investigated the incidents. What I find odd is, Taylor's Theran and has managed to fill your vacant teaching position. Not to mention, he messes up on historical quotes. I can't prove it, but Taylor and his girlfriend are mixed up in this somehow."

"How'd you know about the dead ...?" He didn't finish his thought but gave me a measuring look. "You know other Therans, don't you?" Silence stretched several beats. "The night of the fire. The Dougrey boy, ah, what's his name?"

"Trystan. He's my boyfriend, and he works here."

He clenched his eyes. "Does he know you're Theran?"

"Yes." Caution reared its head. "But he knows nothing about the Remnants or my life story."

His brows shot up toward his hairline. "He's not asked?"

The warning faded from my mind. "He's not pried. I'm sure he's curious, but from the start, all he's ever done is support me."

"I've heard he's different from his father, not that the father's bad." Santos flexed his fingers. "Does his family know you're Theran?"

"No. And Trystan is sworn to secrecy."

"So, the ancients believe you're human—yet you're dating the chief elder's son."

"They're chalking it up to a teenage infatuation."

"Callie, remember what I told you just a short while back." His eyes narrowed. "You're under a microscope so long as you're dating him. Don't let it slip about us. The ancients mustn't find out that the Remnants exist."

A horn honked, and a car came down the drive, but it didn't distract me. I was angry and confused and still wanted answers. "While all of you try to keep your secrets from one another to protect your precious libraries, something's unfolding, and you know it. The ancients know it. Lord Avalon and his son's death are just the start of something more dreadful. Go back to my great aunt and that agency of yours. Ask her what visions she's had. Ask her about Ptolemy's revelation. Ask her what she knows about Sebastian Dougrey's prediction. You told me you'd once worked for the Remnant Secret Service. Use your contacts and find out what's going on." I took a breath of air. "I won't volunteer information about the Remnant Faction, but if Trystan asks, I won't lie."

CHAPTER 36
FACTS, QUESTIONS, & UNCERTAINTY

A breeze stirred, chasing a squirrel up the tree on my front lawn. Trystan's car came to a stop. My heart accelerated as he got out and approached Santos and me.

His smile accentuated his dimple. "Hello."

"Ah, hi." I swung around to face Santos, swallowing my anger. "This is Trystan." I looked back to Trystan. "And this is Mr. Santos."

Trystan leaned in to shake Santos's hand. "It's nice to meet you finally."

"Likewise." Santos sounded more annoyed than I liked.

An undercurrent of tension skimmed my nerves. "Mr. Santos moved his stuff out back."

Trystan nodded. "Cool. I'll be seeing you around, then."

My phone buzzed in my pocket. "Give me a minute. This might be Gramps." I pulled it out and looked at the screen. Immediately, I tucked my cell back inside my purse.

Trystan's brow arched.

I rolled my eyes. "It's Steve." He'd called a hundred times since the cops had arrested him, and I'd ignored every call.

"Well." Santos adjusted his weight, using his cane for balance. "I've got some more unpacking to do. Callie, if you need anything, let me know." He walked away.

My frustration eased the closer he got to the mill. I'd sensed no major red flags while we'd talked. He'd spoken honestly, but facts, questions, and uncertainties still crowded my thoughts.

I trudged up the steps. "Come on in. Do you want a Znapple?"

"I don't have long." The warmth of his hand touched the small of my back. "Callie, how'd you ever convince my dad to give us some peace?"

I turned around. His fingers trailed along my skin, his palm settling on my hip. He was inches from me. I lowered my gaze. His full bottom lip was moist as his thumb stroked my arm. The touch warmed my heart.

"He's got his own agenda. Trust me, it wasn't anything I said."

Trystan leaned in and rested his forehead against mine, wrapping his arms around me in a warm hug. He arched his back and lifted me off the porch.

"The house has been a virtual battlefield the past few weeks. This afternoon, when he visited me on campus, he said he'd met you and decided to give us some space." He set me down, my feet back on the ground. "However,

it came about, I'm grateful." He straightened, whispering, "With the investigation into the murders keeping
him so busy, Dad had to back off on the aptitude tests.
He's been on the phone with the libraries over the past
few days and has had me sitting in on council meetings. He thinks my apprenticeship should start now. He's
even given me a key to the library." He raised his eyes in
a mocking gesture. "It's a token of trust."

"Do you think it's wise to keep things still a secret?"

The wind blew loose strands of hair over my collarbone. Trystan wrapped his finger around a curl.

"According to investigators, three Ashworth students
have reported someone following them. One of them
said that someone tried to drug her drink when she was
out with friends. What's ironic is all of them are Ashworth students who possess powers. Whoever's behind
this and the murders is covering their tracks. Fear is
running deep. Everyone's on guard."

Could Mr. Taylor and his cronies be after control?

"Everyone's scrambling to find motives. Since Lord
Avalon and his son didn't have abilities, their murders
don't seem to fit with these newer findings. An intel-
ligence officer suggested today that the incidents are
two separate matters, as Lord Avalon's older son and
heir has the ability of mind distraction, yet no one's
contacted him. Mind distraction is simple but effective.
One has the ability to interrupt another's concentration,
to distract, and to mentally throw off course, like my dad.
There's more to the power of mental distraction, but I
can explain it another time." His other hand dropped
from my arm, finding my fingers. "I've researched matters, even spoken with an instructor. If you're willing, I'd
like to help you learn the extent of your power. I wish
you'd let Instructor James work with you, but that would
expose you to other Therans. Mr. James had heard of

seers who had dormant powers. Cal, my brother, Sebastian, trusted his sight. Unfortunately, he couldn't predict his death, but his sight offered him a better understanding of the future. You must learn to navigate and control your capabilities. Your sight saved Anna. It might help in the investigation. Are you willing?"

"When do we start?"

Wariness stole into his eyes. "Not tonight."

"When then?" I could've raised the dead with the curses that stacked up in my head. We didn't have time. "Jings, Trystan, we can't keep putting things off. I need to talk—"

Trystan's warm finger came to rest under my chin. My heart constricted as his eyes deepened to chocolate brown, and words disappeared. Trystan wetted his lips. His eyes gravitated toward my mouth. I wrapped my arms around him. Physical strength emanated from him as his warm, soft lips pressed feather-light kisses to my forehead, traveling slowly to my cheek. His words whispered in my ear, "Hmm ... vanilla."

I embraced the refuge of his arms.

"Harrumph."

Trystan jerked back as if a match had burned him, but he kept hold of my hand.

"Didn't mean to interrupt." Max cleared his throat again. "I wanted you to know. I turned off the lights and locked up the mill."

I tucked my head into Trystan's shoulder, trying to smother a chuckle. How embarrassing. "Ah. Thanks, Max."

"See you Monday." Max placed a hat on his head. "You two have fun at the dance."

"Thanks, Max."

Trystan squeezed my fingers. "I've got to run, too."

"Wait." I tugged on his hand as he stepped away. "I want to talk now."

He turned to face me. "It will have to be tomorrow or Sunday. I'm already late, and I don't want to piss off my dad when he's just starting to come around."

They both drove away, and a feeling of loneliness filled me.

CHAPTER 37

KISSES

Gramps's eyes widened, and he set his soda on the counter. "Ah, if I were forty years younger, I'd ask you to prom, dear. I love that dress on you." His smile dissolved as his forefinger circled my face. "This is supposed to be fun. Instead, you look haggard."

"When will you be back?"

"You're troubled. I can tell you're changing the subject." He picked up his drink. "I don't like leaving you, but I'll be home by Wednesday at the latest. Mr. Santos said he'd check in on you. Don't you fret, dear."

He was leaving tonight. I would come home to an empty house.

The doorbell rang. Tesla scurried around the corner, wagging his tail.

"Well, quit standing there. The door won't open on its own. Shoot, now, don't take off until I get the camera and take some pictures."

I opened the door.

My breath froze. Trystan was soooo hot.

I was mesmerized. He wore the blue-black, shimmery suit we'd picked out and a wickedly handsome smile. His broad shoulders filled the blazer, and his royal blue tie matched my dress. In his hand, he clutched a single, short-stemmed crimson rose to his chest, a white silk ribbon dangling from its stem. A lock of dark hair fell across his forehead. My heart squeezed, and my breath returned. His expression melted away all my worries.

The jangle of keys interrupted the moment.

"Here," Gramps said.

Gramps tossed Trystan the keys to the Mustang, then put his hand on the back of the kitchen chair.

"Neither of you asked to borrow her, but I want this to be a special night. Her tank's full. Drive her carefully, and just so you know, she pulls to the right." He met Trystan's gaze. "I trust you with both my girls."

"Thank you, sir. We'll be careful."

After Gramps took some pictures, we left and met up with Erika, Camden, and Anna at the Old Reserve Inn. Anna had insisted on driving herself, as she didn't want to intrude in our space. I ignored the press of people in the dining area, focused on the moment, and pushed away from the worries that tried to creep into my brain. Though, something wasn't right. I scanned the restaurant and saw nothing out of place. I didn't recognize anyone, but tension coiled in my gut.

"Cal," Trystan whispered. "Stop examining the room as if someone's going to jump us."

"You're right. I know." I caught Anna glancing in my direction. I gave her a weak smile. Excitement collided with uncertainty. "I'm just nervous with Gramps's being gone."

Erika swallowed the bite of her food. "We could always go back to your house and skip post prom."

"Not going to happen." I shook my head. "Gramps wouldn't like that."

"Man, an empty house screams of partay." Camden laughed. "We could clean things up really quick. No need for your granddad to know anything."

Camden's words sunk into my head like lightning. "No need for your granddad to know anything." That had to be it. Keeping secrets from Gramps and Trystan was stressing me, but I couldn't open up about them—not all of my secrets.

"Sorry, Cam. But I'm not having any last-minute party."

We enjoyed our meals and headed to the prom. Trystan parked Gramps's car next to another Mustang—a much newer model with all the bells and whistles. Cars packed the school parking lot. A crowd waited outside the entrance doors as others craned their necks to watch us get out of the Mustang.

Trystan's eyes flashed. "This'll be a blast."

"Are you trying to convince me or yourself?"

"Tonight's special." He winked, but I could hear the reservation in his voice. "It's not every night I get to dance with you."

Recent homicides intruded on my thoughts, but I had to constrain them and act normal.

"Did I tell you I'm a klutz in heels? Dance with me at your own risk."

We entered the school. The splendor of white lights traced the New York skyline around the lobby, and colored lights glowed on a spectacular dance floor, surrounded by plants of different heights in the outer corners. Music flowed from hidden speakers. We stood on the outside looking in at hundreds of teenagers crowded on the floor.

"You're so beautiful." Trystan's thumb rubbed my palm.

My toes curled. Warmth ignited, sending sparklers through my body. "Thanks."

He squeezed my hand. "Come on. Let's find the others."

Camden, Erika, and Anna swarmed us. Sandy had a new, not-slimy guy on her arm.

"My bestie." Erika pulled on the end of her swooping braid. "You look fantastic with all that glitz and sparkle around you."

Anna slid up next to me. "Next time, I'm buying flats. These shoes are pure torture."

"Wear them long enough, and you'll get used to them," Sandy said as she trailed off with her new boyfriend, and Jessica showed up on Tony's arm.

"This place rocks." Tony looked over his shoulder and smiled at Jessica. "Let's grab drinks."

Camden jerked his thumb over his shoulder. "I like this song, Erika. Come on."

Erika, in a whirlwind of giggles, disappeared with Camden. Her red dress hung perfectly, and the sequins around the bodice emphasized her slender figure. And Anna's glamorous garb struck me. Her new hairstyle enhanced her neck, and the green lace that covered her shoulders gave her the appearance of a magical princess.

Trystan leaned toward me, his arm around my waist, and whispered, "Tonight, all your slow dances are mine, agreed?"

Before I could respond, two things happened. Taylor emerged from behind a fake palm tree with another guy who had reddish-brown hair. The strobe light flashed, giving me glimpses of Taylor's grim facial expression as he kept pointing outside. The other guy kept nodding. Then Logan moved, blocking Taylor like an unwanted pest.

I stiffened. I hadn't expected Taylor to chaperone the dance.

"Callie, you look great," Logan said with a megawatt smile.

"I agree." Trystan gave me a weak smile as he glanced over my head at the faces behind us.

"Ahh, thanks."

Logan's eyes flickered with frustration to Trystan and immediately back to me. "Can you dance?"

Avoiding Logan was impossible, but I'd do anything to circumvent a scene. "Ah, yeah, sure." I released Trystan's hand. "I'll be back in a few."

Trystan nodded.

Seconds into the song, Logan leaned in toward me. "Steve called me. He actually apologized to my dad for taking one of the cars from the lot. Guess the threat of a jail sentence has knocked his ego down several pegs."

"Where does your brother fit into all of this?"

"Dylan's an idiot." Logan swung his hips awkwardly from side to side, drawing spectators. "He talked Steve into it. Dad's threatened him with the military, but Dad's all talk. It'll never happen. Steve told me you haven't been answering his calls."

"Logan, don't spoil a good moment by bringing up Steve anymore." This dance couldn't end quickly enough. I had to change the subject. Talking with Logan was like dodging land mines—I didn't know what safe territory was. "Who sings this song?"

"It's Tyler Marson's new song. He's really cool."

"I like the beat." The music droned on while the conversation fizzled. Even though Logan was actually being nice, I wanted to ditch him and find Trystan.

I glanced around and saw Trystan at the opposite end of the lobby from Taylor. Trystan's back was pressed against the brick wall, scanning the crowd as he conversed with Anna. The homicides had all three of us nervous, though Taylor had me jumpy.

When the song finally ended, I tried to head over to Trystan, but Tony and Jessica distracted me, drawing me into their little circle for a couple of dances. Finally, the DJ played a slow song, and I slipped my way over to Trystan. Though, dancing had been a good distraction and a way to keep my eye on Taylor. He hadn't abandoned his corner near the palm tree since the brown-haired boy left.

Tonight was great. However, a disturbing edginess lurked in the recesses of my mind. I was drowning in the pressure of maintaining all these secrets. I had to talk with Trystan about Mr. Taylor and Samantha.

"Come on, let's dance." Trystan guided me back toward the floor, and my thoughts evaporated. He eased my troubled thoughts of Taylor. My mind worked in overdrive. It's not like Taylor wasn't part of the school staff—he had a reason to be here.

Trystan's warm hands slid around my waist. We skirted the edge of the floor as the second song played. He pulled me against him, and I rested my head on his shoulder. Someone must've opened the doors because a cool breeze caressed my skin.

Camden, Erika, Anna, Trystan, and I danced late into the night. Other friends came in and out of our small circle, but the five of us stayed together. The moment a slow song played over the speakers, Trystan's arms encircled my waist.

Eventually, the night was winding down, and people collected by the door. Some had already left for post-prom.

"Can we get a drink?" Trystan asked.

"Sure." I followed him through the corridor to the refreshment table. We grabbed a pop each and exited through the double glass doors to the courtyard, where we stood near the brick wall.

I sipped my drink as the fresh air awakened my senses. Trystan craned his neck, stretched up on the balls of his feet, and looked over the school grounds in every direction.

"What are you doing?"

He stepped toward me, leaving but an inch between us, and took my cup.

"Come on."

We ditched the sodas in the trash and stayed tight to the corner of the school by the darkened trees as we walked, far from the parking lot lights. The breeze toyed with the bottom of my gown.

The music faded into the background. He stopped and pulled me to his chest, his arms wrapped around me like a glove. The breeze continued to blow, cooling me. I pulled my hair back behind my ear and met the hesitant amusement in his eyes.

He released one hand, and his finger traced my jaw. "Have you ever been kissed on the lips?"

I shivered, shaking my head, reluctant to admit my lack of experience. "Have you?"

His finger trailed down my face to the back of my arm until both his hands again circled my waist.

"No."

It's amazing how one simple, single-syllable word could make a person feel so special. His hands didn't roam. He just held me close. His fingers caressed my back. I pressed my face into the neck of his shirt, just below his ear, inhaling his musky, spring-like scent.

His touch, so unfamiliar, felt so right.

He moved in until his chin touched the side of my face. I went up on my toes. His lips slowly–lightly–brushed mine, and my arms circled his neck. His mouth became softer as mine opened to his deepening kiss. The pressure from his lips melted my resolve as a shock of electrical current cascaded through my body.

Trystan stopped, and I gasped for a breath of air against his mouth.

"This relationship," his thumb brushed my lips, "is even more special than I could've imagined."

A loud computerized beep charged the air, and lights flashed from the parking lot.

Trystan jerked away from me. "What the–"

"Oh, no. Isn't that where you parked Gramps's car?"

We dashed across the school grounds into the parking lot and pushed through a crowd of peers to find the Mustang next to Gramps's had keyed marks along the fender and hood.

Fear wormed its way through me. Taylor! Did he have the reddish-brown-haired guy damage the Mustang–the wrong Mustang? If so, why?

It took over half an hour before we could leave, as the cop cars blocked our way. We stayed with Anna, Erika, and Camden. No one said anything about the damaged Mustang. Finally, the cops left.

Trystan tugged at his tie. "Hey, I'm going to drop off Callie at her place so she can change." He looked at Erika and Camden. "We'll meet up at the party." And then he looked at Anna. "Do you want to follow us back to Callie's house? We can wait for her to get ready, then head home to change for the party ourselves."

Part of me wanted to scream, *we can't go to a freakin' party*. The other part of me questioned if I was even thinking right. After all, Taylor hadn't left the school. He could've been speaking to any one of our classmates. And who's to say it had anything to do with damaging a car? Someone else could've keyed Van Decamp's vehicle.

Trystan clenched his jaw. The killings had us all nerved up.

"Are you sure I won't be intruding?" Anna gave a weak smile. "I feel like a third wheel around here."

Camden snickered. "You would've had a date if you weren't so picky."

Anna's shoulders drooped. "You were all selective and got lucky."

Erika blushed red, accepted the compliment, and leaned into Camden. "See you all shortly."

"Come on." I bumped my elbow into Anna's side. "Follow us back."

A lingering group still hung around the damaged Mustang. They moved for us as Trystan backed up. Anna followed us out of the parking lot in the other vehicle.

I clamped down on my nerves. My overactive imagination was out of control. Not everything that went wrong had to connect to the killings. Ugh! I needed to focus on the good things in life.

Cars passed us. Their headlights illuminated the inside of the Mustang, including Trystan. I mentally traced the contour of his face, stopping at the fullness of his lips. I touched my mouth with my fingertips. I'd experienced my first official kiss tonight, which was amazing. This was the best night *ever*. *Best* kiss ever.

CHAPTER 38

DAGGER

O nce we hit my drive, an intense, threatening feeling pulled my gaze to the property across the mill. It was too bright. I'd left the loading dock light on, but brightness stretched onto the grass across the lawn, opposite from where the beam was set to illuminate. The double wooden doors under the overhang were open.

I leaned forward in my seat. "Something's not right."

Trystan parked the car well before we reached the house and leaned closer to the wheel. "Didn't your gramps leave already?"

"Yes, Gramps left, but Max shouldn't be here."

"Would Mr. Santos have keys to the mill?"

I glanced at him. "No."

Tap, tap sounded from the driver's side window. Trystan rolled it down.

"Quit talking," Anna murmured. "I'm dying to ditch these pumps."

Trystan rested his arm over the steering wheel. "Shh. We're trying to figure out why the mill's open when it shouldn't be."

Anna crouched down enough that I could see part of her face through the window. "Can't be too bad—the dog's out."

I glanced up. Anna was right. Tesla sat on the loading dock floor. I shivered. My intuition threw me a warning.

"That's odd. He shouldn't be out." I opened the door, got out, and scooped up the hem of my dress to keep it from dragging on the gravel on the way to the mill. Trystan and Anna followed.

"Anna, call Colin—*now*," Trystan said.

Anna pulled out her phone and dialed Colin, keeping pace with us.

Tesla whined from the loading dock platform. As we approached, his snout lowered, meeting mine.

I dropped my gown and stroked my fingers through his coat of fur. "He must've been up in the woods. He has burrs on the underside of his belly. Did Gramps forget to lock you up?" I lowered my hand and approached the steps.

"Your grandfather might accidentally forget to lock up the dog, but not the mill."

Trystan's words caught my attention as my foot touched the bottom step. I swallowed my anxiety and pushed the warning aside, taking the second step. Thankfully, Gramps's car wasn't here, so he must've left.

Trystan's hand latched onto my wrist, stopping me. He slid in front of me and climbed the staircase. I crept alongside him. He pushed at the entrance door, which creaked open, giving us a view of the office.

Tesla pushed past us, his body rigid, ears drawn back.

Trystan stuck out his arm and blocked me from moving forward.

"What in the heck?" The drawers all down one side of Gramps's desk were open, as were those in the filing cabinet. Both chairs were clear across the room, and business papers scattered the floor.

My breath lodged in my throat.

A six-inch knife stabbed the wall, pinning a folded paper next to Trystan's name on the board. Its wooden, two-toned handle, with dark and light inlay, sported a crest with the image of an eagle, its wings spread wide, its talons clutching a single star.

Tiny hairs on the back of my neck stood at attention. "That's the emblem on Ella's blanket."

Trystan turned to me, placing his hands on my shoulders. "You recognize it?" His eyes burned with concern.

I glanced over at Anna. She stood outside, twenty feet from us. I bit into my lip to stop the flow of words, closing my eyes.

Anna's shoes clicked along the concrete. "Colin's on his way."

I inhaled, opened my eyes, and whispered, "I've tried to talk–"

"Not hard enough." His dark voice chilled the air.

"You haven't made it easy, either."

Trystan's hands dropped from my shoulders. He took two long strides to the board and yanked the knife from the wall. I snatched the dagger and paper from him, turning it over in my hand, knowing what I would see–the same seal embedded in black wax.

I broke the seal and unfolded the letter.

STOP DATING THE HUMAN. OR WE WILL WIPE THE SLATE CLEAN OF POLLUTED BLOOD.

Cryptic words, but the meaning smacked me. Whoever had written this note assumed I was a polluted human. No one but Trystan, Gramps, and Mr. Santos knew I was Theran, and Trystan still believed I was a half-breed.

The glint of the knife brought my past haunts to life in my mind. Could I survive another attack? How would I protect Trystan and his family? Gramps? The folded paper grew damp in my cold hands. I looked back at the single sentence and read it again. The words seared themselves into my brain. Mr. Santos had been right—Taylor's group was watching us.

"What's it say?" Anna approached us and asked.

I ignored her and met Trystan's blazing eyes. I held out the paper to him.

He took it and read. His fingers trembled.

A knock came from the side of the mill. "Trystan?"

"In here, Colin."

Tesla sat on his haunches near me.

Colin entered the office. "What happened in here?"

Trystan closed the distance between us and slid his hand around my wrist, seizing the knife from my grasp. "What do you make of this?"

Colin took the knife. Anna hovered at his side.

"It's old." He placed the dagger on his finger above the hilt. "And well balanced, but I've never seen this symbol before." He looked at Trystan and me. "Is this why Anna called?" "Not just that. Look at this." Trystan handed over the creased paper.

Colin and Anna examined the note. Colin lowered the paper and caught my eye over its top edge.

"Callie knows we're Theran." Trystan's words brought silence to the room.

The silence increased the tension, twisting my nerves tighter. Trystan and Colin held a brief but severe staring match.

Colin's nostrils flared. "Of all the asinine things. You expose us and, at the same time, risk her life through association."

Nails scraped along the floor as Tesla moved to touch my leg. He snarled.

"Stop, Colin!" Trystan raised his hand. "There's more to this than you know. What I want to know is why they are trying to discourage me from dating Cal. Why did they nail it in the wall here? Heck, Max could've found it. Why not leave it at our house?"

"Because you work here," Anna said.

"No," Colin snapped. "Either they've gotten desperate or reckless. And the longer this is drawn out, I'd say both."

"That's exactly what I thought."

"It's almost as if they want to get caught. Or ..."

Colin's words had muted to the background. Something niggled at my consciousness. My eyes narrowed in on the hilt of the stiletto. The crest. Ella's purple blanket. How'd Tesla get out? No. No. Did someone find the chest?

"*NO*." I bunched up my skirt and dashed down the mill steps toward the house, a herd of footsteps at my back. Without thinking, I ran through the open door into the kitchen, stopping just before I tripped over the books scattered on the floor. Papers from the secretary drawers covered the ground and couches. The light stand was on its side in front of the wood burner. Smashed on the floor was one of the two pictures of my parents and sister, the portrait torn in two.

I darted out of the living room and pushed open my bedroom door. The chest sat, *untouched*, below curtain-covered windows.

Trystan came up behind me. "Talk to me."

I looked over my shoulder.

Emotions flickered across his face. I couldn't identify them. He stepped back, away from me. The air around us chilled as Anna and Colin flanked him. United they stood.

I turned the rest of the way around and tentatively slipped my foot back, hearing the tap of my heel hit the floor. I closed my eyes.

My perfect night had fractured into chaos and confusion.

"Cal, talk to me." Trystan's words were softer, but his undertone carried weight.

I stepped back, hitting the backs of my thighs against the bed. I collapsed onto it under the weight of my fatigue. I opened my eyes to see the dress pooling around me. Tesla sat on his haunches at my side.

Colin gripped Trystan's forearm. "Trystan, I don't like this. Why would elders leave a dagger with a threatening message at her house when your dad's fully aware of your infatuation with her?" His eyes narrowed. "In case Trystan hasn't told you, Callie, we don't date humans. He's broken a rule by being so involved and protective of you. And someone's pissed." His hand flipped in the air. "But something's not right here. This isn't the council's MO."

"Maybe it's from the murderers," Anna said.

"The photo—it's the bad guy who took our pictures. It's got to be."

"What're you talking about?" Colin asked.

"The photo." I squatted, pulled books out from under the bed, and opened a paperback. "Here." I passed a wrinkled photo with our scored-mutilated images to Colin. "The day we met at school. Someone took this picture. I got it from Hanson before we left Coccia House."

"And you're now just showing this to us?" Colin glared at me.

"Wait! Don't get mad at me. How was I to know it wasn't a classmate hating on me? Or Lizzy!"

"Didn't you say something about a bad guy? Not classmate?"

"Dang it!" I grimaced. "I don't know. One minute, Hanson's handing me this photo with my face scored right through the image—"

"Our faces, Callie," Trystan said. "Not just yours."

"Yes." Guilt prodded me. "But I didn't know you guys well. And then I'm getting prank-restricted calls. Dead bodies start surfacing, and now, this threatening note. What was I supposed to do?"

Trystan stomped his foot. "Talk. Open up."

"It's clear," Colin said. "Callie's not safe."

"Wait a minute—"

"No, you don't get it." Colin looked down at me. "If Trystan dumps you, you've got a chance to survive this mess. You're guilty through association with us. But you can't let it slip we exist—not to anyone, Theran or human."

Guilty by association? This wasn't making sense. This wasn't logical.

The ancients and Mr. Taylor's group don't know I have a birthmark. But, if their sole purpose was to separate us because they thought I was human, how did the symbol from Ella's blanket fit in? Words piled up on my tongue, and my mouth popped open, ready to spill.

"Trystan, give me tonight. Alone. Please." I looked at Colin. "I'll explain everything to him."

"No," Colin yelled. "This has to stop. Nothing can come of your relationship. Trystan is so obsessed with you that he threatened to leave us a while back. That's part of the reason my uncle let him go to prom with you. You have to let him go, Callie."

"It can't be guilt by association, Colin." Moisture filled my eyes. My secrets caused nothing but pain. "Because my face is sliced through on that picture just like yours. And that was three hours after meeting you."

Colin's brows formed a V.

"There's stuff *you* don't understand."

"Leave us alone," Trystan said. "Give us tonight to figure it out."

"How can you interpret this then?" Colin dropped the picture and held out the knife. "It's a bold threat on her life, and we don't know who made it. She's dead if you keep dating her. There are several lifeless bodies as it is. Let's not add hers to the list."

My eyes slipped, looking toward the trunk. I stretched, sat up, and glanced at Colin. "I need tonight, alone with Trystan."

"No."

Anna gripped Colin's shirtsleeve. "Give them a chance to talk."

Colin shook the note and fanned it in the air over his head. "What if they come back?"

Trystan faced them, another staring match. "It's an order." Trystan's steely voice froze me in place. "I outrank you, Colin. You will wait until tomorrow when I will come to a decision."

"Fine." Colin placed the blade and note on the dresser. "You've got a couple of hours. We'll be back. And we're staying the night."

I nodded, walked over to my purse, and pulled out the house keys. "This will let you two back into the house."

I put the key in Colin's palm. "Can you lock up the mill on your way out?"

Colin's eyes softened. "I don't want anyone hurt." He looked past me to Trystan and Anna. "Do you understand?"

I bit my lip. "More than you realize."

I followed them out to the kitchen. No one said a word. Once they left, I locked the door and slid to the floor—a sob lodged in my throat. Trystan's arms came under my knees and around my back. He lifted me from the floor, carried me to my room, and sat on the chair with me in his lap. I buried my face in his shoulder as tears spilled over.

He lifted my chin and pushed the wet strands of my tear-soaked hair from my face. I studied the penetrating warmth of his eyes.

I inhaled and was thankful for my bedroom's familiar surroundings. Dark curtains blocked the view from outside the house, and Tesla curled up at the end of the bed.

"Keeping my secrets has cost you."

"I was willing to keep your identity private from my family, but this threat changes everything."

With my fingers, I pushed his dark curls back from his face. "I haven't lied to you." I scooted off his lap. Discomfort settled on my shoulders, but the compulsion to confide in him overwhelmed me. Kneeling in front of the chest, I opened it. "I didn't find this until after we'd met. My mom had sent it to my grandparents two weeks before she died." I wiped my damp palm on the purple blanket before taking it out and laying it across my knees. "Because I'd predicted their deaths. Nana and Gramps kept it for me." I pulled out the leather-bound book that contained my mom's note. I handed it to him. "Some of the stuff written in there, you can't repeat yet."

He nodded and sat on the floor next to me, accepting the small book. His finger ran down the thin spine. He carefully opened it and studied it, often flipping back to previous pages. His facial expression changed from unease to bewilderment.

Silence spread.

My gut clenched tighter with concern.

His gaze flickered between the writing on the page and my face.

Finally, he rested the book on his lap and slid his palm over it. "This is a lot to swallow." His eyes caught mine. "Both your parents are of the strongest bloodlines of the ancient Therans." His fingers fanned through the edges of the book. "Both families still sit on the Council of Elders." He held the brown manuscript up. "Wow. When you said you needed to talk, I never imagined you'd tell me of the existence of another group of Therans." He lowered his head. "Man, Callie. I can't wrap my mind around this. There's another complete group of us out there. They've managed to keep their bloodlines clean for a thousand years longer than we have. This Remnant Faction could be much stronger than us since their sole purpose was maintaining pure bloodlines." He leaned back against the dresser. "That note stabbed into the mill wall doesn't reflect the feelings of every ancient. Until now, I didn't know of any Theran hating humans. We all serve a purpose. Humans are some of the most loving people, but Colin's right. Whoever sent that threat has issues with humans."

"I don't have proof, but intuition tells me that the Avalon murders, that note," I tilted my chin toward the dresser, where Colin had laid the dagger, "and my past are linked." My fingers toyed with the frayed edges of the purple blanket. "Look at the knife's hilt. It matches the crest on my adopted sister's coverlet."

Trystan snatched up the dagger and the note again and sat back on the floor next to me, his leg bumping mine. "You think they're the same crest?" He tugged the coverlet. "My interests have never covered reading up on family crests, but if Colin doesn't recognize it, then it's got to be a symbol created more recently."

"Why would Colin be so knowledgeable about symbols?"

"He's not." Trystan drew up his leg and rested his elbow on his knee. "His interests are in weaponry, old and new, but most old armaments have markings like that or a family crest."

This was totally out of my realm of understanding. By American standards, the mill was old. For that matter, anything over a century was old. But Trystan spoke of things several centuries old.

"Trystan." I picked lint off the corner of the blanket that covered my dress. "Mr. Taylor, he's Theran."

He rubbed at an eyebrow.

"He's got a power I don't understand—as does his girlfriend, Samantha." The coverlet slipped between my fingers. "I've witnessed them using it."

His jaw dropped.

I raised my palm to stop him from speaking. "It's happened twice—once when you were with me—the other with Anna. I've caught him in lies. I wouldn't be surprised if he sent the threat. Especially if you're from one of the strongest bloodlines. They wouldn't want—"

"Us together, being intimate."

A swirl of embarrassment hit my cheeks. I raised my head as he ran his thumb over the emblem in the blanket. "If my visions are correct, Taylor's not the mastermind behind the deaths. My guess is Taylor's group has several motives. And, from the looks of that threatening note, you're one of them."

"Hate to say it, but I know you're right." Trystan searched my stare, digesting my words. A calculating light flickered in his eyes. His switch of the topic didn't surprise me. "Both your parents were crimson-blood, making you a pure-blood. You predicted your parents' deaths." His voice softened. "You possess the ability of premonition. You're some sort of radar detector, able to sense if someone's using power." He raised Mom's letter to me. "Cal, your mom's note mentions your birthmark is different. How?"

I touched my sweetheart neckline, separating the extra layers of chiffon that decorated the bust line.

Trystan swallowed and lowered his eyes. "Your mark. Where is it?"

I shifted, leaned forward, and pulled my hair over my right shoulder. I reached behind, unzipping my dress until the front of my bodice dropped low, and cool air caressed my back. I clutched the material at the front, stopping it from exposing me, and tugged at the chiffon with my other hand until I'd dragged it loose.

I lost myself as his finger traced along the crimson edge of my birthmark. I trembled under the warmth of his touch. "Why am I different?"

"That ... I cannot answer," he murmured in my ear. "But your mark is beautiful. I love how the red divides the luminous lines into both sides of the big star, and the smaller star is so tiny." I shivered as his hand traveled lower on my back. "And this is your scar." His warm palm pressed against my bare skin. "You're crimson-blood."

A frisson of bubbles popped in my stomach. "On the jeweled box where I found the ring, there's a crest—one with two stars, like my birthmark. It's in the chest."

He leaned in and kissed my shoulder. "You should go change clothes. I'll take a look at the box."

I stood, wrapped my arm around my chest to keep the dress up, and slipped into the walk-in closet, closing the door behind me. I dropped my dress, which pooled at my feet, tugged a shirt from a hanger, and slipped it on. Once I slipped into jeans, I opened the door to find Trystan sitting on my bed, staring at the box on his lap.

His eyes shimmered with surprise. "Grab your shoes. I know where we can find some answers." He placed the box on the floor next to the chest, and we left the house.

CHAPTER 39

ASHWORTH LIBRARY

The door opened, and I gave myself a mental shake. What was I doing? I flipped the flashlight button on my cell and held it toward the ground. A tiled path became visible between wooden pews on both sides of the aisle. Our shoes clicked against the floor, echoing in the church. The moon illuminated the stained-glass scenery high above on the sanctuary walls.

"This gives me the creeps. Had you told me we'd be breaking into a house of worship, I'd never have come."

"We're not committing a crime. Remember, my dad gave me a key."

"Yeah, and I'd lay odds he never intended you to use it at two in the morning. If we get arrested, I'm blaming you."

He chuckled and aimed his phone's beam of light at the corridor floor. "The only ones who'll know we're here are the statues, and they won't say a word."

I shivered and reached for his hand, fumbling with his fingers until they interlocked and gave a squeeze. "This is freaky."

"Trust me. You'll like it."

We picked our way through marble columns until we reached the end of the pews. Trystan's beam shone on a wooden door. I raised my cell to illuminate the same space and moved the light away from his to broaden our view, revealing three ornate wooden entries.

He leaned into me. "This is the confessional. Only one of us can go down at a time. Do everything I tell you."

I swallowed. This was the last place I'd figured on finding information about my jewelry box.

He opened the door on the right, revealing a small wooden bench at the back of the tiny room. A thin, black fabric hung on the left wall, separating the rooms, and a sconce fixture on the opposite wall. The room was equal to the size of a porta-potty.

"Remember this keyless entry-code sequence: seven, seven, three, three. Okay?"

"Wait. What about the key your dad gave you?"

"Oh, it's easier to bring you this way. Someone could figure out we'd come down here if we used the other entrance. Hardly anyone knows this route." He smirked. "Anyhow, this is more fun."

This is crazy. "Okay, so I'm supposed to remember seven, seven, three, and three."

"Once this door shuts, it resets the number sequencing," Trystan murmured, reaching under the light switch to a small dial. "Twist this seven times to the right—always right first. Then, seven to the left, three to the right, and three to the left. It's simple—once the elevator descends and the door opens to the library, get out and wait for me there. There are several miles of underground passages."

I bit my inner cheek. "Can't you go first?"

"No." He shined the light into the confessional. "Wait for me outside the elevator."

I stepped into the small room and sat on the bench. Trystan shut the door. I shined the beam up toward the sconce. I turned the switch to the right and heard a click, then a second click. I completed Trystan's directions. Immediately, the floor jerked, and the seat began to lower. The black curtain disappeared above my head as I descended.

"Talk about weird," I whispered.

The elevator jolted again, and the door disappeared into the wall. A musty scent penetrated my nostrils, making me gag. I aimed my light at the ground, then stepped out into a dark space, after which the door slid back into place, closing. Cold seeped into my body, and goosebumps crept up my spine. It must be twenty degrees cooler down here than it had been up above. I wrapped my arms around my middle, smothering the light beam from my cell.

Darkness surrounded me on all sides. Anyone could be out there. Why'd I listen to him? He should've come down first. I dropped my arms and shined the light around me. I immediately jumped back, gasping. The light had revealed a white face. Several marble busts sat on podiums along a wall.

"Jings." I shuddered.

A minute passed before the door opened again.

"Sorry, I took so long. That elevator needs moderniz-ing."

His cell shined a ray on the far wall, illuminating a row of forty or more switches. Trystan stepped away from me and flicked them all on. A succession of lights came to life, echoing in space. The lights lit up a wall that stretched into a long hallway, where fifty or more pictures hung from floor to ceiling.

"They call this Historical Hall. Every picture here reflects some great past event. You can look at them later, but I want to show you something. Turn off your light and follow me." He wove his cool fingers through my sweaty ones and led me down the corridor. "What I want to show you isn't too far from here."

Historic snapshots shown in the pictures on the wall are Egyptian, Chinese, and Greek. Some, I couldn't make out. They'd have to be worth a fortune. Even the carved wooden frames encasing the pictures were priceless. Twenty paces from the elevator, I tugged on his hand.

"What's this painting?" Flames appeared to cover the entire work of art, which displayed a burning building close to the sea, and ships scattered on the ocean.

"It's a reminder of the lives lost during the Fire of Unknown Cause during the War of Knowledge. You know, humans believe Julius Caesar started the inferno. After reading your mom's pages, I know it was actually the Remnants, and that's how they escaped." He chuckled. "Did you know your family's related to him?"

"We're related to Caesar?"

"Yep. He was one of the greatest military commanders in history."

Trystan stopped in front of a thick Egyptian rug, spanning about four feet by four feet, encased in glass. Interwoven threads portrayed a picture with faded colors of terracotta, light greens, and gray-blues. What looked to be three Egyptian rectangles were in the background of the tapestry, with mounds of desert sand around them near the sea. Woven into the material near the bottom was a large building. Hieroglyphics lined the border on all sides. Other objects—I couldn't tell what they were—were depicted throughout the mural.

Trystan released my hand to point at the image. "This was my mom's favorite work of art. She'd bring me down here when we came in from California to visit Dad and explain stuff about the images. See that." Trystan pointed at the odd rectangles. "If you look closely, you'll see depictions of Egyptian gods and priests offering sacrifices to them. And look here." Trystan pointed to a small square whose threads were similar in color to those of my jeweled box. "Your container looks to be a replica of this box."

"Wow. The likeness is amazing."

"I'd like to know why your great aunt wanted you to have the box."

Me, too. I twisted the band on my finger. "It's the ring." I raised my finger.

He clasped my hand. The warmth of his skin contrasted with the chilly air. "It's strange to me someone would make a misshapen ring with a flat area near the stone." He looked at the canvas and my ring, then shrugged. "Come on. While we're here, I want to see if we can figure out your mark."

We rounded a corner, and I gasped, standing on the threshold of what looked like an amphitheater–a Greek Coliseum. The underground room's dimensions expanded to the size of a football field, and several tiered platforms descended into the earth. Wooden benches covered each raised area. Large stone columns stretched to the ceiling and disappeared behind the lower lights.

"I would never have imagined a place like this could exist below ground," I whispered.

I placed my hand on a cold, marble stone resembling an Olympic torch and gazed at forty or more monstrous stone pillars that filled the room in various places to the pit.

"What are these?"

"When they have meetings, they light the fire bowls at the top. It's cool. The basins are made of soapstone and weigh over a thousand pounds."

"I guess it's handy, especially if the lights go out."

He chuckled. "Try playing down here without flashlights. Aunt Selma always made sure the three of us brought our cell phones after we lost Anna hiding down here once."

On the dais, on my right, were seven ornate, high-backed chairs. Covered in dark purple material, each one resembled a throne, and each high back depicted a family crest.

"Wait a minute." I walked around to the front. Trystan followed. "The chairs ... they're the same purple as my sister's blanket, but none of these have the symbol of the eagle on it."

He chuckled. "You'd have to be crazy to even think about looking for a similar crest here—that's where the elders sit." He pointed to the second chair. "That's my dad's seat. From the Ancient Faction, your mother's ancestors sit here, next to him, and your father's ancestors," he pointed toward the end, "sit the second seat in, on the far side."

My eyebrows rose. "Assigned seats."

He extended his hand, and I grabbed it. "The strength of a family's bloodline impacts where they sit and to what extent they control the ancients' movements."

"It's intimidating." I followed Trystan around the platform. The place was a virtual museum. Paintings hung everywhere. "Jings." We stopped at a canvas depicting a woman with coiled snakes for hair. "She's ugly."

He leaned in and looked at a golden label. "Leonardo da Vinci's *Medusa Shield*."

"I wouldn't consider it art."

"Lord Avalon bought it off the black market some time ago. The story goes it's one of Hitler's pieces they managed to steal during WWII."

"Why would anyone want so many pieces of art? I mean, I like history, but this is a massive collection."

"My mom summed it up like this. Each artifact tells a story, and, by preserving them, we are preserving someone's existence."

"I'd buy something less frightening than Medusa."

"It's sad. Lord Avalon had been inventorying collections in Alexandria, Egypt before he was killed. Some of them have gone missing."

"Wasn't he a librarian?"

"And an art lover." Trystan grinned. "Come on. We're never going to figure out your birthmark if we keep talking about all this other stuff."

We walked to a place where rows of bookshelves extended out from a central hub, like spokes on a wheel, passing row after row, stopping before each shelf. Trystan read from the paneled ends, which were written in English with other strange lettering beneath them. Tables were in the center of every aisle.

We moved into a passage. One-third of the way down, he said, "I don't know where to begin. Latin or Greek might be best."

I leaned against a table. He pulled a book from the top shelf. Dust floated in the air. The thick, bound volume had gilt edging. Some pages looked tattered. He tipped his head to read the spine of another manuscript and pulled it out, too. Twenty minutes later, he had seven books on the table. He scanned book after book. My butt hurt, and my eyes dragged as I watched his finger move up and down pages.

He slammed another book shut. "Dang it, this is frustrating. There must be something down here showing why you have two stars on your back. But all I'm coming up with are dead ends. And we must get back. Anna and Colin will be at your place soon."

"They said they'd give us a couple of hours. Please, try another language." I straightened as he went right back to searching through the books. I walked along the aisle, dragging my fingers over the hardcovers and passing one shelving unit after another.

He still sat, looking at a book.

Gazing down, I noticed a purple feather on the edge of the bookshelf. I picked it up. What's this? It felt as soft as a bunny.

"Trystan?"

He made eye contact with me. "Hmm."

"Why's there a bird's feather down here?"

"You've got me." He chuckled, making eye contact with me. "None of us understand it. For centuries, we've found the feathers. Long ago, when they'd find them, they'd make writing quills. Now, they collect them in a jar of dust. Another one of those mysteries for the Room of Legends."

Freaky. No sky around, yet I find a feather. I pocketed it.

A breeze tickled the hairs on my neck.

Whack!

I spun, catching my breath, and froze in place. A book fell from the top shelf with the force of a bat hitting a ball. Is there a ghost in here? My eyes darted to the dark corners of the aisle floor and above.

"What the—" Trystan said what my lungs failed to allow me to speak.

"A-a book fell from the shelf."

"You can't knock over the things."

"I didn't, Trystan." I swallowed. "That book is fifteen steps away from me."

Trystan looked behind him. "Is someone here?"

"Let's get out of here."

"No, just wait a minute." Trystan slipped by me, picked up the book, and returned it to the desk.

I made a noise, but Trystan silenced me when he flipped open the book–the same book that dropped from the shelf–and pulled a purple feather from between the open pages.

"That's no bookmark."

Strained silence filled the space between us. He read the bookmarked page and flipped it over several times.

He cleared his throat. "It's more than a bookmark, Cal." Trystan jabbed his index finger at a tattered page. "This is it. Your mark."

I returned to his side, feeling an uneasiness as if eyes watched us. I gazed across the table, the edge digging into my hip. A picture: two stars–one larger, one smaller–filled the top of the page. The bottom of the sheet was meticulously lined, with dark ink writing flowing with a weird symbol below the stars.

"Does it say anything?"

"I haven't gotten far. Give me a minute." He examined the sheet. Again and again, he looked at me, turned back, and read more. His smile dissolved into a perplexed frown as he leaned over the table. He captured my stare and the color drained from his face.

"If this is right, you have a mythical mark."

"Mythical? What's that mean?"

Shadows crossed his eyes. "It's an ancient protector's mark—rumor has it, Ptolemy was one. Also, some even say the *last* protector. Your crimson-blood heritage must be strong. I still can't believe I thought you could be a half-blood." He ran his hand through his dark hair and pinched the bridge of his nose. "Legends have always fascinated me. After I metamorphosed last year, I discovered I could read ancient scrolls. That's how I found out I could translate. I've interpreted passages from every script and tome I could get my hands on. Since Sebastian demanded we keep our powers a secret, I couldn't risk someone catching me deciphering. Still, up until this, I'd only heard scuttlebutt about protectors, never anything concrete. What knowledge there was seems to have died out as the number of translators decreased. And now, the few that can translate aren't focused on myths." His brows furrowed. "The last known report of protectors existing was around the time of the burning of the Alexandrian Library. It's written right here." He tapped the page with his index finger. "Protectors defended the library, fighting. They were believed to be our last hope and line of defense. They kept the library from being completely destroyed." His Adam's apple bounced in his throat. "Supposedly, they're seen around times of cataclysmic events. They're the strongest of Therans, possessing mythical powers."

The gravity in his voice was like the bang of a judge's gavel.

He stared at me in speculative silence.

Hollowness surfaced within me.

Panic consumed his expression. "Your seal must remain a secret. If other Therans discover you exist, it will create pandemonium our generation has never seen."

My heart bounced with excitement. "You won't tell anyone about my mark?"

He extended his arm across the table and placed his hand over mine. I straightened as his other hand pushed back my hair and brushed my collarbone. His warm fingers slid to my shoulder and massaged.

"No. I won't."

Relief surged through me. I swung my arms around his neck and pulled him into a hug. His arms encircled my waist.

He leaned back. "Cal, my brother had a reason for Colin, Anna, and I not to reveal our powers, so your mark will remain our secret. But the other information can't be kept from my family for long. It affects everyone. I've made more headway listening to you than the investigators have made in weeks. If your instincts are correct about Mr. Taylor's involvement, we have to lay low and collect information." His warm lips pressed against my forehead. "After the threat, you're a walking target."

Tightness built up in my chest. Would I be ready to protect myself? Others? Could I use my shield?

"Things don't add up," I murmured, thinking of Mr. Taylor. "Why are they hunting those with powers?"

"That's why everyone's freaking out. They don't know who's behind this, and the elders can't find a motive for the murders. It's all confusing."

"Answer something for me. If the ancients, long ago, were trying to guard the Golden Chamber and Room of Legends and all these paintings, treasures, and," I released my hand from his neck and pressed my palm on the book, "the libraries, wouldn't they have more protectors or soldiers than, what, three percent of the Theran population?"

He stepped back. His eyes narrowed to slits. "You'd think so. Kings always had vast armies. Even now, countries have huge armed forces, but how'd you come up with the exact figure printed in the book when you don't read Latin?" His finger tapped the worn page.

I lowered my gaze.

"Out with it, Cal."

Sighing, I looked back up at him. "My parents' friend, my only acquaintance from the remnants, is my ally. He explained to me the different roles in Theran society and told me, long ago, it was believed protectors numbered only about three percent of Therans."

For several seconds, he said nothing. A faint smile passed his lips. "Mr. Santos?"

I battled to steady my hands.

"You trust him?" A hint of concern entered Trystan's voice.

Without wavering, I said, "Yes."

"We'll talk to Mr. Santos sometime. But we better get back to your place. I don't want to give Colin another reason to be ticked off."

A *fluttering* movement stirred my hair.

I jumped, letting out a squeak of fear. "What's that?"

"I didn't hear anything."

"No, no, I felt something."

"Cal, nothing's down here." Trystan chuckled. "I think you're watching too many scary movies."

Bat? Birds? Whatever it was, I didn't like it. Words died on my lips as we moved from the aisle. I scanned the top of the bookshelves until we neared the thrown chairs, shivering in the chill of the library gloom.

An hour later, I sat on my couch in my sweats, wrapped in a light blanket. Colin and Anna had returned with food. Anna sat at the table, and Tesla begged for scraps. Trystan leaned against the counter. His gaze darted between his cousin and me.

"Peace offering." Colin tossed a hamburger at me. He sounded thoughtful. "I don't like that we argued."

"Thanks, but I'm not hungry."

"Mmmmm." Anna dropped her hand, lowering her sandwich to the table. "Just in case you're wondering, my parents think I'm staying here until your granddad returns. And Trystan, they believe you're staying with Colin on campus with some friends. Dad said it was one of the safest places." She shrugged. "At least, that's what we're telling them." Anna's eyes sparkled with mischief. "Oh, and I texted Erika. She's cool with us not showing up. I guess post-prom wasn't as much fun as she'd thought it would be."

So, everyone's staying here for several days. Ugh! I never liked my space invaded, but even I knew there was security in numbers.

Too tired and stressed out, none of us talked. I crawled into bed with Anna beside me. The guys took the couches.

Fatigue dragged my eyes shut. Suspicion washed through me, and fear snaked around me, pulling me deep into the clutches of despair. Ghost book? Protector's mark?

CHAPTER 40

PERSONAL HELL

*E*verything turned black. My brain pounded in my skull. *Coldness surrounded me, and blazing fingers reached into my lungs, stealing my air. I kicked my feet, fighting to reach the surface, thrashing against the pain.*

I gasped a mouthful of air. My teeth snapped. I opened my eyes, squinting against the pain in my head. My peripheral vision was dark as if I were looking through a shadowy tunnel. At the end of the dark scope, an image of morning light came into focus, brightening my view. My blue blanket draped over my legs. I was in my bed, in my bedroom. I closed my eyes, inhaling the faint scent of vanilla.

The bed bounced, jostling us. I couldn't think—couldn't feel. I was hazily aware of someone's touch on my shoulders. I inhaled again.

"You're okay, Cal," Trystan said.

Relief surged through me. I was alive.

"It's me." I opened my eyes and met Trystan's stare. "I'm going to drown. I saw it. My vision—it's me, floating in the water. I don't want to die." I closed my eyes and crawled into his lap. His arms encircled my waist. "I hate it. These visions are so cryptic." I inhaled again, calming myself. "It's a huge boat ... the one I fall from. The premonition played through everything so quickly. I only saw the name, *Freedom*, on the back." I dropped my face into the curve of his neck, ignoring our surroundings.

"Trystan, what's going on?" Anna asked.

I opened my eyes to see Anna standing beside Colin, her face pale.

"Tell us," Colin said.

Trystan cupped my chin, prompting me to look at him. "Everyone heard what you said about the vision."

I cringed and lowered my head back into the curve of his neck, wanting to disappear.

Tesla's nose nuzzled my thigh. Someone cleared his throat from the opposite direction of Anna and Colin. I dragged my face from Trystan's neck.

Mr. Santos rested against the doorframe of my bedroom. He stood near a silver-haired woman in a blue pantssuit, her sapphire eyes twinkling with tears.

"They arrived about five minutes ago," Trystan whispered. "After we'd cleaned up the mess at the mill."

Someone was bound to find out about my visions at some point. I took a deep breath, resigned to the fact that my life was more public now.

The gray-haired woman broke the silence. "I am Miss Anstley, your great aunt." An uncertain smile tugged at her lips. "You have your mother's eyes."

My fingers dug into Trystan's shoulders, crumpling his shirt. So, this was my mom's aunt. The woman who passed her genes to me but who, up until now, never attempted to contact me. I took a deep breath. Now wasn't the time to be angry.

"You're related?" Anna pointed back and forth between Miss Anstley and me.

"Trystan, what's going on?" Colin's razor-sharp tone cut at my frayed nerves.

Trystan took my hand from his shoulder and squeezed it. "This is Callie's great aunt, Miss Anstley." He raked his finger through his hair with his other hand. "And her teacher from last fall. Mr. Santos, Miss Anstley, these are my cousins, Anna and Colin Dougrey."

Colin raised an eyebrow. "Great aunt?"

"Yes," Miss Anstley said. "I wish we were all meeting under different circumstances." The sad smile on her lips thinned. She walked toward the chest. "But it seems like we've picked a good time."

I shifted on Trystan's lap. Miss Anstley held the dagger hilt in her palm. I disentangled from his embrace and snatched Mom's book off the floor. While they may have witnessed me having a vision, I couldn't let them read her book and find out I had a *mythical* mark.

"Why are you here?" I asked.

Miss Anstley raised the threatening note. "A few days ago, you issued a challenge to Mr. Santos, suggesting he use his contacts to discover what is happening with the murders. From the looks of this dagger, it's time we met."

"Are you here to help?" I asked.

She raised her index finger. "Yes. We need answers. All of us."

Anna rubbed her chin, her cheeks regaining color. "My uncle can take care of this."

"Yes," Mr. Santos said. "I'm aware of Lord Dougrey."

Anna sucked in her cheeks.

Mr. Santos stepped forward, leaning on his cane, and looked straight at me. "We don't know exactly against whom—or against what—we're fighting. It could be any-one outside this room. Callie's already collected more information than other Therans have figured out. If she trusts you," Mr. Santos looked at Anna, Colin, and Trys-tan, "I'm game to work with you. Especially after last night, Theran security found Lord Sanderson's daughter murdered. We've gotten ahold of her phone records, which show someone contacted her hours before her death. Lord Tresmeire's daughter indicated that Amelia Sanderson was terrified in the hours leading up to her death."

Miss Anstley cleared her throat. "But I won't risk ex-posure of the Remnants' Faction till I must."

"Murderers?" Anna muttered, her eyes seeking Trys-tan's stare. "That's why Sebastian didn't want us to tell anyone our—"

"Don't." Colin grabbed Anna's shoulder and jerked her backward. "They're total strangers."

I stepped away from the chest. "The word is Remnant Faction, and they tell the truth. I'd know if they'd lied." Without my ability to read voice inflections, I'd be sus-picious like Colin.

Anna pulled from Colin's grip and turned toward me. "Wait. You're Theran—so, that's why Trystan's refused to listen to his dad and stop dating you. He knew all along you were Theran."

As vulnerable as I felt opening up, I didn't back down. "I'm crimson-blood and a remnant descendant."

Colin waved a finger toward me. "Why should we believe you?"

"Don't be stupid." Trystan pushed himself off the bed. The comforter fell to the floor. "She's the reason Anna's alive, and you just witnessed her having a vision." Trys-tan stepped toward me. "Besides, I can testify she's got a seal."

Swirls of embarrassment colored my cheeks. Why'd he have to reveal something so personal? It was bad enough my stomach still hadn't settled since my vision, and then he had to dig the hole deeper and let people know I showed him my mark. Jings, now everyone thinks he looked at part of my chest.

Trystan gave Colin a challenging stare. "Anna's right. Sebastian knew something hideous was coming down the pike. Now, things are lining up."

Miss Anstley pierced Colin with a deadly look. "And the murderers have no idea that an army of Theran remnants exists, whose bloodlines are powerful. More powerful than the ancient's bloodlines."

Anna stepped forward. "I can lay hands on an injured body and heal physical infirmities."

"That is different from your mother's gift." Miss Anstley blinked.

Colin swung around and faced Anna. "Keep your mouth shut. You can't give away our secrets." He rocked back on his heels and turned to glare at Trystan. "Give me time to get a mental grip."

Colin's silence made me more aware. I needed to know Sebastian's vision.

Colin stomped past Santos, elbowing him in the arm. Everyone followed except Trystan. I lifted the journal and scanned the pages, gently removing the two pages that revealed my mark.

Trystan nodded. "Come on."

Trystan and I left my bedroom and approached Colin. He sat with his head lowered in his lap, his fingers linked together at the back of his head. "Read this." I dropped Mom's note on the sofa. "Please."

"I'll do it." Anna lifted it from the cushion.

Miss Anstley tilted her head, giving me a questioning look.

I stepped forward. "It's my mom's last written note to me, explaining everything about my existence." I gazed over at Mr. Santos. "So, are you working this case now?"

"Yes, I've come out of retirement, but all remnant Therans are on the case."

Miss Anstley held up the note we'd found stabbed into the wall of the mill. "You've been threatened."

"I got it last night." With trembling fingers, I grabbed a rubberband from the table and pulled my hair into a messy twist. Every fact I'd learned, I measured against my gut intuition. "My guess is that it comes from Mr. Taylor. He doesn't like humans. He knows Trystan, Colin, and Anna are Theran and believes I'm a human with polluted blood. But, if my visions are correct, Mr. Taylor doesn't pull the strings."

Anna gasped. "The history teacher?"

Methodically, I broke the details down for everyone and explained the vision of the elusive man's shattered face, and my intuition was warning me that everything stemmed from him. Lord Avalon and his son's murders, Lord Sanderson's daughter's murder, people being hunted for their powers, and the threatening note all had connections to Taylor and Samantha. In addition, the mark on the dagger matched the one on my sister's blanket. I didn't give details about having searched Mr. Taylor's pockets or spying on their house. I also skipped telling them about my mark and other powers. I wasn't ready to drop my mask entirely. It was hard enough to digest last night's information. Anyhow, no one needed to know we'd been inside the library.

"So," Colin said, getting to his feet. "We're relying on your intuition that these three dead bodies are the result of some teacher at your school, his girlfriend, and some mysterious man. Why should I believe you? How do I know we're fighting for the same cause?" He looked over at Santos, who leaned against the living room wall. "I don't even know if you're Theran."

Mr. Santos snickered and put his cane against the wall. He raised his shirt and revealed his mark.

"You should know." He turned and looked at me, ignoring Colin. "Samantha confronted me at the hospital. She saw my mark when they undressed me. She commented about never having met me before. She's currently under the assumption I spent most of my time before the accident working in the Italian library before moving here to teach high school." He glared at Colin. "It's not false."

"Okay, so you're not human." Colin paced in front of the wood burner. "But that doesn't mean we're fighting on the same side."

"Stop it. Give'm a chance." Anna slapped the book shut and looked up at Colin. "It makes sense. Don't you see? Sebastian prepared us for this. It's why it's been so vital our powers didn't become public knowledge. He told us not to reveal our powers because, if we had, the bad guys would be after us. Think about it. Isn't it odd all three of us developed our capabilities early? And look, Callie's got powers, too. This isn't a coincidence—even I can see that." She tilted her head. "But how's Sebastian's vision fit into this mess? He never mentioned the remnant group."

This moment was pivotal.

I'd never met Miss Anstley, but I knew she wasn't lying. She wanted to help. This was the first step for me. "What did Sebastian's vision reveal?"

Colin stopped pacing but said nothing.

I pointed to Santos and my great aunt. "They've managed to stay hidden. Maybe for the same reasons that the three of you weren't to reveal your powers." I looked at

Colin, daring him to challenge my logic. "We have the element of surprise on our side."

Miss Anstley sat on the couch. "You're intelligent. Mr. Croskney's done a fine job raising you." She drew in an audible breath of air. "You will never know how much I wanted to be a part of your life, but I couldn't risk going against your parents' banishment and drawing attention to you." She looked at her hands. "I see he's made sure you got the ring. I've no idea of its purpose, let alone why you were to have it, but it left a strong impression."

I rubbed my thumb on the inside of my finger, twisting the band while everyone stared at me.

Miss Anstley pursed her lips and looked between Colin and Anna. "I touch things and get glimpses into the future—that's how I knew my great-niece was to have the box with the band. The limitation is that I must have contact with a tangible object." She ran her finger along the wooden inlay of the dagger. "I don't recognize the eagle symbol here, but I'd like to try to get a mental imprint from this."

Colin's eyes widened. "Have you ever worked with the police?"

Miss Anstley smoothed out a wrinkle in her pants suit. "We don't work with law enforcement. We have strict rules against exposing our abilities. Anyway, my capability is limited. I don't always get a vision."

Colin sat on the sofa next to Anna. "We googled the symbol last night, thinking it was part of some family's coat of arms, but we couldn't find anything. If you isolate the eagle from the star, knowing the single star represents Therans, then the eagle emblem could mean *freedom* also, *ruler of the skies*, *victory*, and *quest seeker*."

Colin's research results eased my anxiety and confirmed my suspicions. "I believe it's a personalized symbol. Someone created it, and it's been around for at least twenty years. That's how old Ella, my sister, would've been."

"Good work." Miss Anstley grinned, looking at the blade. "Now, please give me a moment. I'd like to see what snapshots, if any, I can collect from this." She closed her eyes.

Silence stretched, broken only by Tesla's tags clunking against the bowl as he ate.

Miss Anstley repositioned the stiletto in her hand and laid it across her palm, the sharp blade making contact with her skin. She shook her head and switched the blade to her other hand.

"I can't capture a fresh mental image." Seconds later, a strangled cry came from her lips. She recoiled. "Chains ... and several large feet, linked by shackles." She set the knife on the end table and flexed her fingers.

Concern and appreciation saturated me. Her willingness to reveal her gift confirmed my intuition's itch of her commitment to work with us. I crossed the room and knelt on the floor before her.

"Are you okay?"

Miss Anstley wiggled her fingers at her side. "I don't understand. This couldn't be a fresh image. Restraints of that sort are medieval."

"Criminals are still chained up when they walk." I glanced toward the doorway and saw wary lines caressing Santos's face. "Aren't they?"

Startled, Miss Anstley encircled my hands with her warm ones. "No. These shackles were rusty and old. They looked like they'd been made from iron."

"Calerine." Santos rubbed his chin. "The knife is old, but your powers don't allow you to see the past."

I let out a breath of air, not allowing myself the time to take back the words. "Let me try."

"No." Trystan jerked forward in his seat. "I don't like this. What if you see something hideous?"

Mr. Santos thumped his cane on the floor. "She's seeing the future, not drinking poison." Mr. Santos's tone sizzled with annoyance. "We've got to work together and use what powers we have to solve this mess before someone kills again."

Miss Anstley patted the back of my hand. "I've taught two others from the Remnant Faction how to use this technique. Each individual works at a different pace. Some glimpse only the past. Some see the future. It takes time to master the skill, to hone a level of peace, and you can't believe everything you see." She shrugged. "Visions aren't for the weak and are subject to change. I'm sure you understand that. Are you sure you want to try this?"

CHAPTER 41

VISIONS

Although the mid-morning sun brightened the living room, the stares from everyone in the room brought goosebumps to my arms. I attempted to see the vision as five pairs of eyes zeroed in on me.

Trystan crossed his arms, tapping his foot and scrutinizing my face. He'd taken on the role of my self-appointed protector, but I had no choice. I had to do this.

I looked back at Miss Anstley and pulled my hands from hers. I swiped the dagger from the table and shifted from the floor to the couch. I stared at Trystan, searching his face. He said nothing.

I pulled in a long, steady breath. "I'm ready."

"Remember, you're in control," Miss Anstley whispered. "You can drop the knife and break the mental images from pressing upon your mind if they get too intense. There are no guarantees this will work."

I nodded.

"Take another deep breath," Miss Anstley said. "Inhale through your nose and exhale slowly from your mouth. Close your eyes. It's easier to stay in contact with the vision that way. Seal your mind to your surroundings and focus your thoughts on the object."

For a long moment, I drew strength from Trystan.

I took a deep breath, exhaled, and lowered my eyes to the knife in my palm. I closed my eyes. Everything disappeared. A droning hum engulfed me.

"The face is shadowed. I can't make out what he looks like. It's breaking, splitting down the center into jagged halves. The larger piece shows ... dirty feet, shackled. Hmm. They must be men—their legs are muscular. They're walking ... five of them. I can't see anything but their calves. They're walking to a set of steps, wooden stairs. The chains restrict the width of their steps. Someone has fallen."

A wooden bat smashed fingers against the steps.

I jerked. "Jings." I swallowed. "It's giving me a panoramic view now. Thousands of emaciated, disfigured bodies in muted gray clothes clutch at a barbed-wire fence. It's weird, but they're motionless ... like scarecrows in a black-and-white photo. People are huddled together, and snow is heavy on the ground." The muscles in my hand tightened around the knife. "I don't like this vision."

"Focus on odd or out-of-place details in the setting." Trystan's voice registered an octave higher. "What about the men? Turn your mind to them."

Trystan's voice eased my heart rate.

"The last man's feet have reached the wooden platform. It's shoulder height to a figure in the background. I can't make out anyone's face in the distance. They're distorted, hazy."

Like a lightning storm, the pictures blew up, forming a close-up snapshot.

"Oh, my ..." The hilt of the knife snapped in my hand. "There's a gallows–a masked man's p-placing nooses around their n-necks before trapdoors in the platform." For what seemed an eternity, they stood on the raised area.

I dropped the broken knife. It thudded on the wooden floor and echoed in the numb chambers of my heart. My breath lodged in my throat. Fear filled my pores. My instinct screamed at me–this was our future. It surprised me. I'd never thought the knife could act as a sort of talisman.

Slowly, I became aware of voices in the background of the room. A grip seized my hand.

"Cal, I'm here."

I felt a mental tug. While I clutched Trystan with one hand, I thrust my other palm up.

"Wait. The vision shifted. It's rewound, showing me the shadowed man's face again, splitting into halves. Other pieces are shattering. It's focusing on the smaller piece." I caught my breath and forced myself to face the next vision. "It's pitch black ... my hands have hit something solid–a wall. It's cold, rough, and sharp under my palms. I'm descending the stairs. The temperature's cold. I'm feeling along the edge with my fingers. The steps are wider and closer to the wall. My right foot doesn't need a full step before it makes contact with the ground, and I can now touch both walls with my hand." I paused. "It's like I'm going down a spiral staircase into the depths of the earth. I've hit a flat surface. Air is stirring my hair. The room has opened up, I can't feel the wall to my right. It has disappeared."

A chill crawled up my spine. "This is a wider hall, more like a room. It's still dark. I can feel a light breeze on my face and ... Ow."

"What?" The tension in Trystan's voice put me on edge.

"I'm okay. I bumped into something. It's still dark, but at my side, something is odd about the wall. There's some sort of shelf on the wall. It feels flat, like a rough board ... oh, there's the edge. It runs the length of my body." Not wanting to bruise my knee again, I reached out a hand, encountering the cold, rough surface. "Stone." My hands followed the curve of the rock, up and over my head. "A stone arch at eye level curves over the flat surface I hit." I inched past the arch, using the wall as a guide. "I'm going deeper into the room now." For more than a minute, I reported nothing. I felt only the jagged wall under my fingertips and the stone floor under my feet. "There's another arch in the sidewall like the first one. It feels about the same length. This one has something in it, under the arch. It's a cold, oddly-shaped ball, with holes ... it resembles a bowling ball."

Lightning crashed on the heels of my vision.

Within the vision, the mental picture thrust me forward. I clutched Trystan's hand tighter.

"The vision's taking me around corners too fast. I don't know where I'm going." With a blinding flash, a golden light froze, forming a vivid snapshot.

I gulped. "Golden figures ... m-my height, hundreds of them. They're standing around the perimeter of a large room. The f-faces of the statues are stiff but lifelike. There are figures of men and women carved on the far stone wall, behind the imposing gold figures. On the two opposite walls, I don't know what you'd call them ... more arches. Ahhh ... wow. There are two Egyptian coffins in the center of a sunken room, with an odd sapphire-stone altar of sorts between them." My shoulders tightened. "It's the same size as the two sarcophagi and has intricate gold etchings, but I can't make them out."

A feeling of foreboding swept through me, chilling me like a brisk winter's wind. The object between the sarcophagi was sapphire blue, like my ring. I opened my eyes.

Anna gaped, and everyone was focused on me.

Miss Anstley ran her hand down her thigh. "This is uncharted territory, even for me. Everything bears weight. You can't even neglect the shards. The vision with the shackled men and the Egyptian sarcophagi are clearly linked, but I don't understand why."

Colin grabbed a Kleenex from the end table. He wiped the sweat from his forehead and looked at Trystan. "Are you going to tell them, or should I?"

I waited for someone to respond.

Despair shadowed Trystan's eyes. His thumb stroked my knuckles. "The first vision you described—the one with people walking to the gallows—Sebastian *saw* the same thing, although he never described the faces of the people. But the Ancient Faction felt the threat. It's what the ancients are trying to uncover." His thumb stopped moving. "Sebastian saw the future using inanimate objects, also."

"Interpreting visions involves a degree of speculation," Miss Anstley said.

"Could any of this relate to Ptolemy's vision?" Mom had planted the seed in my mind. I had to ask.

Miss Anstley closed one eye and squinted through the other, watching us. "No one knows for sure what he witnessed. When one tells a story, and it hasn't been written down, yet it's repeated for months, years, decades, then centuries, it takes on a life of its own. Someone changes it, adding or subtracting from the original content and putting his or her personal stamp on it. This is one reason why ancients, for the past two thousand years, have concentrated harder on maintaining concrete records of mortal knowledge and preservation of rare possessions."

Miss Anstley raised her eyebrows. "Unfortunately, some things weren't written, leaving behind legends, myths, and untold mysteries. Written history, paintings, bards, and rare jewelry offer proof of various existences, at least to some extent. However, treasure hunters and thieves have destroyed some historic works. That is why ancients aim to keep treasures buried below ground." She lowered her shoulders. "I'd hate to speculate about something from so long ago. The one consistency in Ptolemy's vision is the threat of imminent death. Whatever the actual content of the vision, it was powerful enough to convince the Remnant Faction to pack up and leave the ancient Therans thousands of years ago."

A sob escaped Anna. "If Callie's right about this connection, could he be planning to kill all Therans?"

Miss Anstley leaned forward and picked up the broken knife hilt. She set the pieces on the end table to her right. "I believe the first vision is the most pertinent, as people are being hanged."

"So, what do we do?" Colin asked. "Why can't we go after them? Maybe Mr. Taylor and Samantha can lead us right to the bastard."

"No." Trystan released my hand and stood. "Back up—we're missing something. When Callie told us about the first vision," his words came out methodically, "She was a spectator, not a participant. She watched what was transpiring at the gallows. Yet, the vision you experienced this morning—the drowning—and the other vision of the Egyptian burial tomb—you felt it. All of it. The water. The wall."

"He's right." Miss Anstley tapped her chin. "This is a tangled web. Deciphering visions is subjective. One must lean on one's intuition in such matters as the emotions surrounding the vision. Feelings carry as much weight as what one sees."

I rubbed my forehead, trying to ease the pressure behind my eyes. "Why do the men move as they walk to the gallows, but no one in the background holding the fence moves? For that matter, why would men march in the snow wearing no shoes, wearing only thigh-length, long-sleeved, purple robes?"

Trystan's eyes pierced me.

Colin's breath caught.

Anna squealed. "No, you said their faces were hazy."

I lowered my hand. "Yes, the faces were hazy, but not their clothes. Trystan said to look for things that were out of place. I wouldn't have paid attention, but only a lunatic would walk barefoot in a blizzard yet dress in long-sleeved clothes."

"No, the robes." Trystan's sharp, glittering eyes bore into me. "They're only worn by the seven elder lords during meetings within library walls."

A tic started in Colin's jaw. "Sebastian never saw faces, and he never commented on the clothes and bare feet. The Ancients' Faction had no idea who would be targeted, but Trystan's brother saw six men, not five, walking to the gallows."

Anna bit her lower lip. "We must tell my uncle what Callie saw so the elders can protect themselves."

"Don't." Santos leaned with both hands on his cane. "The murderer's connected to the ancient Therans. One thing the enemy has proven is he can slip between the cracks." Santos cleared his throat. "This is why Sebastian warned you all about keeping your powers a secret. And don't forget Callie's now a target."

I cringed at hearing the word *target* and my name used in the same sentence. "Seven Theran elders," I mumbled under my breath. "One dead lord, five at the gallows, and one lunatic on the loose." The picture made sense. Felt right.

No one moved.

Trystan broke the silence. "Are you suggesting an elder is behind this?"

I closed my eyes, thumbed through my vision, and scanned the images on the sidelines and other out-of-place facts. "Think about it. Whoever is behind the murders must be powerful and influential, someone used to giving commands and having them obeyed."

Trystan gripped the back of his neck. "She's got a point. And, with the rightful elders killed, their heirs would inherit their parents' seats, but they wouldn't know how to run the council because of lack of training. Even those of us in the apprenticeship program would struggle. It'd be total chaos."

Santos adjusted his stance. "It would, also, be the perfect time to take over control of the Council of Elders, what with the confusion surrounding Lord Avalon's death."

"It could be any one of the elders." Miss Anstley slumped onto the seat as if weighted down by our topic.

"Callie." Anna's white fingers clenched the pillow on the couch. "Could you talk to each of them, maybe get a glimpse of the truth behind their words?"

"That's risky," I said. "Each elder would have to talk about Lord Avalon's murder for me to gauge the truth of their words. It wouldn't take long for them to figure out I was searching for answers."

The tip of Santos's cane hit the floor with a thud. "We've got to catch this elder in the act. We can't convict anyone on one person's empathic ability or visions. There's got to be concrete and tangible evidence."

Colin leaned forward on the couch. His fingers laced together. "What do we do from here?"

Miss Anstley patted her lap with her palms. "I'll set the remnants to start watching the elders and have Mr. Taylor and Samantha followed. At least this narrows down the scope of whom we're seeking."

"I'll look into the tomb." Santos tented his brows. "I've got a feeling that Callie's described the lost library we've searched thousands of years for. Rumor has it rare meteorite sapphires were hidden there."

Colin lifted his eyebrows. "How could you lose a library?"

Mr. Santos stretched his leg to the side. "People die, maps disappear, and centuries of distorted stories cripple the truth."

"And yet, you believe it still exists?" Colin asked.

Santos dug his fingers into his thigh and massaged it. "There was a map, which our remnant ancestors took with them under cover of the fire after the War of Knowledge, but it disappeared during WWII."

"Under Hitler's tyranny," Trystan said. "And you think Callie's vision may deal with this lost library?"

"There is a chance." Miss Anstley tapped her fingers on her knee. "But there's lots of speculation about the use of the map and how it works. Some believe it doesn't work unless you have a seer. And the stories from seers before us say that they couldn't get a read or vision from the map." She looked at me. "You shouldn't have experienced the second vision. The object—in this case, the knife—acts as an antenna during the time you maintain contact with it, but you'd dropped it between mental pictures. What I find interesting is your second vision. I've never witnessed one having a premonition without contact with an inorganic item—you dropped the knife before witnessing the Egyptian burial chamber—and, also, you physically experienced it and another vision."

So, people had noticed the power of my visions. I could hear it in Miss Anstley's quizzical tone. I couldn't reveal my shield, and dropping my mask was out of the question. I wasn't ready to reveal my mark, either. Trystan didn't even know the extent of my ability. Anyway, there were enough questions. I didn't need to add more to the mix.

"Understanding the significance of this lost library doesn't matter," I snapped. "We need to stop the first vision."

Colin's eyes narrowed. "I'd like to ask Uncle Michael what object Sebastian held when he channeled his vision. Maybe we could find the owner of the object before he strikes again."

"The elders would have taken that into account." Santos leaned with both hands on the cane again. "Callie's right. We've got the element of surprise on our side, but they're slippery, and remember, we don't truly know if an elder is behind this. No one outside this room should know, other than the remnants who will investigate."

It didn't take long for us to commit to working together. The recent murder, my intuition of events, and the need to find the culprit before he struck again—all these circumstances bound us.

Both Colin and Trystan explained their abilities to Mr. Santos and Miss Anstley.

"Strength is not uncommon." Miss Anstley drew her lips into her mouth. "It's a wonderful power to possess. It's a gift to have any capability at all, but for one to have two or more abilities." Her eyes flashed between Trystan and me. "That is rare, although not unheard of. Hmm. Now, if memory serves, Ptolemy had two gifts. Sight and something to do with freezing liquids. Now, that I recall, it really wasn't freezing liquids. If historical records are correct, he couldn't see the future if not for drawing the moisture from objects. His power was stronger the more he drew moisture from objects, but it was short-lived. Rumor had it that he suffered greatly after experiencing a vision."

Colin's brow arched. "I've never heard of that ability."

Miss Anstley looked at Mr. Santos and back at Colin. "Strange things have happened, and we don't always understand them."

"I couldn't agree more." Santos muffled a chuckle under his palm. "One thing's for sure. I would hate to fight against the four of you, but I believe there's a higher power at work here, and I'm very hopeful." His eyes slanted to me.

Tesla barked and darted for the kitchen door. I got up and pulled back the living room curtain. "It's Dr. Dougrey."

"Shoot. Mom's here." Colin stood. "Why's she here?"

Trystan stood. "You've got me."

I shrugged. The Dougreys followed me into the kitchen. Santos went farther into the living room and stood near Miss Anstley.

"Calm down, boy." Tesla circled my legs in anticipation. I opened the door. "Hi, Dr. Dougrey."

"Hello." She blinked. "I've tried to text my kids. No one's answered."

I gestured with my hand. "Come on in."

"Thanks." Selma crossed the threshold.

"Sorry, Mom." Colin leaned over and patted Tesla on the head. "I left my phone in the car."

Selma's smile faltered at the corners. "Your dad and I would like the three of you home tonight." She glanced at me. "We've received some bad news."

She avoided mentioning the death of the Sanderson girl, but I'm sure that's what she was referring to.

"Can Callie stay with us until her grandfather returns?" Anna gripped the kitchen chair. "I told her I'd stay with her since her granddad's gone."

Hesitation flashed briefly in Dr. Dougrey's eyes. "Sure, but it's finals week, so I want you studying."

"Thanks. We can study together."

Dr. Dougrey left my house.

Later, I called Sheriff Travis to let him know I'd be with the Dougrey family for a few nights. It's the least I could do with Travis being one of Gramp's besties.

My mind eased, knowing I wouldn't be confronting the nights alone. However, I'd be under the microscope.

CHAPTER 42

DORMANT POWERS

Trystan's version of boot camp kicked my butt. For three days, he gave me a crash course in self-defense training and treading water. Not to mention, it was finals week, and Gramps was returning from his meeting tonight. I was exhausted, and living under the Dougreys' roof was difficult. Still, we'd managed to study for finals and occasionally slip away to practice.

Half-crouched, Trystan leaned to the side, shifting his center of gravity. Bo staff in hand, he swung low. I lurched backward, but the tip of his weapon nailed me in the back of the legs, knocking me to the ground. Pain vibrated through me.

"Darn it, Cal. Do whatever you must to stay alive. Hit. Bite. Kick. Fight. Now, get up and widen your stance. We're practicing this again."

"Give her a break." Colin sat on a boulder. "She's been at it three hours. Ease up."

Trystan set the weapon at his feet and tugged his shirt over his head. His muscles glistened with sweat. He dragged the T-shirt down, wiping his face.

"Amelia Sanderson wasn't given a break. Callie's got to fight."

"You're going to kill her before they even get a chance to try. Look at her, man. She's tired. We don't even push our third-degree black belts this hard." Colin pushed himself off the rock, walked over, and placed his hand on Trystan's shoulder. "She's with us, and we'll protect her, but her body has got to rest. You've pushed her hard. Now, chill out."

Trystan picked up the staff. "We don't have time. We might have a chance if Dad knew who owned the book Sebastian held when he witnessed that vision."

"The ancients couldn't figure it out back then. What makes you think we could figure it out now? Our enemy has been planning this for years. Sebastian's vision may have prepared us, but we didn't understand it at all until we saw Callie's vision. We've got a chance now."

"Yeah, with Cal as bait." Trystan stabbed the tip of the Bo into the ground. "I don't like any of this. Mr. Santos has remnants watching Taylor, but they can't get close enough to him because all the schools in the district are locked down tight since Governor Sanderson's daughter's murder. Security's even tighter at Ashworth, where his daughter attended classes. They've managed to search Taylor's house, and not even a scrap of paper revealed anything."

Trystan flicked his wrist in the air. "We can't justify planting our agent inside the school because there are only two days until summer break begins. The elders won't do it. The only good thing is the superintendent has hired patrols to scout the school, but they stick out like a pimple on someone's nose, riding around in those black cars. Sad thing is none of them are our agents, so they're most likely no use anyway." Exasperation creased his forehead. "And Samantha's so boring. One of our guys fell asleep while watching her house."

"Give the remnants time to dig something up." Colin spread his hands wide. "Right now, enjoy your time together. At least your girlfriend's still here." He lowered his eyes. "Mine leaves Saturday for the entire summer. Forget the world and take a break." Colin picked up his towel from the rocks where the other equipment lay scattered on the ground. "Callie's granddad comes back tonight. You two should hang out. Just enjoy your time together. I'll carry this stuff back to your car and return it to the gym."

Colin's support of the remnants was awesome. At first, I'd given up hope, but after he'd witnessed my visions and our group conversations, his perspective had completely changed.

"I'll drop Trystan off later." I dug the tip of my toe into the dirt.

Colin disappeared through the trees. I sat and leaned against the boulder as two monarch butterflies landed on a branch behind Trystan.

I closed my eyes, feeling the sun's heat kiss my face. "I haven't slept the past few nights. My mind feels like I've run a 10K, and my body's limp ... and if Steve calls again, I'm filing phone harassment charges." I knew I was being unrealistic—I couldn't keep ignoring his calls.

"You're bottling up your anger. You should've told me to stop pushing you so hard. I'm sorry." Those two words were full of remorse.

"What are you thinking?"

Trystan lowered his body next to mine and plucked a long strand of grass. "Life's not guaranteed."

"Trystan."

He gazed at me. "I don't want to see you hurt."

I leaned into him, unable to respond, for I knew life had an expiration date.

He wrapped his arms around my waist. "I'm glad my aunt let you stay with us. It made things easier with your granddad being gone. Seems like Santos appreciated it, too."

"I think your aunt knew I didn't want to be alone." I made circles on his forearm with my index finger. "You know, Gramps has really appreciated your family letting me stay, especially after I mentioned the break-in. As excited as I am to see him, I dread telling him about that threatening note." I met his stare. "Man, I wish I could find some clarity to these visions. They're not complete pictures. Every decision seems to hinge on intuition. What if I can't figure out who's behind the break-in?"

"You're not fighting this alone, Cal," Trystan whispered in my ear. The sound of his voice eased my tangled nerves.

"I know, but I feel like I'm missing something crucial. I can't take it. My mind's darting all over the place, making speculations." I pulled at my hair. "I admit, the powers have come in handy lately, but it'd be nice to understand the true meaning of the visions."

"Your brain's fried. You should think about something else." Trystan rubbed my back while I rested my head on his shoulder. "How'd you feel after meeting your great aunt?"

I couldn't bring myself to call her aunt. She was nice, but it didn't feel right. "Miss Anstley seems cool. It's great she's willing to help. It's hard, though, knowing I've had a blood relative all this time—one who could've answered some of my questions growing up. Dang, those banishment orders, I hate them." I pushed away from him and rolled onto my back, feeling the cool blanket of grass beneath me. "And I wish these powers came with an instruction booklet. Everything's confusing, and interpreting my visions has become harder. What if I read them wrong, or my radar system doesn't alert me? Or the dang shield ..." The wind robbed me of my muffled last few words.

Trystan touched a finger to my mouth, stopping the flow of words. Leaning in, he kissed me. Warm fuzzies burst into flames. He withdrew. "Your emotions are raging all over the place, and you've got every reason to be concerned. I didn't want to comment on it this Sunday with everyone else around, but when you described your visions the other day, it reminded me of Sebastian and how he felt trying to learn how to control his power. It made me wonder if you're getting stronger, if there's still more to your powers."

I tilted my head to the side.

Trystan's eyes converged on mine. "Instructor James could be right. You might have dormant powers. Part of me wonders if we'll ever make sense of all this. I also wonder if your mom's letter is right, that you're an example of Therans evolving with the times."

"So, you think my mom was right? Powers develop to meet the demands of the future?"

"Cal, I don't know what to think exactly. I've gone over it in my mind. The book said protectors are seen in times of cataclysmic events, then, you had your weird vision with the burial chamber." He exhaled. "I'm lost, like you."

I moved my forearm to block the brightness of the sun. "I hate this pressure. Last night, I woke up drenched with sweat. Anna didn't sleep, either. The visions keep repeating themselves, pawing at my mind. Anna couldn't stop asking questions about them and about Mr. Taylor. Between your cousins' questions and your dad driving me nuts, scrutinizing my every move, I've barely had a moment's peace. It'll be nice having my space back. Speaking of which, your dad wasn't happy when I got out of the car Sunday. He must've questioned your aunt later that night. He doesn't like me."

"Dad's being an idiot. His life revolves around profits and elder responsibilities."

"I'm glad your aunt calmed him down. If he'd sent me home the other night, I don't know what I'd have done."

"It helps that Dad believes I'll relinquish my title to my uncle if he tries to interfere in our relationship. It pisses him off."

I didn't want to fuel the growing animosity between the two of them. One day, his dad would know me—truly know me. This divide had to stop.

"Give him a break. In his eyes, you're dating a human. It's got to be embarrassing for him. He doesn't understand us." I tugged on his hand and drew his eyes back to mine. "Besides, your dad's worked his butt off trying to help the elders find the murderer, and you know he's got less to go on than we do."

"I know. But he angers me." His eyes lowered to our linked fingers. "I was never good enough. Now, you're not good enough. But I still feel a sense of betrayal keeping information from him." His eyes met mine. "Are we doing the right thing, leaving him in the dark?"

I sat up. "An army's working on this. If we tell your dad, we risk him telling someone. The murderer is powerful. And close enough to have someone kill a lord in Egypt and a couple of people here. Your dad's investigators haven't found one person who's traveled back and forth from Egypt to the United States. There are Therans on both sides of the ocean, jumping at someone's command. We're doing what we must. I trust Mr. Santos." Anxiety crept back in. "This conversation's freakin' me out. Can we talk about something else? Tonight, I won't have you guys around to help if I need rescuing. It's just Gramps and me."

Trystan pulled me into his arms. A peaceful sensation washed over me as the awkward moment eased. Time slid by, and we fell asleep. I woke as the sun rested in the west, above the tree line. I'd experienced the best sleep I'd had in days.

"Mmm." Trystan stretched his arms above his head. A smile skimmed across his lips. "I'm gonna miss fighting you for the bathroom in the morning. You're cute when you wake up."

Two butterflies fluttered around us. One landed on my forehead. I blew a puff of air, and it took off and joined the other, dancing above the green grass.

Trystan chuckled and gave me an ornery, crooked smile.

In a flash, Trystan's palms gripped my rib cage, and his fingers were tickling my sides. I thrashed on the ground like a fish trapped in a fisherman's grip. I pushed his hands away, trying to dislodge from his grip, but it didn't work. A giggle escaped my lips. He released me. His hands rested on the grass, on either side of my face. With the brightest of smiles, he chuckled.

"It's good to hear you laugh again."

I kissed the tip of his nose.

A mischievous grin caused his dimple to show. He leaned toward me and captured my lips with his. His fingers curled under my neck. I closed my eyelids as his lips teased my mouth for the longest time.

I sighed, feeling my heart race with excitement. I opened my eyes, and he pulled back. The lazy sun dipped behind the trees.

"Hey." I pushed on Trystan's shoulder, and he groaned. "I'd love to stay here, but Colin took your car. I've got to get home, and I'm hungry."

Ten minutes later, I pushed open the door to my house. Tesla bolted from the living room and greeted us. Trystan walked across the kitchen and fanned through some pages from my English book, which I'd left on the table after studying. "When's your next test?"

"English and history are back-to-back on Friday, with a half-hour break between them." Both of us avoided saying Taylor's name. The thought of being near him drained me.

"Let's celebrate together after the exams. Let's meet at Coccia House."

"Awesome. Sounds good." The clock on the kitchen wall chimed. "Oh, I've been meaning to ask you. Did you get an invite to Sandy's new boyfriend's graduation party?"

"Yeah. I'm surprised he invited us. He doesn't know us."

"He invited us, so Sandy's got some of her friends around."

"That's nice," Trystan said. "Let's talk about it later. I've got to get home."

I locked the door to the house, and we jumped in the Jeep. A warm sunset highlighted the sky. Birds swept low near Trystan's driveway as we pulled in.

"Everyone's cars are gone." I peered across the dashboard. "We're not that late. Wonder where everyone could've gone."

I got out and shut the door. We'd no sooner walked up the step than a loud voice thundered from inside.

Trystan pushed open the door and grimaced, drawing his face into a frown. I stepped across the entry and froze mid-stride.

"Damn you." His father's words echoed off the walls. "The death toll is rising. I demand you summon all elders to an emergency meeting. My investigators have informed me that Lord Avalon's murderer is hunting and collecting Therans with powers. These are not two separate cases as originally thought. This is one group working against the good of all Therans. There could be an uprising. And if you place any value on my son Sebastian's vision, I'd hurry. We don't know whose necks are on the other end of those ropes."

Guilt rode my nerves, but sometimes secrets were a necessary evil.

His tone softened a degree. "We go back a long way, Lord Anstley. Under the leadership of the enacted Council of Elders, things have run fair for centuries. Until now. We've got to find out who's behind this before it's too late."

Hmm. So, Trystan's dad was speaking with another member of the Council of Elders.

Trystan's head tipped forward, and his brow arched.

We waited in silence for several minutes, listening.

"No, I've turned up nothing regarding the blasted archaeological dig. It's not a pressing matter. The archaeologists aren't digging near Alexandria, so the library is safe. Egypt's laws are tight, and they will protect what's unearthed."

"No, I'm not chasing library myths when future lives are at risk." His steely voice was low. "Yes, my methods may be unorthodox. However, not once have they been anything other than unselfish. I've given my entire life to the council at the expense," silence fell for a moment, "of both my sons. Call the damn meeting. Get every Theran there, or I will." A loud clank sounded from the other room.

I made a sign to Trystan for him to call me tomorrow and headed back to my Jeep. This information proved very interesting.

CHAPTER 43

CHANGES

"Pack your bags. Now. We're leaving." Gramps plunged down the stairs and threw two suitcases onto the living room floor. He clutched a smaller bag, his blue eyes shadowed in fear.

Gramps had come home late last night and assumed I'd stayed with the Dougreys because of the break-in. I hadn't explained the dagger or note until now. If I had, I was sure he'd have left the grain convention and rushed home. I couldn't risk him getting into an accident as Nana had.

"We can't." I stepped around the luggage and grabbed his forearm. He whirled around to face me. "This is exactly why I didn't tell you everything over the phone. You've got to calm down."

"Like heck I do." He thrust the bag at me. "We can't stay here. I've got friends who will hide us. Put your stuff in the suitcase. Maybe they'll forget about you once you're gone and not hanging around Trystan anymore."

"I can't run. They can find us." And kill you.

"I won't lose you, too." Gramps's bottom lip quivered as a tear trailed down his cheek.

I wrapped my arms around his waist, pulled him close, and buried my face in his shoulder. He dropped his forehead onto the top of my head and gripped me tightly. His shoulders began to shake, and my heart clenched tight at hearing his breathing.

"Gramps." I pulled back from him. "I've got no choice. I'm not the only one who's been threatened."

He wiped the tears from his face with the back of his hand and paused. He looked down at our Bible on the stand, the one Nana used to read to me. "I'm scared. But I've got to trust God's given you these powers for a reason. But I can't help being weak when it comes to you. I've lost so much." He let out a breath of air. "Though, I've got to stay strong in my faith."

"I'm scared, too. But I have to trust my gut intuition." Moisture built up behind my eyes at hearing the cry in his voice. "Mom and Dad thought something like this might happen. I must stay. I won't let the others die, not if I can stop it."

For over an hour, he held me on the couch in silence.

<h1 style="text-align:center">CHAPTER 44</h1>

HUNTING AND COLLECTING

Friday dawned. Sunlight slid in around the edge of the bedroom curtains. I'd woken for the fourth time—my sixth consecutive night of broken sleep since we'd found the dagger. More problems mounted, and I wasn't any closer to figuring things out. I pressed my fingers into my lower back and dug at the ache lodged there.

Today was the last day of exams. My exam schedule was so weird. The irregular class times had thrown off my entire week. To top it off, I'd have to see Taylor today for my history exam.

I buried my face in the pillow. Taylor and my exams weren't the only things on my mind—Lord Dougrey's words kept creeping into my thoughts. "Hunting and collecting Therans with powers." Despite this added fear, I was glad we'd overheard the phone conversation. My intuition had been correct—Trystan's dad was honest.

Tesla rubbed his cold, wet nose against my cheek. He whined and licked my face. Slobber stretched from my chin to my hairline.

"Yuck." I rolled over, dragging the covers with me, and wiped my face with the sheet. "I don't need your help washing my face."

A rap sounded on my bedroom door, then it eased open. "Thought I'd heard you stir. I was coming in to wake you." Gramps held two envelopes at his side. "Our passports came."

I flipped the covers back. "Awesome. I'm up for a change in scenery." Too bad it had to be later. Maybe I could easily escape this reality for a while, but my family and friends meant the world to me, and there was no way I was letting them down.

"Come on, boy." Gramps patted his leg. "Half the morning's already gone. I was afraid to wake you after our conversations these past two nights. You need your rest," he squinted at me, "but you've got exams, right?"

A lump formed in my throat. Dread took hold of me. Living in two worlds was confusing. I hated conforming to teenage demands—exams, my job—it all seemed pointless, given that my other world was crumbling.

What sucked was that I'd have to face the day acting as if Taylor was a typical teacher and not someone out to annihilate the elders. At least after these two tests, summer vacation would start. Once it did, I'd have more time to figure things out.

Gramps's frown twisted in concern. "I can call Principal Kennedy and tell him you ain't feeling well."

"No, I'd just have to make them up later." I threw my legs over the bedside and placed my feet on the cool wooden floor. "Besides, Trystan will be there with me."

"All I ask is that you're careful. I want you to stay with someone at all times. Crowds are safer."

I managed an awkward smile and tried to project a calm demeanor, yet all the while, my insides were wilting with anxiety.

CHAPTER 45

ENEMY

I gave Miss Delong my completed English exam and exited the classroom.

The sunlight shone in from the windows onto the hall floor. Some students were taking down posters advertising basketball events that had already happened while others cleaned out their lockers.

I pinched the bridge of my nose. Steve tried to talk to me about the driving incident before class started, but the exam bell rang, forcing us to take seats. This was his first day back. I wished they could've arranged for him to take his exam in the principal's office, with one of the guidance counselors, instead of allowing him to take it with us.

This conversation was another weight that displaced my mental equilibrium. Was I holding a grudge? Was I being unfair?

I made it a couple of steps and skittered to a stop. Trystan's eyes were intense, and only for me. His twisted smile gave me a warm surge of strength. I took a deep breath. He wrapped his arms around me. I hated the thought of facing Taylor—but I wasn't doing it alone.

We walked to my locker. I pulled out the last of my stuff and stashed it in my bag.

A man, dressed in black with a gold security badge, passed us. Since Governor Sanderson's daughter's murder, two security guards with black security vehicles were on staff during school hours.

"Hey, are we still on for tonight?" Trystan approached my other side and leaned his shoulder against my locker. "I'm hungry for pizza."

Food sounded so good. "Yes, sure."

Trystan wrapped his arms around me. "Your body's strung tight," he whispered in my ear and pulled back. His full lips stretched across his perfect white teeth, but his eyes clouded with worry. He looked over my head at Mr. Taylor's classroom. "We'll get through this. Anna's meeting up with Colin later tonight to work on a research project. They all agree. You need to get away from all this stress."

Coded: Colin and Anna were in detective mode, working with Santos and the remnants to solve this mess. And Trystan was babysitting me.

I stretched up on my tiptoes, gave him a thank-you kiss on the cheek, and took a deep breath, swallowing my anxieties. We walked into history class for our last final.

A booming laugh erupted from the back of the room.

Principal Kennedy strode to the whiteboard and gestured us forward. "Come. Come grab a seat. You're one of the last classes to finish taking exams." His grin stretched up into a wink.

Anxiety drained from my body like a stuck balloon.

I hated the wave of relief that filled me. Was I a coward?

The exam bell rang.

Principal Kennedy stood at the whiteboard. "Mr. Taylor's out, and I'm filling in for him. He's got food poisoning. Now, we don't have much time, so let's get down to business. The test is a comprehensive exam."

Trystan bumped my foot with his shoe, and his white teeth shined.

I exhaled, so grateful for Mr. Taylor's food poisoning.

Just short of an hour and a half later, I flipped over my test. A few minutes passed before Trystan finished. We collected our things and wished Principal Kennedy a good summer.

We hoofed it down the steps toward the lobby.

Steve was waiting in the cafeteria at a circular table. I was losing it. Limited sleep and food had begun to play with my mind. If I could get through the day, I would be able to rest tonight, but that meant not ignoring Steve again.

I stopped at the base of the steps. "Since Taylor's not here, can we meet at Coccia House later? I need to talk to Steve."

"I don't know about that." Trystan rubbed the back of his neck.

"Taylor's not here. And I'm with Steve. I'll be fine."

"Okay. Only because Taylor's not here." He gave me a weak smile. "I'm glad you're willing to talk with Steve. Grudges aren't healthy."

"Thanks. Let's meet at six?"

Trystan nodded, and we entered the cafeteria.

"Hey, Steve," I said, my voice tight.

"Hi." Steve pushed back his chair, stood, and picked up his backpack. "How do you think you did on your exams?" Steve's voice was hoarse, and he didn't look at me but fidgeted with the strap of his backpack.

I shrugged. "I don't know. I'm just glad it's over."

"Me, too," Trystan said. "It's been a difficult week. Hey, I'm taking off."

Steve nodded at him. "See you later, dude."

"Catch you later, Steve." Trystan gripped my hand, squeezed it, and stepped back. He scanned the cafeteria, turned, and met my eyes. Reluctance etched his face. "Okay, see you in a few hours." Trystan kissed my cheek and walked away.

A couple of stragglers stood three tables from Steve and me. Some guy with an Ohio State baseball cap sat on a chair leaning against the brick wall, speaking to a girl dressed in black. I cringed. I hated audiences.

Steve looked over his shoulder and jerked his head. "It's crowded in here. Come on, let's get some fresh air." I followed him down the back corridor. He held the door open, and we stepped out into the warm air. Rays of sun were beginning to disappear as darker clouds moved in, hanging low in the distant sky.

We walked away from the school in silence. It was hard to string sentences together when my mind was running a race with other worries. He stopped near the dumpsters. One of the security guards had parked his black car beside the garbage containers.

I hung back on the sidewalk, maintaining some distance. I crossed my arms, and my purse strap fell into the crease of my elbow. The wind blew the tree branches as shadows danced on the ground.

I wracked my brain for something to say, suppressing my frustration. If he wanted to talk, I would talk. "Looks like it's going to rain."

"Yeah." Steve glanced up at the trees, then turned to gaze at me. "I'm truly sorry. We were out on a joy ride. I never meant for anyone to get hurt–"

"No—you never expected to get caught." I sucked in my lower lip and contemplated my words. Steve had been a friend–a reckless one–but a friend. If Nana hadn't died because of someone's careless driving, this wouldn't have hit so hard. But maybe the threat of the charges he'd faced had made him wake up. "Steve, accidents happen, but you were driving the car that ran Trystan and me off the road. We could have died less than a mile from where Nana died. Finding out you–someone I trusted–was driving the car was rough. I know you weren't responsible for Nana's death, but *stop* your stupid driving."

"I'm sorry." He kicked at the ground. "It was a mistake. I never considered my actions. Never thought I could lose you as a friend. You wouldn't pick up my calls. Or call me back. I didn't know what to think. I swear it will never happen again." Steve's hands fidgeted on the zipper of his backpack. "I don't want to lose your friendship."

His words were sincere.

"Don't do it again," I warned him. "Your joyride could've put us in the hospital or worse."

"Callie, I'm sorry." He croaked.

"We're friends, Steve, but be straight with me from now on." My frustration decreased by slow degrees. I sounded more composed. "I haven't been fair. I shouldn't have waited so long to talk with you."

"Thanks, Callie." His voice came out a whisper.

"We'll get through this." I nudged him in the arm, feeling a weight lifted from my shoulders. It wasn't perfect, but a second chance at friendship.

He smiled, his eyes cautious. "You know, since I got arrested, my parents are paying attention to me again. They actually gave me a curfew, and they're finally talking to one another. Dad's got me going to his house when Mom is at work. I wish it hadn't taken me getting into trouble for them to realize they'd been ignoring me."

"I'm glad. How are things working out with the courts?" The wind blew strands of my hair in my face, and I pushed them back behind my ear.

"Uncle Lindy got me a good lawyer. Since I don't have any prior convictions, I might get off with probation for two years, but I'll be in debt the rest of my life helping to pay the school damages." Thunder rumbled in the distance. Steve held his hand out, palm up. "You're right about the rain." He gazed at me. "I'm glad we're okay."

I repositioned my purse as raindrops spit. "We're good." I gave him an encouraging smile.

Steve clutched his bag tighter and looked up at the clouds. "I'm heading home. Can I call you sometime?"

"Uh, yeah, sure."

Steve took a couple of steps back toward the school. "Are you coming?"

"I'll walk." I pointed. "My Jeep's in the parking lot around the corner."

"Catch you later." Steve headed back inside through the doors.

I made my way toward the corner of the school. The wind whistled through the trees lining the rear-parking alcove. An eerie, urgent feeling flared in my gut. Something was wrong. My pulse accelerated.

My shield popped up. A bubble of golden light surrounded me.

Fear sparked. I froze. My breath stopped.

I spun around and faced Mr. Sykes.

The school door automatically closed, positioning Sykes twenty feet from me.

He wore a white T-shirt and an open, black, button-down shirt that flapped in the wind, revealing the handle of a pistol tucked into his jeans. The handle looked real. Dangerous. His lips were twisted in a snarl as if he'd bitten into something rotten.

Death whispered from his gaze.

Panic crashed into my awareness. I stepped back off the sidewalk onto uneven ground and heard a loud thud from a car door. I paused, half turned, watching Mr. Sykes through the sprinkling rain, and saw Mr. Taylor marching onto the curb, having just exited the black security guard car.

Terror shot through me.

They wanted me.

My mouth went dry.

Mr. Sykes had been part of the school backdrop for as long as I could remember. How could he be involved? My mind sputtered, trying to fit him into what I knew about my vision, but I couldn't make sense of it.

Sykes's eyes narrowed in on me as he inched closer. "You didn't honestly think we'd let you date Trystan, did you? You're as polluted as this waste heap." He jerked his thumb toward the dumpster. "This mission has dragged because of your interference."

"Why couldn't you have stopped dating him?" Truthful concern reverberated from Taylor's words. "We warned you."

I wanted to run, but my feet had grown roots. Petrified. Diffuse the situation. Tell them you're crimson-blood. Show them your mark. Even while I was telling myself these things, instinct screamed, *NO*.

My shield intensified. The golden yellow glowed as the red pulsated in time with my heartbeat.

Could I kill?

How could I live with myself if I did?

Couldn't I talk my way out of it?

Sykes lunged for me, wrapping his steely hand around my forearm and jerking me to his side. His fingers dug into my arm, making red mountains between digging fingernail marks.

He dug into my flesh with a strength greater than mine.

"NOOOOO." I stomped the heel of my foot into his shoe. He didn't flinch. He wasn't affected. I wrenched my arm out of his hold and dodged him as the butt of the gun sliced through the air, aiming for my skull, missing me by an inch.

I ran. "HELP. SOMEONE HELP."

"You wench," Sykes roared.

I ran past the black car, but Sykes threw his arms around my shoulders in a death grip.

I squirmed and thrashed against his hold, sinking my teeth into his upper arm—drawing blood.

His grip loosened, and the gun swung wildly in his other hand. I pushed against his body, sending us in a spin-drag for several feet. His back hit the dumpsters. Metal trash bins banged together like a cart on wheels, and screeching, they hit the curb.

The gun dropped to the ground, but his other arm swung around me, tightening, constricting. I couldn't suck in air, couldn't breathe.

"Stop it, Sykes," Mr. Taylor yelled.

Simultaneously, the force of a twenty-ton truck hit my face, whipping my head back.

Sykes squeezed the life from my lungs, and the edge of the world dimmed.

Day turned to night.

CHAPTER 46

CHAOS

Distant voices dragged me from sleep like a jack-hammer pounding inside my skull. I tried to touch my face, but my hands wouldn't move. Something heavy bound them.

Cold fear congealed the blood within my veins.

I opened my eyes. Pain seized me. My right eye opened completely. Trying to look through the left was like looking through a slit the width of a sewing needle. Taylor had one heck of a punch, but it was nothing compared to Sykes's strength. I lowered my jaw, and pain radiated up the side of my face into the hairline. Immediately, darkness surrounded me, except for a faint light around the edge of a doorway. I shook my head to dislodge the cobwebs, realizing the surface I lay on was a soft bed. Somehow, I shifted as if I'd moved, even though I hadn't.

Tears stung my eyes. They'd captured me.

I froze.

Words reached my ears.

"Why didn't you wait in the car like you were told?" Mr. Sykes's gravelly voice set my teeth on edge.

"I'm glad I didn't stay. She gave you a good fight," Taylor countered.

"If you hadn't interfered, I could've silenced her."

"Is that your remedy? Killing?" Something clanked, like metal hitting metal. "You know my orders. I falsified records, posed as a teacher, and screened the Dougrey kids for powers. Those kids have powers. What kind of superpowers, I don't know. But what I want to know is why they haven't told the elders, which is not my job to figure out. I'm done. I plan to leave for Egypt and get to business."

"You'll be waitin' until his lordship gives the orders," Sykes said.

"You act as if the only thing that matters to you is his lordship's orders, and yet, if you had killed the girl, you would've been explicitly going against his lordship's commands." Taylor's voice was taut. "He doesn't rule me. I'm a gemologist, not a murderer."

"Your fingerprints are all over this, just as mine. Quit your bellyaching."

"I hate the idea of that human dating a crimson-blood like Trystan Dougrey. His lordship had no choice but to intercede since Lord Dougrey wouldn't put his foot down with his son, but that doesn't mean killing the girl is the only way. I tried to distract her by offering her a chance to tutor other kids this summer in the hopes I could find a way to drive a wedge between them, but I don't want any part in her death."

"Killing the girl is the only way. We can use her death to make Dougrey's estranged father-son relationship work to our advantage. Trystan will have to believe us once we show him those forged papers implicating his dad for embezzlement. We'll strike when Trystan's weakest. I'll make him see workin' with us is the right thing." Sykes snickered.

I inhaled. Did Sykes have a beating heart beneath that block of ice?

Papers rattled, shuffling in the other room.

"If you think the boy will swing our way after she's dead, then you're nuts," Taylor said. "Trystan cares for her. That's why Lord Kingston's pissed. Anyone with half a brain could see it."

A bark of laughter erupted from Sykes. "We've got it all planned. All we must do is link the girl's death to Amelia Sanderson and allow Mad Jekyll and Hyde to take the fall. That's all it'll take. A simple set-up." Fingers snapped.

"How convenient. Cleveland's notorious murderer gets loose, and you're going to pin the killings on him."

"We busted him out. We needed him to draw the authorities' attention away from us."

"Sykes, you can't honestly think it will be that easy. How do you plan to explain away Lord Avalon's murder and his son's? No Theran will ever believe a human did it."

"We do nothin'. Not every murder case is solved."

"Why does anyone have to die?" Taylor asked.

"Amelia was given a choice. Join our cause or suffer the consequences." Another clanking noise sounded from the other room. "The other recruits have adjusted."

"You're a hired bodyguard, but act more like an assassin." Taylor's voice tightened. "Killing Lord Sanderson's daughter was sloppy."

"I don't care. I've worked as his lordship's bodyguard for thirty years. Then, suddenly, he puts me on this case, where the most excitement I've experienced is fightin' with a human. I'm not waitin' anymore." Sykes let slip a sinister cackle. "It's amazin'—even desperate humans can find hidden strength. I've heard how they get an adrenaline rush durin' tragic situations."

"Your hatred for humans has made your judgments shoddy."

Sykes was beyond stupid if he believed I'd had an adrenaline rush. But was he dumb enough to think he could fool so many people with his cover-up plan for the murders?

A quiet laugh surfaced from Sykes. "My judgment's not bad. Besides, your dowsing power won't keep you alive. Samantha serves more purpose as a lie detector. I don't know what purpose you serve for his lordship, but you're a waste of the air you breathe."

Dowsing? What in the heck's that?

"I don't dowse," Taylor said. "And I don't agree with these tactics. No one should've died. Callie's Lord Kingston's business. But give the girl credit. She saved Anna Dougrey's life. The longer I work with you, the more despicable I find you, Mr. Sykes. Every one of those lives you took mattered to someone. Count me out of any future assignments. Samantha and I'll be on a plane to Egypt tomorrow, and I plan to be excavating by the end of next week."

"You will do as you're told." A low growl filled the room.

At that moment, heels clicked on the floor. "Will you two stop it?"

I strained to hear. It sounded like Samantha's voice.

"You'll wake the girl if you keep yelling, and Elizabeth will come down here," Samantha said. "Picking up the human and Elizabeth at the same time was a mistake. Don't make it two."

"If Elizabeth hasn't learned the truth about her guardian by now," Sykes's gruff tone contained a measure of hatred, "then she's not gonna."

"She's studying to be a nurse, which should count for something," Samantha interjected. "Now, come on. Derek brought back some grub from North Pointe Grill. He's putting the small boat away. So, hurry."

"Does anyone eat anything besides hamburgers around here?" Taylor asked. "Ugh. What I wouldn't give for a glass of wine and some lobster from Maine."

"Give me steak or hamburger any day," Sykes murmured.

"They've set things up in the galley," Samantha said. "Go eat before his lordship gets here. I'll check on the girl."

"Don't worry about checking on her," Sykes said. "She's out cold. Oh, you can thank your pretty boy here." A chair scraped the floor. "He punched her. I would've killed her. She dug her teeth into me. I'd love to throw her overboard."

"Aww, poor baby," Samantha teased. "It's a good thing you had your rabies shot. If you die, we have plenty of recruits who can replace you. We'll be ready to rise against the elders shortly. More importantly, do you two think Trystan will fall for the human serial murderer having killed Callie?"

"Aw, you have such a loving heart." Sykes's sarcasm twisted my gut.

"Samantha, you knew about this setup?" Taylor roared.

"It doesn't matter if Samantha knew or not." Something banged on a surface. "You're either with us or against us. Pick a side or die, Taylor."

"I've picked a side, but I won't kill for it."

"You're an idiot. As we speak, the Council of Elders has allowed humans easier access to the Alexandrian Library. I won't let another decade go by with those vermin infesting our halls. With one wrong turn, a secret entrance could open, and humans could find the underground caverns and learn about us. I won't allow history to repeat itself. It wasn't just humans who got hunted during the witch trials. Our forefathers did."

"You're not my boss, Sykes," Taylor said. "Once we dock, I'm getting off this boat."

"Will you two grow up?" Samantha shouted. "We don't have time for this. Quit your arguing, and let's go up on deck and eat." Their gruff words faded into the distance as footfalls exited the outside corridor.

Boat. Water.

My lips quivered. Fifty pounds of pressure landed on my chest, feeling like someone was sawing through it with a dull knife.

How much time had passed since they took me? By now, someone had to be searching for me. Gramps would've gotten Trystan. They'd hunt for me. But did they remember everything I'd told them from my vision? Would Colin stand up against Sykes's strength? Would they find me in time?

Trystan ... warm teardrops cascaded down my cheeks.

Desperate, I moved my legs and found they weren't bound like my wrists. I twisted my hands and tried to pull free from the makeshift handcuffs. I dug my teeth into the material and spit out frayed pieces. I could do this.

Tap. Tap. The sound came from the door.

I lifted my head from the pillow and peered over the edge of the bed at the light coming through the crack in the door. A flash of blue stormed my vision, moving toward the foot of my bed in the shadows at the opposite side of the room, and then *something* ducked behind a curtain.

What the heck? I blinked at the hidden bulge.

A long snake-like neck with feathers peered from around the drape.

I blinked again.

Like a ghost, the large, blue, feathery creature with long legs vaulted on the mattress. Light from the hall illuminated its thin downward-curved beak. The mysterious creature's bill turned as hot as an ember of coal.

I inhaled. My anxiety increased, pulling my shield forth.

Within a wink of an eye, it leaped from the light into the shadows at the head of the bed. The stench of fish filled my nostrils.

I clenched my eyes shut. I'm seeing things. This isn't possible. I know I'm seeing things.

The bed dipped as the creature shifted its weight. A burning scent filled the chamber. I jerked against the ties, feeling the restraints loosened a little.

Was *it* helping me?

Even if I made it out of here, I couldn't swim off the vessel. Getting control of my nerves, I opened my eyes and slammed down my barrier.

The door hinges squeaked, and more light seeped into the room. A human figure stood in the doorway. Sykes? Taylor?

The bed shook as blue feathers brushed my face.

Again, I glimpsed the creature's snake-like neck before it shimmered into the shadows, disappearing like a ghost. What the—?

I jerked against the still tethered binds and closed my eyes again, faking sleep.

Stay calm. Breathe. Slowly.

Seconds later, icy fingers touched my ankle, moving in circles up my calves.

Where are my shoes?

Fingers squeezed my knee. This wasn't the feathered creature. Don't flinch. They'll know you're awake.

The bed indented at my hip. Heavy breathing hovered above me as hands moved up my body ... neck ... face.

Vomit climbed up my throat. My head was spinning with horrid images.

Hands dug into my hair along the side of my face.

"No bumps on the head." The fingers moved to touch the right side of my face, and a woman with a slight British accent whispered to me. "You're crying. Good, you're awake. Can you move?"

"Yes." My desperate word triggered a gut-wrenching pain in my stomach. I was so glad it wasn't Sykes or Taylor.

"Let me cut your bindings. When my guardian returns, I'll ensure he fires Mr. Sykes. I can't believe he would resort to such trickery. Samantha has always said Sykes loved tampering with women's emotions, but this is beyond fun and games."

Did she really think this was a diversion for them? I opened my eyes. The room allowed a small shaft of light inside, but not enough to discern the identity of my potential rescuer.

She continued to whisper while moving about the room. I listened to the inflection of her voice and lost track of my thoughts until the glint of the silver blade in her hand robbed me of breath. I wanted to grab the knife and break free, but trust in my intuition kept me in place. My life depended on it.

She gripped the ropes between my bound hands. "Ouch! Looks like you worked at getting untied."

"Ah, yeah!" I did use my teeth.

"I saw Mr. Sykes carrying your body on board. I've never trusted him." She placed the knife to the bonds and sawed into the material. "Taylor hates certain people, but he's not as cruel. Samantha has told me hideous stories of Sykes bullying girls, but what he did to you tonight goes way beyond bullying. Until tonight, I'd never witnessed it. I'd always thought it was foolish storytelling on her part."

The ties fell to my legs. "We don't have much time. Come on."

Her tight voice hid nothing. She genuinely wanted to help.

Relief came alive, surging through me. I sat up and clutched my wrists, rubbing the heavy sensation from them. She straightened, and my bed leveled out.

She moved toward the door and whispered. "Can you see enough to follow me? There's a small boat we can board."

I stood. Nausea gripped the pit of my stomach, churning acid and sending me spiraling back onto the bed.

"Come," the harsh whisper broke through my fog.

I took a deep breath and got up, looking around the room for the feathered creature, but couldn't find it. We crept into the hall.

"Sh ... Sh ..." she whispered. "There are stairs at either end of the boat. Keep close. I don't want Mr. Sykes on our trail."

I followed her from inches away, thankful for the carpeted floor that muffled our footsteps. My fingers searched the cool walls as we crept through the narrow passage, passing doors on either side until we reached a large room. It was still dark but for the one lamp standing in the corner, illuminating a room full of white furniture, a large kitchen at the far end, and a staircase that climbed through to the tiled ceiling.

The boat heaved, and so did my stomach. I threw a hand over my mouth, forcing myself to swallow burning acid. My rescuer stood by the windows looking out. I pulled the curtain back farther and peered out. Rain sprinkled the glass. White and red flashing lights sparkled in the distance. Angry water swells increased, distorting the mainland illumination. A pyramid cast light from the shore. I blinked. My brain took half a second to realize it was the Rock-n-Roll Hall of Fame. We must be out on Lake Erie.

I took in the room—more like a museum. Twenty to thirty paintings were stacked on the floor in the kitchen. Boxes lined up, front-to-back, in front of shelves loaded with golden knickknacks, precisely stationed. More paintings hung from the walls. Egyptian-motif wallpaper and weird, rusty metal contraptions hung between the prints, and medieval weapons and swords, staffs, and metal balls covered in sharp spikes hung from chains. The modern kitchen appliances and knives on the counter rounded out the décor, making the room clash.

"My guardian's a collector of medieval devices. He owns several art galleries around the world." She turned toward me. Soft, short red hair curled around her heart-shaped face. Moss-green eyes narrowed in on me. "You're awfully young for Sykes."

I didn't have time to challenge her words. "How do I get out of here?"

"Once we're up on deck, we'll have to lower the smaller dinghy into the water. Last time I saw them, they were eating with the captain."

A loud noise, like the whine of a turbine engine, interrupted us.

"That's the helicopter. He's early. Wait here." She sprinted up the steps and disappeared.

Words stuck to my tongue. I'd barely worked up any anger, not yet having gotten over my shock at finding someone willing to help. Then, she vanished. My mind skipped a beat. Things weren't adding up. Why wasn't she scared? Who else lived on this boat? Why did she help me—and then take off?

I scanned the room, noting a tapestry under the bar near stacks of old books. I knelt before the familiar Egyptian picture and traced my finger over the bumpy, interwoven threads of colors, terracotta, light greens, and gray blues. The last time I'd seen the canvas, it had been hanging in the Historic Hall inside Ashworth Library.

I reached over my head and grabbed the cool granite counter, straightening. I narrowed my eyes, wincing from the pain. My fingers bumped red-inked newspaper cuttings. Several of them were marked with a yellow highlighter. An open manila file, marked Callie Tresham, lay across the counter.

I grabbed it, fanning through the clippings. Article after article about my family's murders had lain there, available for anyone to see, on a countertop next to two coffee cups and a comic strip.

If this red-haired girl lives here, she'd have had access to these papers. So, why'd she help me? Whose side was she on?

I inhaled, holding one of the clippings up. I read the words—murder, three dead. Fire consumed bodies. My vision blurred, and my fingers trembled as I digested the words in the margin in red.

JULY 7TH – MISSION COMPLETED.

July 7th – the day my mom, dad, and Ella died.
   The stench of tobacco tickled my nose.
   I stiffened and dropped the paper to the floor.
   "Tsk. Tsk."
   I wasn't alone.
   "Death is so sweet."

CHAPTER 47

KINGSTON

An ice-cold chill consumed me. I bit my lip, feeling the boat's sway, and turned around.

A man stood in the hallway from where my rescuer and I'd come, his face hidden in the shadows. He leaned against the entrance frame, one leg crossed over his foot in a relaxed, almost bored, pose. He wore a dark suit, white shirt, and red tie. Manicured, skeletal fingers pinched a glowing cigar smelling of cedar. He exhaled. A puff of smoke drifted out from the darkness, where shadows disguised his facial features.

"Rarely do I reveal my identity, but, in your case," the man's voice resonated throughout the vast room, "I have made an exception."

The shadowed man from my vision.

My stomach recoiled. I wrapped an arm around my waist.

He pointed to the counter. "I see you've found the clippings. I had hoped to make an album of them." He uncrossed his legs and stepped from the shadows. Moss-green eyes glared at me, dark around the edges. Webbed-blue veins branched down across his nose to his wrinkled cheeks, and a snarl laced his lips. A self-satisfied scowl grew into a menacing death-awaits-you smile.

I stepped back. His disdain filled me with ice. "W-who are you?"

"You do not remember me?"

I squinted. His identity escaped me.

He bowed. "Lord Kingston at your service." His exaggerated politeness mocked my terror.

Taylor and Sykes worked for this man. "I don't understand."

He flicked his ashes. "Of course, you would not remember me. You were young, after all. Nonetheless, your family stole what was rightfully mine." He shrugged. "And your interference in my plans has cost me time and money."

My shield intensified, brightening.

His eyes narrowed, surveying me. "Allow me to connect the pieces for you. What you learn today makes no difference. It is your last, and the sooner I end this conversation, the better. I have much to attend to." He pursed his lips. "Your parents stole my daughter, Elizabeth. I tracked her down through her dead mother's friends and found your family had adopted her."

I bit through my bottom lip, drawing blood. Reddish-blond hair, and her eyes ... moss green. They were Ella's eyes—she was alive?

"Mind you, finding out that I had a daughter came as a shock, but to have one raised by ... humans." His thin fingers pinched lint from his dark jacket. He held it out, allowing it to fall to the floor beside the cigar ashes. "Needless to say, I detest filth." He tsked.

This man had killed my parents and stolen my sister from me.

The rush of sorrow brought glimpses of haunting memories from my past. I took a deep breath, shoving my anger down inside my grief.

"My lawyers confirmed I would have to fight to get her back. By the time I discovered she existed, she was already eight years old. I was not willing to take any chances with courts in America—that they would not give me back what was mine. So, I took the necessary actions."

His words whirled around in my head. My lungs filled with glass. "Y-you murdered my parents?"

"You do not understand. I have made it my mission to rid the world of evil. It is my purpose in life to... punish transgressions," he flipped his empty hand in the air, shifting his stance.

His flippant ownership of my parents' murders dredged up a burning hatred inside me. Clarity forced its way, surfacing past pain and fears into my mind. I wanted to scream, but pissing him off got me nothing but dead ... quicker.

"You're heartless."

He took a puff of his cigar and expelled smoke. "I like to think of it more as ridding the world of waste." He moved to the table and flicked ashes into the ashtray. "You should have died that night, but the house caught fire before my men could finish their job." He snarled. "Sadly, you did not die from your wounds. Still, your scar should have been a constant reminder, not to mention the beginning of the nightmare existence I had mapped out for you." His brow creased. "Do you know how disappointing it was to return to Ohio with the purpose of destroying Trystan's relationship with his father, but instead, I find an article about your grandmother in the paper. Her accident and the name Tresham—the *very* last name my daughter had had before I adopted her. The accident only propelled me to investigate and search your house. It was horrible to find pictures of my daughter—my child, hugging another man—that was not her father. She should have been hugging me! Your family robbed me of time with my child—my blood child."

He had been in our house that night when I'd had to flick on the control panel in the basement. "You broke into my home."

He lowered his eyes, making me aware of my trembling fingers.

I tucked them behind my back and gripped my wrist.

"Yes." He sneered. "I entered your modest shack. I cannot tell you how disappointed I was at seeing all those memorable pictures around your happy little home when I had gone to such lengths to secure your future misery. It is that hideous hospital. They fired the social worker I had hired before she could carry out my finely crafted plan." He took another drag on his cigar and let out a smoke-filled sigh. "It is sad. Even payment in full has not guaranteed your misery. The human species has devolved into a genetic cesspool. At least the three idiots I hired to finish your parents off followed orders."

"Bastard."

He tsked again, making me cringe. "It was my fondest wish your wretched life would have mimicked my own childhood. You see, a human governess raised me, one whose love left bruises and welts all over me. Unfortunately for my uncle, he did not defend me, so I killed him. I *always* get what I want. I do not know exactly how your grandparents did it, but Mr. Croskney protected you from that existence." He stood in speculative silence. "Now, your involvement with Trystan has undermined my timetable. He should have been mine months ago, but he became infatuated with you. And you poisoned his mind. Mr. Taylor informed me about certain facts concerning Trystan, Colin, and Anna having powers, and for some reason, Trystan's father stopped the aptitude tests before I could discover what types of powers they possessed." He cocked his head, pinching his lower lip between his fingers. "Silencing you will satisfy my revenge while allowing me to get matters with Trystan back on track."

"What matters?" I had to ask, even if I was pushing my luck.

"You are an inquisitive chit." He tapped his fingers on his arm. "You will not understand. Let us say, the world needs to be rid of a few more lords, and I have an adventure to look forward to." He dropped his gaze to the Egyptian tapestry at my feet. A high-pitched cackle escaped him, igniting my nerve endings like a lighted fuse to a case of dynamite. "Humans are such failures, managing only to make my life miserable—you are no exception. Your kind is a threat to your own existence."

I inched toward the exit. "Months ago, you were at Coccia House. You took the photo of Trystan and his cousins. Didn't you?"

"And do not forget—you, too." He adjusted a gold cufflink on his sleeve. "The way that boy looked at you puzzled me."

"The restricted calls—you were the one who called me? Weren't you?"

"You are very observant."

Perhaps, but I wouldn't have known had I not had that freaky feeling of someone watching me.

He stepped closer, stopped, and sucked in the last puff of his cancer stick, then flicked it in the ashtray on the stand.

I crept farther to my right.

He tilted his head back and barked a laugh. "You'll never make it out alive." His eyes sparkled. He took several cat-like steps forward as if stalking prey.

The counter dug into my back.

My heartbeat slid into overdrive, pounding against my ribs. The crimson shield's pulse brightened and consumed the transparent barrier. I kept eye contact with him as my fingers searched behind me for anything. Something.

My fingers latched onto a handle—a knife handle. A sharp knife.

"I am wondering, though." He gave me a contemplative stare. "Why is it you are not surprised when I use the words human or powers?" His lips pulled back, baring his teeth. "He. Has. Told. You. You know about us." His face reddened with rage. "ANSWER ME."

I tightened my grip on the handle of the kitchen knife. "ANSWER ME."

My eyes narrowed, and the crimson flashed to orange and constricted to the size of a quarter.

Lord Kingston lunged at me.

The beam shot across the room, straight at the light fixture. The glass bulb broke, and the room went pitch black. I plunged the knife deep into his flesh.

A scream reverberated throughout the room. "YOOOUUUU *HUMAN*."

I stumbled back. My heart sank at hearing his agonizing growl.

An earthy, iron scent filled the air, and drumming footfalls rushed across the upper deck, echoing on the ceiling.

Vise-like fingers wrapped around my arm. "I've got you."

I whipped my elbow around, hitting Kingston's chest and sending him backward.

An "OOMPH" sounded from across the room.

My chest heaved. I stumbled forward, reeling from the odd rocking motion under my feet. Had I killed him? Acid surged from my gut, up into my throat, and spewed out. Vomit hit the ground, filling the air with a sour stench. I wiped my mouth with my arm.

He moaned.

Run.

Hate and panic drove me. I searched the open air for something to latch onto with my hands. My fingers located a cool, slender object—the staircase railing. I ran up the steps as if the hounds of Hell nipped at my heels.

The door at the top of the steps opened wide.

I stopped cold. One foot, ready to leap to the next step.

My stomach recoiled when my hands contacted a warm, solid body.

Fingers latched onto my hair and dragged me up the last step onto the lit deck.

I wrapped my hand around Sykes's wrist and dug my nails into his flesh.

Sykes screamed. "*YOU'LL PAY FOR THAT.*"

He gripped my head and forced my face toward the boat's deck floor, forcing me into a death crawl, my head no higher than his thighs. He dragged me over a freezer chest.

The rain hit my back as chaos circled the deck.

I scrambled to my feet, my arms windmilling before me, narrowly avoiding collisions with lounge chairs and tables. I tried to keep up with his frantic strides but only managed to trip behind him with every step. He towed me down a set of steps onto a wet surface. Even with my enhanced strength, I couldn't compete with his grip or catch my balance long enough to break loose. The boat rocked, waves lapping through the open gate and onto the slick stern. My heart clenched with fear.

Sykes tightened his grip on my hair. His other hand dug into my shoulder, pushing me to my hands and knees.

"Your watery grave awaits you," he said, forcing my face over the outboard motor.

Heat built up from within my shield's wall and flooded me with a surge of energy.

Sykes released my head.

Lord Kingston screamed obscenities and commands from behind me. "Sykes, I want her dead."

My tears continued to fall, mingling with the lake water that covered my hands. I collected my breath and pushed against the floor. I grabbed the gate and used it for leverage, struggling to my feet and fighting the dizziness that made my surroundings swim. I ignored the shooting pain from my legs and relied on adrenaline to keep me upright.

Several boat lights danced in the distance.

Waves of crimson coursed through my activated shield. I pivoted and faced my nightmare—Lord Kingston—head-on.

His eyes darkened. They bore into me from twenty steps away. Lord Kingston cradled his bloody arm against his chest. A torn, white sleeve dangled from his elbow.

"You human wench. You puked on me." Fury iced each word. With a groan, he released his battered arm, causing it to hang limply by his side. He raised his good arm above his head and made the circle lift-off motion to the pilot.

The pilot on the upper platform moved to the chopper.

Kingston's eyes narrowed to hate-filled slits. "Sykes—make sure her remains are disposed of."

Out of the corner of my eye, I watched a brown-haired boy approach from the port side–Jon, from the fitness club, and oh, my ... he was at my prom, the one who keyed the Mustang.

Kingston groaned. "Jon, get Miss Elizabeth from her room."

The chopper hummed to life, the blades rotating, vibrating the boat under my feet.

Lord Kingston gave a commanding nod, drawing my attention toward the top of the steps, where three people had gathered. Taylor stood under the deck lights, shifting awkwardly, his hands bound in front of him. Jon's brother stood at Taylor's side, knife in hand.

Samantha stood next to him, a black metal gun with a scope in hand.

"Get rid of her," Kingston yelled at Samantha. A wicked grin stretched across his face. "Sykes, do not forget the traitor. We need him."

The helicopter blades picked up speed, creating waves in the water.

From the darkness, two huge spotlights from an approaching ship lit our deck.

"My lord, that's Dougrey's liner," Sykes screamed over the hum of the propellers.

"Get to the helipad. Samantha ..." Kingston moved two fingers across his throat and then ran for the upper platform.

No! Kingston couldn't escape.

A cold, alone feeling seeped inside me, intensified by the wind from the chopper's blades.

Samantha approached, the barrel of the gun pointed at my chest, her eyes glowing with retaliation. She stopped fewer than ten steps away and then aimed at my head.

I swallowed. I *don't* want to die.

The chopper lifted, maneuvering away from the boat. Kingston rushed to the helicopter and grabbed one of the landing skids, causing the propellers to dip before taking off.

Panic crawled up my throat. "Kingston left you behind—"

"Long enough so I can dispose of you."

"*Please*. Don't do this."

"I have no choice," Samantha said. "Do you think Kingston would allow me to live if I betrayed an order? And now, Dougrey's onto us."

In the distance, a loud *croaking cry* ripped through the dark, echoed by the *BANG* of a fired gun.

I jerked, gazing around the deck for the hideous scream.

"What? Where'd that sound come from?" Samantha's eyes riveted on the helicopter.

The chopper dipped and spun toward the water out of the spotlight's view.

BANG!—another shot tore through the conflict from somewhere in the night.

My heart raced in anticipation as I waited and watched the helicopter's red, green, and white lights level parallel to the water. The pilot finally gained control of the chopper as it flew low over Lake Erie toward the Rock and Roll Hall of Fame.

From somewhere on Kingston's ship, another unearthly hopeless *CROAK* echoed louder than the storm.

Samantha half turned, glancing over the water.

I blinked. Blinked again. And I scanned the ship for what made the unforgettable blood-curdling croak.

A fiery spear lifted straight off Kingston's boat and shot across the sky, burning hot like an erratic heat-seeking missile on target. Seconds later, yellow and orange sparks flashed and swallowed the dark of night.

I ducked, afraid of flying debris and spreading shrapnel. The force of the explosion rang in my ears. An acrid cocktail smell filled the air. The falling flame's reflection on the water turned everything momentarily red.

I wiped my face. "Someone must've shot the fuel tank."

"Impossible!" Samantha said. "They're dead."

Hairs on my neck lifted in acute awareness.

Several things happened simultaneously—nothing in slow motion like in the movies. I glanced over Samantha's shoulder. Ella stared at me in horror from the starboard side.

My mind raced, and my thoughts rushed with adrenaline. My shield intensified to a brilliant orange.

Samantha's frown widened into a sneering smile as she cocked the gun.

I narrowed my vision, constricting my shield's weapon, and discharged a beam of light at the gun in Samantha's hand.

She screamed and released the gun. It hit the deck and fired a bullet at the guardrail.

"NOOOO." The single word sliced through the chaos as Ella rushed Samantha from behind, hit her, and then they both plowed into me.

I faltered but couldn't catch my balance. My foot slipped on the wet deck, the stern railing slamming into my thigh, and we flew over the edge.

I gulped air as freezing water swallowed me.

I thrashed, not knowing which way was up, and fought against the weight of my fears.

My vision.

The floating body was me.

I kicked, breaking the water's surface, gasping for breath in a tug of war against the waves that sprang up, forcing me below.

I inhaled, taking in water.

Would they find my body?

I flailed, shooting above the water level again, gasping for air. Bright light hit me, then another wave nailed me and knocked me under.

I sank as pockets of air rippled past my cheeks. Pressure built up in my body, and my arms became heavy. My ears roared. My feeble attempts to move my body were nothing compared to the force of the water's pull.

Floodlights disappeared.

Heaviness drew me deeper, and my limbs went lifeless. Darkness encased me as a peaceful sensation gripped my mind.

Trystan.

Please. I don't want to die.

With that thought, a surge of energy tore through me.

I cupped my palms and lashed out. My warped body arched upward.

Somehow, I broke the surface, gasping for air. I opened my burning eyes, a bright, white light blinded me.

Something bumped into me.

A voice roared over the turmoil. "Don't struggle. I've got you." Ella.

An arm came around my chest and pulled me close. "People are here to help."

I whimpered, one of my hands gripping Ella's arm to my chest, the other fighting to stay above water. I was terrified of slipping deeper into the murky water, terrified of losing her again.

Voices broke through my thoughts, becoming louder. Hands reached into the cold water. I fought against them as they tried to separate me from Ella. She was slipping from my grasp. My mind protested, but words escaped me. I realized they wanted to save me, but separating from Ella *again* drove me crazy. They dragged me across a soft surface and into a dinghy. They hauled Ella onto another small boat.

"I thought I'd lost you when you went overboard. I dove in but couldn't find you." Trystan's eyes were grave as they examined every inch of my drenched body.

The cool air felt like an icy knife. I shivered. He reached behind me and pulled a blanket over my shoulders. I coughed, choking on regurgitated water.

He thumped my back, trying to help my body rid itself of Lake Erie's nasty concoction.

"We need more blankets," Trystan yelled to a guy in the small boat.

I exhaled a painful breath, seeing Ella safe in another dinghy. "I can't believe it—my sister's alive." Joy clashed with muscular pain. I was alive.

Trystan looked over at the dinghy where Ella sat but said nothing.

A man dressed in white with a medical cross on his sleeve examined me, putting another blanket over my shoulders. I floated along, dimly aware of the exchange of conversation around me, answering Trystan but aware that I'd have to repeat most of it.

Seconds dissolved into minutes.

I scanned the dinghies and the water swells but couldn't find her. I glanced at Trystan.

"Where's Samantha?"

"They're still searching." A new sound darkened his voice, and his arms loosened around my shoulders.

"Kingston?"

"He's a goner. No way he could've escaped the explosion."

"But he hung from one of the landing skids." I coughed, clearing water from my mouth. "I stabbed him in the arm—"

"Kingston met a quick death." Trystan's eyes were pensive. "Along with Sykes and the pilot." His arms tightened around me. "I was afraid ... I'd lose you. I never should have left you alone with Steve."

I shivered and nuzzled closer.

Sounds that had been distant rumbled through the night as we neared the ship, and someone shouted, "Gauges show the water temperature at sixty degrees. Get them up here, now."

Dr. Selma Dougrey stood on the deck of a large yacht next to Lord Dougrey. I pulled the blankets tighter. The others on the dinghy rowed us toward the yacht. We closed in on the boat, bobbing in and out of the rescue lights.

"Cal." Trystan's warm fingers stroked my face above my bruised eye. He pushed my matted hair from my forehead, leaned in, and whispered, "There was no way to avoid it. My family knows you're Theran." I cringed. His fingers slid up my arm and over my left shoulder. He sought my mark. "But *this* secret is safe."

My heart slowed its frantic beating, and a cool stillness seeped in.

CHAPTER 48

REVEALED

I looked in the cabin mirror and turned my head—a bluish-purple stain spread across my cheekbone. I poked at my jaw, and pain radiated up the side of my face. The bruise made a stark contrast to the backdrop of the cabin. The compartment boasted plush, white furniture and eggshell-colored walls. Hints of gray stripes covered the ivory bedspread. I resembled the color of a smashed eggplant.

I sighed and ran my hands over my hips, reveling in the warmth of dry jeans and a T-shirt. My wet clothes lay discarded on the floor at my aching feet.

Jings. A sickening feeling churned my stomach, reminding me I was still on a boat–Lord Dougrey's yacht. At least I was no longer worried about becoming the floating body I'd seen in my vision.

A knock came at the cabin door. Fingers wrapped around the edge of the frame. "Callie, it's me, Anna. Can I come in?"

"Yeah, sure." I covered my eye with my palm as she rounded the door. The bruise made me so self-conscious.

"Hope those clothes work for you. I grabbed some stuff from your closet."

"You didn't think ...?" I'd drown.

"I didn't know what to think." Anna pushed her lips into a pout. "That morning, when I witnessed you watching yourself drown, you were describing what happened in the vision so fast. It was hard to absorb everything, but I remembered you saying visions were unpredictable, and that gave me some hope, that is until you went overboard and disappeared into the water. I'm so glad you're okay." Her lips drew into an exaggerated frown. "Man, your eye looks miserable."

"Your mom left about five minutes ago. She said it'd take a couple of weeks for the bruising to change."

Anna's eyes brightened. "I can help with that if you want."

I cocked my head.

Anna approached. "I haven't had much practice. I tried it on a bird that had fallen from a tree. Its wing healed, but for some reason, it couldn't fly afterward." She placed her warm palm over my eye and closed her eyes. Immediately, an electric pulse transferred from her hand to my wound.

The muscles over the bruise twitched and tightened. I watched my reflection in the mirror. My skin contracted, tugging at my upper lip. Beneath her fingers, my skin transitioned from blue-purple to green at the edges. The swelling gradually subsided. A slight yellow tinge flared, faded, and cleared, leaving me with a clear complexion.

The sensation felt so weird. I traced my healed nose and eyelid with my finger. "Thanks. Not to sound ungrateful, but, um, how'd you do that?"

"I don't understand it myself. Uncle Michael said something about cell regeneration." Anna stepped back to inspect her handiwork.

"It's a cool power to have." I swiveled to face her and rested my arm on the back of the seat. "I'm curious. How'd you guys find me?"

Anna sat on the edge of the bed. "While Trystan was waiting at Coccia House, he noticed Steve meeting with Erika and Camden. He asked Steve about you, and Steve said he'd left you out back of the school. Trystan called me immediately because he couldn't reach you, and he asked me to find Colin. Then, he headed off to alert Mr. Santos while I hunted Ashworth for Colin, and we alerted my parents and Uncle Michael." Anna fumbled with her fingers in her lap. "It took Colin pushing over a tree in the backyard to convince our parents to take us seriously. They couldn't believe we'd kept our powers a secret from them. It was even harder to convince them you were Theran." She chewed on her lower lip. "I'm sorry, Callie. We broke our oath to you. We didn't tell them everything. Nothing about the remnants or you having the sight."

I swallowed. She'd confirmed Trystan's confession.

A knock sounded on the door. "You girls about done in there?" Trystan gave me a ghost of a smile as he entered. "You look much better. I'm sure it's easier to see with being healed."

I nodded. "Thanks. Anna was explaining how you guys found me."

Trystan gazed down at me. "How much has she told you?"

"She's said a lot, but I still don't understand how you knew which boat I was on."

"When you didn't show up at the restaurant ..." Trystan's voice rose an octave. "I found your grandfather and Mr. Santos. Mr. Lindy's connections with the Lake Erie boat marinas and the clue from your vision—*Freedom* being the name of the boat—led to a few phone calls. Finally, at the fifth one, a dock-repair worker remembered Lord Kingston's boat, which fit the general description, was docked off North Harbor Marina. Once we'd heard that, we notified Miss Anstley, and everyone hurried over."

Trystan glanced at something behind me, sucking in a breath of air. He picked up a picture on the stand beside the armoire.

"Who are they?" I asked.

"Sebastian, with me and our mom." Trystan's tight words surprised me.

Two boys, one about two years old, sat on a woman's lap. The other boy looked to be about twelve, and he bore a striking resemblance to Trystan. The woman was beautiful.

"These are my dad's private quarters." Trystan set the frame back down. "I've never been in here before. I about died when Dad told you to take this room to change in. He's very private." Years of resentment radiated through Trystan's voice.

"Yeah, I've never been in here, either." Anna stood. "But I think in his way, he's trying to show he cares."

"You might be right," Trystan said to Anna. He held out his hand to me. "But right now, we've got to talk with the others. Come on."

I grasped his hand.

We exited the suite and walked across the hall into a bright, cheery room.

CHAPTER 49

PENSIVE

The black of night hung heavy outside the open blinds. Lord Kingston's boat's size and layout weren't much different from Lord Dougrey's, but the décor separated them completely. Instead of medieval devices on the wall, this boat displayed photographs of warm sunsets, a sparkling chandelier hanging over an ornately carved wooden table, and tricked-out, flashy kitchen knobs.

Nine people waited for us in the large living room.

Lord Dougrey was speaking with a man wearing a grim expression and a captain's hat—the kind with gold-leaf stitching. Miss Anstley and Mr. Santos stood side by side but apart from the other Dougreys. Mixed expressions plastered their faces as they stared at Colin, sitting on the loveseat with his arm around Ella.

Gramps stared at Ella as though she were a zombie out of *The Walking Dead.*

Uncertainty stirred inside me. Why was Colin's arm around my sister?

Lord Dougrey cleared his throat. "It's good to see you again, Callie."

His practiced formality left me uneasy like I'd stepped into the principal's office–and provided a clear indication of the long night that we had ahead of us. Battle weary didn't begin to describe how I felt as I looked about the room at everyone's faces, seeing them riddled with questions–questions only I could answer.

Lord Dougrey motioned for us to sit on the couch near Gramps. I hugged him and sat down, with Trystan settling on my other side. Anna swiped a cushion from the couch and parked herself at my feet.

"I see your eye has healed quite nicely–and surprisingly quickly, too." Lord Dougrey's eyes lowered to me. "It seems my niece possesses a useful ability, and you all have a few secrets." He put his hands behind his back and began to pace the floor. "As much as it surprises me to find one of those secrets happens to be you're Theran, it also brings about much relief. For my son's sake, I'm glad to know your affection for him is not *completely* doomed. However, I have many questions, not all of which Miss Anstley has had time to answer. Although, from what I gather, she's your great aunt?"

I nodded. It was easier to listen than to speak. Lord Dougrey's words were tight, but a layer of warmth showed through his tough exterior. I didn't get the feeling from reading his voice inflections when he spoke of Trystan's and my relationship that he disliked humans like Sykes, Taylor, and Lord Kingston did. However, it was clearly a relief to him that I was Theran. Lord

Dougrey's distress appeared to be caused by other matters.

Lord Dougrey stopped pacing and faced the eight of us. "I don't condone the choice the four of you made to keep secrets from me." He looked at Anna, Colin, Trystan, and me. His eyebrows furrowed. "You had no right to keep secrets."

"Rubbish." Trystan clenched his fist. "You're so desperate for one of us to have some great power like Sebastian did that you set us up to take the skills tests. Your eagerness could've gotten us killed."

"I know." Lord Dougrey cleared his throat. "But, in my defense, Trystan, at the time, I thought my decision was right. I make life-changing decisions every day for my company and the council. I didn't think this was any different. Had you all come clean about your powers and this other information of which Miss Anstley has spoken, I would've made a completely different choice. I had a suspicion you were all keeping secrets—with your odd behavior—which made me more curious, especially when you all became upset about taking the skills test. However, I do believe having followed Sebastian's request to keep your powers a secret could be the reason you're all here right now, alive. It's heart-wrenching to lose a child, let alone to have one murdered, yet that is what has happened. Amelia Sanderson's death is proof those with powerful gifts aren't safe."

I'd never expected to hear such emotional words coming from Lord Dougrey. I grabbed for Trystan's hand and curled my hand over his balled fist. This was surreal. Lord Dougrey was opening up, and Ella was alive.

I wanted to swallow her in a hug. She'd saved my life, but Kingston's words reverberated in my head. "I like to think of it more as ridding the world of waste." Did Ella believe humans were a waste, too? But then, why would she have risked her life to save mine, thinking at the time that I was human? No, no—it couldn't be. More thoughts exploded in my mind. If Ella hadn't jumped in and saved me—twice—last night, I might not be here now. My intuition told me Ella wanted to help me, but whose side was she on? Kingston had raised her. His values could've contaminated her thinking.

I fought against the concern that was eating away at my thoughts, leaned into Trystan, and whispered, "Anna told me that you and Colin didn't tell anyone in your family about my powers. Did Colin tell Ella?"

He shook his head. "I don't think so."

I turned to Ella and Colin. I had to get her to talk. "Ella, why would you save me?"

"How could I not? Sykes was cruel. He'd have used you as a toy. Anyhow, I'd never leave a defenseless person." Ella's expression was wistful, pleading. She moved closer to Colin. "I didn't know who you were when I untied your wrists, and when I came back to get you after not finding my guardian, I heard what he said to you. Every word. He ordered our parents' deaths, b-because he wanted ... m-me. Mr. Kingston saved me from the fire that night. Mom and Dad died—were murdered." She wiped a tear from her cheek. "All these years, he acted as though their death had been an unforgivable crime, yet it was nothing but a charade."

"Wait a minute, you're sisters?" Lord Dougrey asked. "Why am I—"

"Stop, Dad." Trystan's retort stopped Lord Dougrey from interjecting further.

My eyes didn't leave Ella's face.

"Mr. Kingston told me you'd all died from the fire." Ella gripped her forearms. "It was the worst time of my life. I never thought to question him again. I'd seen the newspaper clippings of the murders, which were painful enough. I didn't want to relive it by asking questions." She looked at Gramps. "He told me my whole family was dead. Everyone. That's why I didn't look for Nana and you, Gramps. It was a difficult year. I'd lost everyone I loved. Mr. Kingston adopted me and sent me to live abroad in England and, later, Italy, but I hardly ever saw him. He has always gone on business trips for his art galleries. He left me with a governess for most of my life." Her accent sharpened. "I never knew ..." she paused. "I didn't know our parents weren't my biological parents until today." A tear trickled down her face. Her words crackled like brittle leaves. "I-I can't believe Kingston's my biological father. How'd you find out?"

Gramps leaned forward. "Your mom left a note for you girls. She explains some things in it."

Ella's eyebrows drew together.

"Ella, I'll let you read the note later."

The consistency of her words and the fact that I remembered what she had said about Sykes when she rescued me gave me the comfort I needed.

Colin's dad, Mark Dougrey, took a sip of water from his glass, gazing at Ella and Colin. "And how long have you two been seeing each other?"

After listening to Ella's truthfulness, I noticed the slight changes in Mark Dougrey's voice inflections.

"We've been dating for a few months," Colin answered. "Although we first met overseas and secretly remained friends. We didn't want her governess to find out."

Mark set down his water glass and made direct eye contact with Ella. "Did Lord Kingston force you to date my son to spy on my family?"

What part of "secretly remained friends" did he not understand? Ugh. How could she spy on the Dougreys for Kingston when he didn't even know they were friends?

"No." Colin stood, shooting dagger eyes at his dad. "How could you even ask if she was a spy? Why would she risk her life to save Callie?"

This wasn't going well. Everyone was too defensive.

Ella wiped away a tear. "Don't get mad, Colin. They've got a right to ask questions." She looked over at Colin's dad. "N-no. As I said, Mr. Kingston didn't know we were dating." Ella tugged on Colin's shirt sleeve, and he sat back down.

My heart ached for her.

Colin looked straight at his parents. "Trystan's the only one I told about us, but Anna found out because she's constantly eavesdropping. Anna brought it up over dinner the night you met Callie." Colin and Ella eyed one another for a second. He mouthed a few words to her, but I didn't hear them.

Ella nodded, biting her trembling lower lip.

Colin's brows drew together. "Since we're dumping our secrets, you might as well know Kingston told Ella she's a half-blood."

Intakes of breath whistled around the room—Gramps's head jerked back at their reaction.

"Half-blood? Your mother is human?" Lord Dougrey asked.

"Who cares if her biological mama is human?" Gramps's eyes narrowed to slits. "I'm human. I don't get all this half-blood stuff. What's it matter, now? She's here, and she's my granddaughter."

"Your concern is noted, Mr. Croskney." Lord Dougrey tapped a staccato rhythm with his foot. "But it does matter to Therans—as does our anonymity. Humans don't always have an accurate account of Earth's history, and Therans have yet to uncover all her secrets. We have fought for centuries over circumstances involving half-bloods, and I don't care to witness a repetition of such destruction. You don't understand our civilization, and it's evident that some matters will need to be explained later. You're strictly on a need-to-know basis."

"But how do we hide a half-blood?" My great aunt's retort unnerved me. "Think of the scandal."

"Hide her?" I squeezed Trystan's hand so hard I thought my bones would pop through my skin. "She's a living, breathing person. How could you even say that?"

"I'm thinking of what's best for everyone," Miss Anstley said. "And what will happen if others discover she's a half-blood."

"Yeah, right." Colin's veins stood out along his neck. "You're thinking of everyone *else* but not of Ella. Half-blood or not, every Theran on campus knows she's Lord Kingston's adopted daughter. There won't be a problem. No one need know she's his flesh and blood."

"Whether you like it or not, Miss Anstley." Lord Dougrey crossed his arms over his chest. "Ella is your niece's sister and your niece, too. And she is part of Colin's life. She shouldn't be punished for Lord Kingston's decisions." Lord Dougrey shifted and gazed at Ella. "The circumstances of your birth are unfortunate, but the shame belongs to Lord Kingston and not to you." He paused for breath before continuing. "However, I believe if your circumstances become known, Miss Ella, it would be the scandal of the century. There have been no known half-bloods for hundreds of years. Lord Kingston is known to be one of the least human-friendly Therans of our time, and for him to have fathered a half-blood is almost inconceivable. What's in the best interest of all of us is that this is no longer a topic of discussion. No word on this subject will leave this room, and if the word does get out, I will, as of right now, consider Ella under my protection."

"And mine." Colin's voice was tight, his eyes hard, as he glared at Miss Anstley.

I released Trystan's hand and walked over to Ella. "Our parents loved you. You are the daughter of their heart. Gramps and Lord Dougrey are right. It doesn't make a difference. I know you're telling the truth. Whatever happens, you've got us."

No one in the room challenged Lord Dougrey. Therans might not condone human-Theran relationships, especially when a child is involved, but a looming scandal seemed to far outweigh any relationship issues involving Ella being a half-blood.

Ella's shoulders dropped a fraction.

My heart constricted in my chest, seeing the pain reflected in her eyes. I stood and faced Lord Dougrey.

"She speaks the truth, like everyone else in this room." I pointed to Miss Anstley and Mr. Santos, making my message clear. This couldn't drag on forever. I needed to level with all of them about my powers, but I wouldn't explain about my mark or shield. Until I figured out how to use the shield's power, it'd be my secret, but I had to gain the Dougreys' trust. "I can read voices and tell if they speak the truth, although I can't determine one's purpose or what, if anything, they choose to hide."

"You're a voice reader?" Lord Dougrey stammered. "And a remnant, like your great aunt?"

"Yes, my parents were from the Remnant Faction," I hissed with frustration. "But I'm Theran, and I won't take sides."

"Don't forget, Lord Dougrey." Miss Anstley's eyes pierced his lordship's gaze. "I may have told *you* about the remnants, but you've sworn to keep *our faction's existence* a secret."

Lord Dougrey nodded.

I covered my mouth, yawning. Some details need to be cleared up before I embarrass myself by falling asleep on the floor. "Lord Dougrey, Kingston killed our parents, ruined my life, and tried to claim Ella's. He hired humans to commit our parents' murders, thinking it'd keep his hands clean. And all because he thought my mom and dad were humans, unfit to raise Ella. My grandmother's accident, meeting your family, and dating your son put me under the microscope, which allowed Kingston to rediscover me. It seems that your involvement with me disrupted Lord Kingston's plans, which he only revealed to me out of hatred and because he assumed his confessions would die with me." I made eye contact with Lord Dougrey. "Kingston planned to exploit your estranged relationship with Trystan and make him useful for his personal agenda. From what I overheard from Sykes, Trystan's valuable because Sebastian had the power of sight, suggesting Trystan had a strong chance of developing a great power, too." I dipped my chin toward Anna and Colin. "He knew they had powers. Mr. Taylor can screen capabilities—he's also got some other ability that Mr. Sykes referred to as dowsing." Thank goodness my shield had protected me from Mr. Taylor finding my secrets. "Mr. Sykes is Lord Kingston's bodyguard and does most of the dirty work. He's sick," I looked at Ella, "and Taylor hates humans like Lord Kingston and Sykes do, but, in a weird and twisted way, Mr. Taylor saved my life. He was hesitant to kill, and he must've argued with someone because Kingston called him a traitor. I don't know what Lord Kingston wants with Mr. Taylor, but he seems rather important—"

"Not important enough." Lord Dougrey countered. "They left Mr. Taylor behind when they flew off, and we boarded their boat. Mr. Taylor refuses to speak. Until he does, he will remain with my security detail."

Someone knocked on the door.

"Enter," Lord Dougrey commanded.

The ship's captain opened the door, carrying a handful of files. "My lord, the ship, *Freedom*, has been secured and rafted off ours. And we found these locked in Lord Kingston's suite office." He handed a pile of files to Lord Dougrey, keeping two in his hand. "I also thought you'd like to know that, according to this file, the paintings we discovered on board were bound for one of Lord Kingston's galleries in Egypt." The captain paused, surveying the room. "Permission to speak freely, sir?"

"Granted." Lord Dougrey's chest heaved.

"Kingston's a very disturbed individual." He held the other folder out to Lord Dougrey. "We found this."

Lord Dougrey jerked the folder from the captain's hands, opened it, and scanned the information. His face paled to a ghastly white, and curse words assailed the air.

Mark Dougrey and Mr. Santos asked, "What?" in unison, both walking toward Lord Dougrey and peering over his lordship's shoulder. Mark Dougrey grimaced, and Mr. Santos's white knuckles betrayed an intense grip on his cane.

Lord Dougrey closed the file and gave the rest of us a solemn look. "It seems Lord Kingston kept close track of his victims. These files contain information on human killings, alphabetically, with snapshots of their demises."

Ella buried her head in Colin's chest, sobbing.

Concern radiated through my mind. How much could Ella handle? Not only had she had to discover that her father had stolen her, lied about her adopted family, and murdered her adoptive parents, but now must she also accept he was a mass murderer.

"That information doesn't leave this room until I say so." It was an order from Lord Dougrey, meant for all of us.

"Yes, my lord." The captain lowered his face. "You should know—we've searched but can't even find the woman who went overboard."

"Her name was Samantha," Lord Dougrey said. "Keep searching. Do not give up."

"She's been in the water for a long time. The likelihood of her still being alive is slim."

"Have you any news on the remains of Lord Kingston and Sykes?"

"No, my lord. Coastguards will send a dive team to investigate the waters."

"Keep me posted on both matters." Lord Dougrey dismissed the captain.

"Affirmative."

"Who shot down the helicopter?" I had to ask.

"I shot at it twice." Lord Dougrey shook his head. "And I don't regret it. I thought to force them to land, but I have no idea *what on earth* could've caused it to explode as it did. It makes no sense."

"I got no idea." Gramps shrugged. "Not even with my military experience do I know what that was. It looked like someone shot off a flare gun."

"Yeah," Mark Dougrey said. "But flares don't zig-zag all over the place."

"Good riddance to Kingston and his henchman." Miss Anstley slapped the table beside her. "My compassion is for Lord Avalon's family and the other families Kingston murdered. Right now, our focus should be on the planned executions with men walking to the gallows. And now, this file appears with even more slaughtered victims. Blowing up the helicopter is too merciful a death as far as I care for him. The vile man should've suffered."

Lord Dougrey's head shot up. He glared at Miss Anstley. "Who told you of Sebastian's vision?"

"My great-niece witnessed it," Miss Anstley said. "She has the ability of sight, as do I."

"Both of you?" Lord Dougrey stammered.

"Yes, they're both seers." Trystan's eyes darkened as he challenged his father's gaze. "And no one outside this room will find that out."

"I see there is still much I have to learn." Lord Dougrey pinched his nose with his fingers. "What can the bastard's purpose be? Why kill Avalon and his son and Miss Sanderson?" Lord Dougrey flung the folder onto the countertop. "And why would he steal all the artwork from the libraries?"

"My guess is so he could make money from stolen goods," Trystan said.

"That would explain why he killed Lord Avalon and his son." Mr. Santos paused. "Somehow, they must've figured it out." A flicker of panic crossed his pained expression. "All I know is hatred consumed him."

"My informants," Lord Dougrey said, "indicated Kingston hunted and collected Therans with powers. For what purpose, I can't imagine. But I couldn't agree more, Kingston has intense feelings of hostility. The common thread between Mr. Sykes and Mr. Taylor is their hatred for humans."

I sat down. "If my visions and intuition are correct, Kingston planned to kill all the elders and seize control of the council." I recounted several details of my prediction to the Dougreys, including the fact the victims had all been wearing purple robes, like those of the elders, and that there were only five men walking to the gallows in my vision, as opposed to the six in Sebastian's vision–leading us to determine that it must've been another elder masterminding the mass hanging. The more I spoke, the more the realization dawned. "Lord Kingston had been hidden in my visions because he'd always remained in the shadows, dictating and controlling others. That's why I couldn't make him out in my visions. His obsession with getting revenge on my family pushed him over the edge, forcing him to reveal himself and delay his plans."

"Yes." Lord Dougrey's face twisted into a grimace. "After what I've seen tonight, nothing would surprise me. Kingston may have been a cruel man, but in a trial, he couldn't have been tried on the subjective information of a seer."

"The explosion saved us having to go through a trial."

"Sadly." Lord Dougrey tapped his fingers on the open file folder. "Justice would've been better served in a Theran court of law. He died too easily for the misery he left behind. And he left enough incriminating evidence for us to have used in a court to put him away for the rest of his life."

Dr. Dougrey cleared her throat and gazed up at Lord Dougrey. "Michael, we must get these kids home. This has been a rough day."

"Yes, I agree. We all need rest." Lord Dougrey held up his hand, stopping Dr. Dougrey from standing. "However, before anyone leaves this boat, I want to make something clear to all in this room." His eyes flickered between Ella, Miss Anstley, Mr. Santos, and me. "Some of my closest friends are humans. Please believe me when I say Lord Kingston's hatred of humans is not a common opinion amongst the Ancient Faction." His hard gaze trapped mine. "I hope someday you will forgive me. I only did what I did to protect Trystan's and your heart. I was desperate to keep my son from dating you, Callie, and yes, it was because I believed you to be human. But not because I didn't like you." He cleared his throat. "I care ... care for you, for humans, and Therans. However, I know what's written in our history—the witch trials. The centuries of tragedy that came from *our powers* being misunderstood. Therans have managed to stay safe now while existing among the humans because our secrets and lives are guarded." His eyes bled with deep worry. "I can't tell you how relieved I am that you are Theran and can be with my son."

I nodded, not exactly sure how to respond to his last statement. Behind Lord Dougrey's brick exterior, he had a beating heart. Hundreds of emotions suffocated me at once. Some feelings I couldn't even identify, but the strongest emotion of them was relief—they accepted me.

I shivered, peered over at Ella, and exhaled. Colin's protective embrace seemed to be all that held Ella together. I wasn't the only one who looked ragged.

Trystan wrapped his arm around me and pulled me against his side.

I looked into his dark, Hershey-chocolate eyes and whispered, "My future is so uncertain."

"You're not alone anymore, Cal." His words filled my heart. "I'll keep you safe."

I flinched, feeling a burning sensation ignite my birthmark at the same time Trystan pressed his palm to his chest. "That's weird."

"You felt it, too?"

"Yeah. That's odd."

"You're telling me." I kissed his cheek, yawned, and snuggled beside him on the couch. While the others spoke, continuing to work on our shared problems, I closed my eyes, pressed my palm to his leg, and felt the cold grasp of his familiar touch. I discovered more about my life in the last months after meeting Trystan than I'd learned in the first seventeen years of my life. And without a doubt, I had more to learn.

Dang, I was still learning how to embrace my powers, but I avoided execution and helped halt the plans of a ruthless man who'd killed my parents. I'd always viewed death as an enemy because my parents were taken too soon—Kingston's demise ...

A knock came on the door.

"Enter," Lord Dougrey said.

I opened my eyes.

The captain returned with a scowl on his face, not saying a word. He gazed at everyone in the ship's room, then glanced at the floor before meeting my stare.

"What is it, Captain?" Dougrey asked.

"We've searched Kingston's boat, my lord." The captain scowled, shaking his head. "There's no sign of ammunition in Kingston's arsenal that could've destroyed that chopper. There's *no plausible* explanation for the explosion."

"I fired two bullets. That caused the explosion."

"No, my lord." The captain shook his head. "That particular helicopter has a self-sealing rubber bladder surrounding its fuel tank. The bullet couldn't penetrate it." The captain opened his clenched palm revealing several long blue singed feathers. "But there are instances of birds striking aircrafts, and larger birds can intrude into the cabin or cockpit area, incapacitating or disorienting the pilot and causing the helicopter to crash but not explode. And nowhere have I ever heard of birds in the northeast with long blue feathers like this."

Dougrey removed the singed feather from the captain's palm. "It's completely unexplainable."

Silence hung heavy in the cabin. No one could clarify what we witnessed with the explosion and unusually *weird* missile.

And there's no way I was going to try to even explain a feathered creature that moves like a ghost between shadows—no way on earth. Why'd the creature try to help me? What powers did the feathered creature have that it could've destroy a helicopter?

"Thanks, Captain," Lord Dougrey said. "You're dismissed."

"My lord?"

"Yes?" Lord Dougrey asked the captain.

"Cleveland police found a homeless man on shore with a bloodied torn shirt. The vagrant claims he gave one of his shirts to an injured man in exchange for the tattered silk. He also alleges another injured man accompanied him."

"Nooooo!" the words slipped from my lips as anger stiffened my spine. The knowledge of Kingston still living and being able to destroy more lives ate at my sanity.

Trystan held me tighter in his grip.

The conversation washed over me as dread squeezed my heart.

Lord Dougrey grimaced. "Get every TSS agent on this matter. NOW!"

"I thought they couldn't survive the explosion," Miss Anstley whispered.

"My professional experience," the captain said, "tells me Lord Kingston could've survived if he fell into the water before the explosion, but Sykes ..." He shook his head.

"They're both swimmers." Ella's voice was not but a whisper. "They won't stop until they kill again."

I closed my eyes. My heart raced as a force of anger ripped through me, and my stomach roiled with nerves.

My life was a tangled web, and even the depth of knowledge I'd obtained in the past forty-eight hours hadn't relieved the weight of apprehension in my mind.

Tears of pain and frustration caressed my cheek. As the voice inside my head screamed, recoiling inside my brain.

No. No. No! Kingston couldn't have survived. He couldn't!

A sudden pain shot through my body, echoed immediately by Trystan's tight grip around my waist.

I shifted against his strong control—knowing hurting him wasn't my purpose—but trying to combat his safety hold. After a moment, I stopped trying to get out from under his clasp, biting hard upon my lip until I scanned the room of voiceless, judgmental faces ...

There was a quote from Edmond Burke I couldn't shake: *All that is necessary for evil to triumph is that good men do nothing.*

EPILOGUE

Other pieces, black as night, descended to the ground, carrying a foreboding weight. Each shard exploded, shattering into millions of pieces.

I felt a level of desperation as my brain tried to catch each one before it hit the ground. I knew that each shard told a different story ...

Large swollen, red-rimmed eyes with blue lashes blinked. A tear fell and splashed in the puddle at its talons, where a blue feather floated.

If you enjoyed the story, I'd love to
hear your thoughts!
Please consider leaving a review--
your feedback is priceless.
Thanks a million!

Cyndi xoxo

OTHER BOOKS BY CYNDI BREC

The Therans: Scarred Legends

Available Now

Forbidden love blossoms between Victoria and Cyrus, but the elders demands and a mischievous feathered creature reroute their dreams. They have two choices: surrender or run.

The Therans: Scarred Secrets

Available Now

Visions Haunt Callie Tresham. Nothing she's done helps to stop them. Her struggle compels her to spill her guts in a journal. Except in high school, some consider private property public interest.

The Therans: Scarred Lies

Available Now

Resident Alien
short story one, prequel
Dinner out with Callie Tresham's grandparents makes for an unforgettable Christmas Eve, some might even say heroic—yet, beneath the surface, nothing is as it seems.
Scarred Lies, Resident Alien is a 3,000-word short story.

Bathroom Confession
short story two, prequel
Callie Tresham stumbles into the boy's bathroom and lands in a heap of trouble. She finds that not all lies are written on stall walls.
Scarred Lies, Bathroom Confessions
is a 2,500 word short story.

The Therans: Legends Never Die

Book 2 in The Therans Series — Coming Soon

> **Buried Legends. Deadly Secrets. And a Love that Haunts the Heart.**

WHERE SECRETS BURN BLOOD RUNS COLD. REVENGE CARVES A DEEP SCAR.
Theran protector Callie Tresham uncovered the origins of her volatile powers and worse, the brutal truth behind her parents' horrific murder—the monster responsible. Every secret is a weapon, exposing deadly threats that catapult her on a quest against her nemesis.

AMIDST THE DANGER, A FIRE IGNITES, TEARING DOWN CALLIE'S WALLS AS LOVE AND ACCEPTANCE BATTLE FEAR IN HER HEART.
In this powerful sequel to *The Therans: Secrets Beneath Scars*, Callie travels the world, visiting ancient cities crawling with danger and deception. Among the shadows of towering pyramids and beneath the shifting sands of the desert lies a labyrinth of secret tombs.

WHAT SHE FINDS IS LEGENDS AREN'T STORIES BUT SECRETS BUILT TO HIDE THE TRUTH.
Filled with mysterious riddles, treachery, and heartbreak, *The Therans: Legends Never Die* finds Callie working through the dark ties to her past while training for her life's purpose. Meanwhile, an otherworldly creature stalks her with mischievous motives.

THE TRUTH DESTROYS LIES, BUT WHAT'S THE PRICE OF UNCOVERING IT?

Legends Never Die is for fans who crave romantic fantasy with rich lore and high-stakes tension—think Brigid Kemmerer and Shelby Mahurin layered with ancestral mysteries, secret bloodlines, and Forbidden libraries of legend.

SHADOWS

A TEASER CHAPTER FROM THE THERANS: LEGENDS NEVER DIE

Cyndi has secured
a 5-star rating from **Readers' Favorite**.

I fisted my hand around the tattered newspaper. Lies, nothing but lies. For some reason, I couldn't get rid of the obituary—it was a part of me I kept tucked away in my wallet. The frayed paper comforted me, and now it fueled my parents' unjustified deaths.

"Jings." I scrubbed an unsteady hand over my face. "Is this what it comes to? Stealing my way into a church?"

I gripped the confessional knob and looked over my shoulder at the empty pews and the two-tone gray floor tiles. People found peace within these white-painted walls—the same walls that held centuries of secrets soaked in ancient archaeology underground.

Why couldn't I find peace? Why?

The entire town knew about my family's deaths but didn't know the truth. Journalists recorded their interpretations of the facts about the three men who'd killed them and their prison sentence.

I don't know what's worse, not having my parents here or the reported lies of their murder. Lies that masked vital truths.

"Dang it! What am I doing here?" I mumbled the words. "If I can't trust accurate reporting from newspapers, what makes hunting for answers about my powers below ground any different? I don't know the source, writer, or author of those pages either."

I leaned forward, the newspaper slipping from my hand onto the church floor. I tightened a shaky palm around the confessional knob. I closed my eyes and slid my other hand over the shallow indentations carved into the worn wood. I stopped and opened my eyes. My heart slowed as a cool stillness entered me. I couldn't fix my broken past. I had to face the future, no matter the consequences.

I sucked in a breath of air and opened the confessional door. The hinges came alive with a sickening screech. A spidery sensation crawled over my skin, igniting my shield's defenses to flicker.

Footfalls echoed. "May I help you?"

I spun, hearing the metal of the doorknob groan, and released the handle.

A figure approached from the side entrance. "Why, Callie. I didn't recognize you."

"Ah, hi, Mrs. Sundries."

Mrs. Sundries lived a couple of miles from us. Erika, her daughter, was my best friend.

"I'm surprised to see you here."

"The lights were on in the educational wing. Thought I'd stop in." It wasn't a lie. I couldn't tell her I'd come to search the library cavern for answers about my powers.

"Yes, we were working on vacation Bible school for July." Mrs. Sundries stepped closer and picked up the newspaper clipping I'd dropped on the floor. "Is there something I can help you with? Our priest doesn't hear confessions at this hour."

I exhaled. "Um, no, I'm fine."

"Fine?" She lowered her eyes to the article in her hand. "I've known you for years. You're still grieving for your grandma and parents."

I fisted my hands. I wanted justice.

From the outside, my life journey looked easy and smooth. But inside, a restless fear stirred my thoughts. Days ago, my parents' murderer, Kingston, abducted me and sentenced me to death, but he'd failed to kill me.

Mrs. Sundries leaned against the oak stand and glanced at my hands. "Anger is a natural process of working through your emotions, a feeling we must endure. Your history is compounded by your parents' deaths and your grandmother's car accident. It's all still fresh. Before my brother overdosed, I had never known grief. Anger consumed me, too. I know it's not quite the same thing, but you'll work through this. You have your grandfather."

My heart constricted at remembering Erika telling me about her uncle's death. Grief spared no one. "Why'd they have to die?"

"That I can't answer. We're not given all the answers to life's questions."

New Cumberlin Falls, Ohio, was my sanctuary. I thought nothing changed here. However, that theory crashed after Nana passed, and I met my boyfriend, Trystan, six months ago. He'd revealed another world to me, one completely hidden from humans.

"Come on." She gave a weak smile and linked her hand through my arm. "I'll walk you out." Mrs. Sundries's prod-walk-prod left me no room to go against her wishes.

I bit my inner cheek, wanting to turn around and take the hidden confessional entrance to Ashworth Library.

We reached the narthex as a van pulled up in the church's turnaround.

"There's my hubby." She faced me. "I'm glad you're finding comfort in our church. You're always welcome to come to service. Erika would love it." She stared at the tiles and puffed out her cheeks. "You've lost more in life than what most experience." She returned to the seriousness of the moment before. "I can see in your eyes that you feel raw. The pain won't disappear immediately, but you will discover *new* memories to help soothe your soul. Surrender your problems to God. I knew your grandmother well. She wouldn't want you to suffer. I'm willing to listen if you ever want to talk." She reached for my hand and placed the newspaper article in my palm.

"Thanks." Despite the thousands of unanswered questions that crowded my mind like cancer, I couldn't talk. I didn't want to talk. My life wasn't normal. I wasn't normal. At least not according to Webster's Dictionary. I didn't fit the standard or the common type of anything.

I couldn't explain. I'm Theran—a descendant of those from the Island of Thera—a human hybrid, born with a birthmark different from other Therans.

Therans—some with supernatural powers—fought to keep secrets hidden from humans.

Sadly, humans couldn't digest the intangible, the unearthly, the unhuman. They absorbed scientific, black-and-white information easier.

I gave myself a mental shake. Get it together. I tucked the article in my pocket before I opened the church door. My muscles contracted against the wind's chilly bite. The purple sky transformed into a vast expanse of black. Storm clouds covered the moon. A crack of lightning split the skyline.

"Looks like we're in for a rough night." Mrs. Sundries pulled keys from her jacket pocket and inserted them in the slot. "I've got to lock up."

I started down the ramp, but something *dark* moved by the side exit door of the educational wing.

"Wait!" I stopped. I wasn't sure what it was because I'd caught the quick movement out of the corner of my eye before it disappeared. "What about the other guy?"

"There's no one else here. We're the last ones out. Our meeting ended over half an hour ago. Anyhow, the doors will allow anyone out of the building but not in."

I waved goodbye to Mrs. Sundries and dashed to my Jeep. Once inside, I locked the doors, making sure to hear the succession of clicks. I studied the educational wing, still lit by emergency lights. Nothing was there.

Mortality shadowed my every step, and it seemed that eyes watched me everywhere.

Before leaving the parking lot, I gazed at the stained-glass windows above the church's exit, depicting Jesus crucified on the cross, and was reminded that loving people existed. Good people existed. While I knew this, evil threatened to destroy my faith in the kindness of humanity.

AUTHOR'S THOUGHTS ...

Dear Readers,

I wish to express my thanks to all the readers who have helped make my dream come true. Thank you!

Callie's story demanded to be told—visions of scenes kept crawling into my mind, each more vivid and compelling than the last. I could see the events unfold, and the details of her life story insisted on being brought to life through words. I jokingly say Callie kept whispering in my ear, sharing her secrets, joys, and sorrows. I kept a notebook beside my bed and used my phone's flashlight to capture the scene's breakdown and emotions, bringing my mental images to the page. Some nights, my husband would beg me to turn off the lights, but I kept saying, 'Just give me a minute,' or I'd run down the steps to complete the scene so as not to keep him awake. After a while, my thoughts were so anchored into my character that I could sit at the computer and visualize the events. Secrets and mysteries seem to be a common theme in the storyline—that's why 'Secrets Stab Deeper Than a Blade' stands as the tagline.

Another reason visualizing the stories came so easily is that I have an amazing daughter—whom Callie is slightly molded after—who kept me anchored in the real life of a growing kid and teen. Erica would constantly challenge my thinking and feed me ideas, and I am forever grateful for her incredible support and love.

Oddly, I never considered myself a writer, more a storyteller. The idea for this book came unexpectedly—I always wanted to write, but I wasn't confident when I started. However, faith and perseverance helped fuel my fire. It doesn't hurt that I am so intrigued by *Legends, Myths & Lies*—A secret truth or mystery is hidden inside these tales. Ultimately, carving out a secret civilization around legends wasn't easy, and layering it with an organic, believable backstory added some difficulty. History was a huge added benefit as we owned a historic water mill then—I anchored Callie's story in an existing historical setting. Then, I would research legends and myths to carve out a fictitious story invention to substantiate Callie's story world.

The combination of being a co-owner of a historic 200-year-old mill and my research on the story background has given me a strong stance for preserving history. History—monuments and historical sites—connects us to our cultural heritage and bridges the past. They are symbols to be treasured, respected, and appreciated—no matter what is right or wrong, we can learn from every situation.

Two quotes that fueled my story writing were: 'The past cannot be undone, but the future is yours to shape—Anonymous in the end, we will remember not the words of our enemies, but the silence of our friends.' ~ M.L. King Jr. and 'Those who do not learn from the experience of history are doomed to repeat it.' ~ George Santayana.

My fictitious Theran world's purpose was crafted around these two quotes, which give significance to Callie's future and Theran's ultimate purpose. That's where the importance of my saying comes into play: 'Bound by secrets, Therans shouldered the weight of history to serve and protect pages that transcend time.'

I am just a storyteller who can write the images from my mind onto paper about a girl who plays a significant role in Therans' history. Ultimately, though, we are all stewards of history. Our job is to preserve history for the future growth of cultures. After all, where would we be as a civilization without knowledge?

I hope, dear friend, you can see the significance history plays through Callie's journey as the story progresses into Legends Never Die.

Readers fill my world with joy and excitement! I truly appreciate you taking the time to read. Thank you for joining me on this fantastical journey. If you liked the story, please consider leaving a review. Reviews are so important to authors and I would greatly appreciate it. Thank you.

Take care, my fantastical friends. Air hugs!
Cyndi Brec

SOCIAL MEDIA INFORMATION

Dare to find out more ...
Legends, Myths & Lies Newsletter:
https://cyndibrecauthor.wordpress.com/
https://www.facebook.com/CBrecFantasy
https://twitter.com/CyndiBrec
https://www.instagram.com/novelnook.cyndibrec/
https://www.tiktok.com/@cyndibrec

ACKNOWLEDGMENTS

I learned that writing a book is more complicated than I ever thought but just as rewarding, especially because of the friendships I've made along the way.

None of this would have been possible without God's strength to make this dream a reality—Thank you!

I want to thank my hubby, Richard. He's been my biggest supporter and stood by me during every struggle and successful moment. I thank him for his continued love and support when I was MIA at dinner and he got stuck with the dishes. His sacrifice in explaining scientific concepts, discussing endless plausible story situations, and bringing me my unending bottles of peach Snapple or French vanilla iced coffee was true love. Thanks for always supporting my crazy, harebrained ideas. You are a dream hubby with the kindest and most loving heart.

My appreciation goes out to my children for their help. My son was sooo instrumental in helping; his practical knowledge in discussing fight scenes was so important! I couldn't have done without my daughter's advice, who served as a rough model for Callie! The encouragement and love from both of you is greatly appreciated. I love you two to the moon and back!

I owe an enormous debt of gratitude to authors Linda Morgan and John Newton, who held my hand from reading early drafts to giving me advice on every step of the manuscript adventure. And trust me, Linda's had several journeys with me—you are so special! John sometimes questions *our* sanity, but he's along for the ride in every crazy-cool way that matters. Plus, I'd like to thank Chrissy Hartmann, who, after endless hours as a virtual co-worker, has juggled challenges and weird conversations with me, all with a smile. Lol You've got some fantastic developmental editing skills—Thank you very much!

Also, a massive debt of appreciation goes to Ruth Reifsnyder, my friend and prayer cheerleader; Ryan Schultz, a visual whiz; Cary Harter, a punctuation queen; and Max Fischer, an editing guru. You've all been inspirational, and a piece of each one of you is inside *The Therans* series. You gave so much of your time to help me clarify concepts and world-building and lift me up when doubt dragged me down. This book wouldn't have been possible without all of you. Everyone has helped make this story vision come to life.

I'm also immensely grateful to Jeff and Rachel—dear friends—for creating my author logo, beta-reading my books, and just being "you." I want to thank Sheriff Travis Hutchison for his advice, the Wayne County Fire Department for their guidance, and Coccia House for allowing me to use their establishment name to add credibility to Callie's story, not to mention their delicious pizza. This pizza saved dinner many nights!

Again, this book is what it is because of people like Becky Elk for her long hours of reading and edits (Guinness, too), Julie Ann Lindsey for her insight and shop talk, Mary Ellis for her inspirational encouragement, and Tacey Malone for photo insight. Carly Scott, thanks for being a great beta reader. I appreciate all of you!

Michael Evan, thank you for helping me set up a strong strategy for reaching readers. Your support has been great!

Publicist extraordinaire – Cristina Deptula. Thanks for all the support, guidance, and encouragement. You've done a great job reaching out and contacting interviewers and influencers to get this series off the ground.

And without a doubt, Jonas Saul asking you a crazy question at a writing conference proved to be a blessing in disguise. Your guidance in this writing journey and friendship have been inspirational. You've been a mentor to me in many ways. Thank you for your endorsement.

Dom Brighton—more than once, you've put the biggest smile on my face.

I am also honored by other fellow authors' endorsements—thank you.

I'd also love to thank my *dear* friends and readers for taking the time to read this story. I sincerely express gratitude to everyone for helping me chase my dreams!

BEYOND THE LAST PAGE...
IT'S YOUR TURN

S tories spark best when shared. These questions are designed for book clubs to dive deeper—exploring the characters, debating their choices, and discovering what the journey means to you together. But even if you're reading solo, they're here to help you reflect on the story in your own way.

1) *The Therans: Secrets Beneath Scars* blends romance, mystery, and real history. Why do you think these three themes are often connected in real life? Can uncovering secrets from the past help us better understand who we are or how we love today?

2) The opening of the book is raw and emotional. Why do you think stories sometimes begin with pain? How do hard beginnings reflect the real world, and what can they teach us about anger, resilience, empathy, or survival?

3) *The Therans: Secrets Beneath Scars* is inspired by ancient myths, varied cultures, and fantasy legends. Did you notice the historical elements and locations the author used for world-building? Why might it matter to create a fictional female character who is peaceful and wants the truth? How can fiction help us imagine better ways of living together?

4) Author Cyndi Brec used an authentic historical setting and influenced her story with a lost civilization. In world-building, the purpose of the Therans was to be stewards of history. What can we learn when authors mix the old with the new? Moreover, how does this help us see that history isn't just something behind us, but something we carry forward?

5) Throughout the book, characters face moral dilemmas, painful truths, and hard choices, while also learning to take responsibility for their actions. Can we overcome these moral dilemmas in real life while discovering our identity, for example, by attending college? How can fiction help us become more passionate in the way we would react to each other in different family dynamics?

6) *The Therans: Secrets Beneath Scars* is rooted in ancient Greek Literature and hints at a sci-fi vibe like *Star Wars*. The Therans in *Star Wars* were once known as listeners; now an author has reimagined them as stewards of history. What do you think when authors reimagine mythological or legendary beings into new roles? How do these kinds of characters help us think about truth, memory, and the way we carry knowledge across generations?

7) Characters in the story struggle to trust others or let people in, especially after loss and trauma. Why do you think it can be so hard for young people who've experienced pain to form new friendships? What can stories like this show us about healing, breaking down

walls, and the courage to trust, or the friend who never gives up?

ABOUT CYNDI BREC

Cyndi Brec is a debut novelist of *The Therans—Secrets Beneath Scars*, book one of the *The Therans* series. Also, author of *Scarred Secrets* and *Scarred Lies*—short stories.

An Ohio native, Cyndi lives with her best friend, her husband, her two crazy-fun-loving kids, and her embarrassingly energetic dogs, who find unending trouble.

Her experience as a Recreational Therapy Technician for the Geriatric psych and mentally challenged, love for travel, and creative story building has given her many facets to draw from when world-building.

Cyndi never thought of herself as an author, more of a storyteller. Her love of history was part of the driving force in writing the series, but more so, mythological stories that stretched across civilizations and time. The secrets hidden within those legendary tales cultivated an unending list of questions and inspired Callie's story.

Soon: *The Therans: Legends Never Die* novel.

www.Cyndibrec.com

www.ingramcontent.com/pod-product-compliance
Lightning Source LLC
Chambersburg PA
CBHW022020300726
48970CB00003B/979